The One I Love

ANNA MCPARTLIN

PENGUIN BOOKS

PENGUIN BOOKS

Published by the Penguin Group
Penguin Books Ltd, 80 Strand, London WC2R ORL, England
Penguin Group (USA) Inc., 375 Hudson Street, New York, New York 10014, USA
Penguin Group (Canada), 90 Eglinton Avenue East, Suite 700, Toronto, Ontario, Canada M4P 2Y3
(a division of Pearson Penguin Canada Inc.)
Penguin Ireland, 25 St Stephen's Green, Dublin 2, Ireland (a division of Penguin Books Ltd)
Penguin Group (Australia), 250 Camberwell Road, Camberwell, Victoria 3124, Australia
(a division of Pearson Australia Group Pty Ltd)
Penguin Books India Pvt Ltd, 11 Community Centre, Panchsheel Park, New Delhi – 110 017, India
Penguin Group (NZ), 67 Apollo Drive, Rosedale, North Shore 0632, New Zealand
(a division of Pearson New Zealand Ltd)
Penguin Books (South Africa) (Pty) Ltd, 24 Sturdee Avenue, Rosebank,
Johannesburg 2196, South Africa

Penguin Books Ltd, Registered Offices: 80 Strand, London WC2R ORL, England

www.penguin.com

First published in Ireland by Poolbeg as *So What If I'm Broken* 2009
This edition published in Penguin Books 2010

1

Copyright © Anna McPartlin, 2009, 2010
All rights reserved

Set in Garamond MT Std 12.5/14.75 pt
Typeset by Palimpsest Book Production Limited, Falkirk, Stirlingshire
Printed in Great Britain by Clays Ltd, St Ives plc

ISBN: 978-1-844-88190-1

www.greenpenguin.co.uk

Penguin Books is committed to a sustainable future
for our business, our readers and our planet.
The book in your hands is made from paper
certified by the Forest Stewardship Council.

PENGUIN BOOKS

The One I Love

For Donal, and for all the fans of Jack

Throughout *The One I Love* you will come across the lyrics of the fantastic and inimitable Jack L. Jack's people have kindly arranged for readers to download two of his songs for free. To get them, simply type the words 'Finding Alexandra' in the subject line of an email and send it to download@jacklukeman.com

Chapter 1

Universe

Oh nothing lasts for ever,
you can cry a million rivers,
you can rage it ain't no sin
but it won't change a thing,
'cos nothing lasts for ever.

Jack L, *Universe*

Alexandra, 21 June 2007

Tom,

When you are shopping can you pick up the following:

— Bread
— Milk × 2
— Water × 4
— Spaghetti
— Mince (lean! Make sure it's lean and not the stuff they call lean and charge half price because it's not lean. I want lean cut right in front of you and I don't care how much it costs)
— Tin of tomatoes
— Basil
— Garlic

– Wine, if you don't still have a case or two in the office and make sure it's not Shiraz. I'm really sick of Shiraz.
– If you want dessert pick something up.

I'm meeting Sherri in Dalkey for a quick drink at five. She has the Jack Lukeman tickets so I took money from the kitty to pay for them. I'm taking a ticket for you so if you don't want to go text me. I'll be home around seven thirty. Your aunt called, she's thinking about coming to Dublin next weekend. Try and talk her out of it. I'm exhausted and can't handle running around after her for forty-eight hours straight. Your aunt is on cocaine. I'm not messing. An intervention is needed.

Oh, and washing-up liquid. We badly need washing-up liquid, and will you please call someone to get the dishwasher fixed?

OK, see you later,
Love you,
Alexandra
PS When somebody close to you dies, move seats.
God, I love Jimmy Carr.

Alexandra laughed to herself as she put her note up on the fridge and held it in position with her favourite magnet, which was a fat, grinning pig rubbing his tummy. She was damp and sweaty having run five miles, which was a record and she was extremely pleased. She unclipped her iPod from her tracksuit, placed it on the counter and headed upstairs to the shower. There she sang Rihanna's "Umbrella", and did a little dance move before washing shampoo out of her hair.

Forty-five minutes later she walked down the stairs with her shoulder-length hair perfectly coiffed. She was wearing black trousers, tucked into her favourite black high-heeled boots, and a fitted black blouse complete with a large bow. She stopped at the hall mirror and applied lipstick, then rooted some gloss out of her handbag and applied that too. She stared at herself in the mirror for a moment or two, sighed and mumbled something about Angelina Jolie crapping her pants. She smiled at her own joke while putting on her jacket. She picked up her handbag and went out of the door.

Alexandra walked along the street and waved at Mrs Murphy from number fourteen. Mrs Murphy was busy sweeping her step but she waved and called out that it was a lovely day. Alexandra smiled and told her it was perfect. She waited for the DART and listened to a man talk to Joe Duffy about cruelty to animals on *Liveline*. It was too sad so she switched from radio to her music collection and only stopped humming along to James Morrison's "Last Goodbye" when she realized that three spotty teenagers were laughing and pointing at her. She stuck out her tongue and grinned at them, and they laughed again.

She sat on the train next to a man in his fifties. He asked her to wake him at Tara Street station if he fell asleep, explaining that there was something about moving trains that always made him sleep. She assured him she would wake him and, true to his word, he was snoring less than five minutes later. Coming up to Tara Street she tapped his arm gently but he still woke with a start. Once he'd regained his senses, he thanked her and made his way off the train. He forgot his bag so she ran after him and handed it to him. He was grateful but she was in a hurry to get back on the train so she just waved and ran.

The woman sitting opposite her grinned and nodded. "My own dad would forget his head," she said.

3

Alexandra smiled at her. "He was sweet."

The woman nodded again. Alexandra got off the train in Dalkey. The woman got off at the same station but neither made eye contact again.

Alexandra made her way through the station and out into the sunshine. She continued straight onto the main street and took the left at the end of the street. After that she took a right and then another left, and after that Alexandra was gone.

Elle, 31 December 1989

Dear Universe,

Please don't send a fiery ball of hellfire comet thing to kill us all. I'm only eight so if I die now I won't get to do anything that I really want to. Miss Sullivan thinks that I could be an artist. If I'm dead I can't paint and I love painting and living. Margaret Nolan says that everyone thinks that we're going to be nuked in 1999 but the real truth is that a flaming ball of death is going to crash into earth at the stroke of midnight tonight. She sits next to me in class and sometimes smells like a hospital. Her dad's a scientist and he told her so she has a good chance of being right. She's already given her pocket money to the poor and says I should do the same so that when our time comes God will think we're decent enough sorts and let us into heaven. I forgot to go to the church to put money in the poor box because I got carried away working on a painting of my family dying in dancing fire. Jane says I'm a depressing little cow. She's always in a bad mood lately. Mum says it's because she's a teenager, she's fighting with her boyfriend and she's got fat. She thinks being eight is the same as being slow but I know Jane is pregnant because they shout

4

about it all the time. I'm not slow and I'm not deaf either. I feel sorry for the baby because if we all die tonight it will never have known life but then again maybe that's for the best.

OK, here are my promises to you if we make it past midnight.

1. I'll be good.
2. I'll do what my mum tells me to.
3. I won't swear.
4. I won't tell any lies unless my mum asks me to (see promise 2).
5. I'll be nicer to Jane.
6. I'll paint every day.
7. I'll help Jane take care of Mum a bit more. (I can't help all the time – see promise 6.)
8. I'll give my pocket money to the poor tomorrow morning.
9. I'll be nice to Jane's baby because I've a feeling I might be the only one.
10. I won't listen to anything Margaret Nolan has to say again.

And, Universe, if we do all die in fire tonight, thanks for nothing.

Yours,
Elle Moore
XXX

That was the first letter Elle Moore wrote to the Universe. She folded it and put it into an old shortbread tin. After her supper she tied her long brown hair in a knot and dressed in her brand-new Christmas coat, hat, gloves and her sister Jane's favourite tie-dye fringed scarf. She made her way down the right-hand side of the long garden where she dug a hole between her mother's roses and the graves of four dead gerbils: Jimmy, Jessica, Judy and Jeffrey. Once the tin was placed in the hole and the earth covered it, she made a promise to herself that if she did live past midnight on that 31 December in 1989, the following year she'd retrieve her letter and replace it with another.

Little did she know it back then but Elle Moore would continue to write letters to the Universe every New Year's Eve for the next eighteen years.

Jane, 5 May 1990

Dear Mrs Moore,

I am writing to you today about my concerns regarding your daughter Jane. I have attempted to reach out to Jane on a number of occasions in recent times but to no avail. As you are well aware I have also attempted to communicate with your good self but that too has proved difficult/nigh on impossible. Therefore I am now left with no choice but to write this letter.

It is clear to the teaching staff and to the student body that Jane is in the latter stages of pregnancy and so it is now urgent that we speak. Jane's schoolwork and attendance suffered immeasurably last term and, as a Leaving Cert student, she now faces her mock examinations unprepared and with motherhood imminent. Jane seems to be incapable of coming to terms with her condition, as it would appear are you, but we in St Peter's cannot simply stand by and act like nothing is happening to this seventeen-year-old girl.

I urge you, Mrs Moore, to phone me or to come into the school and meet with me at any time convenient for you. I cannot allow this silence to continue any longer and so if we do not hear from you within the next week we will be forced to ask your daughter not to return to school until such time as communication has been established.

Over the years Jane and I have had our disagreements. Her flagrant disregard for our rules regarding smoking on school premises and the Irish stew incident that led to a fire in the Home Economics room are only two of the episodes I could mention. As you are aware we've butted heads on many more occasions, especially when she came to school with purple hair or, indeed, during her thankfully short-lived Cure-inspired Gothic phase. This school has a zero-tolerance policy when it comes to the presentation of its students but I must admit, though I was exasperated by her opposition and having to endure debate on many occasions, she conveyed her points ably and with admirable passion. The reason I mention this is that although our relationship as principal and student is chequered I feel it necessary to make it clear that Jane is a very clever girl, bright and articulate, and I have often thought that she could do anything she set her mind to, and in twenty years I have only thought that a handful of times. I am worried for her, Mrs Moore. She has lost her sparkle and her fight. The girl I knew and, despite our differences, have a great fondness for has all but disappeared.

Teenage pregnancy is terrible and absolutely not to be encouraged, but support is not the same as encouragement and with support Jane could continue her studies and fulfil her ambitions. Surely it is not the end for a girl such as Jane.

Please come and speak to me for Jane's sake. Don't leave me with no option but to expel such a talented young girl from our school.

Kindest regards,
Amanda Reynolds (Principal)

Jane finished reading the letter aloud and blew her blonde fringe out of her eyes while waiting on her best friend's response. Alexandra twirled her chestnut hair around her finger and stared at it in silence. After a few seconds she shrugged. "Jesus, who knew Reynolds had a heart?"

Jane felt like crying because her principal had responded to her crisis pregnancy with far more kindness and understanding than her own mother, who had had one tantrum after another since her condition had been revealed months previously. During her latest tantrum she had taken the time to mention how much money she had pissed into the wind by sending Jane to a private school and told Jane in no uncertain terms that her education was over because only a bloody childless spinster like Amanda Reynolds could possibly think that having a baby at seventeen didn't mean the end of an academic career. She slammed the door on exiting the room, not once but twice for effect.

On that afternoon, and for the first time, Jane truly acknowledged the predicament she was in and how badly wrong her life had gone. She realized that she would miss her principal and she would miss school, as well as the opportunity to go to college. She'd miss her friends who, except Alexandra, had drifted away during her pregnancy, and she'd miss Dominic even though he was avoiding her and completely ignoring the fact that she was carrying his child. He couldn't hide his pain from her. She recognized and identified with his haunted expression, and she loved him. Following an argument with his parents, who had dared to imply that Jane was a little whore, her mother had made it clear that if she saw him anywhere near their property she'd attack him with a shovel – and Jane's mother did not make threats of violence lightly.

Once when Jane was seven a man had come to their

door. He was buying and selling antiques. Her mother said she wasn't interested but he had spied an antique table in the hall. He had put his foot in the door and attempted to change her mind about doing business. She reiterated that she had no interest and told him if he didn't remove his foot she would hurt him. He laughed at her. "No can do," he said, and his foot remained in the door. She counted down aloud from five to zero. He continued to push his foot further into her hallway, all the while grinning at her foolishly. It was clear to Jane's mother that this man believed her to be a stupid, incapable woman and that she would not or could not keep her promise.

When she reached zero she calmly reached for an umbrella she kept in the hall and, releasing the door, she pushed it, with full force, into his stomach. Startled, he bent forward, clutching his midriff. She then bopped him on the head not once or twice but three times. He fell backwards, she smiled politely, said good day to him, and left him winded and slightly dazed on her doorstep. Jane remembered the incident well because she had stood at the window watching the man sit on the step for what seemed like a long time before he was capable of getting up.

Her mother had joined her just as he was leaving. "Good riddance," she'd said, with a genuine smile. "You know, Janey, there's nothing quite like giving a smug, arrogant cock like him a good dig to cheer up a dull day." So Jane knew that if her mother had enjoyed giving that cock a dig because he'd put his foot in her doorway she would definitely enjoy slapping Dominic in the face with a shovel for putting his cock in her daughter.

After Alexandra had read the letter a few more times and

lamented with Jane over her mother being a bigger bitch than Alexis on *Dynasty*, she opened the first of six cans of Ritz. Later, when Jane was drunk on one can and Alexandra was on her third, Jane compared her and Dominic's plight to that of Romeo and Juliet. Alexandra threw cold water on Jane's fanciful theory: "It's like this, Janey," she said. "Romeo didn't get Juliet up the pole and then dump her at a disco."

"I know, but his parents made him give me up and —"

"And anyway," Alexandra said, with drunken authority, "as bad as your situation is with Dominic, you don't want to be anything like Romeo and Juliet because *Romeo and Juliet* is a shit love story. Romeo was a shallow slut, Juliet pathetic and needy, their families were killing each other and they were in love one stupid day before they were married and then dead. Romeo and Juliet weren't star-crossed lovers, they were knackers."

"When you put it that way," Jane said sadly.

"Can you believe Miss Hobbs only gave me a C in English? I may not be able to spell 'apothecary' but I have insight. That woman doesn't know her arse from her elbow." Then Alexandra threw up in Jane's bin.

After that they talked about how Jane could win Dominic back but neither came up with a workable solution so they agreed that Jane should just wait it out.

"As far as I'm concerned he's just a cock-artist, but I know you love him so it'll work out," said Alexandra.

"He's more than a cock-artist," said Jane.

"I disagree," Alexandra said, burping Ritz.

"He's the one," said Jane.

Alexandra tapped her can. "He'll come back, Janey. He'll see you in school every day and he'll miss you. Just give it some time." She stopped to throw up again, wiped her mouth and sighed. "That's better. What was I saying?"

"Just give it some time," said Jane.

"Exactly. And, anyway, you still have me."

"I know."

"You will always have me."

"I know."

"Even if I get science in Cork – because, let's face it, I'm not going to get into UCD – you'll still have me."

"I'll miss you," Jane said.

"You won't have to," Alexandra promised. "I'll be home every other weekend and you can come and stay with me."

"I'll have a baby."

"Leave it with your mum."

"She's made it clear she's not a babysitter."

"She's such a cow."

"Yeah, she is."

"I love you, Jane."

"I love you too, Alex."

They were interrupted by Jane's mother, who was even drunker than Alexandra and determined to fight. "Go home, Alexandra."

"I'm going home."

"So go!"

"I'm going."

"So get out!"

"Jesus, what's wrong with you, woman? Can't you see I'm trying to get up?"

Jane helped her friend into a standing position.

"See?" Alexandra said, with arms outstretched. "I'm off!" She wove through the corridor and walked out of the front door. She turned to say goodbye but Jane's mother slammed the door in her face.

Jane's mother turned to Jane. "She's not welcome here any more."

"She's my best friend."

"Yeah, well, kiss your best friend goodbye."

That was the last time Alexandra was in Jane's house. Jane gave birth to a son two weeks later and, although they maintained a friendship for four months after that, when Jane became a mother and Alexandra went to college in Cork they lost contact. Over the next seventeen years Jane often thought of her friend and she missed her.

Leslie, 5 June 1996

Dear Jim,

It's time to talk about Leslie. We both know she's stubborn and cut off and we both know why. When I'm gone you'll be all she has left in this world and I know it's a big ask but please look out for her.

We've talked about you remarrying and you know I want you to find someone to love and to love you. I want you to have a great new life that doesn't include overcrowded hospitals, dismissive doctors, overworked nurses and cancer. I want you to find someone strong and healthy, someone you can go on an adventure with, someone you can make love to, someone who doesn't cause you anguish and pain. Every time I see your face it hurts because for the first time I see that, in loving you, I've been selfish and I understand why Leslie is the way she is.

Leslie is a better person than me. I know you're probably guffawing at that as you read but it's true. She's watched her entire family die of cancer, and when we were both diagnosed with the dodgy gene after Nora's death, she made the decision not to cause pain to others the way Nora caused pain to John and Sarah and I'm causing pain to you. Before cancer she was smart and funny, kind and caring, and she still is to me. Without her care I wouldn't have coped. I know sometimes she calls you names but, trust me, she knows you're not a monkey, so when she calls you an arse-picker, ignore it and be kind.

I thought she was being defeatist. I thought that we'd suffered enough as a family and that we'd both survive. So I made plans and fell in love and for a while we had a great life, but then that dodgy gene kicked in. Now I see you look almost as ill as I feel and I realize that my sister Leslie knew exactly what she was doing when she broke up with Simon and all but closed off. I watched her disappear from her own life. I thought she was insane back then but it makes sense now. She put the pain of others before her own. She watched John and Sarah suffer after Nora and she'll watch you suffering after me, and although she pretends not to like you, she does, and it will hurt her and it will also confirm for her that she is right to remain alone, waiting for a diagnosis that may never come.

I'm her last family and friend. She hasn't even let herself get to know her niece so when I'm gone she'll have no one and that haunts me. Please go and live your life but all I ask is that, every now and again, no matter how rude or uninviting she may seem, call to her, talk to her, be her friend even if she fails to be yours, because she has been there for me, for Mum, for Dad and Nora, and I can't stand the idea that after everything she's been through she should live or die alone.

I know I say it all the time, and in all my little notes and letters about this and that, but time is running out and I need you to know that it's been a privilege to be your wife and, although I feel selfish for all the pain I've caused you, I know I've brought happiness too, so hang on to that and forgive me because, even knowing what I know now, I'd love and marry you again. I suppose Leslie would say I was a selfish truffle-sniffer but I can die with that.

Yours,
Imelda

Imelda Sheehan died at eight o'clock on the morning of 12 July 1996. She was twenty-five years old. Her husband Jim was by her side, holding her right hand, and her sister Leslie was sitting on the opposite side of the bed, holding her left hand. They both felt her slip away at exactly the same time. For Leslie it was familiar: the ocean of grief inside her swelled and rose but she knew what to do: she remained still and allowed the pain to wash over her. For Jim it was so shocking: one second his wife was alive and battling to breathe, the next dead and silent. He let Imelda's hand go and stood up quickly, so quickly that he nearly fell. He steadied and hugged himself. He stood in the corner of the room as the doctor and nurses approached to confirm time of death.

Leslie sat with her dead sister Imelda, holding her hand for as long as they would allow her to. Jim cried and his parents, brothers and friends made a fuss of him. Leslie sat alone and frozen. She knew that the physical pain, which made her heart feel like it was about to explode and her ears ring until she feared they'd bleed, would dissipate in time, just as the tide would turn and, with it, Imelda would drift further and further away until she was a distant memory. It only served to make her loss greater. Leslie had just turned twenty-nine.

Jim asked Leslie to read at the funeral but she refused. He asked her to sit beside him and in the first pew, when she'd attempted to sit at the back of the church. She told him she didn't want to shake hands with the people whose hands she had shaken so many times before, but Jim was not taking no for an answer: she found herself sitting beside her brother-in-law with a heavy heart and the all-too-familiar swollen hand from those whose earnest sympathy had ensured they squeezed too tight.

When the priest asked if anyone would like to speak, Leslie stood up. This surprised her and those around her, especially Jim who hadn't even been able to get her to do a reading. She found herself standing without reason. The priest asked her to come forward but her legs refused to comply with his request. He waited and the congregation waited, and Jim nudged her and asked if she was all right. *What the hell am I doing?* she asked herself, as she started to move towards the altar. But once she was on the altar and standing in front of a microphone the words came easily.

"I am the last of the five Sheehans," she said. "Four days ago there were two of us, me the middle child, and Imelda the baby of the family. I should have been next, and not just because I was older but because Imelda was the strong one, the one who embraced life regardless and without fear. Over the years she's run five marathons in aid of cancer. I didn't even walk for cancer, not once – mostly I'll avoid standing if I can." She stopped to take a breath. There was a hint of a titter from the crowd. "She fell in love and married Jim, and she always planned to have kids. Imelda always made plans and that's what I admired about her most because even when she was diagnosed with the same cancer that had killed our grandmother, our mother and sister she still made plans. She froze her eggs and they bought a house and when she wasn't in chemo she travelled. Even when she knew her life was coming to the end she still made plans. Little plans that don't mean much to most, like 'Tonight we'll reminisce about the summer we spent in Kerry' or 'Tomorrow when the sun comes out we'll sit in the hospital grounds and watch the people come and go and make up stories about who and what they are.' She even planned her own funeral. She knew exactly what she wanted, the kind of coffin, the flowers, the priest, the prayers, the attendees. She asked me once if I would speak at her funeral and I said no. I'm sorry, Imelda, of course I'll speak for you. I just was scared that I wouldn't know what to say and I didn't want to let you down. So I'll just end by saying this: I miss my dad, my mum, my sister Nora and now I miss my Imelda and I'm so sorry because it should have been me, but I'll see you all again and soon."

Leslie's voice was cracking, her eyes streaming and her nose running. She walked towards her seat and, once she'd accepted a tissue from Jim, she sat with her head in her hands, attempting to regain her composure but finding it almost impossible to do so. Her hair was jet-black, she was slim and, although not a natural beauty, she was striking. The people sitting in the pews behind her felt nothing but pity for a young woman who was merely waiting for her turn to die. Later, by the side of the grave, she watched Jim grieve and if there was something she could have said to make him feel better she would have said it, but there wasn't so she stood in silence waiting for the day to end so that she could disappear behind her closed door and wait for

16

the inevitable. It never occurred to her that she'd be still waiting for the inevitable twelve years later.

Tom, 25 August 2007

Transcript of *Liveline* radio show with Joe Duffy

"I have a Tom Kavanagh on the line. Tom, are you there?"

"I am, Joe."

"Tom, you're trying to find your lovely wife Alexandra."

"Yes, Joe."

"She went missing on the twenty-first of June this year?"

"It was Thursday, the twenty-first of June."

"Tell us about it, Tom."

"I don't know where to start. She was last seen in Dalkey and now she's gone."

"Okay, okay, all right. How about you tell us a little about her?"

"She's funny, she's giddy, she's kind, she's friendly, she's fussy, she's lovely, Joe." *Caller becomes emotional.*

"The police have managed to retrace her steps as far as Dalkey. Can you tell us about that?"

"She left the house in Clontarf around two p.m. She said hello to a neighbour who verified the time. She walked to the station, and three teenagers who were there came forward to say that they witnessed her getting on the train. She's also captured on CCTV footage on the platform at Tara Street at three thirty but she got back on the train. After the stations were canvassed, a woman came forward and identified her as getting off the train in Dalkey. She was captured on CCTV footage again there but after that . . ." *Caller becomes emotional.*

"And after that?"

"She was gone. She's just gone."

"Ah, God, that's desperate. What time was that?"

"It was approximately four p.m."

"And where were you?"

"I was working. We were finishing a project in Blackrock."

"It says here you're a builder."

"I am."

"So when did you realize she was missing?"

"I was supposed to be home by four. I'd promised to make dinner because Alexandra was meeting her friend Sherri to collect tickets for a gig from her. She had left a note saying she'd be home by seven thirty. But I was delayed on site. I didn't get in until nine p.m."

"When did you raise the alarm, Tom?"

"The next morning, Joe." *Caller becomes emotional.* "I thought she'd stayed out with Sherri or maybe that she was pissed off I didn't get home in time to make the dinner so went out again. I was exhausted so I fell asleep."

"That's understandable. What age is Alexandra?"

"She's thirty-five. She has chestnut-brown hair, shoulder length. She was wearing black trousers and a black blouse with a bow on it. She had a black fitted jacket on. She's very attractive, the kind of person you'd remember if you'd seen her." *Caller becomes emotional.*

"And she went missing on . . ."

"Thursday, the twenty-first of June this year."

"And did she have any mental issues, Tom?"

"No, Joe. She was a very happy, well-adjusted, normal woman. She was normal, Joe, ordinary."

"Okay, okay." Joe sighs. "I'm going to ask the obvious, Tom, so forgive me. Is there any chance she took herself into the water?"

"No. No. She wasn't suicidal and the coast guard searched it
    and the police divers and there were plenty of people on the
    beach that day and no one saw her."
"Okay, I had to ask. I'm sorry for your trouble, Tom. I hope that
    maybe someone listening remembers something."
"And, Joe?"
"Yes, Tom?"
"I'll be at Dalkey train station handing out flyers later this
    evening and I'll be doing the same at a Jack Lukeman gig on
    Dame Street next Friday."
"Why there, Tom?"
"She was a big fan, Joe. She never missed a show." *Caller
    becomes emotional.*
"And he's very popular. Lots of people from all counties will be
    there."
"It's as good a place as any to get the word out, Joe."
"God love you, Tom. I sympathize. Good luck to you. We'll put
    Alexandra's details on the website and if you could send in a
    photo we'll post it."
"I will, and thanks for taking the call."
"And if anyone has information on Alexandra Kavanagh, who
    went missing on the twenty-first of June 2007, would they
    contact Clontarf Garda Station and the inspector in charge of
    the investigation is Des Martin. Right, we'll be back after
    these ads."

Tom put down the phone and turned to Breda, his mother-
in-law. She was sitting at the kitchen table, looking frail and
small. She smiled at him through tears. "You did very well,
love," she said.

"You should have left this phone number," Eamonn said,

while pacing. Eamonn was Alexandra's older brother; he and Tom had never really been close. Alexandra's disappearance had served to widen the divide between them. "And you should have said that she was upset about not getting pregnant."

"Nothing to do with anything," Tom said. "She was fine, happy."

"You just didn't want to see it!" Eamonn shouted. "It was tearing her apart and you didn't see it!"

"Take that back, Eamonn," Tom said, walking towards him.

"Take a swing, I dare you," Eamonn said, and braced himself as if for a fight.

Breda called out to the two young men: "Stop it, both of you!"

Alexandra's father stood up from the chair he'd been sitting in outside on the patio. He put his cigarette out and came inside. "Go home now," he said to Eamonn and Tom. "Go home before you both say and do things you'll regret."

Eamonn and Tom nodded and apologized. Breda was crying again. She looked at Tom, who had aged ten years in ten weeks. His black hair was almost entirely grey; his once-sparkly blue eyes were tired and circled by shadows. He had been so pernickety about the way he looked that Alexandra's family, especially Eamonn, had often joked about her marrying a metro-sexual. His suits were always the best of suits, dry-cleaned after one wear and precisely tailored. His hair was perfectly cut, and his face perfectly clean. Off site Tom didn't look like a builder, he looked like a banker. He was wealthy, and although he wasn't extravagant, he left those around him in no doubt about his standing.

Breda noticed his suit was now too big, his hair a mess, and he hadn't shaved in weeks. He was a shadow of the man he used to be, as she was a shadow of the woman and mother she once was. She recognized his suffering because it mirrored her own and she wanted her son, whose anger was more intense than his pain, to stop hurting her already mortally wounded son-in-law. She promised herself she would talk to Eamonn when she found the strength to deal with his quarrelsome nature.

When Tom was leaving Breda hugged him and he could feel every bone in her back. She whispered into his ear, "She's still with us – I can feel it. God will take care of her. She's not alone because God is there beside her."

Tom nodded. "Try and eat, Breda."

He left and got into his car. He sat for a minute or two and was still there when Eamonn came out of the house. Eamonn walked over to the car window and knocked on it. Tom rolled it down.

"I don't care what the police say," Eamonn said. "I don't care what my mother says. It's your fault. I blame you." He turned and walked to his own car, got in and drove away, leaving Tom sitting in Alexandra's parents' driveway, crying like a baby.

Oh, God, please, please, where is she? Bring her home to me, please, please, bring her home! I'm so sorry for everything I've done. Forgive me and bring her home.

Alexandra was then missing nine weeks and two days.

Chapter 2

Fear Is The Key

All the shapes in the dark are playing with your heart,
fear is always near.
It'll never set you free, it'll never let you be,
once you let it in all the fun begins,
'cos fear is all you'll breathe.

Jack L and the Black Romantics, *Wax*

October 2007
The night was damp and overcast. Jane had thought twice about whether or not she actually wanted to go out. It had been a long and tiring day but she had promised her younger sister, Elle, and Elle did not handle disappointment well. The gig was due to start at nine. It was just after ten. They had missed the supporting act and Jack Lukeman would be already on stage. The venue didn't have a car park and, because of a lack of inner-city knowledge and a patho- logical fear of driving the wrong way up one-way streets, Jane parked miles away. As they were so late they were forced to run from the car park to the venue, and just as they turned the first corner the rain came tumbling down. Neither sister had an umbrella. Elle had a hood but as she ran it insisted on falling off her head. She held it tight around her face and continued to run, with Jane doing her

best to keep up in heels and praying she wouldn't break an ankle.

At the door they fumbled for their tickets, but once they had presented them to a doorman with the build of a silverback gorilla and the manner of a brick, he waved them through. "Move," he said.

"Charming," said Elle, and Jane widened her eyes and tightened her mouth, which signalled to her sister to shut up.

They passed a dishevelled man who was considerably drier than they were. He was standing behind the box office, between the lifts and the stairs. He handed them each a flyer with a picture of a woman on it. "If you see her there's a number you can contact me at," he said.

Neither of them looked at the flyer because they could hear Jack singing "Don't Fall In Love". Elle spotted the lift. "We're in the gods, let's get the lift."

"I hate the lift."

"We're missing the show." Elle pouted.

Jane sighed and Elle pressed the button for the lift just as the silverback charmer looked at his watch and started to close the main doors. A woman in a full-length plastic see-through raincoat that was pulled tight around her face and knotted with a toggle at her chin pushed her ticket against the window and her foot in the door. The man considered whether to let her in or to attempt to amputate her foot for a second or two before he opened it, took her ticket and allowed her to enter.

Elle smiled as she saw the walking condom approach her. *Well, that's one way of keeping dry.* The human condom ignored the flyer man's attempt to hand her one and stood behind Jane, who was preparing to entomb herself in a small space. *Don't freak out. It'll be all over in seconds.* The silverback bolted the front door. The man packed away his remaining flyers into a briefcase and stood behind Elle waiting for the lift. The red light appeared over the doors and they heard a dinging sound. Elle was first in, followed by the human condom and the flyer man.

Jane was frozen but only for a second. When she realized that her sister and the two strange strangers were staring at her she made her legs move towards them to avoid embarrassment. The doors closed and Jane breathed in and out slowly and surely. *Ten seconds and it'll be over. Count back to one. Ten . . . nine . . .*

Elle could hear Jack singing clearly: "'Don't fall in love with the girls around here, you give them your heart they soon disappear.'" She sang along quietly: "'They come from country towns and live on Crescent Street and all that they share are the secrets they keep.'"

Jane counted in her head: . . . *five . . . four . . .*

Elle became slightly louder as the song reached its conclusion: "La, la, la, la, la, la, la!"

The human condom and the flyer man stared forward, ignoring the tone-deaf girl who was compromising their enjoyment of the song by obscuring Jack L with her off-key wailing.

Jane continued to breathe and count: . . . *three . . . two . . .*

The lights were the first to go off. The lift ground to a stop with such a jolt that all four passengers automatically braced themselves. Jane stopped counting, Elle stopped wailing and, outside, the music stopped playing. Only Jack L continued to sing. He finished the last line of the song without mike or music. The crowd cheered and roared and

Elle found herself staring from her sister, whose legs had gone from under her and who was suddenly sitting on the floor, to the human condom hanging on to the rail and to the flyer man, who seemed to be holding on to his briefcase for dear life. Outside the crowd were still roaring and it was all so strange and she liked it. "What's going on?" she asked, a grin spreading across her face. "Do you think it's a fire?"

Jane's breathing was becoming shallower and faster so she was in no position to respond. The flyer man told her that if there was a fire the alarm would have rung. The human condom undid her toggle and pulled her see-through raincoat from her head to reveal short black hair streaked with grey and sprinkled with white. "It's a power cut," she said, "probably the damn weather. I knew I shouldn't come out tonight but I just wouldn't listen to myself." She took off her coat, rolled it up, put it into her oversized bag and sat on the floor next to Jane, who was trying her best not to hyperventilate.

"Is she okay?" the flyer man asked Elle, referring to Jane.

"She's got a thing about lifts," Elle said. "Hang in there, Janey." She went down on her hunkers and brushed her sister's wet blonde hair from her face. "It won't be long now."

For some reason the human condom found it necessary to correct her. "Actually, it could be hours."

Jane grabbed Elle's hand and squeezed it hard.

Elle looked at the human condom. "Not cool, Condom. Not cool at all."

The human condom and the flyer man stared at her quizzically, both clearly wondering if they had heard correctly. Before they got a chance to say anything they were interrupted by a man using a loudspeaker to address the audience.

Jane looked around the lift, wide-eyed. "What's happening out there?" she asked breathlessly.

"Shush," the condom said, placing a finger to her lips. "The venue manager is trying to say something on a loudspeaker."

Jane imagined Jack on stage, standing back, allowing the manager to fix his hand-held loudspeaker before making a second attempt to talk to the crowd without the loud screeching he'd nearly deafened them with on his first attempt.

"What now?" Elle asked.

"Hard to hear over the din of the crowd." The human condom pushed her ear closer to the door. "Hah, they're laughing."

Jane guessed that Jack was playing with the venue manager. Maybe he was bounding across the stage like a puppy or bouncing up and down behind the man, high and in performance mode, while the manager fumbled with an ancient loudspeaker, or he was making a joke or scaling the wall so that he could hang from a box while the guy made his long-awaited announcement. Whatever he was doing the crowd were laughing hard.

"What now?" Elle said.

"Still laughing."

The crowd quietened and the condom listened intently as the manager explained that the entire street was experiencing a blackout. He wasn't aware how long the problem would last and apologized because for some reason the back-up generator wasn't working as it should.

"What?" Elle said.

"As I said, it's a blackout."

"So what now?" Elle asked.

"Shush," she said, "and I'll tell you."

She listened as the manager promised the audience he had someone working on it and that if the generator didn't kick in within the next ten minutes they could have their money back. They booed him, and that was when Jack must have taken the loudspeaker from him. "I'm not ready to leave," he said, and the crowd roared their approval.

"Jack's not ready to leave," the human condom said.

"He's not going to play, is he?" Jane said, between deep breaths.

"I think he is," Elle said.

On stage, the guitar player picked out the familiar chords to "Move On", and Jack's haunting voice emerged as clearly as though it was still amplified. In that second he silenced the crowd. And as soon as he sang, his voice resonated in the lift as though he was there with them.

"Ah, Jesus, I love this song!" the condom said, punching the door.

"Makes no difference who you are, love will find you, yeah,
Opera or movie star, love will find your path.
All the money in the world won't save you from that.
All the beauty in the world you can't just cover your tracks . . ."

The audience joined in for the chorus:

"And if you move on it will keep up
And if you jump town you know you'll be found."

"Should we make some noise?" Elle asked, after the group had sat in silence for a minute or two, save for Jane's panting and Jack's singing.

"The bouncer will realize we're in here," the flyer man said, hoping that the bouncer was slightly more conscientious than his earlier encounter with him had suggested.

"The silverback?" Elle snorted. "Fat chance."

"She's right," the condom said. "He was probably too busy picking fleas out of his arse to notice us getting in."

Elle laughed, clearly entertained by the condom's crudity and her ability to pick up on and run with the primate theme.

The flyer man looked at the doors and decided to try to force them apart. He couldn't get his fingers between them, though, and when he'd established that none of the women carried crowbars, or anything remotely like crowbars, in their handbags he started to bang on the doors. This shook the lift and made Jane pant harder, shake and cry.

"Breathe, Janey," Elle said. "You're all right, everything's fine."

Jane wasn't fine. She was experiencing chest pain and fighting the urge to run through the wall.

"If you don't stop shaking the lift that woman's going to have a full-on panic attack if she's not already having one," the condom said to the flyer man.

He turned and looked at Jane's ghastly face, stopped shaking the lift and sat down. "I'm sorry," he said.

Jane tried to smile at him but she couldn't breathe, never mind smile.

"Does anyone have a paper bag?" Elle asked.

The condom said no immediately but the flyer man checked his briefcase. "No," he said, "but try this." He took out a large poster and fashioned it into a sort of bag. He handed it to Elle, who placed it around Jane's mouth and once again instructed her to breathe.

It didn't work. Jane pulled the poster away from her lips and held it tightly against her chest, then she lay down on the floor, cursing herself for choosing to wear white linen, which was now rain-soaked and filthy. *Oh, my God, I'm going to catch a flesh-eating disease from this floor. Oh, sweet God, whatever happens let my face be last to go. I don't want my child saying goodbye to an open wound. Goodbye, Kurt, Mum loves you. Goodbye, Dominic, you're a selfish bastard, a waster and an arse. God, I love you. Why can't you love me? Goodbye, Mother, you're a bitch in your heart but I don't hate you so that's something. Goodbye, Elle, focus on your career, stop doing stupid things and you'll be fine without me.*

Elle viewed her sister prostrate on the floor, rubbing her chest, sweating profusely and breathing at a rate that couldn't be good for a person. Jane had often talked about the possibility of this happening when Elle had bullied her into getting into a lift but she'd never actually experienced it before and, aside from the paper-bag idea, she had no clue what to do. "What can I do?" she asked Jane, who was busy watching herself float up towards the ceiling.

At least I'm off the floor.

The condom made a *hah* sound, stood up and repositioned herself on the other side of Jane, making the flyer man move over in the process. She took Jane's hand from Elle because Jane's other hand was holding the poster against her chest. "You are having a panic attack. You are not dying. No one dies from panic attacks," the condom said.

Jane stopped floating and returned to her body on the floor.

"You can deal with this. Just let it happen and it will pass," the condom said, and Jane listened and believed her. "It's okay to feel anxious. You'll be all right."

Jane's breathing slowed, and for the next ten minutes the condom repeated the mantras and she began to feel normal again. By the time Elle and the flyer man had all but lost the will to live, she was able to sit up and, once her breathing was controlled enough to allow for speech, she thanked the condom. "I'm Jane."

"Leslie," the condom replied.

"Elle," Elle said. "That was extremely impressive. Are you a doctor?"

"No."

"Do you suffer with panic attacks?" Elle asked.

"No."

"So how did you know what to say?" Elle refused to be put off by Leslie's monosyllabic answers.

"My sister used to suffer from them."

"Used to? She got over them?" Elle looked from Leslie to Jane and was about to put her thumbs up.

"She died," Leslie said, and Jane's cheeks once again lost colour, "but not from a panic attack." She smiled at Jane, who nodded gratefully.

Elle focused on the flyer man, who was sitting quietly in the corner. "So what's your name?"

"Tom." He turned to Jane. "Sorry about earlier. I shouldn't have rocked the boat, so to speak."

Jane smiled at him. "It's fine. I'm just being silly."

On stage Jack had been talking and the audience were laughing. He began to sing "Bedsprings" a cappella.

30

"Take me back to your old ma's place
where the bedspring squeaks and your body shakes
and I lose myself before the morning takes me home.
Love me in the doorway I'll love you on the stairs . . ."

Elle started to click her fingers. "I love this song."
Leslie also loved it. *Please, please, don't sing it and kill it.*
Jane straightened a little and decided to sit on her bag.

"It's a bit late to be thinking about ruining your suit,
Jane," Elle said, still clicking.

"I know." Jane sighed, looking at the filthy floor. "I'm
going to need a tetanus shot after this."

Elle noticed Leslie moving to the music and Jack was
heading for the chorus. "Sing it with me, Leslie!" she said.

"No," said Leslie.

"Is 'no' your very favourite word?" Elle asked.

"No."

Elle laughed. *I like you.* "Come on, I know you want
to."

And Leslie did want to, and if she didn't, she'd have to
listen to Elle murder it anyway. So when the chorus hit she
found herself in a lift singing with a total stranger. *This is
not me but I like it.*

"Oh come on down while we're in full bloom
It's big bright night, let's howl at the moon."

Tom laughed at the women, and even Jane forgot her
anxiety for a moment or two to enjoy the sight of her sister
and Leslie howling.

"Whoa come on down we're in full bloom,
Howl at the, howl at the, howl at the moon."

They howled and howled and by the end they weren't half bad.

"Hello? Is anyone there?"

Tom stood up and pressed his hand against the door. "Hello."

"How many are in there?" the voice asked.

"Four of us," Tom said.

"Okay, sir, we hope to have the generator up and running soon."

"Thanks," Tom said.

"Is everyone okay?" the voice asked.

"We're fine," Tom said, looking at Jane, who nodded to signal she was feeling better.

Before the man got a chance to ask another question Jack began "Georgie Boy" and the whole audience were singing along, drowning the lone voice.

Tom sat down.

Jane finally loosened her grip on the poster that was crumpled against her chest. She opened it out and saw a picture of a woman she recognized. She was older than Jane remembered her but unmistakable. "Alex? Alexandra Walsh?"

Tom stared at Jane. "You know her?"

"I used to."

"They were best friends," Elle said, "but then my sister got pregnant at seventeen and Alexandra disappeared. So maybe not best friends after all."

"Elle," Jane said, in a tone that meant "shut up". "She's missing?" she asked Tom.

"Since June."

"My God, that's terrible!" Jane was genuinely upset. She raised a shaking hand to her mouth. "I'm so sorry."

Elle took the flyer out of her pocket and looked at it. "I'm sorry. I shouldn't have said she disappeared. Sometimes I'm an ass. It's genetic — you'd have to meet my mother to understand."

Tom attempted to smile at her, to reassure her that she was forgiven.

"What happened?" Jane asked.

"She went to Dalkey and vanished."

"As in gone?" Elle said.

"Gone."

"Is it possible she . . . hurt herself?" Leslie asked.

"No," Tom said firmly, "it's not."

"I know it's been a long time but I agree with Tom. That just doesn't sound like the girl I knew." Jane sighed and shook her head. Her eyes filled but she didn't cry.

"What do the police say?" Leslie asked.

"They say they're doing the best they can. They've been very good to us, really."

"How's Breda?" Jane asked, referring to Alexandra's mother.

"Devastated — completely and utterly devastated."

"I'm so sorry," Jane said. "Breda was always so kind to me. When I had my son she knitted him a blue blanket. He didn't go anywhere without that blanket for years."

"I remember that — it was manky," Elle said.

"We were trying for a baby for a long time," said Tom. "Alexandra gave up work after Christmas hoping it would help . . ." He trailed off, as if he'd already said too much.

Alexandra would kill him if she knew he was talking about their private life to strangers, even if she had been friends with one of them when she was young. And already so much of their private life had been laid bare.

"It's a nightmare," Leslie said. "An absolute nightmare."

"She was wearing black trousers, a black top with a bow and black boots," Tom said, repeating the information he had repeated so many times before. "She took her handbag. She never really kept a lot of cash on her but she's never used her cards. She was fine that morning, in good humour – she'd planned to meet her friend Sherri in Dalkey at five. She was fine."

Suddenly Elle felt the urge to cry but she couldn't because it would have been deeply inappropriate, yet it was hard to fight the tears. She stayed silent and breathed in and out, much like her sister had earlier. The full enormity of Alexandra's disappearance and Tom's desolation were causing her actual physical pain.

"I'd like to help you," Jane said to Tom. "I know we're strangers but if there's something I can do . . ."

Tom shook his head. "That's kind of you but I just don't know how you can help."

"We'll think of something," Elle said, and looked at Leslie, who stared at her blankly.

"What?" Leslie said, after enduring Elle's attention for what seemed like eternity.

"Aren't you going to help?" Elle said.

"I wish I could," Leslie said, "but if the police can't, I can't, and unfortunately neither can either of you."

"I disagree," Jane said. "I'd rather try than stand by and do nothing."

"Well, good luck," Leslie said, and she meant it.

"Leslie's right," Tom said, moved by the two women's kindness, "but thank you."

"We're going to help whether you like it or not," Elle said. "Besides, you look like you could do with some direction. Handing out flyers at a gig? What's that all about?"

"If you can think of something better, I'd be happy to give it a go."

"I'll put my thinking cap on," Elle said. "I suppose postings in Dalkey are taken care of?"

"Yes."

"Right. I had to ask."

After that Jane reminisced about Alexandra, making the others laugh. She told them about the time Alexandra insisted they sneak out of her parents' house during a sleepover. They'd had to get out of a second-storey window, jump onto the extension roof and shimmy down the pipe. When they'd finally made it to the ground without killing themselves and were busy high-fiving, they'd failed to notice that Alexandra's father was standing in the porch having watched their every move. When he made himself known to them Alexandra stuck out her arms in front of her and, zombie-like, walked towards him, pretending she was sleep-walking.

"And what did you do?" Tom asked.

"I wet myself," Jane admitted, "but Alexandra kept up the act until her dad laughed, and once he did we were off the hook. She could always get out of anything."

"What about the time she stayed with us and Mum caught you both drinking her stash of wine?" Elle said.

"Rose threatened to call the police," Jane said.

"Rose is our mother," Elle said, to clarify it for the group.

"But Alexandra told her that she'd call the police because our sitting-room carpet was a crime against taste."

"Mum nearly lost it," Elle said. "I was in my bed and I could hear her screaming but Alexandra didn't care."

"Alexandra was too drunk to care," Jane said. "She called Rose an old lush and challenged her to a drinking competition." She started to laugh. "I've never seen Rose turn purple before or since." She laughed some more. "Rose walked away. Of course I got it in the neck for the next couple of weeks, but it didn't matter because Alexandra had got the best of the old bat. That kept me going for years."

"Again, you'd have to know our mother," Elle said.

"She did talk about you," Tom said to Jane, having remembered some of Alexandra's stories involving the girl who'd dropped off the grid after having a baby. Alexandra had felt guilty about losing the friendship with Jane. She had talked about reconnecting with her but never found the will or the time.

Leslie was smiling. "She sounds interesting."

"She is," Tom said. "She's amazing." He fell silent and his mind travelled to the dark place. The weight of his worry permeated the small space.

His sadness was overwhelming and Elle became desperate to change the vibe. "What about you, Leslie, do you have a story to tell?"

"No," Leslie said, and smiled because during their short acquaintance she had come to realize that Elle was not the kind of person to take no for an answer.

"Liar," Elle said. "Everyone has a story."

They fell into silence again, lost in their own thoughts.

Tom was still in the hell he'd created in his head. Jane's mind had taken her into the past before Kurt, when she and Alexandra were making plans to travel the world. Elle was busy working out what she could do to make everything better.

"I could set up a website," Leslie said. "We could go viral."

"Now you're talking!" Elle said, and clapped.

"I've no idea what going viral means," Jane said, "but I like the sound of it."

"Jane?" Elle said. "When is my next exhibition?"

"First week in February."

"How soon could we do another?"

"What have you got in mind?" Jane asked.

"Faces." Elle grinned. "How about I paint the faces of missing people, a collection of twelve to include Alexandra? I could start as soon as I've finished this last painting for February."

"I could definitely get media attention," said Jane.

"Good," Elle said. "Let's do it."

After seventeen weeks and two days of hopelessness, recrimination, confusion, frustration, fear and suffering, three strangers opened their hearts to Tom and they were kind enough to pretend they didn't notice when he cried.

Chapter 3

You Can't Get Bitter

It's so easy to be cynical,
you just turn on your TV screen
and everyone tells you who you should be.
When I feel stupid, disenchanted,
those pretty flowers that he planted,
the pollen comes floating down the breeze.

Jack L, *Broken Songs*

December 2007

It was just after eleven in the morning of New Year's Eve and Elle was standing at the back of her garden, knotting her long brown hair before picking up the shovel from the ground. Many years previously her ritual had changed from late evening to late morning because it had got in the way of her social life.

Jane emerged from the big house and made her way down the patio steps, towards her sister, who was unaware of her and busy staring into the middle distance. Jane often noticed Elle stare at something unseen by anyone else but she was sure that, whatever she was looking at, was real and interesting to her. *Weirdo.*

"Morning, soldier," she said affectionately, patting her sister's back before crossing her arms, hugging herself tightly and waiting for the ceremony to commence.

Elle saluted Jane, holding the shovel in one hand and a cigarette between her lips. Jane waited for her to begin breaking the soil but she was slow to start. "What are you waiting for?"

Elle dropped the shovel and walked backwards towards their mother's roses. "I'm just double-checking. I know the spot should be five feet from Mum's rose bushes and eight feet from Jeffrey's grave, but five feet from Mum's rose bushes appears to be only six feet from the bloody grave." She walked forward, toe to heel, counting.

"But those aren't proper feet," said Jane. "As in twelve inches one foot."

"I'm not talking about 'proper' feet – I'm talking about *my* feet," said Elle.

The recount was the same. Elle was displeased.

"Well, does it make a difference? Just dig a bigger hole," Jane said.

"Can't," Elle said, circling the point where she believed her box to be buried. "Last year I nearly lopped Jeffrey's head off."

Jane laughed. "Jeffrey died when you were six."

"So?"

"So that was twenty years ago."

Elle pretended to be confused. "What's your point?"

Jane spelled it out. "Jeffrey's head is long gone."

"I'm telling you it was Jeffrey."

"Not Jessica, Judy or Jimmy?" Jane asked, then laughed.

"Definitely Jeffrey," Elle said, and recounted her steps again. After the third recount she was utterly baffled. "It should be five feet from Mum's roses and eight feet from

Jeffrey's head so how the hell did the garden lose two feet all of a sudden?"

"Maybe it's the shoes you're wearing," Jane said helpfully.

Elle considered this and took them off. In socks she recounted and bizarrely gained one foot. *Christ, no wonder my toes look like stumps.*

"You need to get your feet seen to," Jane said, staring at her sister's hammer toes.

"Will do," Elle said, flexing them, hoping they would stretch back into toe shape. They didn't.

"And you need to give up wearing high heels."

"Won't do," Elle said, and refocused on the ground.

After another minute or two of standing around and arguing over the lost foot she dug carefully, retrieved the old biscuit tin and walked the short distance to her cottage, situated at the very back of the long garden, with Jane in tow. They headed into the kitchen. Jane made coffee while Elle battled to open the rusty old tin.

"You need a new tin."

"No way. It's this vessel or no vessel. It's all about tradition, Jane," Elle argued, then screamed, "Bollocks!" after nearly losing her middle finger to a sharp end of the rusted tin.

A few minutes passed before the coffee was made, the tin was open, the girls were sitting opposite one another and Elle was reading silently. Elle always read the letter silently while sipping her coffee before reading aloud the parts she was happy to share. She laughed and Jane smiled, although she didn't know what she was smiling at, and it was always at this point in the procedure she remembered that sometimes she didn't like what she heard. Elle put down the letter and nodded to herself with a sheepish grin.

"Well?" Jane asked, a tad nervously.

Elle began reading: "'Sunday, the thirty-first of December 2006. Dear Universe. What in the name of fuck is wrong with you?'"

"Strong start." Jane laughed.

Elle read on: "'The icecaps are melting, the ozone is burning, and species are actually dying out, the Golden Toad gone, the Black West African Rhino gone, the Baiji Dolphin gone –'"

She took a breath long enough for Jane to interject, "God, that's awful!" She was referring to the demise of the Baiji Dolphin. She didn't give a shit about the toad or the rhino. "Do you remember when I took Kurt to Kerry for a week and we swam with a dolphin? He was only nine then and it seems like just yesterday."

"Did you swim with a Baiji Dolphin, Jane?"

"No, a regular one."

"Well, then, it's not really relevant, is it?" Elle resumed her place in the text. "'The Pyrenean Ibex, gone.'"

"What's a Pyrenean Ibex?"

Elle thought about it for a minute. "I've no idea."

"Did you Google 'Extinct Species' before writing your letter?" Jane asked, in a tone that approached condescension.

"Of course I did. I'm not a bloody zoologist."

"I just don't understand your insatiable need to Google depressing subjects."

"Because they're important. We may not know what a Pyrenean Ibex is but I can assure you its extinction will have a fundamental effect on the delicate balance of its ecosystem and vice versa."

41

"Do you even know what you're talking about?" Jane asked.

"Not entirely," Elle admitted, "but it doesn't mean I'm wrong."

"Well, it sure as Shinola doesn't mean you're right either."

"Can I read this letter or not?" Elle asked, and Jane nodded, allowing her to proceed.

"'Why aren't you fighting? I'm doing my bit. I recycle, I turn the lights off, I don't even own a TV, but you don't seem to care that this world, which is a really big part of you, is dying. I know it's not your fault. I know it's ours, but we are trying and we'll try harder so stop being such a fucking tosser and adapt or at least bloody try to.'" Elle looked up at Jane. "Wow, I was really pissed off with the Universe," she said. She sniffed and drained her coffee cup, then found her place in the letter while Jane stood up to make more coffee. "'And as for this so-called Celtic Tiger, I wish it would die.'"

Jane placed the coffee pot on the counter with a bang. "Bite your tongue," she ordered. "This so-called Celtic Tiger is part of the reason you can charge forty-five K a painting."

"Yeah, well, I was over it last New Year's and I'm still over it this New Year's," Elle said. She read on silently as her sister busied herself rinsing out their cups. "Okay. My promises for 2007." She looked at her sister. "Please reserve your comments until the end."

Jane grinned and steadied herself. She placed a fresh cup of black coffee in front of Elle and sat opposite her.

"'One: I will learn to play the piano. Two: I'll donate the proceeds of my next painting to Warchild. Three: I'll paint by candlelight. Four: I'll try to help Jane more with Mum. Five: I'll get pregnant.'"

Jane gasped. Elle sighed a little. "Did I get pregnant in 2007?" she asked.

"Not unless there's something you're not telling me."

"There isn't," Elle said, and admitted it was a desire that had passed and she had no intention of getting pregnant in 2008 either. She resumed reading. "'Six: I'll be nicer to Jane.'"

"You're always nice to me," Jane said, smiling.

"I said no talking," Elle said sternly.

Jane pulled her index finger and thumb across her lips to indicate that she was zipping them.

"'Seven: I'll take Vincent to China.'" Elle stopped reading, and both women reflected on what had happened while Elle and her boyfriend Vincent were in China, but it was far too painful for either to rehash it so Elle moved on. "'Eight: I'll grow my own vegetables.'" She stopped and smiled at Jane, who was still ruminating on China but when Elle's eyes met hers she brightened.

"You made a complete mess of that," she said, remembering the amount of money, time and effort Elle had put into growing her own vegetables to end up with nothing but one crop of pretty poor-tasting potatoes, and some carrots that looked like they'd been shipped in from Chernobyl, never mind the damage she'd done to the patch of land closest to their mother's gardenias.

Elle laughed. "Remember Mum's face?"

"'What the fock's happened to my garden?'" Jane said, mimicking her mother's *faux*-posh accent. It was a funny memory and a good distraction from China.

"'Nine: I'll start a pension fund.'"

"You already have a pension fund. I set it up ten years ago."

"Oh, good. 'Cos I didn't start one. Right. Ten," Elle said, and bit her lip.

"What?" Jane asked.

"You might have a problem with this one."

"What?" Jane asked again, becoming quite nervous. "What did you do?"

Elle cleared her throat. "'Ten: I'll take Kurt skydiving.'"

Jane jumped up and pointed at her sister. "Oh, no, you didn't?" Actual tears were springing into her eyes. "You didn't push my child out of a plane?"

"Of course I didn't push him," Elle said soothingly. "The qualified instructor pushed him."

Jane's mouth was open but no sound was coming out.

"He loved it and he's fine and it's over." Elle was wishing she had kept number ten to herself.

"When?" Jane managed to ask.

"End of April, in good time for his birthday."

"Seventeen-year-olds need parental consent."

"Yeah, I gave that," Elle said, holding her hand up.

"How could you give parental consent seeing as you are not his parent and there's less than nine years between you?" Jane asked, through gritted teeth.

"I must look older than I am."

Jane walked to the door.

Elle called after her, "Please don't be annoyed!" But Jane was annoyed and now Elle was sorry.

"You can't just do whatever you want to do, Elle."

"I know. I'm sorry. He'd been begging me for years and I did hold out until he was seventeen."

Jane shook her head. "I'm really pissed off with you."

"I know. Sorry."

Jane opened Elle's sliding door.

Elle shouted after her, "So are you still going to that party with Tom?"

Jane turned to face her younger sister. "Yes," she said, and sighed. "Are you coming?" she asked hopefully.

"I'd rather be dead. Anyway, Vincent's taking me out."

"You could bring Vincent," Jane said, with hope in her voice.

"It's New Year's Eve and you're spending it with the family of a missing friend who you haven't known since you were seventeen. You have got to learn how to say no."

"I couldn't. Breda asked Tom if I'd come and —"

"And she knitted that bloody blanket. Jesus, Jane!"

"Right. I'm going." Jane turned to walk away.

"Happy New Year!"

"Happy New Year," Jane responded, "and, Elle, don't think that because I want you at that party it means I'm not really pissed off because I am."

Elle's intercom buzzed just as Jane closed her door. She picked up the receiver and a man told her he was standing outside the main gate with flowers. She buzzed him in and told him where to find her. She reopened the door and waved to him as he made his way down the garden.

"Elle Moore?"

"That's me."

She signed for the flowers and closed the door. She smelt them and smiled. She opened the card and the smile quickly faded.

Elle,

Like the song goes, I want you, I need you, but let's face it, I'm never going to love you. We've had four good years so let's start '08 with a clean slate.

Yours,
Vincent

Elle's legs turned to jelly, her ears began to burn and her stomach tightened so much that there was no room for her breakfast. She ran to the toilet and threw up, then sat on the floor and gazed at the note with a sense of disbelief that was overwhelming.

For six years running Jane had joined Elle at the back of their garden to retrieve her letter to the Universe and for six years running she had discovered something she didn't want to know. And yet, although her sister had taken her son skydiving after she had expressly forbidden it and she was so annoyed she could have spat, she knew she would partake in her sister's reading again. Five years ago, after a particularly nasty surprise involving her sister and an intended sexual encounter with a prostitute named Cora, it occurred to her that she should dig up Elle's letter to the Universe every January and read it to get a heads-up on what she'd planned for the year. But Jane was terrible at espionage, as had been proved seventeen years previously when she had only managed to conceal her pregnancy from her mother for two hours. "*What's wrong with you?*"
"*Nothing.*"
"*Oh, my God, you're pregnant!*"

If she dug up the letter Elle would find out and she'd never trust Jane again so she couldn't risk it, even though she often stood on the spot that was five feet from her mother's rose bushes and between six and eight feet from Jeffrey's head and was sorely tempted.

For instance, there had been the year that Elle had promised the Universe she'd give money to Comic Relief. She'd watched the show, got drunk and pledged a hundred grand. Jane had argued that, although people all over the world were in need, Elle didn't know if she'd sell another painting that year, and although Ricky Gervais was funny he wasn't that fucking funny. Elle had laughed and called her mean, but it was Jane who paid Elle's bills when she'd squandered all her money by June and had to wait three months for the next big cheque.

There had been the year she'd promised to rescue a dog and ended up rescuing ten from different pounds across Dublin. Two weeks and two tons of dog-shit later it had become apparent to all but Elle that she couldn't care for them. It had fallen to Jane to rehome them and Elle had taken to her bed for two weeks, mourning the dogs she couldn't seem to remember to care for. There was the year she'd decided to run a marathon and forgotten to prepare. She'd made it twenty miles before she collapsed, suffering the effects of exhaustion and a speed overdose. Elle had felt that it was perfectly acceptable to take speed to run a marathon, going so far as to query the doctor as to how in hell he thought she'd make it without.

All of these incidents had caused Jane to deliberate on risking Elle's wrath, but then she'd conceded that even if she knew of Elle's plans in advance there would be no way of stopping her as she was a law unto herself. Their mother said it was her creative nature that drove her to extremes and that neither she nor Jane could ever hope to understand the things that drove her. Jane and Rose didn't agree on much but they agreed on that. Elle was a genius and everyone knew that genius is close to madness and so as long as Elle painted the most beautiful and inspired paintings she would be indulged.

Jane opened the back door and before she got inside and had time to close it Rose was calling her through the intercom that linked her kitchen with her mother's in the basement apartment.

"Jane? Jane? Jane? Jane, it's your mother! Jane! Jane! Jane, have you gone deaf? I know you're there. I saw you come out of Elle's cottage. Jane, Jane, will you please answer me, for God's sake!"

Jane wondered how many times a day her mother shouted through the intercom and abused an empty room. She pressed the button. "I'm here."

"Are you planning on starving me?"

"To be fair, Rose, I've heard that drowning is faster and less cruel."

"I want eggs, scrambled, dry and fluffy. Not wet and slimy. If I see slime I'll throw up."

"I'll be down in five minutes."

"I'm hungry now."

"Oh, fine. I'll go ahead and pull a plate of scrambled, dry and fluffy eggs from my rectum then, shall I?"

"No need for vulgarity, Jane. You weren't born in a barn."

Kurt entered the kitchen in time to witness Jane give the intercom the finger. "Whatever she wants, I'm not doing it," he said.

"Oh, yes, you are," Jane said, in a voice her son recognized as his mother meaning business. The look that twisted her face suggested he was in big trouble.

"What?" he asked, trying to work out what he'd been caught doing.

"Skydiving, Kurt?"

"Oh, I'm going to kill Elle!" He flopped onto the chair and pulled his hood over his head, covering his blond curls, and pressed his hands to his ears.

"Skydiving. You know how I feel about skydiving. I said no. Every time you asked me I said no. No means 'no'. It doesn't mean 'maybe', it doesn't mean 'I'll think about it' and it sure as Shinola doesn't mean 'Go behind Mum's back with Elle'!"

"Oh, Mum, please stop saying 'sure as Shinola' – it sounds retarded. The expression is, 'You don't know shit from Shinola.'"

"I don't give a shit if it is and that's not the point."

"You said it the other day in front of Paul and he thought you'd hit your head."

"Really, I don't give a Shinola. You cannot get away with deliberately disobeying my rules."

"Ah, Mum, back off. It was last April. It's done, over, it was a laugh, it was safe and nobody died."

"Well, you can forget about tonight."

"You can't stop me going out on New Year's Eve!" he said, with scorn.

"No, probably not, but I can withhold funds."

Kurt pushed his hood off his head. "You can't do that. I've promised Irene."

"Tough."

"I can't believe you're doing this to me on New Year's Eve!" he shouted, and stormed out of the kitchen.

"Yeah, well, believe it and you'd better storm back here in ten minutes flat to bring Rose's eggs to her or you're going to be poor for all of January!"

"I hate you!" Kurt screamed at his mother.

"I hate you too!" Jane screamed back, while breaking two eggs into a cup.

Ten minutes later Kurt stormed in, picked up the plate of eggs and stormed out without a word.

Although Jane's authority had been briefly undermined her power was restored, she was fifty euro richer and she had managed to avoid Rose so her mood brightened considerably.

Kurt made his way down the steps to his grandmother's basement flat with her tray in one hand, fishing for the key with his other. He opened the door and went inside. The place smelt of air-freshener, cigars and wine, making his eyes water a little. In the small hall he nearly tripped over a stack of unsolicited post that she kept in a pile against the wall. It was stacked so tall that it kept falling over. He had once asked her why she kept it and she had told him that she was waiting for a member of the Green Party to call to her door so that she could throw the paper at him, douse him in alcohol and set him alight. She had been drunk at the time so Kurt hoped she was joking. He opened the door to the sitting room and his grandmother sat up straight in her chair.

When she saw him, her face broke into a smile. Kurt's relationship with his grandmother was far different from that he had with his mother. Rose idolized her grandson and saved all her grace for him. He laid the tray on the table she kept near the big chair that dominated the room. The chair was referred to as "the throne" by her daughters and she spent most of her time sitting in it. No one dared sit on Rose's chair, not her daughters, not her friends, not visiting dignitaries and not even her grandson, who was one of the very few people that Rose actually liked. Poking at her eggs, she asked after Jane and he lied and told her she felt fluey.

"Well, then, she may stay away — I prefer you anyway," she said, winking. She sampled her eggs and made a face to suggest that she was less than impressed. She always made that face. Usually it was for Jane's benefit but as it had become habit she did it whether Jane was there or not. She sniffed the plate.

"Just eat the eggs," Kurt said.

Rose took a forkful and popped it into her mouth, rubbed her tummy and made a yum sound. Kurt laughed.

"How's Irene?" she asked.

"She's good," he said, and sat down. "Better, she'll be fine."

His grandmother nodded. "Of course she will. So her father's an ass. She has you, doesn't she? Is your mother still determined to go to the Walsh household tonight with Alexandra's husband?"

"She's dreading it."

"Of course she's dreading it. The Walshes have always been complete lunatics. Alexandra was the cheekiest pup I ever met. The mother is one of those holier-than-thou types, the father hasn't done a real day's work since the seventies, and as for her brother Eamonn, that little snot was trying to get into your mother's pants when she was thirteen!" She stopped and took a breath. "And, anyway, she has no business there – the family are grieving the loss of their child."

"She's missing, not dead," Kurt reminded his grandmother.

"Of course she's dead," Rose said. "She's Valley-of-the-Dead dead."

"You don't know that."

"I know this. If someone vanishes without a trace in this day and age they're buried somewhere and it's usually someone closest to them who's done the burying. For all we know your mother's next."

Kurt laughed. "Now I know where Elle gets her imagination from."

"Mark my words. Your mother is getting herself involved in something very bloody sinister there." She pushed the remaining food on her plate to the side and put down her fork. "I've finished."

After that Kurt told his grandmother about his run-in with his mother, expressing how annoyed he was that she was punishing him for something he'd done eight months previously. For once his grandmother was on his mother's side as she felt that anyone who jumped out of a perfectly good plane deserved to be crippled for life. Having said that, she felt that Jane's withdrawal of funds was an overreaction, bearing in mind which night it was. "How much do you need?" she asked.

"Seventy?" Kurt said, testing his grandmother.

"Fifty it is," she responded, knowing full well he was

chancing his arm. She took fifty euro out of her handbag and handed it to him.

"Cheers, Gran!"

She waved him away. He left the basement flat and she watched him through her window as he turned on his iPod, searched for some noise, pressed play and walked down the street, probably deafening himself. *Kids are mad*, she thought. Then she picked up the open bottle of red wine that was resting against her chair. She drained her cup of tea and poured in the wine. She took a sip and smiled to herself. *Happy New Year, Rose.*

Chapter 4

So Far Gone

I'm so far gone that it seems like home to me.
I'm so far gone, have I lost my way or am I free?

Jack L, *Universe*

It was just after eight thirty on New Year's Eve when Leslie got off the train, returning from the bungalow she owned in the country. Her apartment was located conveniently beside the railway station so she wheeled her suitcase past all those queuing for a taxi, turned the corner, tapped her number into the keypad on the apartment-building gate and she was home.

In the lift, she could hear crashing and banging, and the closer she got to her floor, the louder the noise became. She exited and walked towards a bunch of five people she recognized as neighbours. They were blocking the way so she mumbled, "Excuse me." They didn't notice as they were wrapped up in what was going on around the corner. It was then Leslie noticed a fireman. He was standing in front of the group as though he was there to hold them back. Leslie couldn't smell any smoke. She said, "Excuse me," again, but this time the banging was louder.

One of the girls she recognized but didn't know turned and looked her up and down. "Oh, shit!" she said. "She's here!"

Leslie wasn't one for pleasantries but the girl's response to her arrival was slightly shocking. The others gaped at her. The fireman called to his buddies, "Lads, it's a false alarm!"

The gaping neighbours parted and she was allowed to walk through them with her case rolling behind her. She rounded the corner to be met by two firemen standing in the space where she used to have a front door. "What the hell?" she asked.

"It's my fault," the girl who had uttered "Oh, shit" said. "I haven't heard your music in a few days and there was a smell."

A fireman walked through the doorway. "Well, the good news is we have no dead body. The bad news is the cat has shat all over the place."

"I was down the country," Leslie said, a little shocked at the scene.

"I'm really sorry," the girl said, to the fireman rather than to Leslie. "She rarely leaves the apartment," her tone slid from apologetic to accusatory, "and for the past few days no music and then that awful smell."

"You smelt cat-shit and thought I was dead?" Leslie said, in a voice laced with contempt and disbelief.

The girl turned to her, hands raised in the air. "Look, I was just being a good neighbour – you hear all the time about people left to rot and, to be fair, I don't know what death smells like."

"Well, it doesn't smell like cat-shit – and what do you mean 'these people'?"

"Well," said the girl, becoming a little uncomfortable, "loners."

Leslie stood dumbfounded.

"She thought you'd killed yourself," a random man said.

The girl nudged him and mouthed the words "shut" and "up".

"Well," he said, directing his speech to the firemen, "everyone knows that New Year's Eve is a big night for suicides."

"Am I going to get charged for this call-out?" the girl asked.

"Don't give them your name, Deborah!" the man said.

"Brilliant, Damien," she said, walking away and shaking her head. "Thanks for that."

The firemen gathered their gear; the five people disappeared.

Leslie entered her doorless apartment and sat on the sofa. Her cat, which had apparently recovered from its gastrointestinal malady, jumped on her lap and together they surveyed the pile of cat-shit matted into the carpet near the electric fire. Then the realization of how she was perceived in her building hit Leslie like a ton of bricks. *I'm the crazy-loner cat lady, who drops dead and rots in her apartment.* The irony was not lost on her as she had only recently rejoined the society she had shunned for so long.

A mere two months before this night Leslie had been sitting in a chair opposite her oncologist. He had cared for her mother and both her sisters through their cancer. He had also been testing Leslie twice a year for more than twenty years. He was smiling. "Good news," he said. "You're clean as a whistle."

"Right," Leslie said. "Fine. Thanks." She stood up to leave.

"What's wrong with you?" he asked.

"Nothing. Apparently I'm clean as a whistle."

"You sound disappointed."

She sat. "Well, would it be odd if I said I was?"

"Very odd."

"I'm sick of waiting," she said. "I'm sick of waiting for this stupid tick-tocking time-bomb to go off."

"Oh," he said. "I see."

"The truth is, when Imelda died I stopped living." She hunched her shoulders. "Now I'm a woman about to turn forty with a cat for company. I thought I'd be well dead by now but yet here I am, alive and lonely." She smiled at her doctor to assure him she wasn't going to cry. He must have been shocked at her revelation as it was possibly the most she'd ever said to him.

"You know that you might never get cancer," he said, "but a lot has changed in recent years. Although I'm not a huge advocate of preventive surgery I can give you some brochures."

She looked at him. "We talked about this years ago. You were adamant it was just self-mutilation."

"A lot has changed," he repeated, "and, besides, I might have thought differently if I'd known how you were feeling or if you'd given even the slightest indication of the effect this worry was having on your life."

She stared at him and asked abruptly, "Are you talking about a double mastectomy?"

"Yes. And in your case I'd recommend a full hysterectomy also, for peace of mind."

"Wow," she said. "Jesus. Holy crap." She nodded. "Give me the information."

This new prospect was daunting but even as Leslie pulled out of the hospital car park she had made up her mind. *I'm going to do it.*

It was around that time that Leslie also decided she'd

had enough of being lonely and tentatively she had stepped back out into the world. As she was a web designer who worked from home, she decided instead to rent an office in town. She had yet to move on this but the plan was in place. As she had no friends she decided to visit museums and art galleries so that, even if she was alone, at least she was outside and partaking in life.

It would be a slow road back but, thanks to that night stuck in a lift, not as slow as she had first envisaged. Elle had become a fixture in her world over the past two months and to a lesser extent Tom and Jane. She had created a website for Alexandra and was in contact with Tom, giving him updates, and Jane filled her in on how the exhibition idea was coming along so that she could blog about it. But Elle wanted more than her help. Elle wanted her friendship and, although it was unnatural to Leslie to be a friend to a woman so much younger, she had become fond of her. So, the fact that she had so recently ventured back into the world and actually made friends meant that the comments from her annoying neighbour served to really bug her. "I'm not a loner, Deborah!" she shouted at the wall. "I have friends. I go out. I have a life."

Someone coughed. It was the caretaker. "Sorry to disturb you," he said.

"It's fine," she said. "I was just talking to the wall."

"I'm here to fix the door," he said.

"Okay," she said. "Please forgive the smell. I'm about to clean."

"Will do," he said, and got to work.

Much later, after the caretaker had hastily fitted a new door, Leslie poured a glass of wine, picked up her phone and dialled a number she hadn't dialled in more than ten years.

"Hello?"

"Jim?"

"This is Jim."

"Hi, it's Leslie Sheehan."

"Leslie – Jesus! I can't believe it's you!"

"I know. It's odd. I hope I'm not intruding."

"No, I'm just sitting in."

"Me too."

"Happy New Year, by the way!"

"Happy New Year."

"So, what made you call after all this time?" he asked.

"I don't know – well, it sounds stupid."

"You're sick?"

"No, no, not sick," she said. "I'm thinking about having preventive surgery actually."

"I think you should," he said, without missing a beat.

"Wow."

"If Imelda'd had that choice I know she would have done it."

"That's what I thought."

"Are you scared?"

"No."

"Have you got anyone in your life?"

"No."

"Do you want me to be there for you?"

Leslie couldn't believe it. She hadn't spoken to Jim in so many years and before that she'd usually been rude or standoffish. "That is really kind of you," she said, "but no."

"So why have you called?"

"I just wanted to hear your voice," she said, and laughed a little. "People are mad, aren't they?"

Jim laughed too. "Yes, Leslie, people are mad."

After that she asked him how he was and what he was doing and if he'd ever remarried. He was fine, doing well and, no, he hadn't. He'd seen a Russian woman for a year but she'd returned to Russia when her father had died six months earlier.

They spoke for about fifteen minutes and before she hung up she promised to call him to arrange to go out for a drink.

"You see, Deborah! I'm going out for a drink, with a man, very soon!" she shouted at the wall once more. "I am not Crazy Dead Cat Lady, not today and not tomorrow!"

The cat stared at her from its freshly washed and pine-scented bed. Leslie looked at her watch and as it was only nine she opened her computer and watched three episodes of *Desperate Housewives* Season One, before hitting the hay around eleven thirty.

"Yeah, Happy New Year, Deborah, and up yours!"

Tom beeped the horn and, within seconds, Jane appeared. She waved, closed the door and ignored her mother's face, pressed to the basement window, when she turned to shut the gate. Tom had got out and opened her car door. She buckled up while he made his way around to his side. He got in and thanked her for agreeing to come to the Walshes' with him, explaining how awkward it had been since Alexandra had disappeared. She wondered why he put himself through it and he admitted he had a soft spot for Alexandra's mother, Breda.

They got to the house just after nine and Alexandra's younger sister, Kate, opened the door. She hugged Tom and said a polite hello to Jane. The last time Jane had seen Kate she had probably been no more than ten so she wasn't surprised when she didn't recognize her. They entered the hallway and Jane felt as though she had stepped back through time. The carpet was still brown with red diamonds, the telephone table still had two yellow telephone books under it, the walls were still dotted with holiday photos from the seventies and eighties and at least three included her. She was ushered quickly into the sitting room.

There, sitting on the green velvet chair by the window, was Breda. The chair was the same but Breda had aged well beyond her years. Having begun her family young, Breda couldn't have been older than sixty-five but she looked ninety. Her face was wizened and her tall frame shrivelled. Her hair was white and cropped. Her hands, clasped and holding rosary beads, were so thin they were transparent, revealing blue and purple veins and knuckles that appeared knotted.

She saw Jane, smiled and held out her hand. Jane took it and felt a little weak.

"Jane Moore," said Breda, "you've grown into such a beautiful woman."

"Thank you, Breda. It's lovely to see you again."

"And Tom tells me you've been so good helping him find my Alexandra."

"I'm only setting up an exhibition to highlight her case and the Missing of Ireland." Jane was embarrassed and wished she was in a position to do more.

"You were always such a lovely girl. Alexandra will be

so pleased to have you in her life again." She was crying but her tears were silent.

From the corner of her eye Jane noticed Eamonn enter the room but Breda still had a firm grip of her hand and deserved her full attention.

"Still so blonde," said Breda, and flipped Jane's shoulder-length hair.

"It has some help, these days," Jane said.

"Do you remember Alexandra's hair?"

Jane nodded.

"She had the richest chestnut hair, so glossy," said her mother. "It was just above her shoulders when we saw her last but the police say it could have changed now. I hope it hasn't. She had the most beautiful hair."

"Mam," Eamonn said, "Jane doesn't want to hear that."

Jane turned to Eamonn and nodded hello. "It's fine," she said. "I understand."

Breda let go of Jane's hand. "You should get a drink." She looked at Tom, who was still standing at the door. "Tom, you should get Jane a drink."

Tom took Jane into the kitchen where Kate, her husband Owen, Eamonn's wife Frankie and Alexandra's father Ben were standing around the counter. Frankie welcomed Tom with a hug and Ben nodded to him. Kate offered him a drink but Tom said he'd make it himself.

Ben shook Jane's hand and thanked her for coming. "It's great to see you. How's that boy of yours?"

"He's fine. He's seventeen now."

"My God, time passes quickly. It seems like only yesterday yourself and herself were giving us a run for our money."

Jane grinned. Although he was older than his wife he

still managed to look ten years younger. He sported a full head of grey hair and he rubbed at the grey stubble on his chin. He was heavier than he had been years before. She remembered him as fit and sporty but those days were long gone. His shirt buttons strained over his paunch, and when he'd approached her he'd walked with a limp.

Some neighbours arrived and sat in the sitting room with Breda. The house seemed full and empty at the same time. Tom handed Jane a glass of red wine. Tony Bennett was playing on the stereo. No one talked about the fact that Alexandra was gone. They referred to her often and included her in stories about the past, which was where, it seemed, her parents now resided. Tom talked with his in-laws' neighbours, Frankie, and Owen, but it was difficult not to notice coldness between him and Alexandra's brother and father. He spent some time with Breda, who hugged him warmly and whispered something into his ear.

Half an hour before midnight he found Jane in the hallway, studying a picture on the wall. "That was taken on a day out in Bray in 1983," she said. "It was such a hot day. The beach was mobbed and we'd run into the arcade and onto the bumpers just to cool down. Alexandra ate so much candy floss she puked pink all the way home."

Tom looked at the picture and recognized Jane. Her hair was so blonde it was almost white and plaited to her waist. She was hugging Alexandra whose wavy chestnut hair shone in the sun. Both girls were facing the camera and grinning so hard they had dimples. "It's a funny old world," he said, but nobody was laughing.

Midnight came and went, the New Year was celebrated

and when the clock struck one Tom and Jane made their excuses and left.

In the car Jane asked Tom about his relationship with Alexandra's family.

"Ben and Eamonn need someone to blame," he said.

"Why you?"

"Why not me? She's my wife."

"And what about Breda?"

"Breda blames herself."

"And you?"

"It depends on the day."

When they got to Jane's house he stopped the car and thanked her once more for coming. "It meant so much to Breda."

She told him she'd be in touch the following week with an update about the exhibition. He nodded and she got out of the car. She closed the gate behind her and waved. He drove off and she made her way up the steps of her house. She could hear Bing Crosby singing "You Are My Sun-shine", punctuated by laughter and chat from her mother's basement flat. She didn't stop to say hello. Instead she went inside, took off her shoes, which were pretty but painful, poured herself a whiskey and took it to bed.

When the clock turned midnight Elle toasted the sky. She spun around the beach in bare feet with a bottle of vodka pressed to her chest. When she stopped spinning she fell onto her arse, still managing to hold onto the bottle. She got up as quickly as a drunkard can and sprayed some alcohol on the fire so that the flames danced higher and higher. The car engine had already exploded so now she and a homeless man, who called himself Buns, watched the shell burn out. She sat beside him and clinked her bottle against his.

"Happy New Year, Buns!"

"Happy New Year, my dear!"

They sat in silence, listening to the flames crackle and the low hush of the sea as it swept in and out. Elle lit a cigarette and passed it to him. He refused with a wave of his hands. "Those things will kill you."

She laughed a little. "Sleeping on a pavement in December will kill you quicker."

"Ah, well, it's January now, so roll on spring!" He took a slug from the bottle of vodka the strange girl had bought for him. "Vincent must be a right bastard," he said, after a minute or two.

"Depends who you ask," she said, getting up and dancing around again.

"How much would you say that car cost?" he asked.

"Around forty grand." She could have answered with a precise figure if she had wished to as she had bought Vincent the car.

"Jesus. He'll be sorry he messed with you."

She smiled. "That's the hope."

They both heard the police sirens. Buns drained his bottle dry before the cops could take his booze off him. Elle continued to dance to the music she could hear in her head. The police approached them cautiously but Elle smiled and waved them over as though they were at a party and she was asking them to join in. Once they had established that Elle had stolen her ex-boyfriend's car and burned it out they put her and Buns, who happily claimed to have been a willing accessory, in the back of the car. Buns was delighted he would have a night inside or even two if he was lucky – he'd seen the weather forecast in the window of Dixons electrical shop and the temperature was set to fall below zero.

Elle was focused on the sights, sounds and smells around her. Everything seemed so vivid; she was giddy, high on revenge and adventure. The city moved quickly past the window and the siren pealed, not because there was an emergency, just to get through the drunkards on the streets. The car smelt of disinfectant and she breathed in deeply. Buns smelt of something else entirely, a little sweat, a little oil, a little damp and a little puke, and still she inhaled and smiled as though it was the sweetest perfume.

"I've never been in a jail cell," she said, excited by the notion. "I've always wondered about it."

The female guard looked over her shoulder. "Well, you won't have to wonder any more."

"True." Elle smiled to herself.

Jane woke with a start. Kurt was standing above her with his hand on her shoulder, shaking her. "Mum, Mum, Mum!"

She bolted upright in the bed. "Kurt?" She looked at the clock beside her bed, which read 4:10 a.m. "What the hell?"

"It's Elle. She's been arrested."

Jane stared at her son blankly; the words that had come from his mouth seemed to have lost their meaning. "Excuse me?"

"Sit up," he ordered, and she noticed he was slurring but at that moment her teenage drunken son was the least of her worries.

"Did you say 'arrested'?" she asked, silently praying she'd misheard him.

He nodded.

She swung her legs around, sat on the edge of the bed and held her head in her hands. "Oh, for fu–" she said, then sighed a sigh that seemed to come from her very core. "Where is she?"

"Clontarf."

"Clontarf," she repeated, and got out of bed. "And why not? Clontarf is as good as any place to get arrested."

Kurt watched his mother talk to herself and bump into things while trying to locate something to wear. She said "ouch" twice and "for fu–" a number of times before he took his leave so that she could get dressed.

Jane entered the sitting room in search of her handbag. Kurt and his girlfriend Irene were lying on the sofa together, listening to music.

"Hi, Jane," Irene said, with a grin that suggested she had imbibed one too many alcopops.

"Hi, Irene," she said. "Does your mother know where you are?"

"She's in Venice," Irene said, slurring a little.

"Nice."

"Not really," Irene said. "She found out that Dad was sleeping with some woman he met on the Internet and she's gone over there to spend as much of his money as possible before she kicks him out of the house."

"Oh, my God, that's awful," Jane said, truly shocked and momentarily forgetting her sister was in a jail cell. "Are you okay?"

"I'm fine." Irene waved her hands dismissively.

"Well, if things get a bit rough at home you can always come and stay here – in the spare room, not Kurt's."

"Ah, Jane, that is so nice of you, thank you." She burped. "Excuse you!" she said, pointing at Jane, then burst out laughing. Kurt laughed too.

Jane raised her eyes to heaven and grabbed her bag but before she left she stood in front of the pair, wagging her finger. "No sex in here, no sex in your room, no sex in this entire house. And don't think I won't know because I will know." She left the room.

Irene looked at Kurt and wagged her finger. "And yet she didn't cop that we've just done it on this sofa."

Jane heard them laugh as she exited the house. *Of course they're laughing. It's four in the morning, they're seventeen, drunk and awake, and they've probably had more sex in the past five hours than I've had in two years.*

Once in the police station Jane waited for more than two hours before she even got to speak to someone. It was then she was informed that her sister faced possible charges on counts of theft and arson. Jane closed her eyes and didn't speak for what seemed to be the longest time. The policeman queried as to whether or not she was all right.

"I hate my life," she said.

"I know the feeling."

After that she sat in the waiting area for another hour. She was freezing and tired and so pissed off that she actually wanted to weep. The man beside her smelt of feet and the woman opposite stared at her in a manner that suggested she might wish to hurt her. Jane would have loved to be bold enough to square up to the stranger and demand of her an explanation as to what she wanted, but she didn't have the balls. *The story of my life*, she thought, keeping her head hung low to avoid her aggressive opposite's gaze.

Elle appeared a little after eight o'clock. She was yawning and stretching. She grinned when she saw Jane, who stood up, grabbed her sister's arm and dragged her out of the station.

"Do not grin, do not speak, do not even bollocking whimper!" she ordered Elle, who seemed to be veering between alarm and amusement. "I am cold and tired and I've just about had it up to here. So shut up."

"Okay," Elle agreed.

They sat into the car. Jane started the engine.

"Can I smoke?" Elle asked.

"Shut up," Jane said.

"I'll take that as a yes, then," said Elle, lighting up.

Jane drove in silence. Elle smoked and stared out of the window. When they were less than a mile from the house, Jane pulled the car into the side of the road and parked. She turned to her sister and began the rant she had practised while sitting in the police station and attempting to avoid being head-butted. "You have done some unbelievable things in your time – stupid, stupid things that have left me wide eyed and open-mouthed – but, my God, this one has really topped the lot. You burnt out Vincent's car? No, hold on, you *stole* and then you burned out Vincent's car? What is wrong with you? How insane does a person have to be?" She noticed tears streaming from Elle's eyes, which silenced her.

Elle took the card out of her pocket and passed it to Jane. Jane read it aloud: "'Elle, like the song goes, I want you, I need you, but let's face it, I'm never going to love you.'" She looked away from the card and faced her sister, who was still crying. "'Like the song goes'?" She looked back at the card. "'Let's face it'?" She shook her head. "Oh, Elle!" She pitied her sister because even though Vincent was a pig Elle loved him deeply. "Let's face it," Jane repeated, "he's obviously back on drugs."

Elle didn't respond.

Jane handed the card back to Elle, whose nose was now running. She took some tissue from her pocket, wiped Elle's nose and hugged her. "It's all right, Elle, we'll sort it all out." But she knew there was nothing she could do.

Elle shook her head. "He's really gone this time, Janey." Then she sobbed on her sister's shoulder until her tears ran dry.

Chapter 5

Authentic Fake

Pillows bursting at the seams,
feathers floating like dreams,
naked on the wooden floor,
night porters banging at the door,
and we just turn the music up.

Jack L., *Broken Songs*

January 2008

Although it was cold the sky was blue and there wasn't a cloud in sight. Jane favoured cold, dry days but they were so few and far between. She wasn't a fan of central heating as it made her skin itchy. She liked a nip in the air and couldn't understand when her son complained that he was cold – she had spent so much money on clothes for him yet he had the audacity to stand in front of her in a T-shirt and boxer shorts wondering what it would take for her to put on some heat. The kitchen was warm because she had spent the morning baking. Kurt came in, rubbing his hands together and blowing into them for effect.

"Put on a jumper and jeans," she said, with her back to him.

"Who's coming?" he asked, ignoring her and putting on the kettle.

71

"Tom and Leslie."

"Oh, them." He made a face.

"'Oh, them,'" she repeated, amused. "What's wrong with them?"

"He's haunted and she's a bit of a freak," he said, spooning coffee into a cup. "Oh, and Gran thinks he's a murderer."

"For God's sake, stop listening to that twisted woman!"

"Well, you can't say it hasn't crossed your mind."

"I can say it hasn't crossed my mind," she replied. "Alexandra disappeared when Tom was in work, and he has witnesses."

"So it has crossed your mind but you're satisfied with his alibi," Kurt said, pointing his spoon at his mother.

"Fine." She put her hands up. "I'm satisfied with his alibi."

"Lots of people have good alibis, and then that alibi turns out to be crap."

"Kurt," Jane said, "please stop calling Mammy's new friend a murderer." Kurt laughed a little. He always enjoyed it when his mother attempted to talk down to him. "Okay, but be careful. You don't have the best track record as a judge of character." He poured boiling water into the cup and gripped it tightly. "God, Mum, it's freezing in here."

He left to go to his room and sit at his computer with his duvet wrapped around his body and arms while his hands remained uncovered and unencumbered. Jane remained in the kitchen, cleaning the spilled coffee granules from the counter while keeping an eye on the oven and clock.

This would be the third time Leslie and Tom had come to her house to discuss their project's progress. Elle had been there both times before but she was taking her break-up with

Vincent pretty hard. When Jane had spotted the "Gone Fishing" sign on her door earlier that morning, she knew it meant that Elle might be away for a week or a month. She wasn't sure how she was going to break this news to Tom.

Tom had become incredibly excited at the last meeting when Elle had revealed the painting she had done of Alexandra. He had previously given her a box of photos of his wife and she'd gone through all of Jane's from when Alexandra was younger. After she'd spent a week looking at the woman's face, she spent another week capturing it. According to Tom, Jane and even Leslie she had done so beautifully.

"I made her look sad," Elle had said. "I hope you don't mind because I know she's a happy sort but I think she needed to look sad."

"I don't mind. She's beautiful," Tom said, staring at the painting, which leaned against Jane's kitchen wall. "How did you do that? How did you make her look lost?"

Elle had stared at the face she had come to know so well and hunched her shoulders. "I don't know."

Tom bit the side of his mouth so hard there was an indent in his cheek. He nodded and looked at Elle. "You're incredible."

Elle loved it when people complimented her. She'd blush and say she hated it but her heart would flutter, her pulse would race and, for a moment, she'd feel a great high, which she'd come down from all too soon.

Leslie had created a fantastic website – www.findingalexandra.com – which incorporated Alexandra's most recent photos and a map of her last movements. She'd even managed to attach the CCTV footage from Tara Street and

Dalkey DART stations. She had created a blog space for Tom to update if and when he wanted, a chat room for anyone who might wish to post a comment and, of course, there was an email address for anyone with information. Tom had been overwhelmed, especially when she revealed the link to Jack Lukeman's website. When she clicked into Jack's site there was a link to findingalexandra. Tom was dumbfounded. Jack's website even mentioned Alexandra and asked his visitors to check the findingalexandra site to work out if they had seen her.

"How did you manage that?" Tom asked.

"I designed Jack's site."

"Wow, that's fantastic. Absolutely fantastic."

"And you said you couldn't help!" Elle teased.

"Well, I'm glad you're happy," Leslie said, a little chuffed with herself.

"How did you get Jack to agree?" Jane asked.

"Alexandra's a Jack fan and I got Myra in his office to agree, and once she agreed it was pretty much done and, by the by, they asked if there was anything else they could do."

"You are shitting me?" said Elle.

"No," Leslie said. "And I'm not sure I even know or care to know what shitting a person is."

"Of course there's something else they can do," said Jane suddenly.

"Yeah," said Elle, beating Jane to it. "Jack can sing at the Missing Exhibition opening."

"It would make the PR a cinch," said Jane.

"I'll talk to Myra," said Leslie.

Tom didn't know what to say. He was bowled over. In the few short weeks he had known these three women, his search for his wife had taken on a whole new life and he could hardly express his gratitude to them.

Jane smiled at him when he became tongue-tied and slightly tearful. "We'll find her," she promised.

Now, less than a month later, her promise appeared slightly premature, if not a tad arrogant. Elle was missing in action and that meant she wasn't painting, and if she wasn't painting the exhibition might not happen in April as had been planned, and if the exhibition didn't happen in April Jack wouldn't be available to play until after he'd finished with the European festivals in September, and he was key to publicity. She had tried to call Elle but to no avail. "Gone Fishing" meant no contact.

Jane felt sick at having to disappoint Tom, and Leslie after all the work she'd put into promoting the exhibition on the website, and she wasn't even sure if she should tell them. *Maybe I'll give it a week*, she thought. *I'll give it a week and see what happens and then, if I have to tell them and break Tom's heart, I'll do it. Damn it, Elle, this is no time for your selfish crap – come home.*

Leslie was the first to arrive. Jane opened the door and Leslie pointed to the basement and asked if Jane knew who the old woman was.

"My mother."

Leslie nodded. "Oh," she said. "She has Tom."

"Sweet Jesus! There's coffee made. I'll be a minute." Jane took off down the front steps like a hare before Leslie could respond.

Tom was sitting in a chair opposite her mother when she burst into the room as though she was a gangbuster. Rose was swirling liquid in her mug and Jane prayed it was tea. Tom was silent, his hands clasped and resting on his knee.

"What has she said?" Jane asked Tom.

"I asked him if he'd killed his wife," Rose said. "I further inquired as to whether or not he had any intention of killing you."

"Oh, God." Jane closed her eyes for a moment to compose herself.

"I said no on both counts," Tom said and, thankfully, he seemed a little amused.

"You see, Jane?" said Rose. "We're only having a nice quiet chat. There's no need to run down here like your anus is on fire."

Tom laughed a bit.

"Tom," Jane said, "time to leave."

He stood up.

"Rose, I'll talk to you later," said Jane.

Tom said goodbye to Rose and followed Jane out into Rose's small hallway where he managed to kick over her stack of unsolicited mail. He stooped to pile it back together and, before Jane could tell him to ignore it and move on, her mother shouted from her sitting room: "And, Tom dear . . ."

"Yes?" He moved back to the doorway.

"If my daughter happens to go missing, you'll die roaring. I'll make sure of it," she said, in a sweet and airy tone, as though she was promising to take him out to dinner.

"I understand."

"I'm so sorry," Jane apologized, as she drew him away from the door and slammed it. "I really am so very sorry."

"It's fine," Tom said.

"You need locking up!" she screamed at her mother,

through the closed sitting-room door. She opened Rose's front door and Tom followed her into the cold air. He was a little miffed and a little entertained.

Jane was pissed off. "Sorry you had to witness that."

"It's fine," he said. "Worth it. After all, without you and Elle I'd still be handing out flyers at gigs."

Oh, God, Elle! Come home, for Christ's sake, just come home!

Jane smiled at him and pretended everything was okay. He followed her up the steps and into the house. They went to the kitchen where Leslie was hugging her cup of coffee.

"Is the heating broken?" she asked.

"I'll put it on." Jane went into the hall.

Kurt heard the familiar clicking and came out of his bedroom dressed in his duvet. "Oh, yeah, Mum, you'll put on the heat for visitors but not your only son. Nice one."

Jane ignored him and, after taking a detour into her bedroom to quickly smear her face with moisturizer for extra-dry skin, she made her way back to the kitchen in time to hear Leslie inform Tom that the hits on the findingalexandra site had increased by seventy per cent since they'd linked up with Jack Lukeman's.

Jane offered them a choice between carrot cake, chocolate log and coffee queen cakes and brewed fresh coffee. Once they'd complimented Jane on her baking skills, Leslie revealed that before she'd left her apartment she'd received an email from someone who believed that they'd spotted Alexandra at a Jack Lukeman gig in London the previous week. "I think it's important not to get excited," Leslie warned, producing a printout of the email. "It could have been anyone."

"But it could have been Alexandra," Tom said. "Please read it."

She unfolded the printout.

Tom lowered his head so that he could focus on the floor. "'Hi, my name is Michelle Radley. I work at the Pigalle Club in London. Last month Jack Lukeman was playing. It was a busy night, two of the girls were off sick and the toilet attendant didn't show up. There was a young girl who'd had too much to drink and she was getting sick in the toilets. I was called in to help her but the club was so busy I couldn't really stay with her. So a woman that looked exactly like the one in your picture said she would. We talked for a minute or two. She said her name was Alex. She really did look like the woman in your picture but she was thinner and her hair was shorter. When I returned to the toilet she and the sick girl were gone. Jack Lukeman is returning to play a show on Saturday, 1 March, and I'll be working so I'll watch out for her. If you would like to give me a telephone number I could phone you if she returns. Regards, Michelle.'" She added her own number as a PS.

Leslie stopped reading and looked at Tom, who was still staring at the floor. She looked at Jane, who was wiping her hands on a tea-towel for a little longer than necessary.

"This could be it," Jane said, and threw the towel onto the counter.

"It's her," Tom said.

"Hang on," Leslie said. "Hang on one second. This is a thin, short-haired woman who just looks like Alexandra."

"She called herself Alex," said Jane.

"But Tom told us she hasn't called herself Alex since she was a teenager," Leslie said.

"But helping a drunken girl in a toilet is something she'd do," Tom said.

"It's something a lot of people would do," Leslie said. "I really think it's important not to get ahead of ourselves here. We should just pass the information on to the police and let them handle it."

Tom looked up from the floor. "I'm going to London for the show."

"I'll come with you," Jane said.

"Really?" he asked.

"Absolutely." *It's the least I can do, considering my sister has gone AWOL.*

"Oh, for God's sake," Leslie said. "You pair haven't listened to one word I've said."

"We have," said Tom. "Look, Leslie, I will pass on the email to the police but I can't just leave it at that. We're so close!"

"But you might not be," said Leslie.

"But we might be," said Jane.

"I give up!" Leslie got up and cut herself another slice of carrot cake even though she'd been watching what she ate since Elle had sat her down in a coffee shop the week before Christmas and told her that not only did she need her hair dyed and styled and a complete new wardrobe but she should lose a minimum of six pounds. When Leslie had argued that she was happy the way she was, Elle was having none of it and asked her new friend one simple question: "Do you ever want to have sex again?"

Leslie had thought about this question for a long time before answering because she really wasn't sure. It had been so long since she'd had sex with anything that wasn't battery-operated that it seemed like it might be a little too much work. After serious consideration, during which time Elle

79

had managed to finish her cappuccino, order another, go to the loo and send two text messages, she had admitted that, yes, she probably would like to have sex again in her lifetime.

"Well, then," Elle had said, pointing to Leslie's head and moving her finger downwards towards her toes, "sort yourself out."

"I'm not that bad!" Leslie had argued.

Elle agreed that she wasn't that bad, going so far as to comment that in fact, for a woman in her early forties, she looked quite good.

"Thanks a lot," Leslie had said, once again wondering why she was allowing herself to be friends with a girl in her twenties.

Elle had smiled at her and, after rummaging through her bag for a few minutes, had taken out a card that was bent and covered with bag dirt. She cleaned it off, straightened it out and handed it to Leslie. "That's my hairdresser. She'll take care of you."

After thinking about it for about a week, Leslie had decided to get her hair done but had put it off until after Christmas to avoid the crowds. Her appointment was for later that afternoon. She halved the slice of cake, then ate half of the half because since Elle had mentioned her thickened midriff she'd become conscious of it. "Where is Elle?" she asked, after pinching some crumbs together and popping them into her mouth.

"Working," Jane lied.

"I'm really looking forward to her exhibition in two weeks," Leslie said. "She showed me some of the paintings last time we were here. They're stunning and just a little bit frightening. Love them."

"Yeah," Jane said, nodding, "she's a genius." *Stop nodding, Jane.*

"Would it be okay if I called in on her for just a moment before we leave?" Leslie asked.

"No," Jane said. "I'm really sorry," she added, "she's just so busy with the exhibition pieces."

"But I thought she'd finished those paintings?" Tom said. "Is she working on the Missing Exhibition already? I thought you were still waiting on permission from the families."

"No, she has some work to do for this upcoming show – she's a perfectionist. And we are still waiting on permission from the families – although that man missing from Clare, Joe something, his family have come back and said they would love to be involved." *Oh, Christ, I hope she comes home in time for the show in two weeks.*

"Okay," Leslie said. "I'll call her later."

"Fine," Jane said, "but don't be surprised if she doesn't answer. When she's in the zone the whole world could be collapsing around her and she wouldn't notice."

"Right," Leslie said, and let it go at that. "Probably better to leave her be."

Jane nodded enthusiastically. *Stop nodding, Jane.*

Tom left soon after. He had promised to go on-line to book the tickets and accommodation for the London gig and insisted on paying for it. Jane had then insisted that he and Leslie take home slices of carrot cake, chocolate log and a biscuit cake she'd spotted in the fridge that she'd made two days previously and forgotten about.

Tom hugged both women before he left. "Thank you," he said, "thank you. Thank you. Thank you." He sighed and smiled, then turned and walked down the steps, leaving Leslie and Jane standing together at the door. They watched him get into his car and waved to him as he drove off.

When he was out of sight Leslie turned to Jane. "So what's really going on with Elle?"

For somebody who didn't spend a lot of time with people she was incredibly intuitive. "You'd better come back in," Jane said.

Jane brewed another pot of coffee and told Leslie about Elle's New Year's Eve.

"Good God," Leslie said, "could she go to prison for that?"

"I have to meet that snivelling little snot Vincent next week to sort out compensation. Basically if we buy him a new car he won't press charges and if he doesn't press charges hopefully the DPP won't either."

"'I want you, I need you, but let's face it, I'm never going to love you,'" Leslie said, shaking her head in disbelief. "Just when I thought it was safe to go back in the water."

Jane explained her sister's inexplicable passion for the man who had mistreated her from the day they'd met and how, having an inexplicable passion of her own for the father of her child, she understood and sympathized with her sister's misguided love. "You can't choose who you love," she said.

Leslie thought about it – it made her crave more cake. After that Jane explained that whenever things got on top of Elle she would hang the "Gone Fishing" sign on her front door. It signalled that she needed peace and quiet, time away from everything and everyone, and until she was ready to face the world again she would be off the radar.

Leslie was aghast that Elle would just disappear like that and couldn't understand why Jane indulged her. "That's extremely selfish," she said. "What if you need her?"

"I leave a voice message and hope she picks it up," she admitted, before dismissing Leslie's concerns, noting she was simply happy that Elle gave her a clear indication of what she was up to so that she didn't have to worry. Although, of course, she did worry but not as much as if Elle disappeared without warning.

It took Leslie a few minutes to grasp the significance of Elle's latest fishing trip and it only became clear when Jane recounted the time two years earlier when she had failed to return for two months.

"Will she paint while she's away?" Leslie asked.

"She hasn't before."

"But the Missing Exhibition is scheduled for April!"

"She'll be home — it's important, she'll get it done," Jane said, but Leslie could tell she wasn't convinced.

"And if she doesn't?"

"Well, we'll just have to find Alexandra in a club in March," Jane said, and knew her proposal sounded weak.

"It's not her," Leslie said, "and even if it was it doesn't mean she's going to turn up in the same place again."

"Don't be so negative."

"Can't help it — it's my factory setting," Leslie said, and smiled.

"Elle will come home," said Jane. "Hopefully in time to deliver twelve stunning paintings and, if not, we'll sort it out. I'll sort it out."

"I should warn the Jack camp."

"No, don't say anything — please just give it a week. Let's

get over this exhibition first and then we can worry about what happens in April."

Leslie nodded, and after that she wondered how Jane would cope if Elle didn't turn up to her own exhibition.

"Actually, sometimes it works out better," Jane told her. "In case you hadn't noticed, my sister can be a bit of a handful."

Leslie had noticed so the conversation ended there. It was too late to get her hair done so she phoned the hairdresser to reschedule while enjoying a brisk walk through the park to undo some of the damage Jane's cake had done to her hips.

Tom's business was suffering and not just because he'd lost interest in it. His company had completed a large development in south Dublin in mid-2007 and he'd been looking for more land but planning was getting tougher and, if he was honest, the houses he'd just finished hadn't been as quick to sell as the previous two. He had decided to bide his time and wait for the right project. Then Alexandra had disappeared, and after that, the only thing he'd been looking for was her. He'd lost most of his building staff in the second quarter of 2007, only retaining a few men for snagging. The plumbers and electricians he'd contracted had moved on to work with others, and by the time he'd got stuck in a lift his company was reduced to himself and Jeanette in the office. It was quite clear that the business was dead and eventually Jeanette received her severance pay.

The risk-taking and swagger that were needed to build and preside over the once-successful business he'd built from nothing had left with Alexandra and, in an environment where the clouds of recession were gathering, Tom Kavanagh had simply lost his nerve. After ten years of blood, sweat and tears, when the doors of his company finally closed in Christmas week Tom walked away without looking back once. His only focus was finding his wife. He spent hours on-line on her website, blogging and adding pictures as Leslie had shown him. He looked at missing-person sites every day and made calls to shelters all over Ireland and the UK and sent them emails with Alexandra's face attached. He ensured that Interpol had all his wife's details and insisted on following up every tiny little piece of information the police were investigating. He was so hands-on that in the end his liaison officer, Patricia Lowe, had to tell him in no uncertain terms to back off. He still handed out flyers and tacked them to posts and trees.

When he wasn't searching he visited Breda and told her about all the things that people were doing to find Alexandra.

"You're a good man," she'd say, "and we will get her back." Breda was sure that Alexandra was alive and well, just a little lost. She knew this because she'd prayed to God to keep her daughter safe and in sixty-odd years God had yet to let her down. Tom hadn't believed in God until his wife disappeared but afterwards he found his mother-in-law's trust and hope comforting.

"She's not alone, Tom," she said, over and over, "she's never alone."

Alexandra's father didn't talk about God or anything at all. Instead he sat in the garden and smoked one Marlboro after another. In the evenings he went out to the pub with his friends and they talked about football and politics, the state of the world and anything but his missing daughter because every time he thought about her his guts twisted, his head ached and his heart threatened to stop dead.

Tom would always make it his business to go into the garden and say a few words to him, and he was polite but a little cold in his response.

"How are you doing?" Tom would ask.

"Fine."

"It's freezing out here. Are you sure you wouldn't be better off inside?"

"I'm fine."

"Breda seems good today."

"She's fine."

"Can I do anything?"

"You're doing all you can."

"I'm sorry."

Tom ended every short interlude with his father-in-law saying, "I'm sorry", and every time the man would nod and say nothing.

In the car on the way home from Jane's, Tom wondered whether or not he should call into his in-laws with the good news but then thought better of it. He'd wait and maybe in March he'd be bringing his wife home. He knew in his heart that Leslie was right to be cautious and that the likelihood of finding Alexandra in a club in London was a million to one, but he didn't care because a million to one was better odds than a million to none.

Tom had never been much of a drinker but since his wife had vanished he drank every night because he couldn't sleep unless he was intoxicated and even then his sleep was disturbed and he was restless, kicking and sometimes yelling out. When he didn't drink he'd lie in bed afraid to close his eyes because when he did he'd go to the dark place. The scenarios were always different and yet they were the same: his wife was hurt, she needed him and he wasn't there. In one Alexandra was tied up and dirty. She was face down on the floor and her arms were twisted behind her back. Her face was streaked with dirt, blood and tears, she had a hole in her head that was caked in blood and she was crying out, calling his name, and over her a shadow loomed, a monster playing with a knife, and she would beg Tom to find her before the monster cut into her again. In another he'd see her in a tiny windowless room; she was surrounded by concrete walls and a black steel door with a tiny flap at the bottom. She was in the corner hugging the wall and there was nothing but silence and a tray of slop that she couldn't eat. She was so thin that her bones stood out and she'd call to him that if he didn't find her soon she'd be gone. There was the one where she was drugged and tied to a bed and men were coming and going, screwing her, and her head would roll and her eyes, red raw, would call to him to save her, but he couldn't because he couldn't see where she was. He'd claw at his face and hit the side of his head and roar and bawl and scream and rock until he was so tired that all he could do was lie very still and stare at her smiling picture hanging on the wall. And with each night that passed he'd live another, more twisted and painful nightmare.

Since Tom's secretary Jeanette had lost her job she had called in on a number of occasions to check up on him. The first time she had appeared he was drunk and wearing what appeared to be uncomfortably snug tracksuit bottoms. "I didn't know you even owned a tracksuit."

"I don't. They're Alexandra's."

"Why?"

"I wanted to walk a mile in her shoes but they didn't fit."

"How drunk are you?"

"Very."

She'd come into his house and run a bath, and when he refused to get into it she'd insisted. Her insistence and freakish upper-body strength ensured that ten minutes later he was soaking in bath oil while she cleaned his kitchen and sitting room of takeaway cartons and empty bottles. He'd fallen asleep and she'd woken him, and when he realized he was naked and in the bath he became embarrassed, but she made light of it and handed him a towel. "I've seen worse on site," she said, and she wasn't lying: she'd caught a plasterer taking a dump behind a tree and when she closed her eyes she could still see arse-hair and excrement. She'd also walked in on brickie Barry Brady receiving a blow-job on his lunch hour, not once but twice, and he was a pig about it, winking at her and asking if she wanted to join in. Even thinking about it made her want to go back in time and punch him.

Tom asked her to leave the bathroom while he covered himself up and he briefly wondered how to dissuade her from coming to his house again.

Jeanette had worked for Tom for four years and she'd developed a crush on him within a week of joining his company and, of course, he knew it. Before Alexandra had gone missing, Tom had been warm and funny. He was the kind of man and boss who didn't need to feel superior to those working for him. He'd drop a coffee on her desk as he was passing, always remembering how she took it, no milk, one sugar, and every now and then he'd bring her something sweet. It wasn't just her, he'd do it for the others too. In fact, when she thought about it, for a man who ran a profitable company he spent a lot of time making coffee. He would listen to her when she spoke and he'd tell her what a great job she was doing. He wasn't available back then, he wasn't even looking for sex, more was the pity, because Jeanette would have done him on the photocopier in week one if he'd asked her. At least, that was what she'd told her pals Lily and Davey in the pub the night before she'd decided to visit him at his home that first time.

"Uncomfortable," Davey said, "and technically impossible. He'd be the one doing you and you'd only be leaning on it. But I suppose you could say that you'd invited him to do you *over* the photocopier."

"Shut up, Davey!" Lily said.

"I was only saying."

"Yeah, well, don't say. Go on, Jeanette, you'd have done him on the photocopier in week one . . ."

"Well, that was it, really."

Lily punched Davey in the arm. "You always do that! Interrupt someone when they're saying something interesting just to say something totally boring, throwing off the person who actually has something to say!" She punched him again.

Davey rubbed his arm and then he said something interesting. "Okay then, elephant in the room, he offed his missus."

Jeanette didn't believe it possible. "No way."

"Of course he did. Nobody just disappears."

"People disappear all the time, knob jockey!" Lily said.

Jeanette shook her head from side to side. "Nothing could make me believe that he did anything to her."

"Well, my advice to you would be to stay away until we know that for sure," Davey said.

Lily nodded. "He has a point. Better safe than headless in a suitcase floating down the Dodder."

Jeanette had no intention of staying away and, even though the sparkle in Tom's eye had been replaced with a terrible sadness, God help poor Jeanette, she fell deeper in love.

She waited for Tom to emerge from the bathroom, and when he did and he was clean and his house was clean and there was real food cooking in his oven and she was talking about the job interview she'd just had and looking for some music, he felt normal and calm and it was nice, if only for a while. When he'd sobered up she poured some wine and they sat together and ate. When they'd polished off the bottle and were halfway through the second, and after she'd served a dessert that neither of them ate, she gazed at him across the table and slowly, hesitantly, took his hand in hers. "What more can I do?" she asked. While retaining his hand, she walked around the table and sat on a chair at his side. Now he was facing her, his hand still in hers, and her other hand was sliding up his thigh. His pulse raced, and her heart was racing too, as she asked him again, "What can I do?" and he was staring into her face and eyes and the kitchen fell away as he reached for the back of her head and pulled her into him and they kissed.

The next night in the pub she'd re-enacted it for her pals Lily and Davey.

"Jesus, that's like in a film," Lily said.

"Exactly like in a film," said Jeanette. And she believed herself.

Davey was less impressed. "You're playing with fire." But he was ignored.

"What happened then?" asked Lily.

Tom had pulled Jeanette onto the floor and they'd kissed again and her pants were off before she could say, "Take my pants off," and his were around his ankles and he was on top of her and inside her and their tops were still on and it was over quickly, which was a good thing because the tiles were freezing. When he was done she could see his regret and shame so she acted fast before he could ask her to leave and file their encounter under "mistake". They both pulled up their pants. She took two cigarettes out of her bag and lit both of them. She asked him to sit next to her on the floor. He complied out of a combination of guilt and a genuine desire for a cigarette, despite having been off them for five years.

When he was sitting and puffing, she straddled him. "I know what you're thinking," she said.

"I doubt it."

"You're thinking, Jeanette is a nice girl and I'm grateful for the tumble, which was badly needed, but how the hell do I get her out of here without making her cry?"

He shook his head, and she smiled. "Something like that," he admitted.

"I like you," she said.

"I'm a mess."

"I know. I'm not blind."

"I'm married."

"She's not here."

"Please go home," he said, and she knew she'd spoken out of turn.

"Okay." She nodded. "I'm sorry." And she was sorry. She was sorry he was so sad and she was sorry for poor Alexandra and she was sorry for herself because although she was desperate for him to love her she knew he never would. *I had to try*, she thought, as she closed the door behind her.

"Jesus, you could have waited," Davey said the next night.

"He's right," Lily agreed.

Jeanette knew she'd blown it so a phone call from Tom came as a shock. He rang her from his car on the way back from Jane's.

"Tom?"

"Good news," he said. "I have a lead on Alexandra. It's not much but it's something."

"Oh, that's great," she said, and brightened. "I hope it works out." She meant it.

"Look, I wanted to apologize for that night," he said. "I should never have done that."

Jeanette thought about how kind he was to call. After all, she had preyed on him — he was vulnerable, lost and drunk and she'd seduced him. *God, I love you.* "It wasn't you, it was me," she said, "and I appreciate you apologizing but you've nothing to apologize for."

"I wasn't that drunk."

Jeanette's heart leaped a little.

"Could we be friends?" he asked.

"Yeah," she said, "I'd love that."

"Would you like to come over tonight?"

"I'd love to."

When she put the phone down she jumped around the place because even if Tom genuinely thought he was looking for a friend he wasn't, and he might be naive enough to think the night would end with a kiss on the cheek but she wasn't.

I need to shave. Whoohoooooooooo!

Jeanette arrived soaked to the skin. It had been raining on and off since six o'clock and she had left her second umbrella in a month on the bus. Tom opened the door smiling. She shook herself off in the hall before noticing that he was wearing an apron. "What's going on?" she asked, following him into the kitchen.

"I cooked." He put on a glove and grabbed a large fork, opened the oven door and turned a roasting leg of lamb.

"I can see that," she said, sitting at the counter while he opened some wine. She poured it into two glasses and handed him one.

He clinked his glass against hers. "I'm going to find her," he said.

"Alexandra?"

"No – Amelia Earhart," he said, and grinned the way he used to grin before he lost his wife.

She wondered who Amelia Earhart was while he attended to the vegetables.

Jeanette drank from her glass until it was empty, then held it out for more. Tom topped it up.

"I've met these women," he said, "and they're amazing – they're helping me. I don't even know them."

"That's weird. Why?"

"Jane was Alexandra's best friend years ago when they were kids and her sister Elle is an artist and she's going to do an exhibition. She's painting the faces of missing people. She's already painted Alexandra and it's really beautiful. And Leslie's set up an incredible website and they've got Jack Lukeman on board and now this lead in London –"

"Jack Lukeman the singer? What is he? A part-time private eye?" She was being sarcastic but although Tom noticed he didn't care.

"No, he's going to sing at the exhibition. Jane says it will increase media interest."

"Well, it sounds like you've got a lot of new friends, so why did you call me?"

"I missed you." He wasn't lying. He had become very fond of Jeanette during the four years they had worked together, and if he was really honest with himself, he missed the attention she gave him. He missed feeling like a man, a sexual being, and even though he promised himself that he would never allow what had happened before to happen again it was nice to be around someone who was attracted to him. Tom missed many things about his wife and one of the things he missed most was being wanted.

"I missed you too," she said, and in her head she was singing, "Here comes the bride, all dressed in white . . ."

Later, after they'd indulged in passionate sex, the kind of sex that Jeanette had always suspected Tom was capable of, they lay in silence and darkness just breathing. "What are you thinking?" she asked.

"It's blissfully quiet in here," he said, pointing to his head.

She smiled at him, leaned over and kissed his cheek. "You're welcome," she said.

She went into the bathroom and he could hear the shower running and he reminisced about the last time he'd lain in bed and listened to the shower running and his wife was singing "I Can't Stand The Rain", attempting a very bad impression of Tina Turner. Tom closed his eyes, just as he had when he was having sex, and for the second time that night he pretended the woman who had been in his bed and was now in the shower was his wife. For the first time in thirty weeks and one day Tom slept peacefully.

Chapter 6

Little Man

Take the world off your shoulders,
little man, little man, little man.

Jack L, *Universe*

February 2008

Elle had been lying in bed for twenty days. Twelve days after New Year's Eve she had taken a taxi to a hotel in Kildare. When she arrived someone took her bag out of the car as she paid the fare. She signed her name on the form that the receptionist handed her, took her key and followed the man with her bag up to the third floor and into her room. She tipped him and he left.

She undressed, put a do-not-disturb sign on the door, and got into bed with the curtains drawn. The only time she had got out of bed in those twenty days was to pee, apart from when the maids came in. They knocked every second or third day and she'd get out of her bed and sit on the toilet while they cleaned the room. When they were finished she'd get back into bed while they cleaned the bathroom. Some days she ate something small and some days she didn't eat at all. The television remained off and days and nights blended into one. Some days she was numb and without any kind of coherent thought; other days her mind raced so much that her head hurt and she felt the need to put pressure on her ears. Her phone remained off. There were days that she cried rivers, other days she simply breathed in and out, in and out, in and out, each breath becoming more and more laborious until every cell in her body hurt, so that even lifting her arm was almost impossible.

The manager knocked on her door after she'd refused the maids access for the sixth day in a row. He waited for a response but was met with silence so he knocked again. She was either ignoring him or sleeping so he knocked a third time and louder, and in her head, for the second time, she screamed at him to go away. As the manager didn't read minds he made the decision to enter the room. He was accompanied by one of the receptionists to ensure that there was no misunderstanding as to the intention of his visit. He entered slowly with the girl following. Elle was lying on her side. He called to her. She remained still. The girl seemed to be of a nervous dispos-ition so the manager smiled at her to reassure her everything was fine. He walked around the side of the bed and Elle's eyes were open and staring. She was pale and because the blankets were tucked under her neck it was unclear whether or not she was breathing. The girl mistook her for a corpse and screamed. Elle moved her eyes to focus on the screaming girl, whose nervous disposition had been blamed long ago on her twin brother, who had often chased her while pretending to be a zombie. Seeing the corpse's eyes move sent her over the edge so she screamed again loudly and ran out of the room, down the hall and stairs and out of the front door of the hotel, leaving the manager alone and decidedly uncomfortable. *Thanks for nothing, Sheena.*

"Are you all right, Miss Moore?" he asked.

"How many times have I told you to leave me alone today?"

"None."

"Are you deaf?"

"I'm not deaf."

"I just told you to leave me alone at least twice if not three times."

The manager decided not to argue. "Is there someone I can call?"

Elle slowly raised herself up in the bed; the blanket dropped, revealing her naked breasts. The manager turned red and looked away.

"If I wanted you to call someone I would have asked you to call someone," she said, leaving the blanket at her waist.

The manager turned from red to a funny purple colour. He covered his eyes because he could still see her in the mirror and she knew he could still see her because she was watching him through that same mirror. "Do you like what you see?" she asked.

"Sorry?" he said, in a voice that had gone up one octave.

"My tits," she said. "Do you like them?"

The manager did like them. She had a lovely, rounded, pert, full pair but there was no way in the world he was going to say that and he wasn't going to tell her he didn't like them either so instead he did what any man in his right mind would do: he ignored the question. "I'm sorry to disturb you," he said, "but we need to know that you are okay."

"Now you know."

"If there's anything we can do for you?"

"You can go away."

He nodded and left the room.

She lay down, tucking the blanket up around her chin, and she lay perfectly still in absolute darkness.

When capable of coherent thought Elle reminisced about all the things in Vincent she had loved. His face: she had fallen in love with his face the first time she'd seen him across a crowded bar. It was a strong and pretty face and he had old man's eyes, deep, dark, chocolate eyes, nestled behind lush eyelashes so thick and long that any woman or drag act would sell themselves for them. His curly brown hair: she loved that it was always messy and sexy and soft, putting her hands through it, playing with it. She loved his height: he was taller than her but not too tall, and they could always kiss comfortably even on the rare occasion she wore flats. She loved his hands: soft and manicured and always perfectly clean. She loved the things he did with his hands and how those hands made her feel. His laugh: when he laughed his eyes leaked water and he threw back his head and slapped his thigh and it was a throaty, giggly laugh that encouraged her to join in. His mind: she missed him reading passages out of newspapers and books to her, she missed watching him read his books and the way he screwed up his face when fully concentrating and bit at his thumb before changing the page. Vincent was never without a book and all his jackets had pockets big enough to hold at least one. She missed the poetry that loving him brought into her life. She missed the fights where they'd scream and roar at one another, where she'd smash a plate and he'd stamp his foot and punch the wall. She missed making up, ripping at one another's clothes and the heat between them

99

and the way he often bit her lip and the feel of him inside her, his rhythm and the way he looked at her afterwards when they lay still and sticky. She missed herself: the silly, giddy part of her that she shared only with him.

He had tried to end it in China and, deep down, she had known that he loved what she represented rather than who she was. He was an out-of-work model, studying design by night, and she was a successful artist – and with success came a lifestyle he had become accustomed to. In a small city like Dublin, Elle was a big fish ensuring minor celebrity status and entrance to every VIP room. Vincent loved the champagne lifestyle, not Elle. He had never loved Elle, just as the note had said. He had wanted her, she had always been certain of that, he most definitely had needed her, as she had paid for his lifestyle for years, but he was never going to love her, no matter what she did to keep him. China had been a reprieve and ever since she'd been waiting for the other shoe to drop.

Elle's love had died and it was all she could do to keep breathing.

The hairdresser put her hands through Leslie's short crop, and when Leslie confirmed that she had cut her own hair for quite a few years, the hairdresser admitted that the thought had certainly crossed her mind, then called over a fellow professional so that they could confer on the best course of action to minimize the damage Leslie had done.

"God almighty, did you use a bowl?" the other woman said.

"No."

"Well, you might as well have. I've seen Trappist monks with better hair."

"What's your name?" Leslie asked.

"Sophie."

"Well, Sophie, if I wanted to be insulted I'd sing for Simon Cowell. As it is, I just want my hair restyled."

"Fine," Sophie said curtly.

"And, Sophie?"

"Yes?"

"No talking."

"So you don't want me to tell you what we're going to do?"

Leslie could tell that Sophie wanted to slap her. "After that," she said.

The first woman walked away, leaving Sophie to it. Sophie then explained to Leslie that she could no longer get away with black hair because of her age and the pallor of her skin, but she could give her a nice copper tone. Leslie was fine with that. Sophie called over the two young girls, Esther and Julie, and after she'd spent a minute explaining what she wanted them to do she walked away and they got to work. As instructed, they didn't address Leslie. Instead they chatted among themselves about an apartment block that had gone up near the salon and whether or not Julie should buy a one-bed apartment in the inner city with her boyfriend Joseph for €390,000, especially as it was only possible with a 100 per cent mortgage.

"You should just go for it," Esther said.

"Yeah, I mean, what have I got to lose?" Julie said.

"Are you insane?" Leslie asked, and the two girls looked at her in the mirror.

"What do you mean?" Julie asked.

"How long have you been with Joseph?"

"A year."

"What age are you?"

"Twenty-one. I'll be twenty-two in April."

"What rate are you buying your mortgage at?"

"Don't know."

"How much will you be paying back per month?"

"No clue."

"What's your rush?"

"I need to get on the property ladder."

"You're twenty-one. You've got another ten years to get on the property ladder."

"Yeah, well, I want to do it now."

"Look, it's none of my business but around here, well, let's be honest, it's a kip. You don't want to pay three hundred and ninety K for a one-bed apartment in a kip, especially when you're paying back a hundred per cent mortgage, no doubt on a non-competitive rate and with a boy you've only been with for one year. It's madness."

"It's not a kip around here," Julie said indignantly. "I grew up around here. My ma lives around the corner."

"What happens if you can't afford the mortgage?"

"But we can."

"What happens if mortgage rates go up and you can't afford the mortgage?"

"We're going for a fixed-rate mortgage," Julie said, delighted she could answer at least one of the annoying woman's questions.

"What if you lose your job?" Leslie asked.

"I'm not going to," Julie said, looking around uncomfortably.

"What if you split up with your boyfriend?"

"We're happy."

"Happy now, but in six months' time with a ridiculously large mortgage to pay in an apartment the size of a box of matches you might not be. In fact, if I was a betting woman I'd put a hundred euro on it not lasting the year."

Julie started to cry.

"What is wrong with you?" Esther asked Leslie, and she took Julie into the break room.

Sophie reappeared and silently resumed dyeing Leslie's hair.

"Is Julie okay?" Leslie asked. "I was only trying to help."

"No talking," Sophie said.

Leslie shook her head. *Fair enough.*

When the dye was finally washed out, after what seemed an eternity, the girl who'd originally consulted with her returned, scissors in hand. She worked quickly and silently and Leslie relaxed. She blow-dried and fixed with a little wax. Then she stood back and Leslie looked at herself.

Although she was forty and had a few age spots on her face and chest, she still had a tight jawline and protruding cheekbones. The copper worked against her brown eyes and the short, elfin style suited her features. The girl was smiling. Some other girls, not Julie, came over and all said they had done a fantastic job and Leslie agreed. *Not bad. Not bad at all.*

Bolstered by her new look she stopped at a makeup counter in Brown Thomas. The girl did her makeup while describing to her what she was using to cover her troublesome areas. She'd asked for something natural and the girl did as instructed: dark eyes, light lips, flawless skin. By the end of it she looked and felt like a new woman and was so impressed she ended up spending more than two hundred euro on the products the girl recommended even though she would never be able to re-create the look at home.

She checked her watch and it was after five. She decided to grab something quick to eat upstairs in BT's before she'd head to the pub where Jim would be waiting. When she'd asked him to Elle's opening she'd felt good about it, but now that the time had come she felt slightly regretful. It had been so long since she'd seen him, almost a lifetime had passed, and they had never really been that close. *What the hell am I at?* she thought, as she queued for a table.

Jane spent the day running around. She started by picking up boxes of wine from the wine merchants. She dropped them off at the catering company, then went to the gallery and hung the paintings. After that she went to a music shop and picked up some music that fitted the theme of the exhibition, "Angels and Demons". As most of the angels and demons were copulating, she chose a mix of metal and classical. After that she got her hair done, and after that she returned to the gallery to set out tables and to load the CD player. When the place was spick and span, the paintings secure on the walls and the tables ready for the caterer, she drove home to shower and change.

She heard Kurt laugh in the kitchen and then she heard Dominic's voice and he was laughing too, and she couldn't remember the last time she and her son had laughed together. She entered the kitchen and Dominic stood up and surveyed her before hugging her. "You look great."

She smiled and told him he didn't look so bad himself.

She inquired as to what was so funny but neither her son nor his father was willing to share the joke. *In-joke bastards.*

"Are you hungry?" Dominic asked.

"I'm not cooking for you. I'm too busy."

"I know. Kurt told me you have the exhibition tonight so I brought pizza."

"Ah, thanks but no, I'll just have a coffee."

Kurt got up and checked the pizza, which was cooking in the oven. It was ready so he plated up. Dominic and Kurt ate their pizza and Jane drank her coffee.

"So, Elle's gone fishing?" Dominic said.

"Afraid so. Still, it's probably for the best. I've heard a rumour that Pat Hogan is coming."

"Who's Pat Hogan?" Kurt said, with his mouth full.

"Don't talk with a full mouth," she said. "He's a critic that Elle threatened to stab when she was at art college."

"Yeah, well, that wasn't yesterday," said Dominic. "I'm sure it's all forgotten."

"No – it's funny, he loves her work but, my God, she hates him."

"Dad, tell Mum about your new bike," Kurt said, and then he opened his mouth wide to show his mother that it had been empty before he spoke.

"Funny," she said. "What's this about a bike?"

Dominic was grinning like a Cheshire cat. "It's a Harley."

"A road king," Kurt said.

"Black cherry."

"And black pearl."

"It's a real beaut."

"I'd swap my dick for one," Kurt said.

Dominic laughed, while Jane covered her ears and smiled.

"How's Bella?" Jane asked.

"Oh, she's not talking to me," Dominic said.

"Because you're a selfish prick who nearly killed himself on a motorbike a year ago and, having promised faithfully that you would never get on a bike again, you've gone behind her back and bought a Harley?"

"Got it in one."

"Jesus, Dominic, what is wrong with you?"

He grinned at her. "Ah, come on, Janey, Bella's already giving me hell. Can't you just be happy for me?"

She smiled at him. "Okay, I'll be happy for you. Congratulations on your new bike. Please don't cripple or kill yourself."

"Ah, thanks for worrying."

"I'm not."

"You are." He winked at her.

She smiled and blushed a little. *Oh, grow up, Jane.*

"Jane? Jane? Jane? Are you there? Jane?" Rose's voice came over the intercom.

Dominic stood up and pressed the button. "Hi, Rose."

"Who let you in?" Rose asked.

"My son." Dominic smiled.

"I want Jane."

"I'm sorry. Jane is currently not available. Is there something I can do for you?"

"You can go back under the rock you've climbed out from."

"I miss you too, Rose."

"I want Jane."

Jane stood up and pushed Dominic out of the way. "Yes, Rose."

"Have you heard from Elle?"

"No."

Rose hung up.

Dominic turned to Jane. "So, are you going to invite me to this shindig or what?"

"Don't you have a home to go to?"

"Maybe tomorrow when she's cooled down."

"Nice one, Dad. I'll make up the spare room," Kurt said.

Dominic reached into his pocket, took out a twenty-euro note and handed it to him. Kurt pocketed the money and headed out of the door towards the spare room.

"You don't mind?" Dominic said.

"I don't seem to have a choice." But she was smiling, indicating that she didn't mind. In fact, it was obvious she was really happy. *Got a grip, Jane, he married someone else,* she thought, as she made her way up to the shower.

Leslie walked into the bar and, although it had been at least ten years since she'd seen him, she recognized him immediately. He was reading a newspaper and when she tapped him on the shoulder he managed to appear slightly surprised that she'd shown up. He stood up and he was shorter than she remembered. They hugged awkwardly.

"You're taller than I remember," he said.

"Heels," she said, and pointed to her brand-new pair of black wedges.

"Jeepers, the last time I saw you you wore nothing but sneakers."

She didn't tell him that this was the first time in years she had worn anything but MBTs, which, basically, were posh sneakers that made her work harder when she walked.

They sat down and he asked her if she wanted a drink and she said a white wine would be lovely, and he went to get one, and she was alone waiting for him to come back and her heart was racing and her palms sweating. He had aged around the eyes and he'd shaved his head. He was thinner than she recalled but he still had his dimples, the ones that had made Imelda go weak at the knees, and the warm smile she had loved so much.

What do we talk about? I hope I don't make him cry. That last time I saw him I made him cry. Why did I do that? What's wrong with me?

As it turned out, they had little or no trouble finding things to talk about. He came back with her wine and she asked him what he had been reading about and he told her and they talked about it and then they moved on to books, and they both liked to read and shared a taste in books so that gave them at least another hour of great conversation. Neither liked the cinema so they discussed why they didn't and then Leslie attempted to persuade Jim about the benefits of broadband. She couldn't believe he was not yet converted.

"So you've never sent an email?"

"No."

"That's amazing."

"Is it?"

"And you've never surfed the net?"

"I wouldn't know how to – besides, I don't have the knees for it." He laughed at his own joke.

"If only that were funny, Jim." She shook her head. "You're a dinosaur, my friend."

"Sorry, I'll try to do better." He smiled. She had called

him a friend. Imelda would be happy. "What about you?" he asked. "Still thinking about surgery?"

She nodded. "I've been to three specialists since we last spoke, and I'm doing it."

It was strange that Jim was the only one she had told, but then again it wasn't that strange. After all, who would understand better than him? She was hardly going to tell her new friends and didn't have anyone else in her life.

"When?" he asked.

"July. The first of July." She nodded to herself. "That's the date they've given me."

"It'll be hard. You'll need help."

"I'm going from the hospital to a nursing-home," she said, smiling. "It's a really nice place. It'll be fine. I'm a big girl."

"You're not as strong as you think you are. They're going to take your womb and your breasts," he hunched his shoulders, "and that's not fine."

For the first time since Leslie had decided on surgery she felt her eyes fill. It had been such a relief to think that she would no longer be burdened by an imaginary time-bomb ticking loudly in her head. She would be free and that was bigger than a pair of breasts and a womb she was almost done with anyway. But at those words and the way Jim had said them – "They're going to take your womb and your breasts" – she felt a fat tear drop from her eyelid onto her cheek and slide down to her chin. She stopped it with her hand before it made its way to her neck.

Jim saw her single tear and made no apology for causing it. He needed to know that she understood the gravity of what she was doing because, although he agreed with her decision, it had occurred to him, having known her of old, that she wouldn't allow herself to think or talk about the pain it caused her. They sat in silence and sipped their drinks.

After a while Leslie looked Jim in the eye. "Do you remember your wedding day?"

"Like it was yesterday."

"Imelda insisted I be bridesmaid and even though I kicked and screamed she got her way. She made me wear peach, which is a colour I detest, and the hairdresser piled my hair so high on my head that I looked like Marge Simpson."

"I remember." He grinned.

"We got dressed together, we got our makeup done together and we drank a glass of champagne and we laughed at my dress, even though she swore she loved it. We talked about the future and all the babies she was going to have."

"Oh, don't," he said, and closed his eyes.

"I wrote her a poem and she laughed so hard she held her ribs." She smiled at the memory. "What was it again? 'Imelda sighed, Imelda cried, the day she met Jim the Ride – He was short, she was tall, he took her up against the wall.'" She thought for a second. "'She had style, he had wit, he really thought he was the shit!'" She laughed a little. "I can't remember . . ."

"'Love is blind, that's what they say – it must be, it's her wedding day!'" Jim said, chuckling.

"I can't believe you remembered!"

"She repeated it often enough."

"Yeah, well, I'm no poet laureate but you must admit it has a kind of bawdy charm, even if I do say so myself," she said. "And after the church we all walked through a wood to the reception and it was such a hot day – do you remember how blue the sky was?"

"Not a cloud in it."

"And the band played all the best songs and we danced all night."

"It was a great day."

"It was my sister's wedding and I can honestly say it was my best day. They may be taking my breasts and my womb but for the first time I feel like I have a chance of having my own best day."

Jim nodded and raised his glass. She raised hers. "I'll drink to that!" he said, and they clinked. "And, Leslie, when you need someone, and you will, promise you'll call me."

"Why?"

"Because of a promise I made a long time ago."

"Okay, I will."

On the walk to the gallery they talked about relationships and Jim told Leslie about the women who had been in his life after Imelda. There was Mary, a librarian from Meath. She was a fan of musicals, the works of Shakespeare and, according to Jim, was passive aggressive. They'd lasted eight months, but it was only a year after Imelda and although Mary was a great cook and looked like a slightly chunkier and seriously paler Sophia Loren his heart hadn't been in it. Then there had been Angela. She was funny, smart, attractive and kind. She also had a psycho ex-husband and four kids under the age of ten so, after he'd been punched in the face on the street and warned to leave her alone or he'd be joining his wife in the ground, he decided he needed space. She and the kids moved to the UK a month later and he hadn't heard from her since. Then had come the Russian woman he had told her about on their first phone call. "I really thought we might have a future," he said. "So, what about you?"

Leslie laughed as he followed her across the street.

"Well?" he said.

"No one."

"No one! In ten years there has been no one?"

"Eighteen years, but who's counting?"

"Simon was your last relationship?" Jim was aghast and wasn't too shy to reveal his astonishment. He slowed his pace and took her arm. "I know nuns that get more action than you."

"That's funny because my hairdresser knew some Trappist monks with better haircuts. Coming up short against religious orders seems to be the theme of the day."

"I like your hair," he said.

She smiled. "Thanks."

They entered the gallery and were met by Jane, who was surprisingly calm and collected despite her sister's absence. Leslie introduced her to Jim and they shook hands and Jane complimented Leslie on looking stunning, which embarrassed her, and then she insisted they have a glass of wine and some savoury snacks. The place was packed with people and a lot were crowded around the paintings so they decided to wait until the herd thinned. They sipped wine and chatted in the corner. Jane was playing host and doing a lovely job. She was polite and pleasant to the three critics who came and she made time for all five collectors who had been supporters of Elle since the beginning of her career. She made excuses for Elle and no one seemed to mind particularly, apart from the photographer who was clearly off his face on cocaine and annoyed that he hadn't been informed of Elle's absence, even though plenty of other minor celebrities were there and ready to pose for him.

"This is a joke," he said to Jane. "Where the fuck is she?"

"Freddie," Jane said, "you're not Herb Ritts. Take photos, hand them in to the media desks and shut up."

"That's my girl!" Dominic said, from over Jane's shoulder. He was on his third glass of wine and thoroughly enjoying his night.

Freddie stormed off and started to push a TV presenter and a rugby player together, pointing at them and shouting for them to move this way and that. They complied. He moved on and pushed three blonde socialites back against a wall. Jane made a mental note never to use him again.

Dominic put his arm around her. "Nice event," he said. "Good wine, good food, good music – and who could have guessed Metallica would work so well sandwiched between Beethoven and Bach?"

"It's Rachmaninov and Chopin."

He nodded and whispered in her ear, "And who could guess Metallica would work so well sandwiched between Rachmaninov and Chopin? 'You say tomato . . .'"

"Get off!" She pushed him away playfully.

Leslie appeared with Jim, and Jane made the introductions.

Jane had filled Dominic in on Alexandra's extraordinary disappearance and what they were doing to find her as they were driving to the gallery. He had been really shocked to hear the news – he had been friends with her before he'd got Jane pregnant and dumped her at a disco. After that Alexandra hadn't had any time for him even if Jane did. The last time he'd seen her was just before she moved to Cork to go to college. His son was two months old and he hadn't seen him yet. She'd pushed a picture of Kurt into his chest and told him to look at it. She'd told him it was his son and he should be ashamed. He still had the photo and he had been ashamed but, still, it would be nearly four years before he'd have the courage to knock on Jane's door to visit his child.

Dominic smiled at Leslie and told her she was doing a really good thing in helping to find Alexandra. "She was a great girl," he said.

Later, when all the people had gone and Dominic and Jane were alone, he helped her clear the tables and box up the unused glasses.

"I missed so much," he said, out of nowhere.

"So much of what?" Jane asked, too tired to try to work out what was going on in his head.

"Of Kurt."

"Oh," she said, and sighed. "Yes, you did."

"I was such an arsehole."

"You still are."

She was smiling so he knew she was playing with him.

"I regret every day I wasn't around."

"Well, at least you got to have a life."

"I really left you in it," he admitted. "If I could go back . . ."

"You'd do exactly the same thing."

"Don't say that, Janey."

"You know, I don't think Kurt even remembers a time when you weren't a part of his life."

"But you do," Dominic said.

Jane didn't want to talk about it so she got busy brushing the floor.

"For a girl forced out of school you've done an amazing job here," he said.

"Thanks."

"And, for the record, I would change it if I could just so I could stop you calling our kid after a heroin addict with a death wish."

Jane laughed. "That was unfortunate."

She locked up and Dominic followed her to the car. They got in, and as Jane drove, Dominic fiddled with the CD player. "Dido, no . . . Dixie Chicks, no and no . . . James Morrison, shoot me . . . Ray LaMontagne, Jesus, Jane – Jack Lukeman . . . Remember that night?" He grinned.

"Yes, I remember." She blushed a little and laughed.

Dominic flicked along until he hit track twelve. It began with a bass drum kicking. Dominic and Jane fell into silence and she drove through the dark streets intermittently lit by fluorescent lights of different shapes and colours. The car was warm and outside the rain came tumbling down. She turned the windscreen wipers on and Jack L began to sing.

> "Take me to the edge of town,
> watch the evening veil come down,
> I'll tell you all my hopes and dreams,
> hold your tongue 'cos I believe
> For me there will be only one,
> yeah for me there will be only one."

Dominic turned in his seat so that he could watch her. She saw him staring from the corner of her eye and his gaze made her both happy and uncomfortable.

> "I'll take you to the silver well,
> make a wish, I'll cast a spell

That you'll remain here by my side,
childlike thoughts I cannot hide
For me there will be only one,
yeah for me there will be only one."

"Stop staring," she said.

"Can't help it. I'm remembering that night."

"Well, stop remembering."

"Can't."

"You're married."

"Memories are allowed."

"I wish you'd stop." She was becoming more uncomfortable.

"Sorry," he said. "Unfair." He turned to face the road.

"'Until stars come showering down, till the seven seas engulf this town . . .'"

Jane turned off the CD player and they drove the rest of the way to her house in silence.

Elle arrived home two days after her exhibition had opened. She got out of the taxi, paid the man and walked through the side gate that led to her little cottage at the end of the garden. Her mother was tending her witch hazels. She called to Elle, and Elle stopped and turned towards her. Rose stood up slowly and took off her gloves. She pointed to the garden furniture and Elle sat. Rose joined her. They were both wearing heavy coats but Rose could tell that her daughter had lost a lot of weight.

"Did you have a good time?" Rose asked.

"Brilliant."

"Jane was worried."

"Jane worries too much."

"That's what I told her. We all need to escape every now and then, don't we?"

"We do."

"And you're happy to be home now?" Rose asked.

Elle laughed a little. "And what about you, Mum?"

"I'm as good as can be expected."

"And Jane?"

"She's fine. Dominic's been sniffing around."

"Bored with the new wife already," Elle said, and her mother nodded.

"You know what that means, don't you?" said Rose. "Poor Janey will no doubt make a fool of herself again."

"Well, if anyone knows about being a fool, I do," Elle said.

"Vincent is the fool and if I ever see him again he'll be a fool without a penis," said Rose.

Elle got up. "It's cold."

"That's winter for you."

"I'm going inside now."

"Me too."

Elle walked towards the front door of her cottage and took down the "Gone Fishing" sign. Her mother called after her and she turned to face her.

"Good to have you home," Rose said.

Elle smiled at her, turned the key in the door and entered her cottage. Rose picked up her garden shears and walked down to the basement and to the promise of a nice glass of hot whiskey. She took a large gulp and when her eyes filled with tears she wiped them away and finished the glass. *Please don't frighten me like that again.*

*

When darkness had descended and Jane noticed the light on in Elle's cottage, she ran through the garden and up the path that led to the door. She knocked before opening it slowly and creeping inside. Elle was in her sitting room, cuddled up on the sofa, music playing in the background. Jane sat beside her.

"Hi, Jane."

"Hi, Elle."

"How was the opening?"

"We sold the lot."

"Good. Sorry I didn't make it."

"It's okay. Actually, it made my job a lot easier."

"Oh, good. Did you miss me?"

"I did."

"I'm sorry for setting Vincent's car on fire. I'm sorry for all of it."

"I took care of it."

"I know. You always do." She sighed. "Sorry."

"It's okay." Jane smiled at her sister. "I'm glad you're home. You look tired."

"I'm exhausted."

Jane took Elle by the hand and lifted her off the sofa. Then, arm in arm, they walked to the bedroom where Jane tucked her sister into bed. "You fall asleep now and when you get up I'll make you your favourite breakfast."

"I love you, Jane."

"I love you too, girly girl." Jane turned out the light and left Elle under her duvet.

Jane always called Elle "girly girl" when she was being affectionate. It was a term she'd given Elle when she was a toddler and Jane was a teen. Their father had died suddenly, their mother was on medication so Jane had cared for her sister. She'd pick up after her, play with her, feed her and put her to bed. She'd read her stories and tell her things about their dad.

"Where is he, Janey?"

"He's in heaven, girly girl."

"Where's heaven?"

"Far away up there in the sky."

"Daddy doesn't like heights, Janey." Elle had remembered the day her dad had got dizzy and fallen from a ladder while trying to retrieve her ball from the caves.

"It's okay," Jane explained. "He likes heaven."

"Why?"

"Because it's great."

"Why is it great?"

"Because God's there."

"So?"

"God is really cool. Everybody wants to be with God."

"I don't. I'd rather be here with you," Elle had said.

And Jane had been a mother to her sister since then.

Chapter 7

Chocolate Eyes

Ran out of hope, ran out of faith,
ran out of milk about quarter past eight
I gave up on dreams and regrets,
well I quit smoking but not cigarettes.

Jack L, *Broken Songs*

March 2008

When Elle woke up in Leslie's house in the country to the sound of birds, they were strangely loud, angry and without melody. She sat up, rubbed her eyes and looked towards the window, which was open. Two crows were on the sill, screeching at one another. She got out of bed, stretched and closed the window. So engrossed were they in their dispute that her action went unnoticed.

She could hear Leslie pottering in the kitchen. She had the radio on and was listening to two DJs make a crank call to some unsuspecting dentist. The house was a bungalow. The guest bedroom's walls were paper thin so Elle's bed might as well have been in the centre of the kitchen.

She pulled on her dressing-gown and joined Leslie, who was kneeling on the counter by the sink and cleaning the window. Elle poured herself a coffee and picked up a croissant from the basket in the centre of the table.

When Leslie's father died he had left the house to her mother. When she died she had left it to her three girls. When Nora died the house had been Imelda and Leslie's and when Imelda died the house was Leslie's alone. She had maintained it over the years, and although she travelled to it on average every eight weeks she rarely stayed more than two days because the echoes of a tragic past haunted the place. This was the first time since Imelda's passing that she had stayed longer than a few days, and with Elle for company, she was actually enjoying herself. Elle had been working hard on the exhibition since she had returned from her break, and when Leslie mentioned that she had to make a trip to check on her family home, she had begged to be allowed join her: a change of scenery would inspire and invigorate her. She had been working hard to make up for lost time and Leslie could see that painting the faces of the Missing was taking a toll on her. She seemed to be absorbing their tragedies, and the pain, suffering, hope and hopelessness imbued in her work was also imbued in her. She was quieter than when they had first met and she seemed older. In the few months they had known each other, Elle had gone from being a playful puppy to a sleepy old girl content to sit on the porch.

As it turned out, the town was playing host to a week-long traditional music festival, which initially served only to annoy Leslie. But the first night they had walked into town to a restaurant that Leslie hadn't visited in ten years and they had a pleasant time eating pasta, drinking wine and listening to a young man play the piano accompanied by a girl on the violin and a boy on guitar. Even though neither woman was a fan of traditional music this little group was less thud-thumping, toe-tapping, feet of flames old-school Irish and more new-age folk, mellow and enchanting. The music elevated Elle into a happy place, and since then her mood had continued to lift ever so slowly but noticeably. As part of the festival, every restaurant, bar, park and street corner was playing host to musicians of all ages, and because their first evening had been such a success Elle and Leslie had got into the spirit of the event and by day three they were really enjoying themselves. Leslie's long self-imposed seclusion and new-found *joie de vivre* meant that every day there was a great new discovery, or rediscovery, to be made. An old woodland that she had played in as a child made a beautiful place to walk and talk, and the new coffee shop, which served takeaway hot chocolate to sip and hug as they walked, made it even pleasanter. Leslie had forgotten how beautiful her little town was. She'd forgotten the way the sky looked through the trees and how the light hit the water in the evenings and how friendly the people were when she actually engaged with them.

"So what's the plan for today?" Elle asked, between nibbles.

Leslie turned and smiled at her, took off one of her gloves and scratched her nose. "Well," she said, "I was thinking we'd get in the car and drive to the coast this morning. We can have lunch in this little pub that Simon and I used to go to – it has the best fish in the country. Then we could get back around five and eat here or go out, depending on how you feel, and then there's a band on in Mahon's that could be interesting."

"Sounds good. I'll just get showered and dressed and we can go."

Leslie put her glove back on and resumed cleaning the window.

Elle finished her croissant as she walked back into her room. She picked up her bag and headed down the hall into the bathroom, stripped off and got into the shower. It was while the water was tapping at her head that she realized a weight was lifting and felt her heart begin to soar.

Elle and Leslie spent a lovely if finger-numbing morning walking along the coastline, then stopped off at the pub for their fish lunch. Elle ordered the salmon and Leslie a fish platter, and when Elle saw it she was sorry she'd gone for the salmon but there was plenty for them both so the women shared the assortment of fish and Elle agreed it was the best she'd ever tasted. She asked Leslie to tell her a little about Simon, and Leslie argued that her relationship with him had been so long ago that it was hard to remember much of it.

"You must remember it!" Elle said.

"There was so much going on back then." Leslie was referring to the sickness that had overtaken her world for so long.

"What did he look like?" Elle said, pushing for an answer.

"He was tall and thin and he had big blue eyes the size of side plates. His hair was sandy and he had freckles."

"Was he nice?" Elle asked.

"He was very nice. He was bright and kind and he put up with a lot from me."

"Did he love you?"

Leslie sighed, and thought about it for a moment. "Yes," she said, and she remembered the day eighteen years earlier when she had just turned twenty-two, her sister Nora was dying and she herself had been diagnosed with the cancer gene.

Simon had been waiting for her when she came out of the doctor's surgery. He was pale and his big blue eyes were glassy. She walked towards him and he stood up. She sat down because her legs could no longer carry her and tugged at his hand and he sat again and faced her, and she didn't have to tell him because her face said it all. He put his face into his hands and he wept right there in the middle of the waiting area. Listening to the pain that was so evident in every wail, she knew she couldn't put him through watching her slow and painful death. And so, right there and then, she had ended their three-year relationship. Even when he attempted to contact her intermittently for six months, and although she missed him more than she could say, she was steadfast in her decision and, deep down, she knew that Simon was grateful.

"I think you're brave," Elle said.

"Thanks. Most would say I was stupid."

"Bravery and stupidity are the same thing. It just depends on the outcome and it's not over yet."

"No, I suppose it isn't." She considered telling Elle about her plans to have surgery in July but decided against it because they were having such a lovely day and she didn't want to think about it too much. *Another time. I'll tell her another time.* And as she was thinking that, Elle's face changed and Leslie turned to see what she was staring at. A tall man with curly brown hair and big brown eyes was standing with a blonde woman. He was wide-eyed and staring back, obviously uncomfortable and unsure. Leslie watched Elle maintain eye contact with him and the man hesitatingly making his way towards her, leaving the blonde at the bar.

"Elle," he said, and Leslie detected a shudder in his voice.

Elle didn't have to introduce him. Leslie knew it was the prick who had broken her new friend's heart.

"Vincent," Elle said.

"How weird is this?" He raised his hands in the air. "Of all the gin-joints in all the towns . . ."

"Funny old world," she said. "How've you been, Vincent?"

"Good – you?"

"Great," she said, but it was unconvincing. Neither of them mentioned the car-burning incident and subsequent pay-off. The blonde remained at the bar.

"This is Leslie," Elle said, looking beyond his shoulder at the blonde. "Who's your friend?"

Vincent turned to the blonde and called her over with a nod. She seemed slow to approach so he made the head movement once again. She came across and stood slightly behind him. "This is Caroline."

Caroline smiled. She seemed familiar, but Elle couldn't work out how she knew her face.

"Nice to meet you," Caroline said nervously. "I love your work."

"Thanks," Elle said. "Do I know you?"

"I'm an actress."

Elle nodded. "Of course you are," she said. She looked at Vincent and shook her head. She remembered where she'd seen her before. It had been at one of her own exhibitions. The photographer had made them stand together for a press shot. That exhibition had been just before China.

Vincent attempted to disguise a gulp by clearing his throat.

"We should go," he said to Caroline, who seemed more than happy to move on.

"You should have gone a long time ago," Elle said.

Vincent grabbed Caroline's arm and escorted her out of the lovely pub, which served the best fish in Ireland, before they'd even had a chance to glance at the menu.

Leslie looked at Elle, who seemed lost in thought. "Are you okay?"

"I'm more than okay," Elle said. She sighed and grinned a little.

"You are?"

"He was screwing her all that time."

"And that's okay?"

Elle nodded. "It must be, because I can't seem to make myself care."

Leslie smiled at her young friend and squeezed her hand and Elle's heart soared just a little higher.

Rose had been throwing up all week. She was steadfast in her refusal to seek medical attention but eventually, when Jane witnessed her doubled over, holding her stomach in severe pain and throwing up in her kitchen bin, she'd had enough of her mother's stubbornness and made the call to their family GP. She was flying to London for the Jack Lukeman gig that evening.

Dr Griffin arrived at ten as promised and, knowing he hated making house calls especially to her mother, Jane met him on the steps of her home. Together they made their way to the basement apartment.

"How's she behaving?" he asked.

"Same as ever."

"Still experiencing mood swings?"

"Dr Griffin, what you call her mood swings we call her personality."

She smiled but Dr Griffin just shook his head. He'd been the Moore family's practitioner for years and really cared for the girls and Kurt but Jane was aware that Rose Moore was his worst nightmare. She opened the door and could see him bracing himself as he stepped inside.

Rose was in the sitting room, asleep in a chair. Jane and Dr Griffin looked at one another, both silently acknowledging that it was time to wake the beast.

Jane approached gingerly. She slowly and gently laid her hand on her mother's arm and shook it ever so gently. "Rose."

Rose stirred a little. Jane backed off.

Rose's eyes opened. She focused on her daughter and the doctor. "What?"

"Rose, I'm here to give you a check-up," Dr Griffin said.

"Did I ask you to come?"

"No," he said, and sighed audibly.

"Well, then."

"Rose, you're sick," Jane said, in her most forceful tone, "and I'm not going to let you rot down here so let the doctor examine you."

"How charming of you, Jane, but you're forgetting about a little thing called free will and if I am rotting and I wish to continue doing so that is my business and my business alone."

"Don't make me hold you down, old woman," said Jane.

"You can try."

"Okay, ladies," Dr Griffin said, holding his hand up in

the air. "Rose, please just let me examine you. I won't take longer than three minutes."

"You have two," she said.

A minute later Dr Griffin was pressing on Rose's stomach and she was trying not to scream, but one press too many and she couldn't help but grab his ear and drag him off her. He called out, and Jane extricated him from her mother's closed claw. He stumbled back, rubbing his reddened and bruised lobe.

Rose grasped Jane's hand, squeezed it as hard as she could and pulled her in close. "Don't you dare bring that man in here without my permission again!" she hissed. Tears sprang to Jane's eyes. Rose let go and Jane backed away, rubbing her hand, much as Dr Griffin had his ear.

Dr Griffin packed his bag before turning to Rose. "Your stomach is inflamed and that's what's causing the pain and vomiting. I've no doubt you're suffering from recurrent diarrhoea and possible pancreatitis. And I know for sure that, however uncomfortable you are now, it will only get worse."

"Well, thank you for your medical opinion, Dr Griffin. You know where the door is."

"Stop drinking, Rose," Dr Griffin said. "If you don't you will die."

"I'm an old woman, doctor. It would be incredibly focking odd if I didn't die. Don't you think?"

Rose loved to curse. She loved to pepper her sentences with the word "fuck" but her accent ensured that it sounded like "fock", "focker", "focking" or "focked". She liked that; it meant she was devilish enough to curse but not coarse enough for it to be instantly recognizable.

Jane and Dr Griffin left her alone. She flicked on the TV, then took a bottle and a glass from the cabinet beside her chair. She opened the screw cap and poured the wine into an unwashed glass. She took a sip and rested it back on top of the cabinet, all the while mumbling to herself, "Stop drinking or you'll die. Who does he think he is? I'm seventy-one years old and I haven't died yet, more's the focking pity."

Dr Griffin followed Jane up the steps and into the main house. In the kitchen she made him tea and for the hundredth time he went through the kind of gastrointestinal damage her mother was doing to herself.

"What can I do?" Jane asked.

"Ban the booze," he suggested, as though it was the first time he'd said it.

A frustrated Jane shouted, "I can't! She's got her own money, she's perfectly capable of buying her own and she's got friends who bring her presents of it. They don't think she has a problem, she doesn't think she has a problem. My sister seems to think that, just because she's not in bars or clubs doing shots till four a.m., I'm insane to even suggest she has a problem, and my son thinks she's hilarious. When she falls asleep with the grill on it's old age, when she falls in the shower it's her arthritis, and when I dare to address the problem I'm deemed to be hysterical at best and a 'focking bitch' at worst!"

Dr Griffin laughed at Jane's impression of her mother, then became serious again. "Rose has been a functioning alcoholic for over thirty years but time is running out and her body is slowly giving up."

Absentmindedly, Jane scooped out sugar from the bowl, then poured it back in. "I'm doing my best."

"I know."

"Can I have her sectioned?"

"Your mother isn't mentally ill."

"I know that, you know that, but how long would it take for them to realize that?"

Dr Griffin grinned. They sat in silence for a minute or two, drinking tea.

"It's simple, Jane. If she doesn't stop soon, her health will deteriorate to a point where she'll have to be hospitalized and then she'll be forced into sobriety. Whether or not it's too late to save her is anyone's guess."

"Sorry about your ear," Jane said, changing the subject.

"Does Rose behave violently towards you a lot?"

"No," Jane said, laughing the matter off. "I think you inspired the violence."

"Well, if it gets too much you'll let me know."

Jane nodded. "It's a pity because when she's in good form she's almost fun to be around."

"I'll take your word for it," Dr Griffin said. It had been a long time since he'd seen the pleasant side of Rose Moore, he thought. In fact he could pinpoint the year: it had been the spring of 1983, three months before she'd called him to the house to declare her husband dead. The doctor stood up and fixed his jacket to signal his desire to exit. Jane waved him off and closed the door behind him. Her ring felt tight. She tried to take it off but, following her mother's attack, her finger was swelling fast, making its removal difficult.

The phone rang, and it was Tom wanting to know if she wished to share a taxi to the airport. She agreed because she was running late and she wouldn't have time to leave the car in the long-term car park. The gig was a late show.

They had decided not to fly out until six that evening, which was a blessing because she still had a full day's work ahead of her.

A meeting she had with an artist by the name of Ken Browne ran late. She was really impressed by his work and energy and they ended up talking for a long time, sharing stories over coffee. His bright blue eyes shone as he spoke about his latest painting and he rubbed his bald head and smiled a wide smile that seemed to take over his rugged features. He had been in a rock band for years and it was written all over his face. He was an accomplished guitar player and told her stories about his adventures on the road and how he incorporated music into his artwork. They spent a very enjoyable two hours together and by the end of their meeting they had agreed that he would show his work in her gallery in July.

Kurt appeared in the gallery just after lunch with a packed bag and announced he was staying with Irene for the weekend. Irene's mother was on another post-break-up holiday, and as Irene's dad was too busy boffing his new girlfriend to be interested in his daughter, Kurt felt a responsibility towards caring for her.

"No way," said Jane.

"Mum, I'm going."

"You and Irene are not staying there unsupervised."

"I'm seventeen."

"No way, no way!" she shouted. She always repeated herself and shouted when she couldn't think of something else to say.

"She's upset, I'm not leaving her," he said.

Jane calmed down. "So bring her to ours."

"What's the difference? You're going to London."

"Your grandmother's here."

Kurt started to laugh. "You're serious?"

"It's better than nothing."

"Where's Elle?"

"She's gone down to the country with Leslie for a few days."

"Mum, why don't you admit that you need me to care for Gran and not the other way around?"

"That's not it. She's perfectly capable of looking after herself for two days." She was lying: a list of things she wanted him to do for his grandmother was burning a hole in her pocket.

"Why don't you just tell the truth?" he said.

She didn't know why she felt it necessary to lie except that maybe she didn't want her son to feel obliged to care for her mother the way she did. And now he had caught her in a silly and unnecessary lie and it embarrassed her, so she dismissed him angrily. "Fine, Kurt, go off with your girlfriend! Do your own bloody thing!"

"Fine. I will." He walked out of the gallery, leaving her to stew.

What is wrong with me? Why couldn't I have said, "Son, I need your help this weekend"? How hard is that? It's not hard at all. Jesus Christ, Jane.

She then had to sort her mother's prescriptions and pick up some takeaway menus and cash. When she finally returned to Rose's it was ten minutes before Tom was due to turn up in the taxi.

Rose was displeased. "It's a bit bloody late to be thinking about me now," she said.

Jane ignored her and put the menus on the coffee table beside her.

Rose picked one up. "Jane?" she asked innocently. "Am I Chinese?"

"Don't start, Rose."

"Because I don't look Chinese, I don't speak the language, the only paddy I know is a person and it will be a cold focking day in hell before I eat anything commonly described as flied lice."

"That's racist."

"That's fact."

"You're a pig."

Rose held up the menu. "Well, maybe it's my year." She picked up the other menu. "Indian?"

"I'm leaving," Jane said.

"Oh, yes, I'll have an order of dead babies dumped in a river, followed by some Kama Sutra with a side order of shitting in the streets."

"Stop now, you insane old hag! Eat chips for all I care! Don't forget your medication, and all the numbers you could possibly need are on the fridge."

"Fine, go off and enjoy yourself — leave a sick old woman on her own!"

"Thanks, Rose, I will. Try not to die before I get back," Jane said, with a grin, because two could play the old woman's game.

Rose licked her teeth. She always licked her teeth when she wanted to hide a smile. "Is that because you don't want to deal with the smell?" she asked.

"If I didn't want to deal with the smell I would have turfed you out years ago."

Jane walked out the door and Rose broke into a smile. *Touché, Janey, touché.*

Tom had checked them in on-line so they ran through the airport and joined the queue at the gate. He bought two coffees from a vendor and they managed two sips each before their row number was called. An air stewardess made a no-no gesture at the coffee with her hand and tutted. Neither Tom nor Jane had the will to argue with her so they handed over their full cups and walked through the gate and onto the plane in silence. Once seated Tom took the opportunity to thank Jane once again for coming, and she responded that he was most welcome for the third time that evening and possibly the fortieth since they had decided on the trip.

Tom was nervous. He didn't know what to do with his hands and he kept shuffling in the seat. He had cut his hair, manicured his nails and bought a suit that fitted him. He had shaved and he looked handsome – probably the way he had looked before Alexandra vanished or at least close to it.

Jane was worried that all this effort and hope would not be rewarded. She knew they were clutching at straws, and although she appeared outwardly positive for the sake of Tom's sanity, she worried that she might have contributed to him having false hope. Now that they were actually flying to London to attend a Jack Lukeman gig, in the hope of spotting someone named Alex with a passing resemblance to Alexandra, it seemed more than desperate: it seemed mad.

"The hotel is really close to the venue," Tom said.

"Great."

"Just a walk away."

"Fantastic."

"We could eat there, if you like?"

"Lovely."

"Or we could go out. I'm sure there would be a place between the hotel and the venue. I just don't want to move too far away."

"The hotel is perfect."

"Oh, okay."

"Nice suit," said Jane, after a pause.

Tom nodded. "I thought I'd better make an effort if I'm going to see my girl."

"It's unlikely, Tom, you know it is." She wanted to cry for him.

"I do. Still, you never know."

"Yeah."

He closed his eyes and she read her magazine and they didn't speak another word for the rest of the flight.

The plane landed on time and Tom and Jane quickly found a taxi to take them to their hotel. They split in the lobby and agreed to meet half an hour later. Jane showered and changed while Tom paced his hotel room over and over again, counting down the minutes until he might see Alexandra again.

They met in the hotel restaurant. Jane ordered a steak and salad, and Tom ordered the same, but he only picked at it. Jane tried to allay his anxiety with idle chat. Since his encounter with her mother, Tom had developed sympathy for Jane and had become her sounding-board. She told him about the incident with the doctor, which entertained him, and Rose's reaction to the takeaway menus made him laugh out loud. Jane laughed, too, because her mother was always funny from a distance. She told him about Kurt and their stupid fight and berated herself for being a bad mother. Tom disagreed and told her she was a great mother – but he hadn't witnessed the fight she'd had with her son when he was sixteen and had wanted to leave school to join the army after watching *Black Hawk Down* twenty-five times in the space of a week.

He had approached her while she was working on her computer at the kitchen table. He'd sat opposite her and folded his arms, and when Kurt folded his arms it indicated he meant to talk business. She'd looked up and asked him what he wanted, and he'd told her straight out, as if he was asking for the price of a CD, that he wanted permission to join the army. She had laughed it off at first but it soon became apparent that he wasn't joking. Jane said no. Kurt had refused to accept no for an answer and their argument spiralled so out of control that Kurt called his mother the C-word and stormed out of the kitchen, slammed the door, walked into his own bedroom, slammed that door, locked it and put his music on, blaring. Shocked by his language and red-faced from roaring, his mother had stamped down the hall and banged and kicked at his locked door, calling him a disrespectful little bastard. He had screamed, "I hate you," and she screamed, "I hate you back," and only managed to calm herself down after she'd kicked a hole through the door and broken her small toe.

Tom hadn't been witness to the time she'd left the child in a pram outside a shop and didn't notice until she'd got home and her mother inquired as to his whereabouts. He wasn't there when Kurt was six and a kid aged eight had started to bully him in the school playground. Kurt had confided in Rose rather than her and when Rose told her, instead of taking her mother's advice to back off, she'd barged into the school, grabbed the bully by the neck and threatened to break his legs if he ever touched her son again. It was obviously the worst move she could have made because there was a playground full of witnesses, including a teacher and a visiting nun, and of course the child's parents called to her house and threatened action against her. Following a meeting with the headmistress it became apparent that the best course of action, in light of Jane's aggression to a minor, was to pull Kurt out of the school altogether.

"You got him expelled when he was six?" Tom said, and laughed.

"Mortified," she said. "But when Rose told me I just saw red."

"I can't believe you attacked an eight-year-old."

"Well, I had to do something. Rose told Kurt to wait till the kid had his back to him and then beat him around the head with his bag."

"That doesn't sound like the worst idea."

"She told him to put a brick in it."

Tom laughed again. "I'm sorry for laughing but that's insane."

"I've made so many mistakes with Kurt it's a wonder he's not a little psycho."

"You were so young having him," Tom reminded her.

"Yeah," she nodded, "and my example was Rose."

"My God, that's true. It's a wonder you're not a little psycho."

"It's possible I am," she said.

"I'll bear that in mind."

Tom had been momentarily distracted from finding Alexandra, but then it was time to pay the bill and head to the club so his mind wandered away from Jane again. Silence resumed as they walked to the place that held one of Tom's last hopes.

Michelle met them at the box office. She ushered them inside and was wondering how they wished their search to proceed. "It's a big club," she pointed out, "but I've put the flyers on the noticeboard and all the staff have been given her picture."

"I'd like to sit close to the ladies', if I could?" Tom said.

"And I'll sit at the bar," Jane said.

They had discussed it earlier.

"Look, we've got a pretty comprehensive security system," said Michelle. "Every part of this place is on camera. I could introduce you to Graham – he's our security guard. I've spoken to him and he's happy for you to join him in his office."

"That would be amazing," said Tom.

"Good." Michelle was only too happy to help.

She brought them to a room where a large man in his fifties sat. In front of him were small TV screens, each one capturing a part of the club. He turned and greeted them, and Michelle went off to get two more chairs while Graham pointed out each camera and where it was positioned. "Box office, main door, back door, side entrance, hallway, main stairs, bar, bar till – you won't need to focus on that – stage, audience. That breaks into three – here, here and here," he said, pointing to three separate TV screens, all of which depicted empty chairs and tables. "That one is the balcony and so is that, and over here is the dressing-room area – obviously we don't have a camera in the actual dressing rooms but it's the dressing-room hallway that leads here to backstage, stage right and stage left, and that's it."

Michelle returned with the chairs. She placed them either side of Graham. Then she left them but before she did she crossed her fingers.

"Thank you," Tom said. "You've no idea."

She nodded and closed the door behind her.

"What happens if I see her?" Tom asked.

"You run," Graham said. "Michelle has given me your number so that I can call you if I see her again and guide you through the club on the phone."

"That's great," Tom said. "That's really unbelievably great. Isn't that great, Jane?"

She nodded, then walked over to a counter and made coffee for the three of them as the lads stared at the many screens. First the box office and the main entrance. As they watched people flow through, Graham pointed out that he could zoom in on anyone who sparked Tom's interest, and while Jane's back was turned he provided Tom with an example by focusing on a woman's large breasts.

They studied face after face as people came in through the doors and halls and spread into the various parts of the venue. The place filled quickly so each took turns monitoring a set of cameras. Graham had posted Alexandra's picture on the wall in front of him for purposes of recognition. The venue became louder as the chatter grew and people moved to and from their seats to the toilets and to the bar, and servers began working the round tables where groups were drinking, laughing and talking.

Jane thought how funny it was to have this perspective, to watch people who were unaware they were being watched. She saw one woman lift and separate her breasts when her partner left to go to the toilet, then followed him down the hall and witnessed him turn to stare as a pretty girl walked past him. Another guy waited for his date to go to the bar before he picked his nose, examined the result and flicked it across the room. She pointed at the camera and made a sound suggesting she was appalled. "People are disgusting," Graham said. She saw many brunettes but none of them had her friend's rich glossy hair. Every now and then her heart-rate would increase because she spotted someone who just might be Alexandra, but Graham would zoom in and her heart would slow, and Tom would moment-arily close his eyes and bow his head for the second or two he needed to pull himself together.

Jack L and his band emerged from the dressing room two minutes before he was due on stage. Jack was in a black suit and a red shirt; he ran his hand through his hair and took a drink from his bottle of water. The bass player slapped him on the back and he grinned at him, the famil-iar troublemaker grin that Jane recognized. The door of the dressing room stayed open for a second or two before someone inside closed it. The band walked down the hall and out of shot, only to be picked up on the next camera that focused on backstage.

On stage the lights rose and danced on the velvet curtain. The drummer sat behind his drums, the guitar player picked up his guitar and placed it around his neck, the piano-player made herself comfortable, and they started to play while Jack bounced with guitar in hand stage right on a separate screen. Tom watched the crowd as they clapped and cheered, and some people stood and some stamped their feet, and the curtain rose and Jack walked on. The crowd went mad – he bowed and grinned and raised his hand – the band started up, the show began and Alexandra was nowhere to be seen.

They continued to scan each and every face while Jack sang and told stories and shared a joke with the guitar player, and time passed so quickly and then the gig was almost over.

Jack returned to the stage to sing his encore, but just as Graham turned to offer his sympathy to Tom, Jane noticed a woman with short brunette hair and Alexandra's face emerge from Jack's dressing room. She pointed and called out to Tom, and he and Graham saw her. Tom shot up and Graham zoomed in and Tom started running and Graham shouted for him to turn left at the box office and he did but the hallway was empty. Jane had run after Tom. Graham phoned Tom's number and directed him to the side entrance and he followed the advice and ran through the club, navigating past people who were on their feet and dancing to "Boys And Girls", with Jane hot on his heels. He made it outside to an alleyway and the woman had her back to him and was talking to a man with a laminated card around his neck and Tom called out to her.

"Alexandra!"

And she turned – and for a split second he thought it was her and seeing her took his breath away, but then she walked towards him and the closer she got the less she looked like his wife because the expression on her face was not an expression he'd ever seen before.

"Can I help you?" she said, and her accent was English.

Tom couldn't do anything but shake his head. "No," he said, "you can't help me."

And then he was on his knees, weeping uncontrollably.

Jane stood behind him, staring at the woman who looked so much like her friend on camera but in person and close up seemed shockingly different. *We're so stupid. Of course it wasn't her. It was never going to be her.*

The woman was unsure how to react. The man with the laminated card moved to stand beside her and they both found themselves staring at Tom, who was on his knees and crying, "Where is she? Where is she? Where is she? Where is she? Where is she?"

Jane knelt down and took his hands, then pulled him to her and hugged him close.

"Where is she, Jane?" he whispered. "Where's my girl?"

"I don't know," she said, rubbing his head like she used to rub Kurt's when he was young enough to be soothed rather than repelled by her touch, "but we will find her."

Michelle, tipped off by Graham who was watching the sad scene on screen, appeared and took the English Alex inside, where she explained the tragic circumstances the crying man had found himself in. The English Alex was dreadfully sorry to hear of the man's plight and more than a little freaked at the likeness between her and the picture of the missing woman. She explained that she worked for Jack's UK distribution company and made her excuses as she had somewhere to be. She was gone before at last Jane came in with Tom, whose disappointment had turned into mild shock.

*

Back in his hotel room, Jane insisted that Tom have a strong brandy to calm his nerves. He was berating himself for believing it possible to find Alexandra at a gig in London and saying how stupid of him to think that his wife would be in Jack L's dressing room – after all, the Jack camp had been so good about helping him. That woman was not just thinner, she was rail-thin, and she was taller and, despite certain similarities, up close she was nothing like his wife. He had been fooling himself.

His police liaison officer, Trish, had said as much the last time she called to the house to update him on the investigation surrounding his wife's disappearance. Their unit had analysed the CCTV footage that Michelle had passed on and found that it wasn't a match. He had argued with her that computers were not gods and he knew his wife's face. She had been patient with him and was always kind, but she was adamant that he needed to let go of the notion of finding his wife in a London club.

"I can't let go," he said. "I have to find her."

Trish left soon after and he promptly blocked out the information she'd just given him because, more and more, his mind was visiting the dark place and he desperately needed hope.

Now, as he sat drinking brandy, that conversation came back to haunt him. He apologized to Jane for wasting her time and for breaking down in the alleyway. He assured her he would pay to clean the oil stains from her coat, the result of her sitting on the ground and rocking him like a baby for ten minutes.

She told him he should get some sleep. She kissed his cheek and said they would keep searching.

He held her hand and looked into her eyes and bit his lip. "Tell me something about her."

So she told him about a time when her best friend Alexandra was a little girl, maybe eleven or twelve, and stole an ice cream from the local shop. She'd spent a second or two choosing the one she wanted, placed it under her coat and made her way outside. When the shopkeeper ran after her, calling on her to stop, she turned to him, calmly took out the ice cream and handed it to him. Then she smiled and congratulated him on catching her. "No flies on you, Mr Dunne, no flies at all!" Alexandra had said.

Mr Dunne was taken aback, especially when she pointed out that two days earlier, while he was away from the shop and his wife was behind the counter, she'd stolen a bar of chocolate without any fear of capture. She took it from her pocket and handed it to him. "I practically dangled it under her nose," she said to Mr Dunne, who was now decidedly confused. "To be fair to her, the shop was busy but, Mr Dunne, you can never be too careful – shoplifters are everywhere."

"I'll mention it to her," he said, still unsure as to what was going on.

"You're welcome," she said, and walked down the road.

Mr Dunne stared from her to the chocolate bar and to his wife, who was busy serving a customer. *What the hell just happened?*

Alexandra made it around the corner to where Jane was waiting and, as soon as she was sure that Mr Dunne could no longer see her, she burst into tears. Once she'd recovered sufficiently to walk home Alexandra promised Jane she would never again engage in a criminal act, but although she had scared the pants off herself and was down a bar of chocolate, the encounter was not a total loss because Alexandra had learned something very powerful that day: any lie delivered with confidence and conviction is believable, no matter how ridiculous the circumstance. This self-awareness had really worked in their favour when they were caught poaching while on holiday with Alexandra's parents in Mayo a year later.

"And what about you?" Tom asked. "Did you just wait to see if she'd get away with it before you had a go?"

"Oh, no! I'd successfully robbed three Mars bars from a shop two doors down. It was one of those bars that she gave back to Mr Dunne."

He laughed a little. "So what did you learn?"

"That the hand is quicker than an old woman's one good eye."

When Jane was content that she'd cheered Tom up a little she bade him goodnight.

"Thanks," he said. "I don't know what I'd do without you."

He walked to the door with her and watched her go down the corridor to her room. She could feel his eyes on her back and she smiled at him when she turned to place her key card in the door. She disappeared into her room and Tom entered his, opened the mini-bar again and started drinking. When he saw he'd missed three calls from Jeanette he turned his phone to silent.

When Jane's taxi pulled up to her house her son opened the front door, walked down the steps, met her at the gate and took her suitcase from her hand. "Sorry, Mum," he said. "I should have helped out with Gran."

Jane was surprised and unsure what to say. Instead she just hugged him tight and took the opportunity to kiss his cheek.

"Mum!" he moaned. As they walked up the steps together he put his arm around her shoulders. "I have something to tell you," he said.

"I'm listening."

"Irene's here."

"And?"

"She needs a place to stay."

"What's going on?"

"There's no food in her house."

"Okay."

He stopped at the door and turned to her. "Really?"

"Really. Just make sure she lets her mother know."

"She would if she could reach her."

He followed her inside, she hung up her coat and he placed her case on the floor.

"Are you hungry?" she said.

"We're starving."

"Okay," she said. "Give me five minutes and I'll get busy."

Irene appeared in the sitting-room doorway. "Hi, Jane," she said shyly.

Jane walked over to her, hugged her and kissed her on the forehead. "Welcome."

Irene brightened. "Thanks, Jane, you rock."

"Yes, I do," she said, "and you're in the spare room."

"I know, I know. Don't have sex, not here, not there, not anywhere," Irene said, in a voice that mimicked Jane's.

Kurt laughed and Jane nodded. "Exactly."

She walked into her bedroom, sat on the bed and took a minute to allow the events of the weekend to wash over her. Then she took time to be grateful for her life, as hard as it sometimes was. *I'm one of the lucky ones.*

Chapter 8

Numero Uno

I looked behind the counter,
sofa and the sink,
got down on my knees
and looked under the fridge
but I can't find love.

Jack L, *Metropolis Blue*

April 2008

Dominic had never been very good at relationships. In his thirty-six years on the planet his longest had been three years. He had married Bella six months after he'd ended a disastrous but very passionate affair with a dancer called Heidi. She was twenty-three and liked to take E or alternatively acid on weekends. He hadn't bothered to take E in his teens and twenties with his peers so he was damned if he was going to do it in his thirties. Also he'd witnessed a guy in college attempt to hack off his own foot with a wooden spoon while screaming that the eagles had landed after a particularly bad acid trip, so that was out. Besides, as a respectable bank manager the last thing in the world he wanted was to be found in a club in Dublin off his tits and bouncing off walls or screaming bloody murder while attempting to land himself on the moon.

Heidi resented that he didn't share her interests and he found it difficult to live with someone who was in a bad mood from Sunday morning to Tuesday night. So, class A drugs were blamed for the demise of their relationship. They had fought and she had ordered him out of her flat, and he told her he wouldn't be back and she was happy with that, further promising that if she saw him anywhere near her place again she'd call the police. Obviously he pointed out that calling the police would be a bad idea, considering she shared a flat with a drug-dealer named Seth and spent half her time either going up or coming down. He had walked from her flat to his car and gone to Jane's house. She had made him dinner and provided a shoulder to cry on, because even though Heidi drove him crazy he would miss her. Jane was a great listener. She was always there for him even though when she'd needed him most he hadn't been there for her.

Dominic often regretted the choices he had made aged seventeen but there was part of him that was also secretly grateful. If he and Jane had married, as Rose had demanded at the time, they wouldn't have made it. He would never have gone to university. If he hadn't gone to university he wouldn't now have an extremely well-paid and cushy job in a top bank and he certainly wouldn't be living the luxury lifestyle he'd become accustomed to. He could have kissed goodbye to his cars and his house in Ballsbridge, his chalet in France and the five apartments he was earning high rents from in an exclusive development in Blackrock. God knew where he'd be because, when he was seventeen, his parents had warned him in no uncertain terms that if he didn't go to university and get a degree and follow in his father's footsteps he was on his own.

At the time he was a kid, confused and scared, and although he was high on a drug called love, the reality of becoming a father had brought him down fast. His parents had insisted he stay away from the girl who they believed had become pregnant on purpose to trap him. When their offer of financial support, on the condition that Jane kept away from their son, was rejected by the madwoman who had reared her, they were happy to wash their hands of the girl and child entirely. They were adamant that if Dominic didn't want to pay for university himself he would never speak to the girl again. He didn't want to pay for college himself. He wanted the same free ride that his two older brothers had enjoyed. He wanted the cool apartment he could share with his two best friends, Mint and Brick. He wanted to experience the college lifestyle, the parties, the girls, the clubs, the drink, the sport, the late nights, the crap food and mostly the freedom from a life lived under the watchful eye of his strict parents.

He acquiesced to their demands easily, and afterwards when Jane tried to talk to him he ignored her. When she took the hint and stayed away, he watched her grow under her uniform and it was hard to avoid the terrible sadness in her eyes because she wasn't given a choice. All the ambition that had burned so brightly in her would be lost and all Dominic wanted to do was run away, because Dominic, like their principal Amanda Reynolds, knew that Jane could have achieved whatever she wanted. She could hold a full-scale conversation with Alexandra during the maths class, and if the teacher tried to make an example of her by asking her to explain the theorem on the blackboard, she could do so without so much as a second's thought. Alexandra, on the other hand, would make up something so preposterous that the whole class would burst out laughing. Then she'd take a bow, leaving the teacher too busy trying to regain control to bother correcting her for not paying attention.

Jane barely opened a book and yet she maintained a B average. She could have been an A student with the greatest of ease but deliberately maintained the B because she didn't want to be associated with the class nerds. She, too, had been desperate to go to university and she'd applied to the same colleges as Alexandra, and although it would mean being apart from Dominic, she had secretly hoped that they would both get Cork because that meant she could leave home. Dominic was sorry for Jane and he wanted the best for her because she was cool and they'd had the best two years together, but he was far too selfish to risk his own future to tell her so.

Four years after his son was born Dominic had graduated from college. He had experienced all the things that came with college life, he was on a good starting salary with the bank of his choice and his parents didn't own him any more. He walked up the steps of his old girlfriend's house on their child's fourth birthday. He carried a gift in his hand. Passing balloons tied to the railings, he stopped at the front door and took a moment to collect himself before knocking. He was perfectly prepared for the door to be slammed in his face but it wasn't. Jane opened it with their son on her hip, and even though he'd walked up the pathway and knocked on her door, he was shocked to see her and his son. He tried to raise a smile but he was ashamed and embarrassed so he lifted up the gift and held it out. She looked from him to the gift and then to her son, and she opened the door a little more and invited him in. Thirteen years later Dominic still couldn't work out why Jane had found it so easy to forgive him.

The first time they had slept together again was on the night of Kurt's Holy Communion. He was seven, and in the three years Dominic had been a father to him he and Jane had become close confidants and friends. He was there, dressed in a suit with video camera in hand, when his son came down the stairs dressed in his own little mini-me suit and wearing his rosette pinned to his chest. Kurt was embarrassed and hated his suit and begged Jane to gel back his blond curls but there was no way that was happening, so after a mini-tantrum at the bottom of the stairs, which was later edited out, they made their way to the church as a family. Dominic drove, Jane sat in the front and Kurt sat between his auntie Elle, who was sixteen and going through her Siouxsie and the Banshees "craving for a raw love" phase, and Rose, who kicked the back of Dominic's seat twice, claiming it was an accident and pretending to be horrified at the notion that her daughter could possibly think it was anything else. "I was merely crossing my legs, Jane, and if this car wasn't the size of half a can of beans I'd have been able to do so without nearly losing a knee."

Afterwards they had met up with his parents in a posh restaurant in Dublin city centre and, in spite of Rose getting completely twisted before the main course was even served and in spite of Dominic's parents' coldness, Kurt was happy. He was surrounded by the people he loved because, back then, Jane and Dominic were the centre of his universe and Elle was the coolest person he knew. Dominic stayed until well after Kurt had been put to bed. Together he and Jane opened a bottle of wine and toasted their son's big day. They weren't even through the first glass when Dominic was taking Jane to her bedroom, the same one that she had snuck him into seven years earlier. They both crept as silently as they could because at that time Rose still lived in the main house, and although she was in a drunken stupor, neither Dominic nor Jane wanted to risk waking her and provoking her wrath.

Once Jane's door was locked they kissed and touched and were naked within minutes, lying together on the bed in which their son had been conceived. This time Jane had a coil fitted and Dominic was wearing a condom. Dominic snuck out a few hours later.

The next day he phoned. He was regretful and hoped that their actions the previous night wouldn't ruin the fantastic friendship they'd built up. Jane had promised him that nothing would change and when he'd hung up he was relieved that, once again, Jane Moore had proved herself to be so cool. Of course he didn't see her, broken-hearted, lying face down on her bedroom floor crying for hours. Neither did he have any idea how much she had hoped that he'd give their relationship a chance because, for Jane, what could have been better than a happy ending with the man she loved, the father of her child?

The second time they'd had sex was after Jane's twenty-seventh birthday. Dominic was seeing two girls but it was early days as neither had allowed him access to their bedrooms. Jane had broken up with an artist she'd dated for six months. They were incredibly drunk and if Jane had not woken up on top of Dominic neither of them would have remembered having sex. This was rectified the following night when Dominic brought flowers and chocolates to apologize once again for his pesky penis. Jane opened a bottle of wine, and half an hour after Dominic's apology they were in bed. Over the next year they often got together when Dominic was between relationships or Jane was lonely and having a hard time dealing with her mother, her sister, or their son. By that stage their relationship was firmly in the friends-with-benefits zone, which suited Dominic completely, and Jane seemed happy to make the best of it.

It stopped when Dominic met Gina at a conference held in the Gresham Hotel. She was a country girl, accomplished, nice to Jane and kind to Kurt. They lasted for three years and Jane was sure they'd marry, but when Gina demanded a ring Dominic walked away and found himself in Jane's bed once more. And so their sexual history continued until the last time they'd had sex – the night when he'd split with the tripped-out Heidi.

A week later he'd arrived to Kurt's birthday with his new girlfriend, Bella, and one month later they were engaged. He hadn't slept with Jane since.

Elle felt like a new woman since her weekend away with Leslie. She had continued to work for hours every day, labouring over each face as though she was re-creating it in the presence of God. When the collection of twelve was complete, two of her old art-school contemporaries arrived at her cottage to view them. Fiona and Lori arrived together and Elle greeted them warmly, hugging them, and when Lori pointed out that they hadn't seen her since before Christmas she explained that she had been working very hard. They complained that she hadn't bothered to turn up to her last exhibition and she apologized for her absence, telling them she'd come down with flu.

She made coffee before the unveiling and Fiona admitted they'd heard gossip that Vincent had ended the relationship and she'd burned out his car.

Lori laughed a little. "He deserved it," she said.

"Elle," Fiona said, "he's a user, always was and always will be."

Elle joined them at her kitchen table and poured the coffee. "So what's the story about the blonde?" she asked. "Caroline. I bumped into them recently."

"She's an actress on that stupid drama shot in the UK what's it called?" Fiona asked Lori.

"Can't remember, but I've heard she takes her kit off every second episode," she replied.

"So now he's living off her," Elle said, and grinned. "Lucky girl. Until another source of income takes his fancy."

Lori and Fiona looked at one another and Lori made a face. Fiona turned to Elle. "He married her," she said.

"What?" said Elle. "No! It's only been five minutes. No way! Really?"

"Sorry," Lori said.

Elle was in shock. "He married her."

"Last week," said Fiona. "In a register office, and the afters were in the Four Seasons."

"It's featured in this week's *VIP* magazine," Lori said. "Can you believe that? The only thing important about him is the person he's sleeping with."

Elle brushed it off, telling her two friends that she wished Vincent and Caroline the best, then changed the subject.

After talking some more they followed her to the studio and were both impressed with her work, going as far as to say it would be her best show yet.

"I feel like crying," Lori said, looking across the twelve faces, including Alexandra's – the slight smile made her ache inside.

"It's genius," Fiona said, "and it's such a great concept."

Now that Elle was finished her latest project the girls would allow no excuses and insisted she join them at a party after the exhibition the next night. They left soon after and Elle sat at the baby grand piano that took up half of her sitting room, played some notes and decided it was time she got back in the game.

Jane appeared later that afternoon and they packed up the paintings together. Elle told her about Vincent, and Jane called him some names and wished ill health upon him, but Elle was determined to be over him so her sister's bitching seemed unnecessary. After Jane had left, Elle got into a bath and soaked for a glorious hour. When she grew bored she got out and lathered herself in the richest of creams. She sprayed on her favourite perfume, pulled her hair off her face into a tight ponytail, then put on her sexiest short dress and black thigh-high boots. She left her cottage and walked up the path towards the gate that would lead her to adventure.

Rose was standing outside when she passed. "You look like a whore," she said.

"I plan to act like one," Elle said.

"Well, at least no one can say you're a tease," Rose said, and headed indoors.

*

Leslie had spent the week in and out of hospital, having tests to ensure that she was healthy enough to have her breasts and womb removed. She remarked on the irony of the situation to one of the nurses who, having been on her feet for twelve hours straight, wasn't interested in irony – all she cared about was getting the necessary bloods so she could move on to the next patient and so on until she got home.

Jim had asked Leslie if she wanted him to go with her but she had politely and firmly told him no. He had a job and a life of his own and it wasn't as though she hadn't attended medical check-ups on her own for the past eighteen years. She was in the waiting area, reading a pamphlet on reconstructive surgery and picking at some trail mix, when a tall, bald man in his late forties sat down beside her. He nodded hello and opened a newspaper. They both sat reading for ten minutes or so before he closed his paper and asked her if she had the time.

She looked at her watch. "Just after three," she said.

He sighed. "I've been here since seven this morning."

"Hell," she said.

"Hell," he agreed, and smiled at her a big wide smile, and she wondered how he could smile with such warmth and how he could carry himself with such cheer when it was obvious he had cancer and was going through chemotherapy.

"I'm Mark," he said, and put out his hand. "It's nice to meet you."

"Leslie," she said, and shook it.

"Are you a patient or family/friend?"

"Patient. Are you starting chemo or near the end?"

"That obvious?" he said, rubbing his freshly shaved head.

"It's not the bald head – it's the colour of your skin."

"Ah," he said, nodding. "Off-putting."

"Familiar," she said.

"Do you mind me asking why you're here, seeing as your hair is your own and your skin looks good too?"

"Thanks."

"You're welcome."

Leslie thought about lying or, at the very least, avoiding the question but she didn't know the man and, aside from Jim, she hadn't spoken to anyone about her radical plans so she was honest. "I'm having my breasts and womb removed in a few months to avoid getting cancer."

"You're joking," he said.

"No."

"To avoid getting cancer?"

"I have the gene."

"But that doesn't mean you'll get it."

"I've lost my entire family and my youth to cancer. I'm not willing to lose any more."

"Except your breasts and womb."

"Except them."

"Well," he said, "I've lost both balls."

Leslie was as taken aback by his honesty as he had been by hers. "Ouch," she said.

He grinned at her. "Could be worse. I could have my balls and no penis."

"True," she said. "That would suck."

They laughed.

"Yes, it would," he said.

"So how does that work?"

"You mean sex?"

She couldn't believe that she was engaging in such an

intimate conversation with a stranger, but she nodded to indicate that, yes, she did mean sex.

"I can still orgasm apparently, but haven't tried it yet. Obviously I can't get anyone pregnant and I'll need to inject hormones every few weeks."

"Ah, it'll be pretty much the same for me."

"I see you're thinking about reconstruction," he said, looking at the pamphlet.

She nodded.

"They offered me fake balls," he said.

"Really? Did you take them?"

"No, too weird."

"I don't know what to do," she said.

"Then just take one step at a time," he said.

After a pause she said, "Mark?"

"Yes?"

"Are you married?"

"Divorced."

"Kids?"

"Two boys, twelve and ten."

"Is the cancer gone?"

"That's what they tell me," he said.

"Would you like to go to an art exhibition with me tomorrow night?"

"I'd love to," he said.

"Good," she said. "Excellent."

They swapped numbers and soon after that she was called into her doctor's office. He couldn't help but wonder why she had a stupid grin on her face while he was talking her through the radical procedures she was facing.

*

159

Tom fought with Jeanette on the phone in his car. She was pissed off that he wouldn't allow her to attend the Missing Exhibition and he couldn't understand why on earth she'd want to be there or how she thought her presence appropriate.

"It's appropriate because I'm the one sleeping beside you in bed."

"That is why it is so very inappropriate, Jeanette."

"It's not like I'm going to advertise myself. I'll stay quiet, I'll bring Davey and I'll pretend you're my friend and he's my boyfriend."

"No."

"So that's it?"

"Yes," he said, "that's it."

"Don't expect me to be waiting for you when you get home."

"Okay."

"Bastard!"

She hung up and Tom drove on, wondering how he had allowed himself to get into such a dangerous situation with a young girl who had a stupid crush on him. *I'm so sorry, Alexandra. If only you'd come home to me, this nightmare would end.*

He pulled up outside his parents-in-law's house and beeped. Breda appeared at the door and he got out, ran up the path and put his arm around her shoulders. "You look beautiful," he said.

She smiled at him. "You're a liar but I appreciate it."

Alexandra's father had decided not to attend the exhibition. He didn't feel comfortable in arty circles. Instead he would spend the evening as he always did, with his friends in the pub avoiding his new reality. Alexandra's sister Kate and brother Eamonn were attending with their spouses and travelling separately.

Tom helped Breda into the car and walked around to his side, sat in and took off down the road.

"It's very exciting," Breda said, "all this good work in Alexandra's name."

Tom agreed. Jane had been very pleased with the media interest, and when Elle had insisted that any proceeds would go to the National Missing Persons Bureau it was a major coup for them and a news story worthy of reporting. The fact that Jack Lukeman was taking time out of his busy touring schedule to come and play led to further interest, including a TV magazine show that wished to film a song from Jack and an interview with Tom. He was pretty sick at the notion of having to talk to a camera, but Breda assured him he would be great and that Alexandra would be so proud.

Jane was waiting at the door. She greeted Tom and Breda with hugs and ushered them inside. They were early enough to see the pieces hanging from the wall without interruption. Breda stood in front of the painting of her daughter for the longest time. Silent tears rolled down her hollow cheeks. Tom took her hand.

"I still feel her," she said. "She's still with us."

"I know," Tom said, but he didn't know, and every time he ventured into the dark place, he left it hoping she was gone rather than enduring ongoing torture.

A few minutes later Leslie appeared with a man. She introduced him to Jane, who welcomed them both, then asked Mark to excuse Leslie for a minute. Leslie followed her into the back room.

"What is it with you and bald men?" Jane said.

"Is that why I'm back here?"

"No. Elle's missing. I was hoping you'd talked to her today."

"No. I haven't. I don't believe it."

"The press is relying on her being here." Jane was starting to freak out. "I can't let everybody down now."

"You're not letting anyone down – bloody Elle is. I'll kill her."

Just then Elle appeared in her short dress and thigh-high boots. "Kill who?"

Jane let out a sigh of relief. "Where were you?"

"I have no idea. On a boat and a long way from land, if that helps."

"You nearly gave Jane a heart attack," Leslie said.

"Sorry, Jane. Sorry, Leslie."

"Don't be smart," Leslie said.

Elle hugged her. "I met a boy and I liked him. Of course he's gone now, sailing away on the high seas as we speak."

"Well, good," Leslie said, "good for you. Now go home, change out of the dominatrix gear and have a wash while you're at it."

Elle saluted and Tom was given the job of driving her home to wash and change before the exhibition.

Jane introduced Breda to Leslie and explained who Leslie was and what she had done to help them find Alexandra. Breda was very grateful, Leslie humbled and Mark incredibly impressed by his altruistic new friend.

Then Eamonn, Kate and their spouses arrived and Jane offered them wine and watched as they migrated towards the picture of their sister. Eamonn and Kate stood together, shoulders touching, looking into Alexandra's eyes. When they turned to face the crowd, Kate's eyes were damp and Eamonn looked as if he was in physical pain.

Mark wasn't drinking so Leslie merely sipped a glass of wine. She asked him if he felt well enough to stay and he said he did. She told him she wouldn't ask him again so if he wanted to go he had a mouth and could tell her. He liked that she didn't fuss over him.

Dominic appeared with Kurt and Irene in tow. Jane felt more than a little awkward around Dominic after the night in the car when he'd clearly attempted to seduce her, so his insistence that she invite him to Elle's Missing Exhibition had made her extremely uncomfortable, especially in light of Kurt's recent revelation that things were weird at his dad's house. She managed to put her discomfort to one side and concentrated on Kurt. She was delighted to see her son and wondered what had brought about his sudden interest in one of Elle's exhibitions.

"What you and Elle are doing for your friend, well, it's really cool, Mum," he said.

"Yeah, Jane," Irene said. "Every girl could do with a friend like you."

"Thank you." She was still a little miffed because Kurt had known about the show for months and he'd never seemed particularly interested or impressed before.

"Dad showed us pictures of you and Alexandra when you were our age," Kurt said.

"Can't believe you were a Megadeth fan," said Irene. "I love Megadeth."

Jane looked at Dominic. "What's this?" she asked, feigning a smile.

"Your mother wasn't half sexy in her day," said Dominic.

"Too much, Dad," Kurt said. "Seriously too, too much."

Irene explained that Dominic had shown them the pictures of the Megadeth concert in Antrim that they'd gone to a year before Kurt was born. Jane remembered the pictures: she was smoking and straddling Dominic, and Alexandra was drinking from a bottle of cider and giving the camera the finger.

Kurt nudged his mother, grinned at her, then followed Irene to the drinks counter. They picked up a glass of wine each and raised them to her. She turned to Dominic and shook her head. "What were you thinking?" she said.

"What do you mean?"

"Showing them those pictures."

"Why wouldn't I? They're part of our past."

"Kurt sees me and you and cigarettes and booze and —"

"And he'll run off and get his girlfriend pregnant?"

"Don't make fun of me!"

"I would never do that. Look, all I'm saying is your life isn't his life so just relax."

"It's not him I'm worried about." Jane pointed to Irene, who was rubbing the back of Kurt's neck and whispering in his ear. "It's her."

"What will be will be, Janey."

"Easy for you to say," she said, and went to talk to a representative of the National Missing Persons Bureau.

Jack Lukeman arrived on schedule. He was dressed from head to toe in black and his long coat swung behind him. Leslie greeted him with a hug and introduced him to Jane. He put his hand out and she shook it. He cupped her hand, tipped his head to the side and viewed her as though she was a painting. She blushed. He grinned and let her hand go. "Nice to meet you, Jane."

Jane told him how lovely it was to meet him and then she told him about the many times she'd seen him play, the where and when, how she'd got there, who she'd been with and how fantastic each show was. Jack nodded as though he cared.

Leslie sighed. "Jesus, Jane, as if he gives a shit."

Jack laughed a giddy, dirty laugh and put his arm around Leslie.

"Sorry," Jane said.

"You'll have to excuse her," he said. "She doesn't mix well."

Later Jack and his guitar player played an acoustic set surrounded by paintings of the Missing to a captivated crowd. They sat on chairs under the painting of Alexandra. The guitar player strummed gently and Jack leaned forward, closed his eyes and sang "Metropolis Blue" into his microphone.

"Sometimes I ask myself how did I get here?
Country boy with no change for his fares and city girls are so
*   expensive.*
I wanna go back to the girl that I love, I would go back there if
*   I could.*
I know I should. I need you. My lips ache for your kiss.
I need you and not this hungriness.
I just spend my time hanging around here with the boys, drinking
*   whiskey drinking beer,*
Fool I was thought adventure was near, those easy thrills are so
*   elusive I fear.*

"My heart sings for the one that I love. I would go back there if I
    could, I know I should.
I need you, my tune lacks your melody.
I need you, my eyes no longer see.
I am floating like an autumn leaf, on the whim of a breeze I float
I would give almost anything, a thousand jewels, an enchanted
    view, a billion poems but I'm a fool.
I can barely write a note but we live in hope. I need you for all
    eternity.
I need you, you are my destiny. I need you. I need you."

The audience were silent as though they were in church
and they only clapped and cheered when he opened his eyes
and smiled. Tom wiped away tears. The TV cameras rolled.
    Elle was back, clean and in a subdued black outfit, stand-
ing quietly and respectfully to the side with her sister. When
Jack had finished his set – the photographers were snapping
and the crowd were clapping – she leaned in towards Jane
and whispered, "We've done well, Janey."
    Jane looked at Alexandra's mother smiling a genuine
smile, her sister and brother clapping and charmed by the
talented Mr Lukeman, who had managed to make them
forget their loss if only for a few minutes. She caught Tom's
eye and they smiled at one another. She turned to Leslie,
who was laughing with the latest bald man in her life, and
felt happy.

Jane was about to go to bed when the doorbell rang. She
looked through the peephole, which revealed Dominic.
She thought about ignoring him but then he pushed the
buzzer again and held it down. She opened the door.

"Go away."

He held the door open. "Please let me in."

She let him in.

He sat on the sofa and hugged a cushion. "I think my marriage is over."

"I'm sorry to hear that."

"The bitch just kicked me out of my own house. I mean, is that even legal?"

"Well, it's her house too."

"Is it tits! I've had that house ten years – we've only known each other five minutes."

"Which begs the question as to why you married her in the first place."

"She was pregnant. She lost the baby at eleven weeks."

Jane was shocked. She hadn't guessed.

"As soon as I found out I proposed because I didn't want to be the same fucker I was to you. I wanted to be a good dad, a good man, but I suppose it wasn't meant to be."

"I'm really sorry." She sat down beside him.

"Don't say anything," he said. "Just kiss me."

"Dominic."

"Please, Janey."

And so she kissed him, and she straddled him like she had so many years ago at the Megadeth concert and they had sex on her recently re-covered sofa.

After he came and the condom was quickly disposed of, they sat together and he looked into her eyes and asked, "Do you think we should try for another baby?"

For a second she thought he was talking about him and her, but then the truth dawned. He was talking about his wife, the woman he had married, baby or no baby, and something inside her died. She stood up, fixed her skirt and asked him to leave.

"But I've nowhere to go," he said.

"I don't care."

"But I don't understand."

"I loved you for all these years. I was in love with you, but no more." She walked him to her front door. She handed him his shoes. She bade him goodnight. She closed the door and she walked to her bedroom. In bed she covered her head. She didn't cry because she had done that too many times before. Instead she just lay there and embraced the pain in her heart and told herself, *Enough now.*

Elle had smiled for photographers and made nice with the interviewer. She had shaken Jack L's hand and they had posed together and parted, and when her work was done she joined her pals, Fiona and Lori, at a private party in a club she used to frequent.

"Well, if it isn't Elmore," one other partygoer said. "Long time no see!" Two air-kisses followed. Elle signed all her paintings "Elmore" but only the biggest of arseholes within her circle referred to her as anything but Elle.

She moved through the club and towards the pool table where some guys were playing, sat on the sofa nearby and a waitress took her drink order. She drank and watched the guys play. One in particular interested her. When he finished his game she asked him to join her and had a drink waiting for him. "I'd really like to have sex with you," she said.

"I'd like that too," he said.

"Of course you would."

"Are you playing with me?"

"Absolutely not. Tell me, do you like doing it outdoors?"

"It depends," he said. "What have you got in mind?"

"Come with me," she said, and he followed her through the club, outside and down the street. They crossed the road and as they approached the police station he began to wonder about her, but she pressed her finger to her lips. When the coast was clear she opened the gate that led to the back of the station.

He pulled away from her. "You're insane," he said. .

He heard some noise out front and she pulled him onto the ground under a window through which he had seen five or six men and women, sitting at desks, roaming around, one at the coffee machine and another kicking the fax machine.

"We can't," he said, but she could tell that he was excited because he was leaning against her so she unzipped his trousers and released him. After that there was no going back and if any of the officers had taken a moment or two to look out of their window they would have seen a pool player's freckled arse appear intermittently.

Afterwards, invigorated, Elle returned to the club where she joined Fiona in the loo for a few lines of coke. She drank shots with Lori and, as it was a celebration, she paid for six or seven bottles of champagne for all twenty of her new best friends.

Kurt woke up around seven. He yawned, stretched, scratched his balls through his boxer shorts and headed into the main bathroom. He peed, shook himself off and flushed the loo. It was when he turned to walk from the loo to the door that he saw Elle. She was lying in a bath filled with water. She was completely naked, her lips were purple and she was either asleep or dead.

Kurt roared, "Mum! Mum! Mum!"

Jane woke up with a start. Kurt was still roaring. She jumped out of bed and followed his yells to the bathroom where he had remained frozen.

"Oh, my God!" Jane cried. "Oh, my God, Elle!" She ran to her sister, touched her cold skin and shook her hard.

Elle's eyes opened and she yawned. "What's happening?" she asked.

"Oh, Jesus," Jane said, and sank to her knees. "I thought you were dead."

"I'm really cold," Elle said, realizing she was in a bath of freezing water.

Kurt exhaled and sat on the loo lid. "Holy shit, Elle."

Jane asked Kurt for a towel. The only one he could find there was a hand towel, which he handed to his mother. She responded with a dirty look. "Come on, Elle, time to get out," she said.

"I can't seem to move my legs," Elle said, and giggled.

Jane looked at Kurt.

"Oh, no," he said, because lifting his naked aunt out of the bath was above and beyond the call of duty.

"I need your help," Jane insisted. "I have to get her out now."

Kurt walked up to the bath, flexing his neck and trying not to focus on his aunt's bush. Elle gave him her hand and smiled at him; her purple lips were stuck to her teeth. Jane took the other arm and together they pulled Elle up.

Kurt closed his eyes when he felt his aunt's breast against his chest. "Oh, Mum, this is so wrong."

Elle giggled again.

"Here," Jane said. "I'll take her from the front, you go around —"

"Don't even say it," he said.

Jane and Kurt pulled Elle out of the bath, and while Jane held her up Kurt ran to the hot press and piled his arms high with bath towels. Jane wrapped Elle in one and Kurt helped carry her into his mother's room. Once she was dry and safely snuggled in bed with the electric blanket on, Jane went to the kitchen and boiled the kettle to make some tea for Elle.

Kurt followed his mum.

"Are you okay?" Jane asked her son.

"My eyes, Mum, my eyes!" he said, covering them and pretending to be blinded.

He was playacting so Jane relaxed, content that he wouldn't be scarred for life. "I'm sorry, Kurt. You shouldn't have had to deal with that."

"It's fine, Mum. If it ever happens again I'm moving to France, but it's fine." He was smiling, which suggested he was joking, and after he'd come into skin-on-skin contact with his naked aunt that was the best she could hope for.

"I got lucky with you," she said, and Kurt blushed just like his mother often did.

"Whatever," he said.

"Kurt?"

"Yeah?"

"Don't you think it's a bit weird that Irene didn't wake up?"

"She wears ear-plugs. She says I snore like a pig and you should have had my adenoids out when I was a kid."

"How does she hear you snore from the spare room?"

"Oh, crap!" He grinned and held his hands up. "She's on the pill, I wear condoms and I'm turning eighteen in two weeks."

Jane sighed. "I give up."

"About time," he said, waved her away and headed back to bed to sleep off the image of his aunt's tits and arse.

Jane handed Elle the tea. It was too hot, burning her frozen hands, so Jane kept hold of it and fed it to her shivering sister until it was gone. "What's going on, Elle?"

"Just wanted a bath, Janey."

"You could have frozen to death."

"I was just really tired. Big night."

"Did you take something?"

Elle nodded. "I was having a good time – but I won't do it again."

"Do I need to call Dr Griffin?"

Elle shook her head. "No. I'm just cold, that's all."

Jane tucked the duvet up under her sister's chin. "What am I going to do with you, girly girl?"

"Just love me, Jane, even though I don't deserve it," Elle said, and then she turned around and fell fast asleep.

Jane sat in the room, touching her sister's hand every few minutes until it had returned to a normal temperature. She turned off the electric blanket and the light, then made her way to the kitchen.

Through the intercom she heard her mother calling. "Jane! Jane! Jane! It's your mother!" Jane put her hands over her ears and if she hadn't been scared of frightening her son for the second time that morning she would have screamed until her voice was gone.

Chapter 9

No Goodbyes

I love you now as I loved you then
but it's time to save our prayers,
it's time to say amen.

Jack L, *Metropolis Blue*

May 2008

Breda went to Mass every day and had done so for well over thirty years. Every morning she would wake at seven, she'd wash, dress, drink a cup of tea, and then she would put on her hat and coat and walk a mile down the road to her local church in time for the eight o'clock service. Over the years she had noticed the church becoming emptier and emptier. The young people had all but disappeared and all that was left was a handful of old men and women, most of whom were waiting patiently for the Lord to call them home.

Breda was early so she knelt down and put her hands together and looked up at the statue of Jesus hanging on the cross. She said an Our Father and then some Hail Marys and a Glory Be after that. The church was empty as she looked around. Her knees were hurting and she felt tired and cold. She leaned on the pew and pulled herself into a sitting position, then joined her hands again to wait for the priest and the few last souls seeking solace or saving.

"Dear God," she said, "I look at Your Son on the cross, I see the nails in His hands and feet, the thorns on His head, the blood in His eyes, the wound in His side, and I'd trade places with Him in an instant if You would just give me my Alexandra back. This burden is too great and I can't carry on much longer. I'm begging You as your servant, have pity on me. Show her the way home. I'm leaving now." She got up and bowed before the altar. "I won't be back tomorrow or the next day or the day after that. The day she comes home, that's when You'll see me here again." She walked out of the church, and although bargaining with or, indeed, threatening the Lord had been slightly unnerving, Breda felt that He had left her with little or no choice.

Kurt woke up to Jane, Rose, Elle and Irene singing "Happy Birthday" at the end of his bed. He grinned because his grandmother was wearing a party hat with "18" written on it, Elle was draped in a banner that read "18, Legal and Pissed Already", and Irene was bouncing up and down, blowing a horn. His mum was standing between them, holding a cake with candles blazing and, of course, she was fighting tears. She always cried at every birthday and every milestone so it had been only a matter of time. He smiled, rubbed the sleep from his eyes and sat up.

Jane made her way around the bed. "Blow," she said.

Kurt blew out the candles in one go. Elle, Rose and Irene clapped, and Jane kissed his cheek. "Eighteen," she said, and burst into tears.

A big breakfast of steak and chips awaited him when he was dressed. He sat with his birthday hat on munching his favourite food while his mother, aunt, gran and girlfriend fussed around him. Jane made Rose and Elle some toast while they sat at the table with the Birthday Boy.

Rose was first to slide a present across. He looked at the envelope and grinned. "So far I like it," he said, and opened it. Eighteen one-hundred-euro notes fell out. "This is too much," he said.

She tapped his hand. "It's enough to take you and Irene on a sun holiday after your exams."

"No way!" he said.

"Oh, my God!" said Irene.

"Apparently it's a rite of passage," Rose said.

"Mum?" he said, waiting for her to veto the trip.

"I've heard that Greece is pretty special," she said.

"No way!" he said.

"Oh, my God!" said Irene.

He leaped up from his seat, dragged his grandmother off her chair and hugged her. She held him tight for a few moments before letting go. "You're such a good boy," she said.

Irene jumped up and down on the spot, saying, "Thank you, thank you!" over and over again.

Elle was next. She walked into the hall and came back with a large box wrapped in red paper. Kurt tore at the wrapping. He opened the box and lifted out a helmet. "A helmet?" he said, and Elle grinned and turned to Jane, who sighed and pointed to the garden.

Kurt stood up and looked out of the window. His dad was straddling a motorbike outside. Dominic grinned and waved. Kurt looked at his mother. "No way!" he said, shaking his head.

"Please, I'm begging you to be careful!" said Jane.

"No way!" Kurt shouted, and the back door was open and he was standing beside his dad in two seconds flat.

Dominic handed him the keys and they hugged, then his dad pointed to his mother and told him that the bike was from both of them. Kurt ran in through the back door and hugged Jane. She burst into tears again but this time it wasn't as a result of over-sentimentality but instead a manifestation of disbelief that Dominic had managed to talk her into buying her baby boy a death-trap. Elle handed him the helmet. He hugged her and ran back out to his dad. Together they examined every inch of the bike.

"A Suzuki Bandit 600!" Kurt said. "Holy crap, a Suzuki Bandit 600!"

Jane closed the door and left them to it. Rose kissed her on the cheek.

"What was that for?" Jane asked, startled.

"Bravery. You're learning to let go and that's good."

Jane sat down at the table. "Yeah, I suppose it is. Of course, if he kills or maims himself I'll hate myself for ever."

"You won't be alone," Rose said, and made her way back to her basement apartment.

Elle and Jane went outside, sat on the steps and watched Kurt take off down the road as Dominic waved to him. Dominic turned to Jane and smiled at her. She returned his smile, then got up and walked inside. Elle stood up and went to where Dominic stood watching his son disappear down the road. "What did you do to Jane?" she asked him.

"I married someone else," he said.

"She's finished loving you."

"She is."

"It had to happen some time."

"Yes, it did," he said. "It's truly amazing she loved me at all."

"Yeah, well, the Moore women aren't the brightest when it comes to love," Elle said, and she walked to the gate that took her through the garden to her little cottage.

Dominic found Jane on her hunkers, loading the washing-machine. "Big day," he said.

"It is."

"Our son is a man."

"And still just a boy."

He sat at the table and turned his chair to face her. "Is that why you forgave me so easily? Because you knew I was still just a boy?"

"I forgave you because if someone had given *me* a way out I would have taken it," she said.

"You're the best person I know," he said.

"Please don't try and sweet-talk me because it's not fair," she said, sitting down on the floor.

"I'm not and I know. I know. I've been really selfish."

"I let you think I was fine with being friends."

"But I knew better," he said. "And I feel like a prick."

"Well, feeling like a prick isn't exactly unfamiliar territory for you."

"No. It isn't. What are we going to do, Janey?"

"Well, we're going to be parents to a pretty cool kid, you're going to work on your marriage and I'm going to get a life."

"You're the best person I know," he said again. "You're kind and selfless and cool and funny, and sometimes weird and dangerous, and I really, really wish I loved you the way you loved me."

"I know you do," she said.

"And I will never cross the line again."

"No, you won't."

"But I don't want to lose your friendship."

"Okay," she said. "Let's just take it one day at a time."

He left soon after and Jane closed her eyes. She felt the pain pulse through her. *It's over.*

Because Kurt's eighteenth birthday fell only a few weeks before his Leaving Certificate exams he'd agreed that he'd defer his party until afterwards and so, when he returned from his bike ride, he grabbed his books and, after telling his mum he loved her, he went to school.

Elle went back to bed for a few hours and then to meet Leslie in the underwear department in Arnotts. She had promised she'd help her pick out sexy underwear for a date with the Ball-less Wonder, which was what Elle had christened Mark. "What are we looking for?" Elle said.

"Something sexy."

"Well, obviously something sexy – you don't want to look like his mother. He has enough problems getting a stiffy as it is."

"Yes, that's exactly what I need to hear, thanks so much."

"All right. How about racy red?"

"No."

"Why not?"

"Because I'm not a racy-red person."

"Well, what are you?" Elle asked.

"I'm a sports bra and shorts person."

"Well, that's just not sexy, Leslie."

"Which is why I've brought you."

"Fine, then, you have to listen to me and do what I say or I'm going home."

"Fine," Leslie said, "but if you make me look like a hooker I'm leaving."

Having argued, debated, reflected and conceded, Leslie finally purchased a black lace set. The bra was padded and lifted her in all the right places and the pants were shorts as opposed to the G-string Elle had initially suggested.

She bought Elle lunch to celebrate.

Elle was surprised that Leslie was rushing into a relationship with a man who was recovering from cancer and interested to hear her reasoning. Leslie admitted she was worried that she was making a big mistake but she felt a level of comfort with Mark that she hadn't felt with a man in a very long time.

"What about Jim?" Elle asked.

"Jim is my sister's husband."

"Was her husband. Your sister died a long time ago."

"And?"

"And he's a very nice man. He cares about you – he's a little on the short side but you must admit those dimples are to die for."

"You're sick," said Leslie.

"I am not."

"He's my –"

Elle put her finger against Leslie's lips. "He's your friend, that's all."

Leslie saw it differently, and when Elle realized that she was becoming increasingly uncomfortable, she returned to the subject of Mark. "Why the rush?" she asked.

"I've known him three weeks."

"Exactly."

"You sleep with people you've met in toilets, for God's sake!"

"Don't make me sorry for sharing my adventures with you. Besides, we're not talking about me, we're talking about you, a woman who hasn't had sex with anything that wasn't battery-operated for eighteen years."

"So?" Leslie said.

"So, I'm curious as to what the rush is."

"I'm having surgery on the first of July."

"What kind of surgery?"

"A prophylactic bilateral mastectomy and laparoscopic hysterectomy."

"A what and what?"

Leslie explained the procedures to an open-mouthed Elle.

"How long have you known about this?" Elle asked.

"Pretty much since we met."

"Why are you only mentioning it now?"

"It didn't come up."

"That's the kind of thing you bring up."

"Well, I'm sorry," Leslie said. "This friendship thing is still new to me."

"You're forgiven. But only because you're having your tits lopped off."

"Charming!" Leslie said, and laughed a little.

Now it was clear to Elle why Leslie was in such a rush to have sex with an actual man and a ball-less one at that. She wanted to experience it with all her bits just one last time. Elle wished her friend good luck and told her she'd expect her call the very next day with full details. Leslie had no intention of providing her with anything like the full details but she agreed just so Elle would let her go home. She had so much to do before Mark arrived.

An hour before he was due, the house was clean and she was washed, dressed and looking well, even if she thought so herself. She had wondered about cooking, but she wasn't a cook so it seemed like a much better idea to order in when he came. That way he could pick what he wanted and there would be no chance of him enduring a bad meal.

Jim rang half an hour before Mark was due. "Well?" he said.

"Well what?"

"Are you excited?"

"None of your business," she said, beginning to regret telling him about Mark at all. "Go away."

"Ah, come on, I'm here sitting alone watching a DVD about two homeless drug addicts."

"Okay," she said. "Do you think I should play music or is that really corny?"

"No, it's not corny – definitely play music. What have you got?"

"Lots of stuff."

"Okay, what do you feel like listening to?"

"I don't know."

"Think."

"I can't, I'm too nervous."

"Okay, go over to your CD rack, close your eyes and pick something."

"I don't have a CD rack. I buy all my music on-line."

"Well, what do you do that for?"

"Because I no longer live in the year 1983," she said.

181

"Fine. So close your eyes and click on a song or do whatever it is you do to listen to music."

"Okay. Can I go now?"

"Yes," he said. "And, Leslie?"

"What?"

"Enjoy yourself."

"Thanks."

She hung up, went over to her computer and clicked onto her media player. She closed her eyes and dragged the mouse along the various tracks listed, stopped and clicked, and Alanis Morissette's "In Praise Of The Vulnerable Man" started to play. *Apt.*

She sat holding her cat and waited for Mark to come.

Tom opened the door and found Trish, his liaison officer, standing outside. The house call was unscheduled so his heart started to race and his palms were instantly damp. If he'd allowed himself, he would have begun to shake.

"Calm down, we haven't found her," she warned.

He followed her to the sitting room. They sat.

"*Crimeline* are going to do a reconstruction."

"Okay," he said. "So Alexandra has captured the media's imagination. Finally."

"Finally." She nodded. "It's good news, Tom."

"I know."

"You should thank your friends. Without them . . ."

"She'd just be a number."

"Never just a number," she said, "but media interest always helps – just keeping her face out there helps."

She left soon after. Tom picked up the phone and called Jane. He told her the good news and they agreed to an impromptu celebration, even though Elle and Leslie were unavailable. He suggested that he would cook and she agreed to bring the wine, so at eight fifteen she knocked on his door.

It was the first time Jane had visited Tom in his home and it felt so strange being greeted by pictures of the adult Alexandra, the woman she didn't know. In the sitting room there were photos of their wedding day. Alexandra had made a beautiful bride even in the shot when she'd stuck out her tongue at the photographer. Tom poured wine and they clinked glasses, as was customary. He thanked her once again and told her how grateful he was, and she told him to shut up and that he was boring her. It was true that media interest in the disappearance of Alexandra Kavanagh had increased considerably since their little exhibition, but they were a long way from finding her.

Once again, Tom put all his hopes in the one basket. "This will work," he said.

"Please don't get too excited. It's only a reconstruction. It's good news but that's all."

"I know."

"You're contradicting yourself."

"I don't care. I'm happy."

The exhibition had been a great success in so far as the critics were happy. Alexandra's plight – and the plight of many others – was given a little time in the spotlight and they had made some money for the charity. Originally Elle had put the painting of Alexandra aside for Tom or Alexandra's family, pending Tom's decision, but only five of the twelve paintings had sold and a buyer had offered a great deal of money for Alexandra, so now Jane found herself in the uncomfortable position of having to approach Tom on the matter. If the money was going into the Moore family business there was no way she would have sold the painting, but because the sales were in aid of charity she felt obliged to earn as much money as possible. It had been a shock to her that the exhibition had failed to sell out because Elle had been a sure-fire seller for a long time. Jane had begun to notice a slowdown in sales with some of her other artists, but she had put it down to various reasons and now she was wondering whether or not a change was going to come. This concerned her because while she had banked her money and scrimped and saved, her little sister had gone through it like there was no tomorrow.

Over dinner she broached the subject of the picture with Tom.

"Definitely sell it," he said.

"Oh, great. I'm so glad you feel that way."

"To be honest, it's a bit of a relief. It was just too sad."

"I understand," she said.

"Do you ever wonder about Fate?"

"Not really."

"I do," he said. "I think about that night in the lift and what would have happened if I'd taken the stairs or decided to give the gig a miss. If I'd gone home with my little bag of flyers, I think I'd have lost the will and I'd be gone."

"Don't say that."

"It's true."

After dinner they sat in the sitting room together and Jane told Tom about Kurt's birthday present of a motorbike and how she'd wrestled with it. Dominic had finally broken her but she feared that she might now never sleep again. He laughed and told her she'd find a way – after all, he had. He didn't mention the way he'd found was getting pissed.

Eventually she thanked him for a really nice evening, one she had needed badly. He was getting her coat when the doorbell rang and, thinking it was her taxi, she answered it.

A girl stood in the doorway, looking at her quizzically.

"Who are you?" the girl asked.

"I'm a friend," Jane said. The girl's aggressive tone set her on edge.

"Jeanette, go on into the kitchen and I'll join you in a moment," Tom warned.

"No," Jeanette said, and it was apparent she'd been drinking. "I'm Jeanette, Tom's girlfriend." She put her hand out to shake Jane's.

Jane got such a fright she shook her hand and told her it was lovely to meet her. This took the wind out of Jeanette's sails. Her aggression dissipated and she told Jane it was nice to meet her too, and all the while Tom was biting his lip and praying he was dreaming while at the same time trying to work out a plausible lie to salvage the situation. "Jeanette, please, go and wait for me in the kitchen," he begged.

Jeanette said goodbye to Jane, who was still smiling like a simpleton, and went into the kitchen, closing the door behind her.

"Jane –" Tom attempted to explain, but Jane just shook her head.

"No," she said. She walked out of his open front door and he followed her to the gate.

"You don't understand," he said.

"Oh, I understand," she said. "You're a man, and men

are self-centred, lying, cheating bastards. I thought you were different. I thought you were decent. But you're just like the rest of them."

"Jane –"

"Don't Jane me!" she said, and now she was crying. "In fact, you're worse than the rest of them because you pretend to be better – you pretend to give a shit!"

"I do!" he shouted.

"Your wife is missing, she's alone and lost or hurt or hurting or dying or dead, and what are you doing? You're fucking, that's what you're doing."

She moved to open the gate and he grabbed her arm. "Please," he said.

"Go fuck your girlfriend," she said, "and let me worry about my old friend." She pulled her arm away and ran towards the taxi that was approaching. It stopped, she got in and Tom watched her disappear.

He walked inside his house and grabbed Jeanette's coat from the banister. He walked into his kitchen. He wrapped it around her shoulders, pushed her through his hall and front door and closed it in her face without saying one word. She banged on his window and door for a few minutes, then gave up. She knew that whatever sweetness they had once shared had rapidly turned sour. The next night she'd tell her friends all about it over dinner and they'd tell her he was a user and a tosser and she was too good for him anyway, because he was a broken man.

"Throw him on the pyre and light a match," Davey would say, and Jeanette would laugh and decide that although she would miss him she wouldn't miss his problems so she'd drink to finding a man her own age – sexy, funny, uncomplicated and without a tragic past.

When Leslie didn't call, Elle decided to visit her in her apartment. She buzzed, Leslie let her in and she bounded up the stairs. She sat with the cat while Leslie looked for some teabags because Elle was attempting to cut down on coffee.

"Well?" Elle asked.

"He didn't come."

"He probably couldn't – I mean, I'm not a doctor but cum is semen and semen lives in balls, he is ball-less – *ergo* no cum."

"He didn't turn up."

"Oh. What happened?"

"About an hour after he was due he phoned and told me he was sorry but that he wasn't ready," Leslie said, dropping a teabag into a mug of boiling water.

Elle preferred the bag to be in the mug before the boiling water but she wasn't about to argue. "Sorry," she said.

"The man has lost his wife, his kids and his balls all in the space of a year. He's just finished chemo. I was mad to think anything could happen."

"Not mad. You were just trying to open yourself up and maybe you rushed it with Mark, but that's okay. Next time will be better."

Leslie smiled at her new friend because what she'd said was true. She had rushed into something with Mark. She was so desperate to move on, and to be with someone who really understood what she was going through and it had all been a little too simple. The poor man had his own issues, his battles to win and lose. Elle was right: next time

187

it would be better because next time she'd know better. *I'm not ready and that's okay.*

"How's Jim?" Elle asked.

"Do not bring Jim into this," Leslie warned.

Elle put her hands up. "Okay, Miss Touchy."

"I am not Miss Touchy!"

After Elle had left most of her tea in the cup and Leslie was fortified with a nice hot coffee, they decided to take advantage of the bright, warm day by going for a stroll in the Phoenix Park. Leslie had stopped to look in her postbox when Deborah from Apartment 8a entered the main door. Deborah had managed to maintain a safe distance from Leslie since the incident in which she'd mistaken stale cat-shit for Leslie's rotting corpse. She mumbled hello.

"Well, hello, Deborah," Leslie said loudly.

"Hi," Deborah said.

"This is my friend Elle. Say hello to my friend, Deborah."

"Hi," Deborah said again.

Elle grinned. She'd heard the story on more than one occasion because, for some reason, Deborah's misguided concern for Leslie had really hit a nerve.

"You see, Deborah, loners don't have friends."

Deborah nodded and looked about to see if there was anyone around who could possibly save her if Leslie decided to physically attack. "I'm going now," she said, and made her way to the lift.

"Lovely seeing you!" Leslie called.

Deborah disappeared into the lift.

"You need help," Elle said.

"Yes," Leslie said, "I really do."

They took a stroll in the park and ended up in the zoo

and enjoyed a perfectly charming day together that both women would remember with fondness for a very long time.

On 29 May 2008 the television show *Crimeline* featured a reconstruction of Alexandra's last movements. In the week that had passed Tom had attempted to call Jane but she didn't pick up the phone or respond to his messages. In one of those unanswered messages he reminded her of the date and time of the show and thanked her again for all her support and help in getting him this far along the track. Then he apologized for not being a better man.

Jane had listened to his message a number of times and her anger turned to regret and embarrassment because, as much as she was disappointed that Tom had turned out to be a human being with actual faults, the person she had really been shouting at that night was Dominic. Of course, that was Jane's problem. She couldn't scream and shout at Dominic because she had always been so desperate to win his love that she'd never allowed him to see who she really was and how messed up, sad and lonely, and sometimes bitter and hateful she could be. Because to show him that would be to go against the image of cool, kind, anything-goes Jane, the Jane she had spent the last eighteen years creating for Dominic and Dominic alone. She had taken out her pain and aggression on Tom – poor, desperate, haunted Tom – and she felt really sick about it.

The only silver lining was that she hadn't told Elle or Leslie about her encounter with Tom's whore. Her reasoning had simply been that she didn't want them to be as disappointed in him as she was. She didn't want them to stop searching for her friend just because her husband was a selfish dick. But now it dawned on her that neither Leslie nor Elle would have been as disappointed as she was because neither of them was a silly romantic. While she had seen Tom as some sort of hero, they had merely seen him as a man.

The night of the reconstruction she sat in her sitting room with Elle and Rose, and even Kurt and Irene took a break from pretending to study so that they could follow Alexandra into the ether and with any luck beyond. She had thought about calling Tom just before the show aired but she didn't have the nerve so she left it.

Breda sat on her favourite green velvet chair surrounded by her family – Eamonn and Frankie, Kate and Owen. Even their five-year-old, Ciara, was sitting there quietly, waiting to see Auntie Alexandra or at least the actress who would be playing her.

Alexandra's father smoked a cigarette in the garden, then came inside and sat down in the midst of his family, finally about to face what had gone so wrong.

Despite Breda's invitation, Tom watched it alone.

The reconstruction started and an actress with brown hair, dressed in black trousers and a black shirt with a large bow, carrying a black tote bag, appeared in the doorway of Alexandra's home. The camera followed her walking along her street. An actress in her mid-fifties was brushing the step at number fourteen. Mrs Murphy had been asked if she'd like to play herself but she was too shy and felt an actress would be better. The fake Mrs Murphy called out to the fake Alexandra saying what a lovely day it was. The fake Alexandra agreed that it was perfect and she walked on towards the station and through the turnstiles, then stood waiting for the DART.

The same three teenagers who had seen the real Alexandra sing James Morrison agreed to be part of the reconstruction to win cool points – the eleven months had done wonders for their skin, especially the girl's. The fake Alexandra started to sing James Morrison's "Last Goodbye" badly. The teenagers acted as though they were laughing and one of the boys even slapped his thigh. The fake Alexandra stuck out her tongue and they pretended to laugh harder, ensuring the camera moved away from them quickly. When the DART arrived she stepped onto it and sat beside an actor in his mid-fifties. Across the way an actress in her forties was looking out of the window. The camera returned to the fake Alexandra and the fake older man. He asked her to wake him at Tara Street if he slept. She agreed. There was a shot of the DART moving along the track before returning to the inside. The DART pulled into Tara Street station and the fake Alexandra nudged the older man and told him it was time to get off. He got off and she jumped out of the DART, followed him and handed him a bag. He thanked her and she returned to the train.

The fake stranger sitting opposite, who had been looking out of the window when the fake Alexandra had got on the train, grinned at her and told her that her own dad was as bad. The fake Alexandra mentioned that the doddery older man had been sweet and then they looked away from one another and out of the windows. Another shot of the DART on the tracks and Dalkey station appeared. Inside again, the fake Alexandra picked up her bag, stood up and fixed her clothes before disembarking. She made her way through the station and out into the sunshine. She continued straight onto the main street and took the left at the end. After that she took a right and another left, and after that the fake Alexandra faded from the screen and was gone.

The presenter appeared in front of the screen, which was showing an empty street in Dalkey. He reminded the viewers of the date and time of the incident. He reminded them of the woman's name and reiterated what she was wearing, her height and weight. He asked people to cast their minds back to that day. "The twenty-first of June 2007, a bright, warm day, a day when Alexandra Kavanagh, *née* Walsh, daughter, sister, friend and wife, turned a corner in Dalkey and vanished from plain sight. Someone knows something. If you're that someone, please call." He gave the hotline number, the email and postal address, then moved on to a robbery in Carlow.

Jane, Elle, Kurt, Irene and even Rose sat quietly. Rose was the first to get up to leave, shaking her head and sighing. "She was a cheeky pup in her day but nobody deserves that," she said, and made her way back to her basement apartment and a much-needed drink.

Irene and Kurt made their excuses and returned to their studies. Elle and Jane sat together in the dark. "Wanna go to the pub?" Elle asked.

"I'll get my bag," Jane said.

Tom sat alone in his sitting room, ignoring the texts buzzing on his phone. He drank from his whiskey glass and prayed that the someone who knew something would phone the hotline because he wasn't sure how much longer he could hold on.

Alexandra's father cupped his face in his hands and cried like a baby. This distracted Eamonn, Kate and their spouses from Breda, and while they soothed him Breda stood up quietly and, unseen, walked up to her bedroom, took off her cardigan and folded it. She pulled her duvet down and got into her bed and, except to go to the toilet, that was where she stayed.

Chapter 10

Lost In Limbo

Here we are blind but trying to see
and here we are speechless but trying to sing,
and here we are paralysed but trying to tango,
lost in limbo.

Jack L, *Broken Songs*

June 2008

Jane was doing her accounts in the gallery. When she looked up from her computer screen she was just in time to see an extremely glamorous woman in her late forties enter the premises. It was a hot day but the woman wore gloves and took one off as she came in. "Jane Moore?" she said.

"Yes?"

"I'm Martha, Irene's mother."

"Oh," Jane said, standing. "Hello."

"Hello," she said, and smiled a wide smile, revealing perfect porcelain teeth. "I thought it was about time we met."

"Okay," Jane said.

Martha pulled a chair that was resting against the wall to Jane's table and sat down. Jane put her hand out to shake Martha's but she didn't seem to notice it so Jane sat.

"Well," Martha said, "Irene is so enchanted by you I

honestly don't know who she has a bigger crush on – you or your son."

Jane had no idea how to respond to the woman's statement or her passive-aggressive tone so she remained silent. Martha took another moment to remove her second glove. "It seems she is determined to stay with you," she said, "but how could I compete with a party house where anything goes?"

She smiled another wide smile, and Jane could feel her temper rising and her face twisting, the way her mother's did before she spewed bile.

Martha's smile remained fixed. "So I was hoping you'd give me some tips on how to get her to come home."

"I wasn't aware you'd noticed she'd gone," Jane said, in a tone that matched her mother's at her very snottiest, "but then you were preoccupied with a boy young enough to be your son. I guess mine isn't the only party house in town."

"Funny," Martha said. "I suppose you think I'm a bad mother because I needed to take some time out to recover from a broken marriage. I suppose you think that you're a better mother than me."

"I do and I am," Jane said, channelling Rose.

"Oh, really? I know that you're allowing them to sleep together under your roof, allowing them to drive around on a motorbike together, and don't think I don't know about the drinking."

"In case you failed to notice, your daughter had a birthday in February, and as they're both eighteen, everything I let them do they're entitled to do. I also feed them, clean up after them, listen to them, encourage them and watch over them, so if you ever want to come into my gallery again it will be with the intention of thanking me for caring for Irene, and if not, you'd better be prepared to run. Understand?"

"You know, I met your mother once at a bridge club – she was a nasty bitch and you're exactly like her."

"I'll take that as a compliment," Jane said. "Now get out."

Martha stood up. "My daughter belongs with me." Her bitchy I'm-better-than-you façade was slipping. "How the hell can I compete with you?"

"I don't know how to help you, Martha, and to be honest you haven't inspired me to want to," Jane said.

Martha walked out, leaving Jane to stare after her.

What an ungrateful tart.

It turned out Martha had split with her toyboy and in his absence she missed her daughter. A few days earlier she had approached Irene about coming home and Irene had told her she was happy where she was and didn't want to move, so close to her exams. Martha had tried everything in her emotional arsenal to encourage her daughter to return home but Irene was adamant that she was happy, safe and secure, and it was nice to be in a house where she was cared for. Martha had shouted that she was ungrateful and cruel to use the past few months against her, but Irene insisted that Martha had always been the kind of mother who had been absent whether she was there or not. "It's not your fault, Mum. You are what you are."

Martha was selfish and the whole world revolved around her, but despite these failings she was also kind and charming and fun to be around and Irene wasn't angry with her. She wasn't venomous; she didn't want to cause her pain. All she wanted to do was stay with her boyfriend and Jane until her exams.

"And then?" Martha had said.

"And then I don't know."

"Please come home to me then."

"No, Mum, I'm going to Greece with Kurt."

"For how long?"

"A couple of weeks," she had said.

"And then?"

"And then you'll probably be back together with whatever his name is or someone else."

"Irene," Martha had said, "that's not true."

"Of course it's true," Irene said. "You can't be alone and that's the only reason you want me home."

"Not fair."

"Totally fair. But it's okay – I understand. I'm terrified of heights, you're terrified of being alone. We all have our issues." She had kissed her mother's cheek. "I love you, Mum," she said.

Shortly after, Martha watched her peel off down the street on the back of Kurt's motorbike, and instead of thinking about what her daughter had said, instead of realizing that the girl had a point and that she needed to change if she wanted their relationship to change, she thought about Jane Moore and what a stupid bitch she was for turning her daughter against her.

Leslie had three weeks to go before her operation and the gravity of her situation was starting to take its toll on her. Sleep deprivation made her cranky and she couldn't help but focus on the mutilation her poor body would soon endure. She got out of the shower, wiped the steam from the mirror and looked at herself, resting the palm of her hand on her stomach. With her other hand she cupped her left breast. She squeezed her breasts together, tried to flatten them down, and then she held onto the washbasin and screamed and screamed and screamed.

When Elle knocked at her door she was lying in the foetal position on the floor, crying for all that she was about to lose. When Leslie eventually opened the door, wearing nothing but her robe, she pretended she was fine but Elle wasn't fooled for a second. "Get dressed," she said.

"No."

"Get dressed."

"No."

"Leslie."

"Elle."

"Get fucking dressed."

"No fucking way."

Elle grinned and Leslie couldn't help but smile a little too.

When she was dressed, Leslie wanted to know what Elle had planned, but all she would say was that they were going for a drive. Leslie really didn't feel like driving but Elle was adamant that she needed to run away from herself.

"You can't run away from yourself," Leslie said.

"Of course you can," Elle said. "You'll see."

It was such a hot day and Elle had no idea where they were heading so she pointed the car in a direction and just kept going. She put the top down and music on and ordered Leslie to lie back and allow the breeze fill her lungs and play with her hair. Spending time with Leslie had reminded Elle how short and precious life was, and she felt a great need to make the absolute most of every second before she moved on.

After they had been driving for more than an hour Leslie voiced concern as to when they'd reach their destination.

"We'll know when we know," Elle said.

Leslie sighed deeply and shook her head to signal to her friend that she wasn't happy but, contrary to her actions, she then lay back and when the wind caught her hair she smiled.

The sunshine made every town and village they passed seem prettier, the grass greener, the flowers more colourful, the people friendlier, and the world a little kinder and better. Elle and Leslie were warm, content and looking forward to reaching their destination wherever it might be. When two hours had passed and they were still driving, Leslie wondered whether they would make it back home and Elle assured her that they wouldn't. Leslie argued that she hadn't got a change of clothes or a toothbrush and, most importantly, that she hadn't left food out for her cat.

"We can buy what we need and ring Deborah – she'll care for the cat," said Elle.

"You are joking?"

"No. I know she makes you a little crazy but face facts. Deborah was right about you. You were a weirdo cat-loving loner who could potentially drop dead and rot."

"Excuse me?"

"You're excused," Elle said, "because that's not who you are any more, so forgive and forget and ask her to feed your cat."

"What about a key, smartarse?"

"You have one hidden somewhere in the building."

"How did you know that?"

"Because you're paranoid like Jane, which means you're

one of those 'in case of' people and you're such an unfriendly cow there's no way you gave it to a neighbour."

"It's under the carpet to the left of my door."

Elle raised her hand. "There you go, then."

Leslie rang Directory Enquiries and asked for Deborah James's phone number. They connected her and Deborah answered immediately, "Ashley?"

"No, it's Leslie."

"Leslie who?"

"Leslie, the weirdo cat-loving loner with the potential to drop dead and rot."

"Oh," Deborah said, "you."

"Look, I know this is out of the blue but I need a favour."

"Go on."

"I'm not going to make it home and I haven't left out any food for my cat. I'd so appreciate it if you'd feed her for me."

"Really?"

"Yes," Leslie said, "really."

"Key?" Deborah said.

"Under the carpet to the left-hand side of my door."

"Hmmm."

"Well?"

"Okay," Deborah said. "I'll feed your cat."

"Thank you."

"Um-hum."

"And, Deborah?"

"Yeah?"

"If you poke around I'll know."

"Don't push it, cat lady."

"Okay," Leslie said, and hung up. "Sorted," she said to

Elle, lay back in her seat, breathed in deeply and stretched her arms in the air.

Elle saw the castle in the distance and told Leslie it was calling to her. It turned out to be a hotel. She drove up the winding road that led to the large wooden door. Leslie jumped out and looked around at the manicured gardens, shielding her eyes from the sun while she examined the turrets. "Perfect," she said, and followed Elle into the lobby.

Elle booked them in and they headed up to their room, which was a deep yellow and dotted with small paintings that were rubbish, according to Elle. The twin beds were covered with blankets, the top ones flowery, and in contrast the headboards were covered with gingham. Two pink chairs stood at the end of the beds and both women agreed the décor was vomit inducing yet suited the place. A white wooden-framed window revealed the most beautiful view of gardens that seemed to roll into the sea. Although it was summer the hotel seemed to be all but empty. Leslie and Elle lunched alone in the grand dining room, and when Leslie's mind drifted away, Elle brought her back with talk of a swim. Leslie wasn't too sure as she'd had two glasses of wine, but Elle assured her that the wine would only heighten the experience.

"We've no swimsuits."

"We don't need swimsuits."

"I'm not getting into the sea in my knickers."

"Me neither," Elle said, and grinned.

And before Leslie knew it, she was following Elle through the lawns and trees towards the sea. Elle stripped off as soon as she hit the water's edge, threw her clothes behind her and ran in full steam ahead. Leslie called after her but she was gone and swimming, powering through the waves like a shark chasing its prey. The sun glistened on the water making it sparkle and she was so tempted to feel its softness on her skin. She looked around and there was no one to be seen. *To hell with it.* She stripped off and ran as fast as she'd ever run into the freezing sea and disappeared under the surface only to come up spluttering with her hair all over her face and in her eyes and mouth. "Holy shit! The cold!" she roared.

Elle laughed and told her to swim and she did and, although she wasn't the powerhouse that her friend was, she swam and swam until the cold turned to warmth and she could stop and enjoy the water swirling around her body.

Elle swam up to her. "Nothing quite like the freedom," she said, "is there?"

"No. There isn't."

They were bobbing along and planning the evening ahead when Leslie spotted a boat in the distance. Mortified, she alerted Elle and was about to make a dash for the shore when Elle grabbed her arm and told her to relax. The boat was coming closer and Leslie could see that there were two men on board. "Relax? I'm naked!"

"So?" Elle said, and winked. "Time to get your tits out for the boys."

"Excuse me?"

Elle laughed, then kicked and pushed herself out of the water revealing her breasts. The men whistled and she waved, looking at Leslie who was cringing. "It's now or never," she said.

Leslie thought about it for a split second and before she

knew it she was displaying her naked breasts to an appreciative audience of two. They wolf-whistled and clapped and she was laughing and lapping it up, and when she turned to Elle and caught her eye, they both registered that they were sharing a perfect high. They turned away from the men, swam to the shore, ran out and shook off. They covered themselves, the boys waved, and they responded.

When they had dressed, Leslie lay on the sand in a wet T-shirt and leggings. "Thanks," she said to her friend.

"My pleasure," Elle said, and they both grew silent and stared into the blue sky.

When it got dark they ventured to the local pub. It was a spit-on-the-floor tiny little place, with wooden pews for seats and rickety tables levelled by beer mats. They enjoyed a drink or two before the two men in the boat appeared. Of course, Elle was delighted to see them and immediately invited them to join them. Leslie was mortified, the high-on-adventure feeling she'd experienced earlier turning to embarrassment and awkwardness, but Elle was having none of it.

The men were in their early thirties. They were fishing for a few days and roaming from port to port. They introduced themselves as Adrian and Keith. Adrian was tall and broad; he had mousy brown tousled hair, and stubble on his face. He reminded Leslie of Grizzly Adams. Keith was slightly taller and leaner than his friend. He had long hair tied up at the nape of his neck and big brown eyes just like Vincent's, except they were not framed by Vincent's thick lashes. The two men sat with their drinks in hand and Elle chatted to them as though she'd known them all her life.

"What about you?" Adrian asked Leslie.

"She's too embarrassed to talk," Elle explained, when Leslie left him hanging.

"Why?"

"She's not used to exposing herself to strangers," Elle said.

"And you are?" Keith asked, and Elle laughed but failed to respond to his question.

"Well, trust me, Leslie," Adrian said, "you have nothing to be embarrassed about."

Leslie drained her glass. "Thanks," she said.

By the time the four of them were kicked out of the pub they were friends, laughing and joking and pushing each other down the street under a bright white moon. Adrian put his arm around Leslie's shoulders and she looked at it resting there, then relaxed against him.

"Adrian?"

"Yes?" he said.

"Would you like to have sex with me?"

"Yes, yes and yes again," he said.

"Oh, good," she said. "That's a big relief."

They walked together to the boat.

Keith and Elle left them to it. "How do you feel about a bed in a castle?" Elle asked.

"Sounds like bliss," he said.

"You haven't seen the décor."

They walked on, arm in arm.

"I'm not having sex with you," she said.

"Okay," he said.

"I find you attractive and funny, and ordinarily I would, but I'm very tired and today has been perfect and I'd like to sleep now," she said.

"Okay," he said again, and they walked into her room together and she kissed him goodnight and they jumped into the single beds and were asleep within minutes.

Leslie was standing in the middle of a bobbing boat wondering what she was doing. She heard the toilet light go off. The door opened and Adrian appeared. He walked up to her and she waited for him to kiss her. He fixed her hair and touched her face with his hand, cupped her chin and his lips hovered close to hers. She wished to Christ he'd get on with kissing her because her legs were going to go from under her if he wasn't careful. And when he did kiss her, a deep, wet, soft kiss, she closed her eyes and thought, *This beats the shit out of batteries.*

They made love once, then twice, and after that she told him about her surgery and he kissed her breasts and placed his hand on her stomach as she had done that morning, a lifetime ago, and he told her she was beautiful and that she would always be beautiful and she cried and he held her, and when she was done crying he kissed her and they made love again.

On the morning that Kurt and Irene's Leaving Cert exams started, Jane was as nervous as if it were her own future on the line. Kurt found schoolwork easy – he was like his mother that way. Irene had to work a bit harder but she was happy to do enough to qualify for nursing. He was determined to get medicine. Jane laid out a huge breakfast to feed the pair of them and when Irene was first into the kitchen Jane pulled a chair out for her. "Sit," she ordered.

"I'm not that hungry, Jane."

"You need food," Jane said, and piled pancakes onto a plate.

As Kurt was still in the shower and they had time alone together, Jane asked Irene why she wanted to be a nurse.

"Because Kurt wants medicine," she said, "and even if I studied day and night for forty years I wouldn't get medicine."

"Kurt is your reason?"

"Kurt and I want to go to Trinity."

"But what if you hate it?"

"As long as we're together I'll love it."

"I hope you're right. Otherwise you're going to be cleaning vomit for the rest of your life because of a boy you knew when you were eighteen."

Irene laughed. "You're so funny, Jane!"

Kurt appeared and they kissed, and Jane began to wonder where time was going.

Her son and his girlfriend enjoyed their hearty breakfast while Jane cleaned around them. "Do you have enough pens?"

"Mum, you bought us about five thousand – relax."

"Okay, double-check your bags for calculators."

"Have them," Irene said.

Jane put down the cloth, reached into her bag. She took out a twenty-euro note and put it on the table between them. "Buy some lunch – oh, crap," she said. "Batteries. I forgot batteries."

"What do you need batteries for?" Kurt asked.

"The calculators."

"They're solar," Irene said, and giggled.

"Oh, right, of course they are."

"Jane?" Irene said.

"What?"

"If you didn't have Kurt, would you have gone to college?"

Kurt looked up from his food. It was a question he'd never thought to ask his mother.

"I was thinking about medicine," she said.

"You never told me!" Kurt exclaimed.

"Well, it was just an idea. After all, I didn't sit the exams. I had you two weeks before them."

"I think you would have been a cool doctor," Irene said.

Jane smiled and blushed. "Thanks, Irene."

"Yeah, Mum," Kurt said, "you would have been cool."

"Thanks, son."

"It's a pity you were such a big slut," he said, and winked at her the way his dad did when he said something outrageous and thought it was funny.

Irene and Kurt burst out laughing and high-fived, and Jane couldn't help but laugh along with them. *Cheeky little bastard.*

Midway through the exams, when Irene and Kurt had a day off, Martha invited her daughter and her boyfriend to lunch. Kurt regarded Irene's mother with suspicion but Irene begged him to join them so he did, and he was really glad he had. Martha had reviewed the situation she found herself in with her daughter and decided the only way back into her daughter's good graces was with a present, so at the end of an expensive meal she handed her daughter an envelope.

Irene opened it and it contained two InterRail tickets. "What's this?" Irene asked.

"It's a month's travelling through Europe," Martha said.

"But we're going to Greece," Kurt said.

"For two weeks," she said, "and then you're going to Europe for a month." She smiled her big porcelain-toothed smile. *Anything the Moores can do I can do better.*

"No way!" Kurt said.

"Oh, my God!" Irene shouted.

They hugged each other and then Irene hugged her mother and Kurt shook her hand awkwardly, but when he moved in for a hug they bumped and Martha pushed him off. "You're welcome," said Martha.

Twenty minutes after that Kurt witnessed his girlfriend's mother manipulate her into coming back home on her return from Europe, and as much as he wanted to say something he kept quiet because Irene looked so happy.

At first Jane was unhappy with the notion of her child backpacking around Europe so she called Dominic and they arranged to meet for lunch to discuss it. The rain was coming down in buckets and had been for three days straight. Jane battled her way into the restaurant and shook the rain off. Dominic was waiting. They kissed and it was slightly awkward but both pretended not to notice. She got to business straight away.

"That bitch thinks she's so clever."

"Or maybe she just wanted to do something nice for her daughter."

"She's getting back at me."

"Really? Don't you think you're being a bit paranoid?"

"No, I don't." She sighed. "She's saying in no uncertain terms that if she can't have her daughter I can't have my son."

"You're being hysterical," he said, and then she pulled

the twisted face that made her look like her mother so he backed down. "Or not – you're right and she's a bitch from hell, but at least Kurt gets to do something great."

"It's too much," she argued. "He's never been away from home for longer than a week and that was with supervision – and now nearly an entire summer!"

"He's eighteen," Dominic reminded her.

"I know but –"

"But nothing – my brothers did it, I did it, Brick and Mint did it, and we all came home safe and sound."

"Times have changed," she reminded him.

"Times are always changing. He's not going to war – all he's doing is strapping a bag on his back and going out into the world to have a blast."

"Did you have a blast?"

"Time of my life," he said.

"Alexandra spent two weeks in the Canaries with Siobhan Wilson and Christina Benson. She came home burned alive and with beads in her hair. She said it was the best time of her life."

"Who are they?"

"They were in our class."

"I don't remember them. What was she doing with them?"

"Oh, I don't know, Dominic. Maybe it was because her best friend was sleep-deprived, knee-deep in nappies and on the verge of a nervous breakdown."

"Oh, yeah," he said, "sorry."

"So you think I should just let him go?" she asked then.

"I think that if you're really honest with yourself you'll see you have no choice."

"God, I hate that woman!"

"I don't know – maybe you should thank her."

"For what?"

"Kurt's seeing you in a different light. He appreciates you in a way he didn't in the past."

"What do you mean?"

"I mean he's seeing you through his girlfriend's eyes and, as a mother, you beat that Martha bitch hands down."

"Yes, I do," she said, and smiled. "I can live with that."

It was true. Since his girlfriend had moved into his home Kurt had come to appreciate his mother more.

"You're lucky," Irene told him one day in his room. "You just don't know how lucky you are."

"Easy for you to say."

"No. Not easy. I live with a woman who doesn't seem to notice if I'm there or not, and as for my dad, the last time I saw him was more than three months ago. Your mum lives for you."

"Yeah, well, maybe that's the problem."

"That's not the problem, Kurt. The problem is she gave up her future for you and now you're scared she'll want to keep you."

"Bollocks," he said.

"Okay," she said.

"You're so full of shit, Irene," he said, and she laughed.

"Fine," she said. "Maybe I'm wrong but it's a thought."

Irene was wrong but it made Kurt think. A whole new world was opening up in front of him – opportunity, his first foray into adulthood, leaving home, university, making his own decisions, living his own life. He was so excited about his future and counting down the days until he and Irene were on a flight and leaving their childhood behind for good. And eighteen years ago his mum had been standing in the same kitchen but instead of holding a bag full of pens and a solar calculator she had been holding a baby, and instead of planning trips abroad, preparing for college and a life without Rose, she was stuck in the rut she still found herself in eighteen years later.

Two days after their exams finished and with packs on their backs, Irene and Kurt made their way down the front steps towards Jane, who was holding the car door open. Elle sat on the wall wearing sunglasses, even though it was dull and raining. Rose emerged from her basement and stood by her door. Kurt put his bag in the car boot and went back to kiss his grandmother. She hugged him tight. "Stay safe," she said. "Life is hard enough without you disappearing on me."

"It's only six weeks, Gran," he said.

"Six weeks is a lifetime, my darling. Live well."

"I will."

She let him go and watched him hug Elle, who took the opportunity to slip him an extra few euro.

"You don't have to do that," he said.

"I do," she said.

Irene got into the car, then waved at Rose and Elle, and Kurt joined her. Jane got into the driver's seat and started the car. Elle waved one final time and they were gone. Rose went inside and Elle sat on the wall, smoking a cigarette and wearing her sunglasses despite the rain.

Jane had felt bad for a number of weeks about the way things had ended with Tom and when she eventually found the confidence to call him she left a message apologizing for blowing up. She asked him to call her and told him once again she was sorry.

Tom had listened to the message but he was too embarrassed, too ashamed to call her back. In the few weeks that had passed he had found himself missing her. He missed her smile and the way she twisted her face when she wasn't happy. He missed her laugh and her calm, caring nature. He missed the devil side of her because just when you thought she was a total pushover she pushed back – and, by God, she pushed hard. He liked that. He liked that she was formidable, just like Alexandra, and it made sense that the two had once been best friends because in a way they were similar.

Jane missed Tom so much it interrupted her thoughts. She'd be on the phone to a buyer and she'd think of him and lose concentration. She'd be parking the car and stop dead just to remember a moment they'd shared. Only when someone beeped would she resume normal operations. She'd find herself thinking about him and worrying about him, and at night she lay awake wondering what he was doing, where he had been, where he was going and whether or not she'd ever see him again.

Jane woke up early on 21 June and was up and out before eight. She knocked on Tom's door a little after eight forty-five, and when he didn't answer she pressed the doorbell and held it until she heard him stamp down the stairs.

He opened it roughly, with a big sleepy head, wearing boxer shorts and a "Go West" T-shirt. "What?" he yelled. Then he wiped his eyes, focused and saw who it was. "Jane."

"Tom," she said, and pushed past him into the house.

He followed her into the kitchen where she set about finding the coffee.

"Second shelf on the left," he said.

She located it and set about making some.

"What are you doing here?" he asked.

"We're going to spend the day together," she told him.

"No," he said.

"Yes," she said.

"Jane, I don't want this."

"Want what? You don't want to spend the anniversary of your wife's disappearance with the woman who recently called you a fucking bastard? Fair enough, but tell me what you do want to do?"

"I don't remember you exactly calling me a fucking bastard."

"Must have been in my head," she said.

He sat down at his counter. "I was thinking I'd stay in bed."

"No," she said, "out of the question."

"What do you want me to do?"

"I want you to come to Dalkey with me."

"You are joking."

"I think we should walk the streets she walked and I think we should talk and reminisce and then maybe we could get some lunch, and after that we'll hand out some of those flyers you keep in that black bag of yours by the door, and maybe we'll make our way into town and we'll stay there until it gets dark and this day is over."

Tom thought about it for a moment or two, then nodded. He went up to his bedroom and came down dressed and ready.

They walked together through the village of Dalkey and

as they walked they handed flyers to anyone who would take them.

After a while Jane decided to broach the subject they had both been avoiding. "I'm sorry. I shouldn't have said those things."

"You were right," he said, "perfectly right."

"I was taking out my own frustrations on you," she said, "and while I'm never going to be able to comprehend how a man who loves his wife as much as you love Alexandra could possibly be with that girl Jeanette, I'm still on your side."

"Alexandra's gone," he said, "and I miss her so much I ache, and I'm so terrified that I swear it's brought me to the brink of insanity and I'm just holding on, and for a while that girl helped me do that. I'm not making excuses. I'm just telling you the way it is."

"Okay," she said, "and again I'm sorry." She handed a flyer to a woman pushing a pram. The woman looked at it for a second and crumpled it right in front of them. "What a cow," Jane said, and Tom pushed her ahead.

"I ended it with Jeanette," he said. "Actually, if I'm honest, I treated her pretty poorly."

"What did you do?"

"I pushed her out the door and slammed it in her face two minutes after you left."

"Oh, that is a poor show."

"I blame you," he said, and grinned.

"That's funny," she said.

There had been no developments since the reconstruction aired. The police had received a number of calls after the show but none of them panned out. Tom was at a loss as to what to do next, and part of him wished he could just let go. "How about we get a drink?" he suggested.

"Love to," she said.

Tom put the flyers back into the black bag and together they walked to the pub.

On the last day of June, Leslie sat up in her hospital bed. The nurse had just taken blood and the trainee doctor had taken her history for the tenth time. She was asked if she wanted something to help her sleep but she declined as she wanted to spend as much time with her breasts and womb as possible. She was wearing a nightshirt that Jane had bought for her and under her bed were slippers from Elle. She moisturized her face and put balm on her lips. When the woman across the way tried to make eye contact she pretended to read a magazine, and when the woman disappeared into the toilet, she jumped out and pulled the curtain around her bed.

The woman in the bed opposite had been watching the clock, waiting for visiting hour, but Leslie didn't expect any visitors because she had been adamant that she wanted to be alone.

Jim was the first to appear from behind the curtain with a bag of fruit and a bottle of 7up raised high.

"I told you not to come."

"I wouldn't have expected you to say anything else," he said, and sat on the chair by her bed.

"I can't believe you're ignoring my express wishes."

Jane called out Leslie's name and Jim opened the curtain. "She's here," he said, and turned back to Leslie. "Looks like I'm not the only one."

Jane appeared with a Brown Thomas bag filled with

moisturizer, perfume and a set of candles. "They're from Elle too," she said, "and I know it's weird to give you candles but they smell so good."

Leslie sighed. "Thank you."

Elle appeared, giving out about the toilets. "My God, where are we? Basra? There was blood on the floor. Make sure you wear your slippers everywhere."

Leslie nodded that she would and Jim got up and pulled two more chairs over for the girls. Just as they sat, Tom appeared with a brown bag full of sweets and mints.

"Oh, for God's sake," Leslie said. She smiled and shook her head. "What are you doing here?"

"Why wouldn't I come?" he said. "After everything you've done for me."

Elle got up to let him sit down and she perched at the end of the bed. Jane introduced Tom to Jim and they chatted happily about the building trade dying on its feet. Jim had read an article on the subject and he was interested to hear Tom's point of view. Tom explained he had closed up shop at the end of 2007 and he was happy to see the back of his business.

"So what are you doing now?" Jim asked.

"Well, aside from looking for my wife, nothing."

"What would you like to do?"

Tom thought about it. "I have no idea," he said.

"Well," Jim said, "the world is your oyster."

"I suppose it is."

Jane and Elle fussed over Leslie and she pretended she didn't like it but she couldn't conceal her joy.

"When this is done," Elle said, "and when you're feeling better we'll do something fun."

"Can't wait."

"And you know that if things are a little bleak in the nursing-home, there's plenty of room at my place," Jane said. "The house is so empty without Kurt and Irene."

Leslie couldn't believe Jane's kindness, which took her by surprise. Looking around at the people she now had in her life, she was moved to tears.

Elle squeezed her hand. "You're not alone any more, pal."

"I know," she said. She wiped away her tears and opened the bag of sweets. "Who wants some?"

They all dug in and even though Leslie was too nervous to eat she felt full.

Chapter 11

Simple And True

Like a rainbow after a shower
I don't regret a day, not one single hour.
Ah bring on the bigger things I can't help but follow,
without you by my side my heart would be hollow.

Jack L, *Universe*

July 2008

Breda had refused to get out of bed since the television reconstruction of Alexandra's disappearance. Her daughter Kate gave her bed-baths and her husband sat with her and encouraged her to eat the food that Kate and Eamonn's wife Frankie took turns to cook and deliver. She'd take a few bites but only when her husband pleaded with her and only to satisfy him. It was not Breda's intention to starve herself or to cause pain to the people she loved, and if she could have summoned the mental and physical strength to get up she would have.

"Look, love, it's shepherd's pie," Ben Walsh said to his wife, raising the fork towards her mouth. "Frankie made it according to your own recipe."

Breda closed her eyes and opened her mouth, the food fell in and Ben cleaned off the tiny amount that fell out with a tea-towel. She didn't chew. Instead it just sat in her mouth until it had melted enough for her to swallow.

"Eamonn's downstairs. Would you like to see him?"

She blinked a few times and he wondered if her eyes were dry or whether she was now resorting to communication through the medium of rapid eye movement.

"Kate will be over tonight with fresh clothes and she'll help you wash," Ben said, "and I'll be downstairs so maybe afterwards you could come and join us for a while. I can put a duvet on the sofa. What do you think, love?"

Breda closed her eyes, then opened them and nodded slightly.

Ben smiled at her. "Great," he said, "great stuff. I'll tell the kids."

He took the tray off the bed and walked outside, closing the door behind him.

Breda lay there motionless, waiting for sleep to come.

Ben joined Eamonn downstairs. Eamonn hung up from a call and turned to his dad. Taking the tray from him, he noticed that the shepherd's pie was not even half eaten. "We need to get a doctor out here," he said.

"I know," Ben said, "we will."

"When?"

"When your mammy says it's okay."

"Dad, my mother is in no fit state to decide that."

"She's just sad, son."

"No, Dad. She *was* just sad, but now it's more sinister."

Ben walked outside and lit a cigarette. Eamonn followed him, grabbed a plastic chair and sat beside him. "You can't hide from this, Dad," he said. "You could hide from Alexandra but not this."

Ben stayed silent because his son was right. He had

hidden from the reality of the loss of his daughter for months. He had pushed her away into a tiny corner of his mind because to think about her and to allow himself to feel the emotions he had felt those first few weeks would be unbearable. His pain had become anger, and in the absence of an aggressor he had turned on Tom. He had loathed him since that day more than a year before when Alexandra had walked out of her door and vanished from plain sight. He had decided that even if Tom was working when they'd lost her, and even if he had loved Alexandra, his love hadn't been enough to keep her safe. He didn't care that it was cruel to blame the man who'd driven himself half mad to find her, because the only time he had felt better in the past year was when he was making Tom feel worse.

Eamonn coped by pretending that Alexandra hadn't been as happy as she had pretended to be and that mentally she wasn't capable of accepting her life as it was. She had forfeited a career she'd worked hard to succeed in for a baby that never came. She had tried hormone tablets and four rounds of IVF, acupuncture, herbs and tonics. She had given up smoking, joined a gym, changed her eating habits, and although she maintained a happy and casual façade, he had known she was lying: he had known that she was desperate to be a mother and that every single month and every negative test was eating away at his sister until there was little of the real her left. At least, that was what he told himself because it was easier to believe she had chosen to walk away from her life or even that she'd thrown herself over Dalkey pier than face the horrifying alternatives. And so, while he didn't hold the same anger as his father, a large part of him held Tom accountable for the loss of his sister.

The difference between Eamonn and his father, while they were sitting on plastic chairs in the back garden, was that since the reconstruction and his wife's subsequent withdrawal Ben had understood that Tom was as helpless in the disappearance of Alexandra as he now found himself in the face of his wife's mysterious illness. All the anger that he'd built up to protect himself from true suffering was slowly dissipating, the pain was slowly returning and he found himself experiencing the darkness that Tom had been experiencing all along.

"Call the doctor," he said to his son, after the longest time, "and call Tom."

"What are we calling him for?" Eamonn said.

"Because your mammy's fond of him and he'll come," Ben said.

Eamonn nodded, got up and walked inside with his phone to his ear, leaving his father alone to smoke and breathe through the pain that finally he allowed himself to feel.

Tom arrived just as Kate was leaving. She hugged him and thanked him for coming and he told her he was delighted to be asked. He had attempted to make contact with Breda a few times over the previous five weeks but had been told it would be better to stay away. Ben came out from the sitting room and, much to Tom's surprise, offered him his hand. He shook it.

"I owe you an apology," Ben said. "Alexandra, well, it wasn't your fault any more than it was mine or her mammy's. It was just something terrible that happened."

Tom didn't know what to say. His hands shook and his lip trembled. "Thank you."

Ben slapped his back. "Breda's upstairs. The doctor's been and he gave her something to sleep but she's been awake a while and I know she'd love to see you."

Tom walked up the stairs and into Breda's room. It was lit by one lamp at the side of her bed. The room smelt of fresh blankets and Breda smelt of Kate's perfume. She was thinner than ever and her veins stood out more. He sat in the chair by her bed and took her hand in his. She looked at him but he wondered if she saw him at all. "I've missed you," he said, "and I'm not the only one."

She tried to smile as it was the least she could do for poor Tom who was kind enough to visit her.

"I'm scared," he said, after a minute or two. "I'm scared that you've let your mind go to the dark place and that you've got stuck there. Have you got stuck there, Breda?"

Tears welled in her eyes and she nodded.

"You need to come back," he said. "You need to be strong because we can't lose you too."

"I'm sorry," she mumbled, and even her mumble sounded raspy.

"Don't be sorry. Just come back."

"I can't," she said.

"Why not?"

"'The sacrifices of God are a broken spirit; a broken and a contrite heart, O God, you will not despise.'"

"I don't understand. What does that mean?"

"It means if a broken spirit pleases God that is what I'll give him."

"Breda, you lying here is not going to bring Alexandra back."

"But maybe it will," she said, and licked her dry lips.

"This is madness."

"No," she said. "This is all I can do. I have no choice. My body feels broken but as sad as I am my mind is strong."

"You have to talk to your family."

She blinked and inhaled and licked her lips again. "They don't understand."

"*I* don't understand."

She attempted to grip his hand with hers. "I can't be expected to go on."

"You'll get help now," he said.

She nodded, but she knew it was too late, that nothing and no one could help her now.

"Whatever the doctor says, you'll do," he said.

She blinked.

"You'll be okay," he said, "and we will find her."

She blinked again because Breda had said all that she was going to say.

Leslie woke up in her ward. It took a while for her to come around, and when she did the effects of morphine made the back of her head feel as if it was being swallowed by her bed. She thought about attempting to sit up but couldn't even garner the strength to move her head so that she could look down at herself. Through the narcotic-induced mist she could feel pain but not enough to call someone or seek attention. Her head and heart were both heavy, her insides desecrated, her breasts gone. She didn't realize it but her finger was pressing on a button administering morphine. Her bed was quickly beginning to feel like a tomb and she heard herself screaming, "Ah, for fuck's sake, this is how I'm going to die?"

A nurse appeared quickly, removed Leslie's finger from the button and attempted to settle her. "Just relax, everything went well, you're in good hands," she said.

"The fucking bed is swallowing me!" she screamed.

"The bed is not swallowing you."

"Save me, you fuck-faced motherfucking fucker!" Leslie said, and the woman in the bed opposite laughed.

"Okay, everything's fine, I've got you," the nurse said calmly.

"I'm dying. I've been dying all my fucking life!"

"You're not dying."

"Has anyone ever told you that you look like a frog?"

The woman in the bed opposite put her hand over her mouth to stop herself laughing again.

"It's the meds talking," the nurse said to the woman, who was clearly enjoying the meds talking and was looking forward to hearing more from them.

"Nurse?"

"Yes, Leslie."

"I've gone blind."

"No, love, you've just closed your eyes."

Leslie fell into a deep sleep after that and didn't wake up for another twelve hours. When she did wake she had absolutely no memory of the incident ever taking place.

Jim was the first person she remembered visiting. He was reading a newspaper when she woke. "What's going on?" she asked.

"President Sarkozy has decided to postpone a trip to Ireland to discuss the EU Lisbon treaty."

"Oh," she said, "I forgot to vote."

"Well, you had other things on your mind."

"Yeah," she said, and suddenly she felt like crying – her face was a little numb so she didn't realize that she actually was.

"You're going to be all over the place," he said. "It's perfectly normal."

"Nothing about this is normal," she said.

"In a few weeks you're going to feel so much better."

"But I'm going to look so much worse."

"No," he said, "you're going to look like a new woman, a woman with a massive weight taken off her shoulders."

"I'll have no breasts," she said. "I haven't even looked yet, I'm too scared."

"Take your time, allow yourself to heal, be kind to yourself and then when the time comes if you're not happy you can get implants."

"Like Pamela Anderson."

"No. Most definitely not like Pamela Anderson."

Leslie would have laughed but she was too sore. The drains coming out of her stomach and chest had blood and pus spewing into bottles and it was as uncomfortable as it was unsightly. When the nurse fixed her bed, the sheet covering a bottle fell away revealing its horrible contents to Jim but, if he saw it, it certainly didn't faze him. Of course, he had witnessed that and more, even if it was more than ten years before.

After he left Leslie was sick into a bowl for an hour, every part of her ached, and with every retch her newly stitched skin pulled and burned. When the woman with the trolley asked her if she wanted some toast Leslie pointed to the bowl before leaning in for another spew.

"Say no more, my dear," the woman said. "I'll catch you on the way back."

Elle waited until the third day before visiting her friend. She did this because when she checked Google it told her that day two following an operation was the worst day and she didn't want to make Leslie's life harder than it already was. She arrived with grapes, magazines and a book about self-discovery. She was on her own because Jane had to meet their accountant. She was nervous, unsure what she should say, and for once she was quiet.

"Are you all right?" Leslie asked.

"Shouldn't I be asking you that?"

"Yes." Leslie smiled.

"I didn't sleep," Elle admitted. "I couldn't make my mind stop."

"I've been there."

"Sometimes it feels like my mind is on a treadmill and I'm trying to reach the stop button but I can't, and with every second that passes, I feel like I'm about to fall off."

"What kind of things do you think about?" Leslie asked, glad that they weren't talking about the operation.

"Oh, I don't know – work, Jane, Kurt, me, a woman in the Sudan lying on a dusty floor dying of AIDS as we speak. I think about her and how bloody unfair it is. A horse found slashed to pieces, starved and burned, and I think about that poor gentle animal's suffering. A young boy aged sixteen stabbed in London on his way home from a football match. I think about him and the family he's left behind. A woman who is promised a new life only to be consigned to sexual slavery. I think about her and the hell she endures day in day out. I think about Alexandra and where she could be and what has been done to her, and I think about you and how sad your life has been, all that you've lost and all that you've missed out on. I think about how brave you are and dignified and kind. I think that if I could be like anyone in the world it would be you and I think flat-chested women are huge on the catwalk right now, that kind of thing," Elle said, and smiled at her friend.

"Jesus, that's a lot of thinking."

"Yeah," Elle said, "too much."

"Elle, I like your way of thinking. Now pass me a grape and tell me a story."

Elle did as she was told and stayed until the nurse kicked her out an hour later.

Dominic walked into his hotel and was passing the bar when Elle called his name. He turned to her and said hello before looking to see if she was on her own. He approached her and she asked him to join her as she was having something quick to eat following her visit to Leslie. He agreed, sat and ordered a coffee.

"What are you doing here?" she asked.

"Same as you."

"Really? Why do you have a hotel key card in your front pocket then?"

"Okay," he said, "you've caught me but don't tell Jane."

"Tell Jane what?"

Dominic explained that his wife had thrown him out of their house for a second time in two months more than a week ago. He was resigned to the fact that his marriage was over but not to the fact that he was in a hotel while she was in his house.

"So take it back."

"My solicitor says —"

"Screw your solicitor. It's your house so take it back."

"How?"

"What do you mean, 'how'? Go home, pack up her stuff, throw her out and change the locks."

"What if she's already changed the locks?"

"Go home, break in, pack up her stuff, throw her out and change the locks."

"You're serious."

"Absolutely."

"But what if she calls the police?"

"The deeds are in your name – besides, they'll consider it a domestic dispute and as long as nobody throws a punch you're home free."

"I can't be involved in a domestic dispute. I'm a bank manager."

Elle laughed at the absurdity of his rationale. "I hate to break it to you, Dominic, but the *Herald* isn't parked outside your door waiting for something to report."

Dominic thought about it for a minute or two. He was really warming to the idea. "Will you come with me?" he said.

Elle rubbed her hands together. "I thought you'd never ask."

They drove down the street and Elle reported that Bella's car was not in the driveway. They parked two doors down, at Dominic's insistence, then Elle made her way to the door and he hid behind a tree in front of the house. Elle knocked and waited. After a minute or two she signalled to Dominic that all was clear. He emerged from behind the tree and fumbled for his house key. He breathed deeply and put it into the door, turned it and the door remained shut.

"Damn it," he said.

"Relax," Elle counselled. "Follow me."

They walked around to the back and Elle picked up a rock, took off her jacket and wrapped the rock in it.

"The french doors are double-glazed," Dominic said, still looking around.

"Yeah, but the window in the downstairs loo isn't."

"It's too small."

"Too small for you, fat boy."

"I'm not fat."

"Do you have an alarm?" Elle said.

"Yes."

"Would she have changed the code?"

"I don't even know if she'd know how."

"If she has what would she change it to?"

"I don't know – actually, I do know. She has a terrible memory so all her cards are the same number: double six double six."

"Fine," she said, and hit the glass with the rock encased in her jacket. It cracked. She hit it again. It smashed.

The alarm went off. She cleared all the jagged glass away by chipping at it with the rock. She only stopped when Dominic almost shrieked hello to his neighbour, Rachel Jameson. "Forgotten your key, Dominic?" she said.

"Oh, yes, can you believe it?" he said, and Elle thought he might have a heart attack there and then.

"Always the way," she said.

Elle mouthed "always the way" and Dominic gave her a kick. When Rachel Jameson went indoors Elle took a leg up from Dominic and climbed in through the window. She ran to the alarm, keyed in 6666 and it stopped. "What a moron," she said, as she opened the front door.

Dominic sprinted in and shut the door with a swing. "Take that, bitch!" he said, and giggled like a girl.

"We're not there yet," Elle warned. "Call a local twenty-four-hour window-repair company and tell them you'll give them a tip of a hundred euro if they get here and fix the glass within thirty minutes. And do the same with a lock-smith."

Dominic did as he was told. Elle went upstairs, armed with a suitcase she'd found under the stairs, and started to clear Bella's things. Once the calls were made, Dominic went around the house bagging everything and anything that was Bella's. He kept checking his watch and was alarmed to discover he was sweating profusely. Elle was behaving as though she was accustomed to breaking and entering.

"Don't be so dramatic, Dominic, this is your house," she said, when he commented on her calm demeanour.

The window guy made it in fifteen minutes and had the job done in another ten. Dominic paid him in full and shut the door with another swing. The locksmith followed ten minutes later and he was gone within another thirty minutes. Dominic hopped, skipped and jumped up the stairs to where Elle was bagging the last of Bella's clothes. "I think I love you," he said.

"Yeah, well, hold your horses," Elle said. "Next we need to send her packing."

Dominic carried Bella's cases down the stairs and parked

them beside the front door. Elle checked the clock. It was just after nine.

"What now?" he said.

"Now we wait," she replied.

They didn't have to wait long because ten minutes later Bella's car came into the driveway and she got out. Elle's heart was racing and, despite outward appearances, it had been since she broke the window. Dominic gulped and braced himself. The key went into the lock and came out. It went in again and came out. Bella stepped back from the door and looked at the house as though it would provide some sort of answer. She went back to the door and tried her key again. She walked around to the back of the house and checked the french doors. She cupped her eyes and looked into the empty kitchen. Dominic and Elle waited with bated breath in the sitting room. Bella came around the front of the house once more, stepped over plants and looked through the sitting-room window. When she saw Dominic and Elle she banged on the glass and shouted.

Elle went over to the window and opened it slightly. "What can I do for you?" she said.

"You can let me into my house!" Bella roared.

"But this isn't your house. This is Dominic's house. I know this because I knew him when he bought it and my nephew has spent every weekend in it since he was four years old. You, on the other hand, have been here for five minutes. I trust in that time he didn't sign over the deeds? No, I didn't think so."

"Who do you think you are?"

"Me? I'm someone who pays their own way. You want out of the marriage with Dominic and, to be fair, no one blames you for that but take what's yours. This house is not yours."

While Elle was talking Dominic was placing Bella's bags outside the front door. He closed the door and gave Elle the thumbs-up. "Take care of yourself," she said, and closed the window.

"We'll see about that," Bella said. She stamped through the plants and retrieved her cases, got into her car and drove away.

Dominic stood at the window agog. "I can't believe we just did that."

Elle danced around the sitting room. "It was fun."

Dominic opened a bottle of wine to celebrate and insisted Elle join him. They clinked glasses, relived the break-in, laughed and drank. Just when the night couldn't get any stranger Dominic told Elle she was amazing. Then he leaned in and kissed her, and she responded. Twenty minutes later Elle was sitting on top of Bella's soon-to-be-ex-husband in Bella's ex-bed.

Jane had taken it upon herself to move Leslie to her nursing-home. Twelve days after the operation she gently guided her friend to her car and helped her sit in. She was in a quandary as to whether or not Leslie should wear the seat-belt but Leslie insisted it would be fine as she could hold it away from herself.

Leslie was quiet in the car and Jane understood that she didn't want to chat. Instead she put on the radio and they listened to a morning talk show. When they were close to the place Jane rang ahead so that a nurse with a wheelchair met them at the door. The nurse wheeled Leslie inside and Jane followed with her bags. She was brought to a private room and the nurse helped her into bed and explained how to work the remote control, informed her of mealtimes and said that someone would be around with pain medication in three hours. Leslie grunted and nodded, and the nurse left.

"Well," Jane said, "that all sounds good."

"Does it?"

"What can I do?"

"Nothing," Leslie said. "Nobody can do anything."

"Elle's been Googling this—it's normal to feel depressed."

"I know. She told me."

"I wish I could help."

"Me too."

"Jim will be here later."

"What's that supposed to mean?" Leslie said, thinking Jane was hinting at romance the way Elle often did.

"It means that Jim will be here later."

"Oh."

"Would you like me to help you wash?" Jane said.

"You want to see how I've been butchered?"

Jane was horrified that she would think that. "No. God—absolutely no, no, no!" She was so horrified and so embarrassed and so red that it actually made Leslie smile.

"I'm sorry," she said.

"God almighty, Leslie," Jane said, sitting down, "my life is hard enough without you . . ." She trailed off. "Life is hard enough."

After that Leslie did ask for her help. She hadn't had her bandages changed in five days and she wanted to do it herself but she needed help.

"Are you sure?" asked Jane.

233

"Yes. Are you sure?"

"I offered, didn't I?" Jane said.

She helped Leslie into the bathroom and sat her on the toilet. She filled the sink with warm soapy water and then she helped her take off her pyjama top. The bandages were wrapped tight around her and Jane found the fastenings quickly. She moved slowly and gently and began to unravel them. Leslie held on to the front of them, her hand protecting and concealing the area as it was exposed.

When the final bandage fell off, Leslie dropped her hand and revealed the indents and angry slashes where her breasts used to be. There were holes from the drains and one was slightly infected. Her eyes filled, her nose ran and her lips pursed. "Seeing is believing," she said, as she wiped her eyes. "It's bad, isn't it?"

"It's still healing."

"It's still horrible."

"Look, it is awful but, then, I've an arse that looks like it's made out of cheese."

"At least you're honest," said Leslie.

"Well, I'm a pretty bad liar and you're not the kind of person who's easily patronized."

"Do you think I should get implants?"

"That's your decision."

"Would you?"

"Yes," Jane said. "I probably would."

"It's not an easy decision."

"Neither is opting to have a double mastectomy and a hysterectomy."

Leslie sighed. "With or without breasts I'll never be whole now."

"Wombs are overrated. They can get you into all kinds of trouble."

Leslie laughed. "I'll think about it."

"Good." Jane squeezed the sponge and gently cleaned around the wounds as Leslie took in her new shape in the mirror.

Tom was sitting on her steps when Jane returned from the nursing-home. She got out of the car and he took the bag of Leslie's washing from her. "I've got some news," he said, "about Alexandra."

Jane stopped in her tracks. "What?"

"They found her wedding ring."

"Where?"

"In a market in Wexford."

"What does it mean?"

"I don't know."

"But it's something," she said.

"Yeah," he smiled, "it's something."

She hugged him and he dropped the bags to hug her back.

From her window Rose watched them hold one another tightly. Even from a distance she recognized the look in her daughter's eyes. "Oh, Janey, another unobtainable man! At least you're focking consistent."

Chapter 12

Open Your Borders

A heart starts growing cold if you remain alone.
You gotta take a chance,
You gotta get up and dance,
You know the song.

Jack L, *Broken Songs*

August 2008

Jane missed Kurt more than she could ever have predicted. Every few days she'd find herself standing in his room, looking around but afraid to touch anything in case he noticed and freaked out on his return. One day she lay on his bed and, staring up at the ceiling, she thought about where he was and what he was doing and what kind of time he was having. *Is every day a new adventure? Will he be sorry to come home? Will he come home? Oh, Jesus, he'll definitely come home, won't he? Calm down, Jane. He's on holiday, he hasn't emigrated. Jesus Christ, what if he emigrates?*

She had felt a great emptiness in her house and heart since his departure. She missed Irene, too, because even though she'd been part of their household for a short time she had made her mark. Jane understood that Kurt's extended holiday was merely preparing her for the day he'd leave home for good. She prayed he would get medicine in Dublin because he had applied to Cork, Galway and Belfast as back-ups. If he didn't get to Dublin he'd be gone from home sooner rather than later, and the permanent loss of her son was too great to contemplate.

As the days passed into weeks Jane also experienced a creeping uneasiness. All the thoughts of fleeing home that she had long ago put to the back of her mind began pushing themselves forward. *If he goes I could go. If he's starting his new life I could start mine. I could sell this house. I could put Rose into a home where she wouldn't be allowed to drink herself to death and set Elle up in a cottage in a pretty place somewhere inspirational, somewhere other than down the end of her sister's garden. I could take my life back.*

As much as these thoughts excited her, she didn't dwell on them long because to take her life back would be to put everyone else's in a spin, and poor old Janey wasn't capable of deliberately upsetting her nearest and dearest. Besides, they needed her. It was unspoken but accepted in the family that Rose would be dead and Elle would be in some sort of state-run facility – most likely a prison – without Jane's presence, patience and care.

In the early days of Kurt's life Jane had remained at home because she had no money and nowhere else to go and, although her mother did not provide any kind of assistance when it came to caring for the baby, she did feed Jane and her child. Those first few years of Kurt's life had been the hardest and most miserable of Jane's, but they had ensured that she and Kurt became the centre of each other's universe.

When Elle's talent was becoming recognized, Jane made a decision to learn the business. This was because, according to Rose, a number of people had queued up "to take advantage of Elle", and after Rose had driven them away, Elle was left unrepresented. Jane combed the streets of Dublin looking for a gallery owner to take her on four mornings a week. When she had walked into a small one near Clan-william Street, a man in his sixties had greeted her with a warm smile and she knew even before they spoke that she had a job. Initially he told her he had no work but she pressed him and told him that as long as he was prepared to teach her everything he knew she would work for him for free for a year. He had laughed, believing she was joking, but she was deadly serious so, as long as he didn't mind that she left by midday, he had himself some free labour.

Albert had liked Jane from the first moment he saw her and, being a man who spent a great deal of his time alone since his beloved wife had died, he was only too thrilled by the notion of company. He was also happy to pass on his knowledge. Luckily for Jane he was a teacher capable of making learning fascinating. Jane had been working with Albert for a month before she brought him Elle's paintings. He was blown away, and after Jane had read a book on PR they had a showing, which, thanks to a few tips from the book and Elle having a genuinely interesting angle to encourage media interest, was packed and a huge success. Jane had been working with Albert for four months when she received her first pay packet. They continued to work together for a further five years and were as close as father and daughter when Albert passed away one cold autumn evening. Albert and his lovely wife had never had any children and he was the youngest of his generation, all his family and pals having gone before him, so he had left his business and home to the girl who had brought light and challenges into his final years.

As it turned out Albert's gift of a home and business couldn't have come at a better time because Rose had refinanced the house, hadn't paid the mortgage in a year and the bank was set to take their home from them. Because Rose liked to stick her head in the sand and because she was arrogant enough to think that the bank would wait for her to decide when she was good and ready to get the job that would be necessary for her to make repayments, Jane took over.

She sold Albert's house and used the money to buy her mother's home from her. At first Rose screamed and roared at Jane for trying to steal her house, but when Jane's solicitor explained to Rose in no uncertain terms that if Jane didn't take over the mortgage Rose would be homeless and that in buying her out Jane would be paying her more than a hundred thousand euro in cash, she became far more amenable. There was enough money left to fix up the basement flat, which Rose had let go to rack and ruin, and when the contracts were signed and the money changed hands, Jane became the owner of a large Georgian property, complete with garden cottage, at the age of twenty-seven. By the time she was thirty she had sold the small gallery that Albert had left her, moved into bigger premises and named it after him. Since then Jane had run a successful business – and some would have said that if it hadn't been for her Elle might not have done half as well.

But now, despite owning her own home and running a successful business, Jane wondered whether or not there was something more to life. She thought about all the things she had wanted to do, medicine being one thing, travelling another. She'd never been out of the country longer than two weeks and never further than a beach resort complete with a kiddies' club in Europe. As a girl she had dreamed of adventure: trekking in Brazilian rainforests, surfing off the coast of Mexico or going on safari in Kenya. And although her desire to get into medicine when she was a teenager had been tempered by her desire to get into Dominic's pants, over the years she had grieved over her lost opportunity. She knew that she would have made a good doctor and, God knew, she had the patience. *Maybe I could still do it? Don't be a dick, Jane, you're ancient.*

Jane's intermittent thoughts of escape were always interrupted, whether it was by Rose or Elle. That day Rose was still suffering with stomach problems but, of course, she wouldn't admit it because to do so would be to accept that she had to lay off the booze and she had no intention of ever doing that. "We all have our crutches, Jane," she said.

"Yeah, but most people's crutches don't cripple them."

"I disagree."

Every now and then Rose would clutch her stomach and breathe deeply.

"What can I do?" Jane asked.

"You can distract me."

Jane stood up and broke into an Irish dance.

"Yes, very funny, Janey, you should really have your own sitcom."

Jane sat down.

"Why don't you tell me about Tom?" Rose said.

"What about him?"

"Well, how is he getting on? Have they found anyone who knows anything about the wedding ring?"

"They sourced it to a guy from Kent. He said he'd bought it off a man from Clare, and when they knocked his door down he said he'd bought it in a flea market in Rathmines. He had thought it would make a nice ring for his girlfriend; she'd got confused, thought he was asking her to marry him and then noticed it was engraved with Alexandra's name, thought he was a cheapskate and broke up with him."

"Well, how did it get into a flea market?"

"The owner swears she doesn't know – she had receipts and a paper trail for everything else she'd ever bought or sold. It's like someone just left it there."

"And what does Tom think?"

"He thinks it's hopeful. Maybe she's leaving us a clue how to find her."

"Balls. She's dead, long dead."

"Rose, please don't say that."

"Oh, don't be ridiculous, Jancy, of course she's dead! And if Tom was honest with himself he'd say so – and you can be sure the police have mentioned the likelihood on more than one occasion."

"Let's just stop talking."

"You like him, don't you?"

"What?"

"Tom – you like him."

"He's a lovely man."

"Don't play coy with me, Jane Moore."

"Oh, for God's sake, Rose!" Jane got up from her chair and turned to leave.

"You be careful – you've been a gobshit with men for far too long."

"It's 'gobshite', Rose. The word you're looking for is 'gobshite', with an *e*."

"'You say tomato', Janey, and the point still stands: don't be an eejit all your life. And judging by the dark circles and lines around your eyes, you're not going to be pretty for much longer – so if you want a man get your skates on."

Jane slammed Rose's front door. *God, I hate that horrible old woman!*

Four weeks into her nursing-home stay, Leslie was battling depression. Her surgeon had warned her that it was a possibility and explained why, but reason was hard to hold on to when everything inside her was screaming. She didn't feel like talking and when she could no longer sleep she just sat staring at the TV with a remote in her hand. Elle would sit with her and sometimes she'd talk and sometimes she'd say nothing at all. Jane tried little tricks to brighten the place up, including coloured balloons, a big cuddly toy and scented candles. Tom told jokes, which Jane laughed at. Mostly they were jokes that Alexandra had told him. She'd loved jokes and once she'd heard one she stored it and could regurgitate it at will. He wasn't good at telling jokes and often forgot the punchline so it wasn't necessarily the depression that prevented Leslie laughing. Jim came in every second day. He'd fluff her pillows even if she didn't want him to, fix the bed and poke around her locker, which annoyed her so much she'd be forced to talk to him.

"Will you just leave it be?"

"No, you've an apple in there and it's gone off."

"Just leave it."

"No." He threw the offending fruit in the bin. "I might clean your sink."

"The cleaners will do it."

"Yeah, well, they're not here right now and if you won't talk to me . . ."

"What do you want to talk about?" She sighed deeply, indicating she was not amused by his neediness.

"I don't know. How about flash floods?"

"Flash floods?"

"In Clonee, can you believe it? Cars were floating down the M50."

"Well, it has pissed rain day and night for the past month."

"I hate the rain," he said, looking out at the dark grey sky and the rain hitting the window.

"Yeah."

"I was thinking about going away. A week in the sun before the end of September maybe."

"Good."

"We could rent a car."

"We?"

"You could get some sun on that sickly body of yours."

"Thanks very much."

"You could walk on the sand and soak up the sun," he said, "eat well, sleep because you're tired and not because you've taken a bucket-load of sleeping tablets."

"Stop monitoring me."

"We could go to Greece or Spain or France – I bet it will still be nice there."

"You really want to go on holiday with me?" she asked.

"We're friends, aren't we?"

She nodded.

"And we both need something to look forward to."

She nodded again.

"So when you're feeling better and when your hormones are adjusted, we'll go."

"Maybe," she said.

"Maybe is good enough for now."

After that she slipped away from him again but he was happy enough to have elicited some chat, and on the matter of a holiday a "maybe" was better than an outright "no".

Tom knew he needed to fill his days with more than checking the findingalexandra and Jack Lukeman sites and hounding his liaison officer. His business was dead and buried, and the way things were shaping up for his competitors, he was glad to be out of it. He'd heard on the grapevine that demand for new builds was disappearing at a shocking rate. One builder he was familiar with was close to bankruptcy and another was barely treading water. Once his accountant had finalized his tax and VAT for the end of the business year he had money in the bank and because he'd only rented his offices he was free and clear.

Getting back into building was certainly not something he could consider in the current climate, and he wasn't really qualified for anything else because he had left school at sixteen to work with his dad on sites around Dublin. Tom's mother had suffered from dementia since she was young so from when he was ten she'd had no idea who Tom was. His father couldn't care for her so he'd put her into the best home that money could buy. The problem was that he couldn't pay for the home and for him and Tom at the same time. That was when Tom had left school and they'd worked together to pay the bills. At night Tom would watch TV and his father would drink, and that went on until four years later when he had died of sclerosis of the liver. There was a year to go on the mortgage and Tom paid it off, sold the house and started his business.

He and Jane had discussed their similar backgrounds one night over dinner. She had told him about the father she lost to heart failure and she didn't need to tell him about her drunken mother because he'd met her. She talked about leaving school to have Kurt and how Albert had given her her life back. Tom talked about his poor mother who had lost her mind long before she lost her life and his dad who, unlike Jane's mother, had been a fall down drunk incapable of stopping once he'd started, often disappearing for days on end. He talked about school too and admitted that at the time he had been delighted to leave, not being one of the most academic students and lacking any lofty career ambitions, but in the years since he had developed a keen interest in human rights.

"I know it sounds weird," he said. "A bit hippie-dippy for a property-developer."

"I think the fact that you're using the term 'hippie-dippy' is weirder."

Jane confided in him her fear of living in that big house without her son.

"It's totally understandable," he said.

"It keeps me awake."

"You need to start living for you again."

"And you need to take some of your own advice," she said.

Tom stayed quiet for a moment. "Yes, there's a part of me that knows you're right."

Jane had told him about her doomed love for Dominic as part of the apology for roaring at him the night she had been with him and Jeanette had turned up. He asked her about him now, to change the subject.

"His marriage is over," she said.

"He told you?"

"No, Elle did. He's staying away."

"Good."

"Yeah," she said. "It's actually the first time in fourteen years that I've a break from my son and his father."

"And you're not the slightest bit interested in how he is?"

"Nope," she said. "I'm moving on."

"Good for you."

"What about Jeanette – are you thinking about going back there?"

"Oh, don't! I'm so embarrassed."

"Trust me, I know how that feels."

After they had eaten, they walked together on Grafton Street. They stopped in front of a band playing for coins and watched them for a while, then pottered on. Initially they were looking for a taxi but, as the rain had stopped and they were entertaining one another, they ended up walking all the way to Jane's. When they found themselves outside her door she asked him in.

"I shouldn't," he said, looking at his watch. "It's getting late."

"Okay," she said. "Goodnight."

"Goodnight."

They stood, rooted to the spot.

"We'll do it again soon," he said.

"Great."

"Okay."

"Okay."

Tom bit his lip and Jane exhaled, and in that moment they were so close to kissing, yet so far from it. They heard knocking and turned to see Rose tapping at her window. When she had their attention she pointed at Tom and gave him the finger. Jane and Tom laughed at the crazy drunk and, thankfully, the moment passed.

Elle knocked on Dominic's front door. He opened it and grinned. She walked inside and he grabbed her by the arse. She slapped his hand, then ran to his bedroom with him hot on her heels. He gave chase around the bed, which she jumped over. She ran down the hall into the spare room and around the chair. He tried to grab her but she bobbed and wove and ran to the box-room, where he cornered her. They were both breathing heavily and Dominic pinned her to the wall. "We shouldn't be doing this," he said.

"That's why it feels so good," she said. He kissed her and pulled at her panties and she jumped on his hips, and if it hadn't been for his bad back they would have finished up there, but instead he was lying flat on the floor. Afterwards when she'd returned from her shower and he was still lying there, she wondered if he'd be okay.

"Fine," he said, trying to make light of it.

"Good," she said. "Get up."

He sighed and she helped him to his feet. He rubbed his back and took two painkillers with water. "You're going to be the death of me," he said.

"That's nothing to what Jane would do to you if she found out."

"But she won't," he said, with alarm. "You won't tell her."

"No. I have as much to lose as you, if not more."

Elle sat down at Dominic's kitchen table and poured salt on it.

"So why are we doing this?" he asked. "And don't say fun."

"Because I'm impulsive and you'd get up on the crack of dawn."

Afterwards when she'd gone and he was cleaning salt from his table with one hand and rubbing the small of his back with the other, he promised himself faithfully that he would not sleep with Elle again.

Leslie came out of the nursing-home on a Tuesday. Jim had the summer off from lecturing so he offered to drive her home. Her spirits had picked up a little and she was looking forward to seeing her cat.

Deborah was in Leslie's apartment cleaning out the kitty-litter tray when she followed Jim inside.

"Welcome home," Deborah said. She seemed genuinely glad to see her but then again she had been feeding and cleaning up after a cat for weeks and she hated cats the way some people hated iguanas.

"Thanks," Leslie said, and sat on her sofa because getting out of the car, walking to the lift, standing in it and walking from it to her door had felt like a ten-mile hike. The cat jumped up on the sofa and rubbed herself against Leslie, purring. Leslie stroked her head and looked around. It was good to be home.

Deborah finished cleaning the tray and made her excuses to leave. "It's good to have you back," she said.

"It's good to be back."

When she'd gone Leslie lay on the sofa and Jim made tea. "Will you come out with me on Sunday?" he asked.

"Where?"

"Surprise."

"I hate surprises."

"Indulge me."

"Why should I indulge you? I'm the one who's just been mutilated."

"Will you stop saying that?"

"It's true."

He wasn't getting anywhere so he decided to start again. "Will you come out with me on Sunday?"

"Where?"

"Leslie!"

"Tell me where."

"It's a garden centre."

She sat up slowly because even though she'd spent several weeks lying in bed it still hurt to move. "A garden centre?"

"Yes."

"I may be in menopause but I'm not in my seventies."

"It has a really good restaurant and the forecast is positive for once. The gardens are beautiful."

"I'd rather just stay in."

"Please."

"Oh," she sighed heavily, "fine, we'll go to your poxy gardens."

"Great. And, Leslie?"

"What?"

"You're going to love it." He grinned and winked at her.

She made a face. "I'll be the one to decide that, short-arse!" She laughed a little. She loved calling Jim names and he didn't seem to mind in the slightest.

Sunday arrived and Jim picked her up at midday. She got into the car and he was listening to the radio. Jack Lukeman was talking to a DJ about his upcoming shows. "Oh, shit," she said, "I forgot to post them on the web."

"Do it later."

"No, I can't." She opened the door. "Wait here – it will only take five minutes."

"Leslie, I don't want to be late."

"Trust me, the garden centre will go on without us."

Fifteen minutes later Jim appeared in the doorway and he was not happy. "Move," he said.

"Two seconds," she said.

"One, two . . ." he said, and shut her laptop.

"Ah, come on!"

"Get to the car!" he shouted, and pointed.

"Right. Fine. Keep your high heels on."

They were twenty minutes late. Jim was having a night-mare trying to find a parking space and he kept swearing, which was unlike him, and Leslie was beginning to wonder what the hell he was rushing for. When they finally found a bay he practically ran into the restaurant with Leslie following slowly, mumbling that he was a pain in the arse under her breath.

She saw John first. Beside him his daughter Sarah was eating a burger and opposite them was a woman Leslie didn't recognize. John glanced up and saw Leslie, then stood up, pushing his chair back. Sarah looked up at her father and followed his eye-line to where Leslie stood.

John was completely grey and his face was so lined it made Gordon Ramsay's look Botoxed, and even though Sarah was sitting, Leslie could tell she was tall, like her mother, Nora. She had her dark complexion too.

Jim grabbed her hand and pulled her towards the table.

John put his hand out to shake hers and she took it. "It's lovely to see you, Leslie," he said.

"Good to see you, John."

"And you know Sarah," he said, "although the last time you saw her she was only five."

"Hi, Leslie," the teenager said.

"Hi, Sarah."

"This is my wife, Claire."

Claire offered her hand and Leslie shook it. "It's great to finally meet you," Claire said.

Jim pushed a speechless Leslie onto a chair.

"I hope you don't mind," John said. "We were starving so we went ahead and ordered."

"No," Leslie said, "not at all."

Jim went off to get them some food and she was left with Nora's husband, her daughter and his wife, and she hadn't a clue what to say.

"I didn't know that Jim had kept in touch with you," she said, after a while.

"Yeah," John said. "Together in the trenches and all that."

"I suppose," she said.

"Jim told us about your operation," Claire said. "Very brave."

"Thank you."

"If you think I'm doing what she's done you're mad," Sarah said to her father.

"Sarah!" he warned.

"You've been tested?" Leslie asked her niece.

"Not yet," Sarah said. "Don't want to know."

"That's crazy," Claire said.

"We keep telling her it's for her own good," John said.

"I understand how she feels." Leslie smiled at her sister's child, who was a stranger to her.

Sarah smiled back, glad that someone at least had uttered those exact words.

Jim returned with food and Leslie nibbled it and listened to Sarah talk about her life, her hopes and dreams. "Law, definitely law," she said. "Dad says I could win an argument with Bono on the topic of his choice."

"Like Nora," Leslie said.

"Very like Nora," John agreed.

"If I don't get law I'm going to repeat until I do get it," Sarah said.

"Good for you," Leslie said.

"What do you do?" Sarah asked.

"I'm a webmaster."

"Cool. What kind of websites?"

"All kinds."

"Would I know any?"

"A few gyms, a radio station —"

"Which one?"

"It's a country one that specializes in folk."

"Oh."

"Jack Lukeman."

"The singer?"

"Yeah."

"Wow, I love him!"

"Really?" Leslie said. "I could take you to a gig if you'd like."

"Backstage?"

"I'm sure I could arrange something."

"Can I take my pal?"

"Absolutely."

"Cool."

"Is that okay, John?" Leslie asked.

"It's great," he said, and he smiled at Jim who was sitting with a big smug grin on his face.

"Hey, Leslie?" Sarah said.

"Yes."

"You don't know U2, do you?"

"No."

"Okay, worth a try."

On the way home Jim was still wearing his smug expression.

"I don't know what you're so smug about – that little surprise of yours could have gone very wrong."

"But it didn't."

"Thanks," she said.

"That's what family's for."

"Is that what we are?"

"I like to think so," he said.

"I'm pretty selfish."

"What makes you think that?"

"I cut out John, Sarah and you because I thought I was doing you all a favour but the truth is I was just protecting myself."

"How do you work that out?"

"Sarah's going through what I went through. She faces the same challenges. I should have been there for her."

"So you'll be there for her now."

"Yeah. I will."

"Nora would be happy," he said.

"Yes, I think she would," she said, lying back, "and, Jim, let's do as you said – let's get away to the sun in September."

"Ha ha! That's the spirit!"

When Leslie went to bed that night she thought about Jane, Elle, Tom, Jim, John, Sarah, Claire and even Deborah. She had so many people in her life who cared and wanted to care. She no longer felt alone.

Chapter 13

Everybody's Drunk

I've been biding my time I ain't that gone
maybe one or two or three or four or five or six too many
but it eases my mind and loosens my tongue,
so come on, sister, won't you take my hand,
be my Alice I'll be Wonderland.

Jack L, *Universe*

September 2008

The plane was late, which was typical. Jane paced the airport floor from one end to the other, and as the arrivals area was about half a mile long Elle only spotted her every five minutes or so. Elle sat and read a magazine and drank a wheatgrass shot, hoping it would negate the damage she'd been doing to herself recently. She was on a binge and every other night she'd be found in a nightclub dancing on a table and her top was optional. She was living on a diet of champagne and morning fry-ups, and when Rose questioned her on her late comings and goings she merely replied that life was too short.

Jane appeared, asked the time and then she was gone. Elle flipped the page and there was a shot of Vincent and his bride. He was holding her tummy and she knew the woman was pregnant before she even read the caption because the bloody pose was so obvious. She wasn't even showing and had just had her twelve-week scan. *I hope she loses it.* She turned the page. She started to read another article about being kind to feet but the interview with Vincent was calling to her.

Read me.

No. Go away.

You want to know what I'm doing and how happy I am.

I do not. I hope you get knocked down by a bus and dragged for a really long time.

You want me to confirm that I'm in a perfect happy relationship and that the reason we didn't work was you and not me. I'm stable and you're a lunatic. You need to read it. You need to understand that I'm so much better off without you.

"Fuck you, Vincent!" she screamed, to an airport full of strangers.

The woman beside her with two toddlers picked up three bags, hung them on a double buggy and, with a child holding on to each side of the buggy, scurried to a place far away from the vulgar mental case. Elle put her explosion down to excessive tiredness and promised herself that she would have a bath later and then an early night.

Minutes later Jane returned and flopped down beside her sister. "I think I've just walked about ten miles. Where the hell are they?"

They were more than an hour late and after her walk Jane was hungry. She turned to her sister to ask if she'd like to join her for a bit of lunch upstairs, then spied Martha arriving into the area. Martha spotted her immediately, waved wildly and bared that awful sinister Osmonds-on-acid smile.

256

"Oh, no," Jane said.

"What?" Elle said.

"That woman, Irene's mother."

Elle looked around, saw her approaching and rubbed her hands together. "Oh, yeah, playtime."

"Elle," Jane warned, "play nice."

"Absolutely," Elle said, shaking her head to suggest she was planning on doing absolutely the opposite.

"Jane," Martha said, and air-kissed her. "You look so refreshed after a couple of months without a teenager in the house."

"Martha," Jane said, refusing to respond to the redundant and annoying air-kiss or the barbed compliment. "This is my sister, Elle."

Elle grinned and remained in her seat. "I've heard so much about you," she said.

Martha sat in the seat opposite and removed her gloves. "All good, I hope."

"Nope, all bad, I'm afraid," Elle said, smiling.

"Well," Martha said, "aren't you hilarious?"

"I try," Elle said. "So, Martha, how are things with the kid you were screwing? Back together yet or has he moved on to Betty White? I hear she's a real goer."

Martha got up and walked away without a word.

"You're welcome!" Elle called after her, as a grin spread across Jane's face.

"Who's Betty White?" Jane asked.

"One of the Golden Girls."

"I used to love *The Golden Girls*. Which one was Betty White?"

"Rose."

"Ah, that's right, a pleasant Rose. God, I wish she'd been our mother."

Elle nudged her. "Jane."

"Yeah."

"Look." Elle pointed to the arrivals gate and to her nephew, brown as a berry, his blond locks bleached white. He was waving.

Jane's heart soared as she jumped to her feet and ran to him, managing to leap a suitcase in the process. They met at the barrier and he dropped his bags. They hugged and hugged and hugged.

"It's good to be back, Mum."

"Oh, God, I missed you!" she said, and her eyes were full and of course she was crying because she always cried.

Elle was next to give her nephew a hug. "You look good," she said. "Better be careful or Irene's mother will make a move."

Kurt laughed and looked back at Irene, whose reunion with her mother was slightly tamer and cooler. Her mother air-kissed her and made her stand back so that she could look at her. Then she squeezed her for a second or so. Kurt turned to his mother and shook his head. "Poor Irene," he said. "I'd hate to be going back to that."

Irene ran over to Jane and Elle and hugged them both far more warmly than she had her own mother. "We had a ball – we'd do it again in the morning. Can you believe how well Kurt did in his exams? When we got our results we were sitting at a beach bar. Incredible. Can you believe he's got medicine and I'm going to be a nurse? I just scraped by, thank God. Oh, Jane, this summer was the best time in our lives!"

"I can't wait to hear all about it," Jane said.

"I have to go," Irene said, and seemed a little sad.

"I understand," Jane said. "Come for your dinner tomorrow night."

"Great," she said. "I'll bring photos." She kissed Kurt and ran off to join her mother, who was waiting by the door.

"Are you hungry?" Jane asked Kurt.

"I'd eat a scabby leg," he said.

"I'll take that as a yes, then. Did I tell you how proud I am?"

"About a million times, Mum."

She put her arm around her son and together they walked to the airport restaurant with Elle in tow, pushing the trolley carrying his bags.

Dominic arrived at Jane's just after six. He ran up the steps and Kurt was waiting by the door. They hugged and Dominic messed Kurt's bleached curls. "Jesus, son, albinos have darker hair!"

"Thanks, Dad."

"Great to have you home."

"Sorry about Bella," Kurt said, as they walked into the kitchen.

"Never mind." Dominic smiled at Jane. "Long time no see, stranger."

She nodded. "Good to see you, Dominic." She was hoping her heart wouldn't flutter. She hadn't seen him in just over two months. She had not missed him once and she had told herself categorically and in no uncertain terms that she was to stop loving him. She did feel a flutter – *Damn you, Jane* – and her pulse did race a little, and although this disappointed her she managed to work out in those few seconds that even if she was still attracted to Dominic she didn't love him. She had been glad of the distance, she had enjoyed it, so she could live with a flutter now and then because they were only friends and that suited her just fine.

Jane cooked a family dinner to include Rose, although Elle had made her excuses because Leslie needed help with something she wasn't at liberty to divulge. Rose had promised to be on her best behaviour around Dominic. "I'm not a child, Jane – you don't have to monitor my behaviour."

"Of course I do, Rose. You have the capacity to insult someone with a mere look. I just want this to be nice for Kurt."

"And don't you think I want it to be nice for Kurt? He is my grandson."

"Fine, fine, but I'm warning you, do not bring up Bella."

"Hmmm," Rose said.

At dinner Kurt talked about the various islands of Greece he'd been to, he talked about Paris, Milan, Rome, Barcelona and Amsterdam, at which point he shared a little knowing grin with his dad.

"I saw that," Jane said.

"What?" Kurt said innocently.

"Don't play dumb with me."

"What are you talking about?" Rose said.

"Nothing," Jane said.

"Sex and drugs on every corner, Gran," Kurt said.

"Well, do you hear that, Janey? Maybe you should get yourself to Amsterdam – God knows, you could do with something to lift both your mood and your skirt."

"Rose!" Jane screamed in exasperation, but Kurt and Dominic were holding themselves, they found it so funny.

Rose grinned at her daughter, who mouthed, "You are dead, old woman."

During dessert Kurt talked excitedly about doing medicine in Trinity. He couldn't believe he'd got the scores necessary because study was so boring that mostly he'd just played computer games.

"Your mother was like that," Rose said. "When Janey was seven she got one of those kids' encyclopedias that were so popular in the eighties. She read it in a week and I swear you could ask that kid any question and she'd know the answer. Remarkable, really."

"My God, Rose, that's the first nice thing I've ever heard you say about Jane ever," Dominic said.

"I stated a fact, Dominic, and anyway how's your wife?"

"Rose!" Jane warned.

"She left me," he said.

"Good for her," Rose said. "I'd like to propose a toast to Bella may she find herself a half-decent husband next time around!"

"That's it! One more word from you and you're going back to the basement," Jane said.

Kurt leaned back on his chair. "I really missed this," he said. "I love you, Gran."

"I love you too, darling," Rose said.

They clinked glasses and drank, and it was just like he'd never been away.

Leslie walked out of the dressing room, feeling monumentally self-conscious. She was wearing red swimming togs and a matching red flowing top picked out by Elle. She'd also selected a wide-brimmed white hat but Leslie had refused to wear it. "Well," she said, gesturing to the togs and top, "can you see?"

"No, I can't," Elle said. "You look lovely. I told you, red is your colour."

Leslie looked at herself in the mirror. The top had enough material to conceal that she had no breasts and instead she just looked flat-chested.

"Try it on in green," Elle said.

"It will look the same," Leslie argued.

"No, it will be a different colour and that changes the outfit utterly," Elle said.

Leslie went back into the dressing room. Elle's phone buzzed and it was a text from Dominic: *Just had dinner in Janes. Feel like shit. What are we doing?????* She put the phone back in her bag. Leslie appeared in the same outfit in green.

"Looks good," Elle said. "Buy them both."

"Really? I feel so exposed."

"You're going to be on a beach not at the opera. Buy the clothes, please."

"Okay." Leslie took one last look at herself and secretly she was pleased: without clothes her body was broken, but with clothes she looked quite good for her age. *I can do this.*

After they had spent another hour on Leslie's holiday wardrobe they stopped off for coffee and a toasted sandwich in a coffee shop that Elle hadn't been to since she was a student.

"It's a bit grotty, isn't it?" Leslie said.

"That's character."

Leslie sat into a bench, pushed the table towards Elle and fixed herself in the seat. "Since when has filth become character?" She pointed to a large cobweb in the corner.

"It's a cobweb, Leslie, not a dangling bucket of shit."

"And there goes my appetite."

They were finishing their coffees when Elle confided what she was doing with Dominic.

"Two more coffees, please," Leslie said to the waiter. "You are insane. Why would you do that?"

"I don't know. I can't help it. It makes me feel . . ."

"Feel what?" Leslie asked.

"It makes me feel, full stop."

"Well, stop feeling because it will end in tears."

"It was easy when Kurt was away, but now he's back, Dominic is back in Jane's life. When Kurt was away we could pretend it didn't matter."

"So stop."

"So Jim's all packed and ready for this sun holiday, is he?" Elle asked.

"Don't change the subject."

"Excited, I bet."

"Stop what you're doing," Leslie said.

"I know, I know," said Elle. "Stop what you're doing with your nephew's father, you hillbilly lunatic."

"Well, that wasn't exactly where I was going but close enough."

Leslie was leaving for her sun holiday with Jim the next day and she was anxious about what she'd wear, how she'd look, how she'd feel, whether or not it was too soon and how they would get on. She had thought many times about pulling out but it was actually Deborah who managed to talk her around one day when they met in the hall.

"Why the face?" Deborah asked.

"I was born with it."

"Oh, ha ha ha. What's wrong with you?"

"I'm having second thoughts about going on holiday."

Leslie got into the lift. Deborah followed her and pushed the button for their floor. "You're going," Deborah said.

"I'm scared," said Leslie, "not to mention sore, tired and itchy."

Deborah's demeanour softened. "You've been through a lot. You deserve to have fun."

"But will it be fun?"

"I have no idea," Deborah said, "but it will definitely beat sitting in that apartment of yours and staring at four walls."

Leslie sighed. "I don't do that so much any more."

"Not as much but you still do it."

"I'll go, then."

"I think you should."

"So you'll still mind the cat?"

"Yes, I'll mind the stupid cat."

"Will you be nice to her and give her at least one hug a day?"

"I'll be nice, as in I won't kick her when I see her, but I will not hug her."

"Will you let her rub against your leg?"

"Fine. I'll let her rub against my leg."

"Good," Leslie said. "I'll bring you back something special."

"It better cost more than twenty euro."

Leslie laughed and entered her apartment.

Jim picked her up and they drove to the long-term car park, then got a bus to the airport. Leslie checked her handbag for her passport and tickets so many times that Jim took them from her. They put their bags through and went straight to their gate where they had time for some lunch.

Leslie was extremely nervous and kept tapping her fingers on the table.

Jim placed his hand on hers. "Relax," he said, "we're going to have a great time."

"I can't relax," she said. "I've just remembered I hate flying."

Jim laughed at her and promised that if she got too nervous he'd share his stash of Valium.

"Why do you have Valium?"

"Oh, the doctor gave them to me after Imelda died."

"That was more than ten years ago."

"Yeah, but pills don't go off, do they?"

"I think they do, Jim."

"Oh."

"Still, give me one anyway."

"Are you sure?"

"Positive."

"Okay, but only one."

"Fine," she said.

He opened his bag and tapped a few Valium into his hand. She grabbed two and swallowed them without water. An hour later she floated onto the plane.

*

Jane spent the day with the party organizers. The tent had arrived and was being erected in the back garden. Rose had spent much of the morning shouting for the men to watch her various plants. The booze had arrived and the catering team had set up a good-sized bar. The dance floor had lights flashing around it and the DJ arrived good and early to sound-check. Dominic kept Kurt entertained for the day because although his belated eighteenth birthday party was no surprise Jane wanted everything to be perfect when he walked through the door. Irene arrived late afternoon to see if there was anything she could help with but Jane was pretty happy that everything was right on track and instead they enjoyed a coffee on the patio together because, thankfully, in September it had stopped raining. They talked about the party plans and Irene was so excited she broke into a clap every now and again. When they were all talked out on the party theme, Jane broached the subject of how Irene was getting on at home.

"It's good," she said.

"You can come back here anytime."

"Thanks, Jane. I know you don't get on with my mum but she's not half as bad as you think."

"I'm sure you're right."

"She doesn't make a good first impression."

Or a second, Jane thought.

"She was painfully shy up to her early twenties so sometimes when she's nervous she overcompensates. She was really upset when we got back from the airport."

"I'm sorry."

"She thinks everyone is laughing at her. She feels foolish. She was married to my dad for twenty-five years, he meets someone on-line and she's a laughing-stock. It's hard for her."

"She's not a laughing-stock."

"I wish she believed that."

"She'll recover."

"What makes you think so?"

"Because people do."

"I hope so," Irene said. "I hate seeing her so sad. That guy might have been a user but at least he was a distraction."

"I really like you, Irene."

"I really like you too, Jane, but next time you meet my mum, go easy on her."

"Promise."

"And Elle?"

"I'll hold her back."

Music played from eight onwards, people started to arrive around nine, the caterers served drinks to anyone with a passable fake ID and the kids were going through canapés like there was no tomorrow. Jane was dressed and ready to join the guests but she waited for her son and his dad. They arrived just before ten. The place was full, lights were flashing and the music was rocking. Kurt jigged down the steps into his back garden where his friends were sitting around drinking and having a ball. The group of his closest pals all howled when he approached and they bent over with arms stretched in honour of his excellent party. He played it cool, kissing his girlfriend and slapping the boys' hands. Jane watched from the kitchen window with Dominic over her shoulder.

"You've done a pretty good job there," he said.

"Despite myself."

"You're always so hard on yourself."

"He's special, isn't he?"

"I think so."

"My heart is full," she said.

Tom appeared behind Dominic with a large boxed present and Jane spotted his reflection in the glass. "Tom!" she said, and turned to him. "Thanks for coming."

"Wouldn't have missed it."

She walked over to him and hugged him. "You didn't need to bring a present."

"Yeah, well, I hope he likes it," Tom said, while maintaining eye contact with Dominic.

"I'm Dominic." He offered his hand.

"Tom." Tom took and shook it.

"I was really sorry to hear about Alexandra," Dominic said, putting his arm around Jane. "She was a good friend to us."

"She was a good friend to *me* – she hated you," Jane said. Tom laughed.

"Only towards the end," Dominic said.

"No," Jane said, shaking her head, "way before that – she thought you were a vain, stuck-up brat."

"I'm leaving now," Dominic said. "It was nice to meet you, Tom."

"You too."

Tom turned and smiled at Jane, and Dominic noticed a look in her eye that had once been reserved for him. He walked out of the house into the garden and said hello to a few of Kurt's friends. Once he had made sure the caterers were happy and all was well, he snuck down to Elle's cottage and knocked on her door.

Tom and Jane mingled with Kurt's friends and when she asked him to dance he was horrified and she made fun of him until he agreed. Two minutes on the floor and she knew it had been a bad idea. They sat and watched Kurt and Irene dance wildly around with their hands in the air.

"It seems like a lifetime ago," he said.

"For me it was a lifetime, Kurt's lifetime."

"Alexandra was so desperate for a baby. We tried everything. I wanted to just skip it all and adopt but she was determined to have her own. She wanted to feel life inside her."

"Yeah, well, it was a long time ago but I hated the sickness, the constipation my God, no one tells you about that – the gas, the heartburn, the backache, the pressure on your bladder . . . oh, the piles, and did I mention the heartburn?"

"Yes," he said, laughing. "You paint such a beautiful picture."

"I don't remember enjoying one bit of my pregnancy, and if I'm honest, the first year or two of Kurt's life were from hell but after that something inside me clicked. It took its time but when it did I could never go back to a time without him, you know?"

"No," he said, "but I'd like to experience that some day."

Alexandra had been missing for sixty-four weeks and three days and it was the first time that Tom expressed a wish for the future . . . a future in which he envisaged himself with Jane and not his wife. The thought was momentary but profound.

Jane wasn't living inside Tom's head so she didn't perceive the juggernaut of emotion that had borne down on him with that statement or the accompanying vision and he hid it well.

"I just don't know if I could do it again," she said, staring at her son, hanging his arm around a friend. "My God, I have no idea how I did it the first time."

"You're a great mother, despite forgetting him outside a shop when he was a baby and threatening to beat up his bully."

"And don't forget breaking my toe when I was kicking down his door – that was an especially proud moment."

"How could I? The image will last a lifetime."

The clock turned to midnight and the caterer approached Jane and asked her to step outside. Dominic was standing there, with a cake the size of a shopping centre.

Elle was lighting the eighteen candles. The lighter had run out and she kept shaking it and cursing. "We should have got the one and the eight. Eighteen actual candles are so naff."

"I want to see him blow out eighteen candles," Jane said. She grabbed the lighter from Elle and shook it hard. She got a few more lit, then began lighting one from another.

"My back is breaking," Dominic said.

When all eighteen candles were lit Elle signalled to the DJ. He played "Happy Birthday" while Dominic and Jane walked in holding the cake. Kurt was left standing alone in the middle of the dance-floor as all his friends abandoned him. He covered his face and then blew out his candles. Everybody clapped, then Jane and Dominic took the cake to the side where the caterer started to cut it.

"This is where we decipher who's drunk and who's stoned," Dominic said. "Cake-eaters, stoned, non-cake eaters, pissed."

"Don't be ridiculous," she said.

"You're such a square, Janey," Elle said, gorging cake. "Yum," she said, and giggled.

After midnight everything got a little crazy. Jane was surrounded by sixty drunken teenagers and was feeling a little worse for wear herself. Tom was on his fifth whiskey, and even though there was plenty of food he wouldn't touch any of it.

"Do you want to get some air?" she asked, when the tent was so hot there was steam coming off the teenagers' heads.

"Yes, please."

They walked outside into the cool night.

"Oh, that's better," he said. "You know, I'd love a coffee."

"I'd love a cup of tea," she admitted, "but I haven't seen Elle in a while so first I just want to make sure she's okay."

"You mean you're checking up on her."

"Did you see how much wine she was pouring down her neck? It was like looking at Rose."

"Where is Rose?"

"Her pal's house. She doesn't like groups of teenagers – she says they bring out the devil in one another."

"Right," Tom said, and headed up to the house to put the kettle on.

Jane could see Elle's light was on so she walked into the cottage. The kitchen was empty, as was the sitting room. She called out to her and heard movement coming from the bedroom. To make sure Elle wasn't getting sick she opened the door and saw Dominic attempt to cover his face with the duvet. Elle just sat there as though Dominic wasn't in the bed beside her, hiding when he'd already been seen.

"Hi, Janey," Elle said.

"I don't believe it."

271

Dominic took the duvet away from his face. "I'm sorry."

"You don't mind, do you, Janey?" Elle said. "You're over him, you've moved on."

"Shut up, Elle."

"Jane, look —"

"Shut up, Dominic."

"Janey, relax!" Elle said.

"I'm finished with both of you," Jane said, "completely and utterly finished."

"What does that mean?" Elle said.

"It means you're on your own."

She closed the door and walked out of the cottage, through the garden, past all the drunken teenagers, two of whom were puking into her mother's rose bushes and one who was taking a pee on the graves of Elle's dead gerbils, Jeffrey, Jessica, Judy and Jimmy. She walked into her kitchen where Tom was waiting with fresh coffee and tea. He was surprised when she slammed the door. She covered her face, sniffed and sat down.

"What happened?" Tom asked.

"Dominic and my sister happened."

"They were together?"

"Yes, Tom, they were together in bed post coitus."

"I'm sorry."

"Everybody is always sorry. Don't you get pissed off with people being sorry?"

"Yeah, I do."

"Me too. I am so fucking sick of being sorry, feeling sorry and having people feel sorry for me."

"Me too."

"Dominic is an arsehole. He can't help it, I've always

known and I've always put up with it. But Elle, it's not her. Elle may be a lot of things but she has always been kind, never cruel, and this is cruel – she doesn't even like him."

"Drink some tea."

"I don't fucking want any fucking tea."

"That's two fuckings in the space of three seconds. I think you need some tea."

"I'm sorry, I'm really sorry."

"It's okay. You're just upset."

"I don't love him."

"I know."

"I just don't understand why Elle would do that."

"I don't know what to tell you."

"I'm finished with her. I've picked up after her since she was a kid. I've put her ahead of me every step of the way. I didn't ask for much – in fact I don't remember ever asking for or wanting anything – but Dominic! She knew what she was doing. So I'm finished with her."

Tom handed her the tea. "You'll feel better in the morning."

She shook her head. "No, I won't."

"It's going to be fine," he said.

"How could she do that?" she said.

And it was then that she burst into tears and sobbed and rattled in Tom's arms until she was empty, and when she stopped crying he kissed her and it took her aback, especially as he was in such close proximity and she had puffy eyes, tear-burned cheeks and suspected her nose was running. It felt really nice so she kissed him and then they were kissing each other for a minute or two or ten, and then he pulled away and under his breath he said he was sorry.

"Yeah," she said, and sniffled a little, "of course you are."

He got up and walked out of the kitchen and out of her house, leaving Jane alone and staring out at her son and his pals having a ball. She walked into her bedroom, locked the door, laid her head on her pillow and cried into it until it caused her actual physical pain to continue. *Where the hell did it all go wrong?*

Two days after Kurt's party Leslie returned home from holiday. She was tanned and relaxed and even happy. Despite being sore, tired, itchy and sometimes emotional she'd had the time of her life. They had lain on the beach, and while she'd slept under the sun her body and mind had healed themselves. They drank wine in the evenings, ate beautiful food while looking at beautiful scenery and, armed with the clothes carefully chosen by Elle, she didn't feel odd or weird or freakish once.

In fact, she'd felt good, especially when she caught the eye of a few locals and one particular waiter attempted to chat her up every time Jim left the table.

She'd enjoyed Jim's company – they had fun together, it was easy and freeing; they talked when they had something to say and other times they just relaxed in silence. Leslie's mood had improved one hundred per cent: she felt better, she looked better, the hormones were obviously kicking in and a confidence she hadn't known she had was coming to the fore. Jim called it survivor's confidence. She liked that. She liked Jim and he was more than family. Leslie Sheehan was falling in love.

Chapter 14

I've Been Raining

I've been raining I've been pouring,
there's a hole in my roof I've been ignoring,
I've been washed up idle and wasted.
I know my luck is going to change,
I can almost taste it.

Jack L, *Broken Songs*

October 2008

After weeks and weeks of doctor visits and referrals, Breda was hospitalized. Two days later her husband Ben, her son Eamonn and daughter Kate were called into a consultant's office and told she had end-stage colon cancer. Ben didn't understand what the doctor was saying so he repeated the words a few times, looking at his daughter and son. Kate cried and Eamonn got angry. "She's been sick for months. How the hell was this not picked up?" he said, banging his fist on the table.

"Eamonn, calm down," Ben said.

The consultant had no answer. "It should have been picked up," he said.

"Is that all you can say?" Eamonn said.

"I can't answer for the other doctors you've seen. I can only tell you what I've found. I will say this. I reviewed your mother's medical history and only last year she had a clean bill of health, which means the cancer has spread in a very short period of time."

"How do we fix her?" Ben asked.

"All we can offer is palliative care."

"Palliative?" Ben said.

"She's dying, Dad," Kate said.

"Don't say that, Kate," he said.

"How long does she have?" Eamonn asked, in a whisper.

"Six to eight weeks," the consultant said.

"Ah, no," Ben said, "this isn't happening."

"I'm very sorry, Mr Walsh," the consultant said.

"No," Ben said, shaking his head, "I can't have this – we only lost our daughter a year ago. I can't have this."

"We will make her as comfortable as possible."

Ben stood up and walked to the door. He opened it and went out into the corridor. When he got there he looked for the exit sign that would take him outside. He was half-way down the corridor when he stopped, held himself and sobbed so loud and so hard that a nurse came to assist him. She guided him to a chair and waited with him until his family came to find him.

Ben sat in a big red armchair pulled up close to the bed. When he wasn't sleeping he was holding Breda's hand. His daughter and son took turns in badgering him to eat or drink, take a walk, shower or sleep. He said no every time. He washed with antibacterial soap in the disabled bathroom two doors down from his wife's room. Kate brought clean clothes and he changed in the toilet cubicle. He ate a sandwich in the chair and sometimes Frankie and Eamonn arrived with some warm stew. They hadn't told Breda she was dying, but Ben knew that, deep down, she was all too aware of her situation. She didn't talk much: the medication made her sleep a lot and the Breda he knew had all but disappeared. So he watched his wife lie still and he wondered where her mind was. Was she happy or sad, scared or at peace? Did she even really know he was there? Could she feel his hand? Would she come around and talk to him – did she even want to?

Kate would talk to her, telling her about what was happening and complaining that after an entire summer of rain it was still raining – even for October she couldn't believe how cold and miserable it was. She told her about the liaison officer's latest report on Alexandra and unfortunately there wasn't much news there. The ring seemed to lead only to a dead end. She talked about Owen's job and how, as a member of the management team, he had been forced to let some people go because the company was starting to cut back. She brushed Breda's hair, put moisturizer on her face and Vaseline on her lips. She washed her nightgowns and made sure that she had water, even though she wasn't awake to drink it, because she would be thirsty when she came back.

Eamonn always stood just inside the door, leaning against the wall, watching his mum and waiting for a sign. He was quiet, only speaking when he had to answer a question or ask the doctor or nurse for a status report.

Tom came and went, and it was hard for him because, although Kate was kind and Ben's attitude to him had softened, Breda had been the only member of the Walsh family never to blame or suspect him in the loss of

Alexandra. She maintained his tenuous link with the Walshes and, in her absence, he felt like an outsider rather than family but in deference to her he went anyway.

Things had been slightly awkward between Tom and Jane since the kiss but after Kate phoned him with the news about Breda she was the first one he called. Initially she was hesitant: he could hear it in her voice so he didn't beat around the bush.

"Breda has cancer," he said.

"Oh, Tom, I'm so sorry to hear that."

"She's dying."

"Oh, my God!"

"They say she's only got six to eight weeks."

"Oh, Tom, that's awful!"

"I can't believe it."

"I'm so sorry."

"I thought you were fucking sick listening to people say sorry," he said in jest, and all the tension that had built up that night dissolved.

"Let's just leave it at that, shall we?"

"I'd love to."

"What can I do for Breda?"

"Absolutely nothing."

"God, Tom, I really am so sorry to hear that."

"I know – I know you're fond of her."

"Poor Mr Walsh!"

"Are you going to call Ben 'Mr Walsh' till the day you die?"

"Probably." She sighed. "How's Eamonn?"

"Annoyed."

"Nothing new there, then."

"For once I don't blame him."

"I wish I could do something for her," she said.

"Me too."

After that they agreed to meet up for a coffee the next day. Jane put down the phone and Kurt was standing behind her when she turned. "What's going on?" she asked.

"I'd like to ask you the same thing."

"What are you talking about?"

"Dad says he's not welcome here any more. What the hell?"

"He's not and you don't want to know," she said, walking from the sitting room to the kitchen.

"I really do," he said, following her.

"Do you want a coffee?"

"Yes," he said, sitting down.

She boiled the kettle, scooped the coffee into the percolator and stood at the counter, tapping her fingers on it. Kurt waited at the table with his hands in his hair. "Mum?" he said, when the kettle was just about boiled.

"It's complicated."

"I'm not twelve."

She poured the water into the percolator and put the top on, grabbed two cups. She placed the percolator and cups on the table and sat. Kurt leaned back in his chair, opened the fridge door and brought out the milk. "Well?" he said.

"He slept with Elle," she said.

"Elle Moore?"

"Yes."

"Elle, your sister, my aunt?" he said, pointing to her and then to himself.

"Yes."

"What the fuck?"

"Language, Kurt."

"No, seriously, Mum, what the fuck?" Kurt stood up and paced. "Why? Jesus, they don't even like each other that much."

"I don't know."

"When?"

"It doesn't matter."

"It matters."

"Your birthday party."

"Oh, man!" He sat down. "No wonder Dad's been acting strange."

"I'm sorry, Kurt, but I don't want to see him again."

"I know you love him, Mum," Kurt said.

Jane blushed so red she was embarrassed by her embarrassment. Her eyes filled and stung.

"I'm really sorry, Mum."

"Thanks," Jane said, and pulled herself together.

"What about Elle?" He hadn't seen her in well over a week but that didn't mean a thing as she often disappeared for that and longer.

"She's not welcome here either."

"But she lives down the back of the garden."

"And that's where she can stay."

"Okay. What about me?"

"I don't understand the question."

"I hate what they did to you but he's my dad."

"And I don't expect you to take sides," Jane said. "You're an adult now. You're starting college next week. You can still have a great relationship with your dad, just one that doesn't involve me."

"Okay, but I promise I'm going to give him such shit for this."

"I appreciate that," Jane said, and smiled at her son, "and if you throw in a kick in the nuts I'd appreciate that too."

Kurt practised swinging his leg. "Consider it done. And, Mum, he isn't good enough for you."

Jane's eyes filled again. "Thanks, son."

Kurt left the kitchen and Jane sighed and thought that even if she was about to turn thirty-six and she was alone, at least she had Kurt – for a while anyway.

She poured the coffee they hadn't touched down the sink, and when Elle appeared and stared at her through her kitchen window she ducked. *Jesus, Jane, get a grip.* She stood up and left the room.

Since the party Elle had deeply regretted her actions with Dominic. As soon as they were caught their affair was over. There was no discussion, no debate and no goodbye. After Jane vacated Elle's room they had sat in the bed in silence, allowing her words to sink in. They both knew Jane well enough to hear in her voice the hurt and damage they'd caused and they both knew her well enough to understand that she was serious when she said she was done with them. They both realized that in that moment their happy family was no more. Jane was the glue that had held them all together and the glue had become unstuck. Elle got out of bed and got dressed and Dominic followed suit. She walked into her sitting room, closed the door and cuddled on the sofa with her favourite blanket. He left without a word. Since then she had kept out of Jane's way: she'd slept with the love of Jane's life so that was the least she could do.

She missed her in her life instantly. Jane was one of the very few people she talked to every day and Jane took care of her when she was sick, when she was well, when she didn't want her to and when she needed her to. Jane was Elle's world, and without Jane Elle's world was incredibly empty. Four days after Kurt's party Jane sent Elle a business letter ceasing their working arrangement, withdrawing as Elle's agent and providing her with names of other agents and galleries she could work with. Elle was devastated because Jane knew that she was a ditz with business: the end of their working relationship meant Jane was absolutely adamant that she wanted nothing more to do with her. For the first time ever Elle had done something so bad that there was no coming back from it. Jane had been forgiving her all her life but she'd crossed the line.

She told Leslie when she called to her cottage to pick her up for a planned walk in a local park. Leslie wondered if she should nip up to the main house to ask Jane if she wished to join them and Elle broke down into tears.

"What happened?" Leslie said, hands on hips.

"She found us together."

"Oh, no," Leslie said. "You cannot be serious."

"At Kurt's birthday party, here in my bedroom."

"Oh, Elle, you stupid, stupid girl!"

"I know – I know I'm stupid. I'm an idiot, a selfish little liar twisted in the head." She was banging her head hard with her fist, so hard that Leslie had to grab her hand and hold it tight.

"Okay," she said. "Calm down, sit down and stop banging your head."

Elle sat and wrung her hands. "I've really hurt her, Leslie. I've really hurt her."

"She'll get over it. It might not be today or tomorrow but I promise she will get over it."

"She hates me."

"Well, now she needs to, so let her."

"But I can't cope on my own."

"You're twenty-six. In two months you're going to be twenty-seven. You're old enough and capable enough to take care of yourself."

Elle shook her head. "Not without Jane."

"Yes, without Jane," Leslie said, in her strictest voice. "It's time for you to find your own way because, Elle, if you think living down the back of your sister's garden is a permanent arrangement you're wrong. Things change – and if anyone knows that I do."

"Let's walk." Elle got up from her chair, desperate for a new scene and subject.

"Okay." Leslie put on her coat.

Elle walked to the door and stood outside waiting for her.

"Elle," Leslie said.

"Yeah."

"Your coat."

Elle looked at herself and realized she was standing outside in the cold in a T-shirt. "Oh," she said, took it from Leslie and put it on. "Let's go," she said.

Leslie pulled the door shut and wondered whether Elle would truly be lost without Jane.

The first night Elle slept with Dominic she had gone home and into her studio and started painting. The theme was

"Sin" and she used a lot of reds and blacks and purples and there was a girl succumbing to a man with the devil in his eyes. She'd liked it, so as the month and her affair carried on she'd painted more in that style. She hadn't shown them to Jane before she'd received her sister's letter, and afterwards she wasn't sure what she would do or where she would go so she just kept painting. Lori called her two days before the Ken Browne exhibition in Albert's Gallery and asked her if she would be attending.

"I'm barred," she said.

"Don't be an ass. Your sister owns the place."

"She barred me."

"For what?"

"For sleeping with Kurt's dad."

"Christ, Elle, what are you like?"

"A whore, a hussy, a selfish, twisted little bitch."

"It was a rhetorical question," Lori said, "and, besides, you have to come. I'm hearing a lot of good things about this guy and you know Jane is all business – she won't make a scene, not in the gallery."

"Okay," Elle said, "I'll go."

She decided to go for two reasons, the first being that she had heard Ken Browne was an artist worth watching and the second that she hoped Jane would see how sorry she was and find it in her heart to forgive her.

On the evening of the exhibition she met Lori in a pub down the road from the gallery and they had a drink to calm their nerves.

"This is actually quite exciting," Lori said. "There's a whole new edge to the event."

Elle just hoped Jane would be okay with her turning up.

They waited until they knew the gallery would be busy. Jane was rushing around and the artist was talking to patrons and friends, every now and then stopping to have his photo taken. Lori spotted someone she knew and ran off to talk to them, leaving Elle standing alone. She walked over to a painting and stood in front of it for a long time. It was so beautiful it made her want to cry. She stared at the colour on the canvas, the deep browns, the burnt orange, the translucent white against the brightest blue, and what she saw was scorched earth and she could feel the heat, and under the brightest blue sky in her mind's eye she saw a beginning of all things.

The woman beside her was just as taken with the painting. For her it didn't evoke the dawn of creation but it did match her sofa.

Elle moved on to the next and then the next, and every painting spoke to her and told her its story. They were celestial, brave and beautiful. She could hear each voice individually calling to her from the canvas. *This is real art.* The one that had made her want to cry called out: *This is talent. This has heart and soul. You'll never paint like this. You'll never evoke the emotions these paintings evoke. You are a pretender and soon you'll be found out. Without Jane, you're just a jumped-up cartoonist.*

"Shut up," she said.

The woman beside her looked her up and down. "I wasn't talking to you," she said, and walked away.

Jane appeared behind her. "Go home, Elle," she said.

"Please can we talk?"

"I'm working, and even if I wasn't I have nothing to say to you and there is nothing that you can say."

Elle left and Lori didn't notice because she was too busy bowing before Ken Browne.

Elle went home. She walked into her studio and dragged all her finished paintings into the garden. "You're shit," she said. "You're shit, shit, shit! It's all shit!" She piled them high and doused them in whiskey, then lit a match and threw it and the lot went up in flames. She stood watching.

The flames and smoke alerted Kurt and Rose at the same time. Kurt saw his aunt standing far too close to the fire, ran out into the garden and pulled her away from the flames. "Your work! What are you doing to your beautiful work?"

"It's ugly," she said. "It's all so fucking ugly."

Rose walked down the garden, grabbed her hose and trailed it to a point where she could point it and douse the flames. Elle watched her put out the fire while Kurt held her back. When Rose had finished and there was only smouldering wood left she turned to her grandson. "Put Elle to bed, then come in to me and tell me what the hell is going on around here."

Kurt nodded and took Elle into her cottage. Rose made her way to her basement apartment and waited for him to make sense of Elle's latest episode.

The day after Ken Browne's exhibition Rose Moore walked up the steps from her basement to the main house and used her key to get in. Jane was vacuuming the landing upstairs and stopped when she saw Rose. It wasn't feeding time and there was no special reason for Rose to be out of her chair and up in the main house, so she was concerned. "What's wrong?" she said.

Rather than shout up the stairs, Rose ignored her daughter and walked to the kitchen. Jane parked the vacuum, came downstairs and followed her in. "What's wrong?" she repeated.

Rose sat down on one of Jane's kitchen chairs with a groan. "Well, since you asked, *you* are."

"I'm wrong?"

"Yes," Rose said, "you are."

"About what, Rose?" Jane said, in a tone that suggested she wasn't in the mood for her mother's madness.

"You know what your sister's like – she acts before she thinks, she's impetuous, highly charged, a slave to her emotions. That's what makes her so special."

"Sleeping with the father of your sister's child is not special. It's cruel."

"Because of what, Jane? Because you love Dominic? Do you honestly for one moment think that your love for Dominic is real?"

"Yes, I do."

"Bullshit," Rose said. "Dominic was just the best time you ever had, that's all."

"And whose fault is that?" Jane shouted.

"Oh, here we go again! I'm the bad mother who stole your future. I'm the one who made you have a baby and raise him. You're just a victim of my bad decisions."

"I didn't say that."

"You didn't have to – you've said it all before. And maybe if I had my time again I would have considered getting that abortion and maybe I wouldn't. And, yes, I am a bad mother. There, I said it. Are you happy now?"

Jane didn't know what to say. She was shell-shocked so she said nothing.

"I should have been more supportive. I regret that. I did punish you, Jane. I punished you because I was so angry at all that potential lost. I should have helped you more. Especially that time when –"

"Don't say it," Jane said, then sat silently because Rose's apology had taken the wind out of her sails.

"Do you remember when you stopped calling me 'Mum'?" Rose said.

"The day we received Principal Reynolds's letter and you told me I couldn't go back to school."

"No," Rose said, "that was the day you decided to call me Rose but long after that you'd let the word 'Mum' slip once or even twice a day. It used to amuse me because every time you said the M-word you'd almost kick yourself." She stopped, but Jane knew she wasn't finished. Rose moved in her chair and tapped the table twice. "The day you stopped calling me 'Mum' was the day you walked into the police station with Kurt in your arms and asked if they would take either him or you because if they didn't you'd kill him."

"Stop it," Jane said. "You promised we'd never talk about it."

"They took him and you went hysterical so they drove you to hospital and the doctors sedated you."

"I don't want to talk about it!" Jane yelled.

"Social Services were called, and when they asked me if we had any history of depression in the family, I said no."

"So what? I was just tired. His colic was so bad for so long, and he wouldn't stop crying!"

"I lied," Rose said. "My daughter was sedated and my grandson was in the care of social workers and all I could think about was making sure no one found out."

"Found out what?"

"About your dad."

"What about my dad?"

"Oh, Janey, he was so clever – just as you are! Did you know that he was one of the country's top mathematicians? He had such a great mind. Sometimes he was so happy, the life and soul of every party, and everyone loved him, and sometimes he was so sad that he found moving his head hard."

"Why are you telling me this?"

"He didn't have a heart attack, Janey," Rose said. "He hanged himself."

"No."

"He hanged himself with your skipping rope."

"No," Jane said, "you're lying."

"People didn't talk about such things in those days – it just wasn't something you discussed," Rose said, pale and tired. "I blamed you and Elle." She laughed a bitter laugh. "For the longest time I told myself if you hadn't left the bloody skipping rope out he would never have left us, and you were the oldest so you should have known better. Of course that was madness because it wasn't your fault – you were just a little girl."

"Why are you telling me this?"

"I'm telling you because I can't keep making the same mistakes over and over again."

"I don't understand."

"You got your dad's brain. Elle got his temperament."

"What are you saying, Rose?" Jane said angrily.

"I'm saying that when I look at my younger daughter I see her father," Rose said, and tears ran down her face. "I'm saying that you have to forgive her, care for her, protect her from the world and herself the way I should have protected your dad."

Jane stood up and put her hands on her head. "There's nothing wrong with Elle."

Rose stood up and wiped her face with her sleeve. She straightened and took a moment to collect her thoughts. "It's a lot to take in," she said. "I'll leave it with you."

She walked out, leaving her older daughter both gobsmacked and utterly devastated.

Two weeks had passed since they had returned from their holiday and Leslie decided to tell Jim how she felt. She would have sought advice from either Jane or Elle but as they were locked in combat she decided that honesty was the best policy, and if Jim was going to shoot her down it was best he did it before she fell too hard. She put on a cute little vest top and matching briefs that Elle had helped her choose, then slipped on a pretty black cowl-neck jersey dress and some heels. She applied makeup and fixed her pixie haircut. She put on some music and poured wine, and at seven thirty on the dot her doorbell rang.

Jim had brought flowers and she accepted them gratefully. He complimented her on the smell coming from the oven and she didn't tell him it was ready-made lamb tagine that she was simply heating up. She handed him a glass of wine and he sat at the table while she dished up.

"You look nice tonight," he said.

"Thanks," she said. "I bought the dress yesterday."

"Well, it suits you."

She put his plate in front of him and a plate in front of herself and she sat. "Eat up," she said.

"No need to ask twice. I'm starving."

They ate in silence.

"Is there something wrong?" he said.

"No, why do you ask?"

"Well, usually you're giving out about something or someone."

"That's not true," she said, "and anyway you've been here five minutes and you haven't mentioned one single article you've read today."

"Well, now that you mention it, I was reading the details of the government bank guarantee scheme earlier. I tell you, Leslie, people have no idea how close this country came to bankruptcy a few weeks ago. The good times are officially over."

"Oh, don't say that! I've only just started to leave the apartment," she said, and he laughed.

"Well, right about now I think your apartment is the best place to be," he said, and she smiled. She'd forgotten to buy dessert so they enjoyed coffees on the sofa. She was wondering when and how she'd break the news of her love for him when he put his coffee down and fished in his jacket pocket. "I forgot," he said. "I have something I thought you might like to see."

"Oh," she said, and put her coffee on the floor. "What is it?" She didn't notice her cat shove her face into the coffee, lick her lips and turn on her heel, raising her tail high in the air. She was focusing on Jim digging in his pocket.

"Here it is," he said.

"What is it?"

He smoothed it out and handed it to her. "It's a letter from Imelda."

"Imelda. My dead sister, Imelda?"

"One and the same."

"To me?" she said, pointing at herself.

"No, to me but it's about you. Go on – read it."

She opened the letter and part of her wanted to read it and part of her didn't and she was totally thrown. *Why did he bring this tonight?* She began to read it silently.

Dear Jim,

It's time to talk about Leslie. We both know she's stubborn and cut off and we both know why. When I'm gone you'll be all she has left in this world and I know it's a big ask but please look out for her.

She looked up at Jim. "What is this?"

"Just read it," he said.

We've talked about you remarrying and you know I want you to find someone to love and to love you. I want you to have a great new life that doesn't include overcrowded hospitals, dismissive doctors, overworked nurses and cancer. I want you to find someone strong and healthy, someone you can go on an adventure with, someone you can make love to, someone who doesn't cause you anguish and pain. Every time I see your face it hurts because for the first time I see that, in loving you, I've been selfish and I understand why Leslie is the way she is.

"I'm not that person any more," Leslie said. "I'm trying to change. Why are you bringing me back in time like this?"

"Just read on," he said.

Leslie is a better person than me. I know you're probably guffawing at that as you read but it's true. She's watched her entire
family die of cancer, and when we were both diagnosed with
the dodgy gene after Nora's death, she made the decision not
to cause pain to others the way Nora caused pain to John and
Sarah and I'm causing pain to you.

"She's praising me but I was so stupid, so wasteful,"
Leslie said. "She was right. I was wrong."

Before cancer she was smart and funny, kind and caring, and
she still is to me. Without her care I wouldn't have coped. I know
sometimes she calls you names but, trust me, she knows you're
not a monkey, so when she calls you an arse-picker, ignore it
and be kind.

Leslie laughed. "I'd forgotten I used to call you an arse-
picker."
"And I've tried to," he said, and smiled.

I thought she was being defeatist. I thought that we'd suffered
enough as a family and that we'd both survive. So I made plans
and fell in love and for a while we had a great life, but then
that dodgy gene kicked in. Now I see you look almost as ill as
I feel and I realize that my sister Leslie knew exactly what she
was doing when she broke up with Simon and all but closed
off. I watched her disappear from her own life. I thought she
was insane back then but it makes sense now. She put the pain
of others before her own. She watched John and Sarah suffer
after Nora and she'll watch you suffering after me, and,
although she pretends not to like you, she does, and it will hurt
her and it will also confirm for her that she is right to remain
alone, waiting for a diagnosis that may never come.

Suddenly Leslie felt the tide of sadness returning. "She always knew me better than I knew myself," she said.

I'm her last family and friend. She hasn't even let herself get to know her niece so when I'm gone she'll have no one and that haunts me. Please go and live your life but all I ask is that every now and again, no matter how rude or uninviting she may seem, call to her, talk to her, be her friend even if she fails to be yours, because she has been there for me, for Mum, for Dad and Nora, and I can't stand the idea that after everything she's been through she should live or die alone.

Leslie put her hand to her mouth. She looked from the letter to Jim and back to the letter. She shook her head. "This is why you're nice to me," she said. "It's because Imelda asked you to. You don't have any feelings for me. You have feelings for her. I'm so stupid."

Jim looked confused. "I just found the letter. I thought you'd like to know how your sister felt about you, that's all."

"Well, now I know," she said, "and I'm actually quite tired so, if you wouldn't mind, I'd like to say goodnight."

"We were having a nice time," he said, startled and dismayed. "I shouldn't have given you the letter."

"No," she said, "I'm really glad you did. It's cleared something up for me, so thanks and goodnight."

Jim was standing outside Leslie's apartment with the door slammed in his face before he had time to work out what had happened and it was only when he was halfway home that realization dawned: Leslie had totally misread his intentions.

*

Leslie took the letter to bed, lay with her cat and read the last piece:

I know I say it all the time, and in all my little notes and letters about this and that, but time is running out and I need you to know that it's been a privilege to be your wife and, although I feel selfish for all the pain I've caused you, I know I've brought happiness too so hang on to that and forgive me because, even knowing what I know now, I'd love and marry you again. I suppose Leslie would say I was a selfish truffle-sniffer but I can die with that.

Yours,
Imelda

Leslie let the letter drop from her hand and closed her eyes. *I'm such a fool. Jim has no real interest in me. And why would he want me anyway? I'm half a woman. I'm such a silly, silly fool.*

Tom opened the door and was surprised to see Jane, red-eyed and tearful. "Are you alone?" she said.
"Yes."
"Good."
"Why?"
"Because I want you to take me to bed," she said.
"Jane, I think you need to –"
"Are we friends?"
"You know we are."
"So please do what I ask and take me to bed."
He nodded, led her upstairs, kissed her mouth and took off her coat. He removed his shirt and unbuttoned her blouse, kissed her neck, and when his face was wet from her tears he took her over to the bed and sat her down. He

handed her a pillow to hug and asked her what was wrong. Jane told him about the time when Kurt was fourteen months and he hadn't stopped crying in a week and everything she'd tried hadn't worked and she'd thought she was losing her mind and she'd hated him with a real, palpable, seething hatred and wondered about killing him more than once, she was so tired. Even when her eyes were black and she was zombie-like and skin and bone, not once had her mother relieved her. Not once did she pick up the baby and tell her that it was okay, that she'd take care of him while Jane got some much-needed sleep. Not once did she offer to babysit so that Jane could go out with her friends, and not once did she tell her that everything would be all right.

Jane told Tom about that day when she'd walked into the police station with her son. "I wouldn't have hurt him," she said. "I just needed someone to help me."

"Ah, Jane," he said, and he took her into his arms.

He lay down on his bed and she lay on his chest and she told him about what Rose had said about her dad and Elle. "I should have known Dad didn't have a heart attack. I'm so stupid."

"You couldn't have."

"And Elle – Rose has always been so protective of her and it used to drive me insane. I made one mistake and she punished me for years. Elle messes up time and time again, and Rose always finds a way of making what she's done seem normal and okay when all the time she knows it isn't – and I should have known. How could I have been so blind?"

"Because Elle seems perfectly fine. If you ask me, she's just a little selfish and a little spoilt."

"No," Jane said. "She disappears for weeks and weeks.

She's so exuberant sometimes and at others she's so pensive, so sad."

"We all get like that – it's called life."

"Then there was China."

"What about China?"

"She was in Hong Kong with her boyfriend. They were in some club and they had a big fight. He told her he wanted their relationship to end, that he wasn't happy any more and that it was over. He was flying home the next day. Right after that there was an accident. Elle was hit by a car and ended up in a coma for two days. By the time I got there she'd woken up, but she'd broken her left leg and arm. She was fine but it scared the life out of us. Vincent – that was her boyfriend – was sitting by her bed and so attentive I thought they were still love's young dream but one day when we were getting coffee he told me about their fight and that she'd jumped out in front of the car on purpose."

"And you didn't believe him."

"She swore she hadn't seen the car."

"So you believed her."

Jane nodded. "Who jumps in front of cars?" She was crying again. "I should have known. After all, her father hanged himself with a skipping rope and me, well, Jesus, I threatened to kill my own child."

"You were just crying out for help."

"And what was she doing?"

"I don't know," he said.

She raised her head and looked at him. "How does it feel not to be the most messed-up person in the room?"

"Pretty good." He smiled at her and wiped away a stray tear.

"Well, that's something, then," she said, and he leaned in and kissed her, and they made love twice before they fell into a sound sleep.

Elle answered her front door expecting it to be her mother, who had been up and down to her cottage harassing her since Jane had stopped talking to her.

Jane was standing there, pulling her coat in close to her chest. "Can we talk?" she said.

"Yes, please."

Jane closed the door behind her and, for the first time in her life, she had no idea what she was going to say to her sister.

Chapter 15

Happy Death

A happy death is all I want,
to feel that I have loved someone
and did the things I said I'd do
and lived my life true.

Jack L, *Universe*

November 2008

Breda died on a Tuesday morning at nine o'clock. She was alone. Her husband was in the toilet next door and the rest of her family were in traffic. Eamonn arrived ten minutes after she was pronounced dead, with Frankie running in two seconds later, panting and in need of oxygen. Kate followed within five minutes. But it was too late. Their wife and mother was gone.

"She waited until I left the room," Ben said. "Your mother never liked to make a fuss."

Kate hugged him. "I know, Dad."

She took Ben outside and Eamonn sat with Breda for a while. All the pain was gone from her face, all the ravages of time melted away. Her spirit had moved on and she looked thirty years younger than she was.

"Are you with Alexandra, Mam?" Eamonn said. "Is that

why you had to go?" He left soon after and Breda's body lay in silence.

Tom got off the phone from Kate and rang Jane. "Breda's gone," he said.

"What can I do?"

"Come to the funeral."

"Oh, I don't know." If she hadn't slept with Tom she wouldn't have had a problem with it, but now attending his mother-in-law's funeral seemed in bad taste.

"She liked you."

"Making me feel worse."

"Please come," he said, and Jane knew he badly needed the back-up.

"Okay," she agreed, and hung up.

Kurt came in, threw his bag down in the hallway and stormed into his room. Jane followed him and knocked at his door. "Go away," he said.

"What's wrong?"

"I just want to be left alone."

"Okay."

She walked down the hall and into the kitchen.

"Jane! Jane! Jane! Jane, it's your mother! Jane!"

She pressed the button. "Yes, Rose."

"Come down."

"I'm busy."

"I want to talk to you."

"I haven't time."

"Five minutes."

"You have two."

300

Jane sat on her mother's sofa and Rose poured herself a large glass of wine.

"What did Dr Griffin say?" Rose asked.

Jane had made an appointment to see him in his surgery the previous day. She had waited for a good half an hour because it was flu season and a few times she thought about bolting. When his receptionist told her to go in her feet had felt like blocks of cement and she had had to drag herself to his door.

Dr Griffin smiled at her and she sat down. "What can I do for you, Jane?"

"You can tell me how my father died."

He sat back in his chair, looked at his hands and rubbed his knuckles. "When did she tell you?"

"Twelve days ago. I can give you the hour and the minute too if you'd like."

"I'm sorry, Jane. It must have been a shock."

"You could say that," Jane said. "Why have you never told me?"

"It's not my place, Jane, you know that."

"You were there. You saw him. Rose said you took him down." Tears were welling but she was refusing to let them fall.

"Your dad had a lot of demons."

"And Elle? Does Elle have demons, Dr Griffin?"

He sat up. "What do you mean, Jane?"

Although Dr Griffin had been the Moore family's general practitioner for years, the family member he had had least contact with was Elle. In fact, the last time he had seen her with any kind of ailment she had been twelve so, as far as

Dr Griffin was concerned, Elle was as fit as a flea.

"Rose thinks Elle is like my father."

"In what way?"

"Temperament."

He laughed. "Well, that's natural. We all inherit aspects of our parents. You are sometimes like Rose."

"I am not!" Jane said, with the greatest alarm.

"The last time I was in your house you threatened to kill her."

"That was just talk."

"Yes, but familiar talk," Dr Griffin said. "Just because some of Elle's behaviour is reminiscent of her father doesn't mean there is a problem."

"She stole her boyfriend's car and burned it out. Then she packed her bags and disappeared for a while. She often disappears – she puts a sign on her door to tell us that she's gone fishing and we just wait for her to come back. Sometimes it's days, sometimes weeks. She drinks a lot. Two years ago she nearly overdosed on cocaine and after that she promised faithfully she wouldn't do it again. A few months ago my son found her in a freezing cold bath – she was blue. She said she'd fallen asleep. She throws money away. She has sex with stranger after stranger, and recently she had an affair with Kurt's dad yet for years she barely tolerated him. Sometimes she behaves like there's no tomorrow and other times she acts as though she can see eternity laid out before her and she can't stand it. She lives her life according to a letter she writes once a year to the bloody Universe. And then there was China."

After Jane had finished telling Dr Griffin about the incident in China he was adamant that Elle needed to be referred to a psychiatrist who specialized in diagnosing the kind of condition he suspected Elle suffered from.

"Rose doesn't want that," Jane said.

"Rose shouldn't have a say."

"She said it was only when doctors got involved that Dad hanged himself."

"Your dad was very sick and, no, he didn't get the help he needed but times have changed and I promise you that if you get Elle to agree to see someone it will help – maybe not immediately but it will help."

"I'm scared."

"That's perfectly normal."

"How could I have been so blind?"

"Because we see what we want to see."

"Vincent tried to warn me," Jane said. "All the times I called him names and thought he was shallow and stupid, and he was the only one who really saw her."

"It's easier when you're on the outside."

"I don't know what to do."

"Talk to her."

"And say what? Hi, Elle, we think you're insane?"

"No, Jane, talk to her, listen to her, tell her that you care."

"Oh, yeah, thanks, she'll love that, bearing in mind she threw a shoe at my TV the one time Dr Phil was on. The off/on button still sticks."

Now Jane sat in Rose's basement apartment and they debated what Jane should and shouldn't say to her sister for more than an hour. Rose was adamant that no doctor go near her girl. "They only make it worse, Jane," she said, "and you're so good with her."

"I can't be responsible for her mental wellbeing, Rose."

Rose slapped her thigh. "Which is exactly why I didn't say anything before. You had enough on your plate. Bloody Dominic! The first time I saw his snivelling face I should have knocked his bloody teeth out. He wouldn't have been so cute then."

"You know, Elle isn't the only one with mental problems in this house." Jane stood up and walked out of the door.

"Darling, we're all mad – you, me, stupid bloody Dominic, precious Tom, that poor titless woman, the woman next door, Paddy the postman. There isn't one of us that someone hasn't thought mad at least once."

"Yeah, well, this madwoman is going upstairs."

"Just talk to her. Just be good to her!" Rose shouted, as Jane was closing her front door. *Please mind her, Janey – please don't let them take her, because when they come, it only gets worse.*

The funeral took place on the Friday. Leslie made her way to Jane's and arrived in time to see Kurt running down the steps with toast in his mouth. "Hi, Kurt," she said.

"Hi, Wezwee."

I've been called worse, she thought.

He left the door swinging open for her so she walked inside and called Jane. Jane came down the stairs in black. Leslie looked at Jane and then at herself. She was wearing red. "Is this inappropriate?" she asked.

"No, you're fine."

"Are you sure? We were never particular about wearing black at family funerals but other people are funny about it, aren't they?"

"You're fine." She looked up the street outside for Kurt

but he was gone. "I missed Kurt," she said, following Leslie into the kitchen. "Did he look okay?"

"He was running and spoke with his mouth full – so if that's okay?"

"Irene broke up with him."

"Oh," Leslie said. "I'm sorry to hear that. I know you were fond of her."

"Yeah, well, I'm fonder of my son. I'm actually a bit pissed off with her, which is stupid and childish, I know. He's devastated."

"He didn't look devastated."

"Well, he is. She told him he studies too much, if you can believe that."

"They're young, and young people break up all the time." Leslie poured herself a coffee.

"And I wouldn't mind but he doesn't study that much at all," said Jane. "Obviously more than when he was in school but this is university – and medicine, for God's sake! What did she expect?"

"Jane, are you taking Kurt's break-up a little worse than he is?"

"No. Maybe. I don't know. He won't talk to me about it."

"I don't blame him."

Jane poured herself a coffee and sat with Leslie. "I slept with Tom."

Leslie spluttered, and coffee dribbled down her chin. Jane handed her a tea-towel and she dried her face. Jane took it back, aimed for the washing basket behind her and landed the shot.

"Tom, the husband of the woman we're looking for, that Tom?" Leslie said.

"That Tom."

"I don't know how to feel about that."

"Me neither. I really like him but I don't know if it's because I actually really like him or that I like him because he's unavailable. If my history's anything to go by, it's probably the latter. And then there is the fact that he's married to my childhood best friend, who he loves and is missing. And, if I'm honest, I think she's dead."

"Hah!" Rose shouted, from the doorway. "I knew you thought she was dead all along."

"Rose," Jane said, "have you ever heard of knocking?"

Rose sat down beside Leslie. "How are you feeling?" she said, pointing at Leslie's chest.

"Fine."

"You're so brave," Rose said. "I would rather have died."

Leslie laughed, and Jane silently thanked God for her friend's good humour.

Rose was going to the funeral even though she hadn't laid eyes on the Walshes in twenty years. Jane had attempted to talk her out of it but she was determined to pay her last respects to the woman who had taken her daughter on holiday on many occasions in the eighties.

"But you didn't like her," Jane argued. "You thought she was a holier-than-thou, pain-in-the-arse Bible-basher."

"Jane," Rose said, "that really is no way to talk about the dead."

Jane gave up. Rose was in good form because she loved a good funeral.

"Where's Elle?" Leslie asked.

"She's making her own way."

"I'm really glad you've made up," Leslie said. "She was lost without you."

"Do you hear that, Jane?" Rose said. "She was lost without you."

"Shut up, Rose."

"Darling, if you think you're going to bag a man with that kind of attitude you're wrong. I mean, I know Tom's standards aren't particularly high and he has a penchant for cheeky little cows, but maybe if you toned it down just a tad you'd have better luck."

Jane groaned. "Just go to the car."

They got to the church on time. Jane sat at the back but Rose walked halfway up the aisle because she didn't want a pillar blocking her view. Elle joined Leslie and June. The atmosphere between Elle and Jane was a little strained. Although Jane had forgiven her, Elle wasn't sure why and Jane had decided against explaining her reasoning. Instead she had merely said that blood was thicker than water and that if Elle wanted her to represent her artwork she would, as long as she promised not to set it on fire again.

"I promise," Elle said.

"Why did you do it?" Jane asked.

"It wasn't good."

"You didn't have to burn it, Elle."

Elle stayed quiet for a while. "Do you really forgive me, Janey?" she then asked.

"Yes."

"Don't you want to hear an explanation?"

"No."

"I'm really sorry."

"I know."

Jane left then because she'd felt awkward and still angry and she needed to talk to Dr Griffin before she spoke to her sister openly and honestly. And since she'd spoken to Dr Griffin she'd been biding her time, delaying the inevitable. Jane wasn't ready to face the possibility that Elle had a problem, so how could Elle do so?

They sat quietly waiting for the church to fill and the Mass to begin. In the front pew Ben Walsh was on the outside and beside him was Kate, her arm linked in his. Next in line was Eamonn, then his wife Frankie, Kate's husband Owen, and Tom at the end. There was little or no talking among the main mourners.

Rose got up out of her seat and made her way back to where her daughters and Leslie were sitting. "Push in," she said.

"What are you doing?" Jane whispered.

"It's no fun on your own," she said.

Elle grinned and pushed in.

"Push in a bit further," Rose demanded, so that her view would be uninterrupted. They all pushed in for Rose. She sat in and looked around. "You'd think for such a Holy Joe she'd have a few more to her funeral."

"Mum," Elle said, "don't be such a cow."

"Sorry, darling."

The priest came out and everyone stood, bar Rose. "You won't catch me standing for one of those arrogant church bastards," she whispered.

For the next forty minutes the priest talked and read the same old passages from the Bible that they always read when a person died, they said prayers, knelt, stood, sat, knelt, stood and sat, and then knelt, stood and sat some more. Leslie, Elle and Jane got up and queued to receive Holy Communion. Rose sat where she was. "You won't catch me taking Communion from one of those arrogant church bastards," she whispered. After Communion and before the priest gave the last blessing he invited Breda's family to come up to the altar and talk about her. Ben couldn't find it in him to speak because it was all he could do to stand. Eamonn got up, walked onto the altar and took a second or two to compose himself.

"This is the good bit," Rose said.

Leslie, Elle and Jane ignored her.

Eamonn cleared his throat. "I'd like to thank everyone for coming here today. My mother would have been really pleased with the turnout."

Rose looked around with a face on her which suggested that if Breda would be impressed she certainly wasn't.

"My mother was a good person. She was kind, caring, giving, friendly, happy most of the time. She wasn't jealous or boastful, she wasn't selfish and she wasn't hurtful. She believed in God. She believed in prayer and she came here nearly every day of her life until recently. Most of you know we lost Alexandra in June 2007. My mother believed that God would save her. She believed that He would bring her home. 'She's still with us, Eamonn,' she'd say. 'She'll be home any day, any day now. God will deliver her from evil.' When God didn't deliver her from evil my mother got so sad and so sick that it made me angry about all the time she'd wasted here on her knees. But then I thought, What if God couldn't deliver Alexandra because Alexandra was already gone? What if the pain and suffering of my mother's loss was so great that instead of delivering Alexandra from evil

He delivered my mother instead? Who knows what's real and what isn't? My mother took comfort in believing in a God who could hear her, and I may not be the most religious of people but today of all days and for her sake I'd like to think He did. Thank you."

Elle was crying and Jane squeezed her hand. "That was lovely," Elle said.

Leslie was silent but nodded in agreement. Rose blew her nose.

Jane, Leslie and Elle joined the queue to sympathize with the family.

Jane sympathized with Owen, then Frankie and Eamonn. "That was really lovely," she said.

"Thanks. I hope she would have liked it," Eamonn said.

"She would have loved it."

Eamonn hugged her. "Every time I see you I think of Alexandra. I miss her, Janey."

"I know you do, Eamonn," Jane said, and her eyes filled. "I miss her too." She moved on to Kate, who hugged her and thanked her for coming, and then to Ben, whose blue eyes were swimming. "I'm so sorry, Mr Walsh."

"Thanks, Jane."

She reached Tom and shook his hand, but he drew her into a hug and they held each other tightly – so much so that Kate and Frankie both noticed. Frankie smiled at them. Jane pulled back. "I'll see you in the graveyard," she said, and Tom nodded.

Elle and Leslie were following and shaking hands and Kate reminded Ben that Elle was the girl who had painted all the pictures of the Missing and that Leslie had been behind the findingalexandra website.

"Thank you, girls, thank you so much."

They both nodded and told them how sorry they were.

It was odd but all three women, Jane, Elle and Leslie, felt like they weren't just at Breda's funeral but that they were at Alexandra's too. They discussed it in the car on the way to the graveyard. Leslie was the first to bring it up but the two others were quick to agree. Rose congratulated herself on being the only one who had worked out the woman was dead a long time ago.

"We're not saying she's dead, Rose," Jane said.

"Oh, fine, Jancy — the funeral felt like it was for both Alexandra and Breda and yet you're not saying you think she's dead. Are you in the habit of burying the living?"

They arrived at the graveyard, parked the car and followed the crowd to the plot that would be Breda's final resting place. As they walked in line the heavens opened and heavy rain fell, drenching them all in seconds.

"Oh, for fock's sake!" Rose said, and Jane nudged her.

They walked from grave to grave under a dark and forbidding sky.

Eamonn stood over his mother's grave, soaked to the skin, and he told the crowd who were gathering around him and his family that his father had chosen the casket his mother would rest in, Kate had chosen the flowers, he'd chosen the readings and the music would be chosen by Alexandra. "She loved Jack Lukeman and this is one of her favourite songs. I know my mother would like it and it seems appropriate. It's called 'Rooftop Lullaby'." He nodded at Owen who pressed play on the CD player and everybody stood in silence. Eamonn dropped his head and stared at the coffin in the ground.

"Mother, is there something in the sky?
Something up there that they hide,
a jewel for me and you,
apple trees with falling fruit."

Kate held an umbrella over her father's head.

"Oh Daughter, now I don't know
but I believe that its beauty's beyond words,
it's like a tune that I can't sing
but I've heard it sung by birds.
It's a rooftop lullaby
falling from the sky
sends us to sleep tonight.
It's the apple in your eye
keeps you as sweet as pie,
dreaming through the night."

Kate's husband Owen held his umbrella over her.

"Oh Father, now won't you tell me
if you know where does half the moon go
when it's not up in the sky
it disappears before my eyes."

Ben Walsh stood in silence, looking into the middle
distance, unable to bring himself to look at the box that
held his wife beneath him.

"Oh my son, why does morning break each day
why do people pass away?"

The rain continued to fall on the people gathered in the graveyard and the people outside walking by and trying to get on with their day. It fell in the cities and the suburbs. It fell by the coast and it fell on the mountains ... and under a dark sky, under dead foliage and in a forgotten part of the Dublin mountains, the rain fell so heavily that the earth slid and moved, and under that dark sky, dead foliage and in that forgotten part of Dublin's mountains, a high-heeled black boot poked through.

> *"Oh it's the mystery in truth*
> *it's the innocence in youth*
> *or a rooftop lullaby*
> *falling from the sky*
> *sends us to sleep tonight,*
> *it's the apple in your eye*
> *keeps you as sweet as pie*
> *dreaming through the night."*

Chapter 16

I Ain't Crazy

Life's a little mystery waiting to be solved,
questions they come pouring down with a little pinch of salt,
forever poised to conquer, forever poised to fall
but every time I close my eyes I hear these voices call.

Jack L, *Metropolis Blue*

December 2008

Leslie had successfully avoided Jim for a month when eventually, through his tenacity and refusal to take no for an answer, she gave in and met him for a walk. They walked in silence engaging in a little small-talk, and when they found a little bench by a bandstand they sat watching a young band play to a small group of their teenage friends. Jim told her that he had gone home and felt very stupid the night he had given her Imelda's letter. He further explained that it was not his intention to suggest that the only reason he was in Leslie's life was because his dead wife had asked him to be. Jim hadn't considered for a moment that Leslie would jump to that conclusion but now he felt a bit of a fool for not considering the possibility. His intention had been to show Leslie how brave she was and how proud her sister would have been to see her not only surviving but living. He wanted her to know how happy seeing her surviving and living made him. He wanted her to know that he cared for her.

"But you don't love me," Leslie said quietly.

"I think that I do," he said.

"But?" Leslie said, sensing the word was coming.

"But you've just gone through a massive life-changing operation."

"It's been more than four months."

"That's no time."

"You think I'm using you," she said.

"No," he said. "I would never think that."

"You think we could never have anything because you belong to Imelda," she said.

"No," he said, shaking his head. "I let Imelda go a long time ago."

"But you never remarried," she said.

"Because the relationships I had didn't work out. Age, distance, incompatibility – there were a million and one other reasons that had nothing to do with Imelda."

"Do you think you could really love me?" Leslie asked.

"I do," he said.

"So?"

"So I'm scared. Are you really ready for love?"

"I am," she said.

"Don't just say that, think about it."

"I have."

"Please, think about it again."

"Why?"

"Because I survived losing one Sheehan. I don't think I could survive losing two."

"I'm ready. I'm ready for you. If you'll have me?" she

315

said, and he smiled, showing his dimples, and he kissed her right there on a bench in front of ten teenagers nodding to the worst rock band in the free world.

It was Christmas week, which was always Elle's favourite time of year. She loved spending time in town, walking among the hordes of shoppers and the dancing lights and beautiful window displays. She liked the big twinkling trees and the *faux* snow and the cold crisp air that reddened her nose.

She'd felt strangely contented since she'd spoken with Jane after Breda's funeral. Jane had driven them home and, when her mother had gone for a nap having nearly drunk the Walshes out of house and home, Jane had made her way to Elle's cottage and they had sat and talked. Jane told Elle about their father and what he had done, and contrary to Jane's reaction, Elle's was considered and calm because to Elle her father's actions made perfect sense.

Then Jane approached Elle about her own mental well-being.

"You think there's something wrong with me?" Elle said, and laughed.

"I don't know," Jane admitted, "but when I think about things you've done I worry."

"Like what?"

"You disappear for weeks without a word."

"I'm in my late twenties, I live in my sister's back garden, I'm an artist who requires inspiration, and sometimes I just need to get away."

"You sleep around with God knows who – it's not safe."

"That makes me a slut, not insane."

"You nearly froze to death in the bath."

"Because I was stoned off my face."

"You burned out Vincent's car."

"I remember you saying at the time that you would have done the same thing."

"Yeah, but I didn't mean it. What about the time you rescued all those dogs from pounds around Dublin and couldn't care for them?"

"Okay, I was pretty over-zealous but I dare you to go into one of those places and not want to save all the dogs."

"You give away too much money."

"Because I have it and I don't need it."

"You don't have that much and in case you hadn't noticed the world has changed in the last year. Money isn't falling from the sky any more."

"Okay," Elle said. "I'll be more careful."

"You burned your beautiful work."

"It wasn't good. I just couldn't look at it any more."

"What about China?"

"Ah, Jane, it was an accident."

"Vincent swears it wasn't."

"Vincent is a liar."

"He said you could not have missed seeing that car."

"Jane, I was upset, I was crying, it was raining and I didn't see the car. I need glasses, not psychiatric care."

Jane stayed silent and thought about everything her sister had made light of.

"I'm just a dick. I'll change. I'll grow up," Elle promised.

"Are you sure there's nothing you're not telling me? Because, Elle, sometimes you look so sad."

"We all get sad."

"I know, but —"

"But I'm fine."

"You'll come to me if that changes?"

"Absolutely," Elle said, and saluted her.

"Okay."

And since that conversation Jane and Elle had been on really good terms. The incident with Dominic was all but forgotten and Elle felt a strange lightness, like a weary passenger who knows her journey will soon end.

She made her way through town, buying the best and most expensive presents she could think of. In Brown Thomas she bought a sound system for Kurt that cost more than three grand. She went into Weir's and bought her sister a pair of diamond earrings valued at five grand. She bought her mother a necklace that cost four grand. She bought Leslie the most beautiful silk dress, then had it boxed and paid for it to be delivered on Christmas Eve. She bought Tom an antique desk because it was the kind of thing she thought he'd like, and even though her sister didn't know and he didn't know whether or not they were a couple, they would be some day. She even bought Dominic something: a set of golf clubs and a bag far superior to the ones he'd been using since his twenties. Now that his bank was being bailed out by the government and he was facing possible redundancy, he'd have plenty of time to use them.

Leslie was waiting for her in the restaurant. They hugged warmly and sat. Once they had ordered, Leslie updated Elle on her love life.

"I told you so," Elle said.

"Nobody likes the Told You So Person."

"So, when is he moving in?" Elle asked, knowing it would irk Leslie.

"About a quarter past never," Leslie said. "Living together? For God's sake, Elle!" She shuffled in her seat. "We haven't even slept together yet."

"You are joking?"

"We're taking it slowly."

"Yeah, but, Leslie, there's moving slowly and then there's going back in time."

"It's a big deal for me."

"I know."

Leslie sighed. "I still feel . . . 'Ugly' is the wrong word . . ."

"Mangled?"

"No."

"Butchered?"

"No, but thanks for bringing that up."

"Unfeminine?"

"Yes," Leslie said, "unfeminine."

"Well," Elle said, "you are sitting here beautifully made up, with your copper pixie hair perfectly coiffed, you've got your finger and toenails manicured and painted, and you're wearing a beautiful jersey dress to the knee that shows off your great legs, which are finished off with a pair of black high heels. When I first met you, you were a human condom in bad shoes. Trust me when I say that you're far more feminine now than you were then."

Leslie smiled because Elle was right. They were halfway through their main course when she told Elle that she and Jim were talking about going to Florida for Christmas. "What do you think?" she asked.

"That you should do what makes you happy."

"Then I think I should go."

"Brilliant," Elle said. "I'm so happy for you and I'm

319

proud of you. You're a fighter, Leslie. Not all of us are."

Leslie left the restaurant an hour later. Briefly she thought about Elle's demeanour and it dawned on her that her friend seemed altered – calmer, more considered, happier, resigned, even – but then Jim waved at her from across the street and she forgot about Elle.

When Elle got home she took great care to ensure that her presents were wrapped perfectly. She took time writing the cards as she wanted everyone she loved to know how much she loved them. She put them under the tree that Jane had made Kurt carry in from the car. Earlier Elle had got out her box of decorations and she and Jane had gone through them. Jane pulled out the papier-mâché angel she had made when she was ten. "I can't believe you still have this," she said, looking at it.

"I love it," Elle said, taking it from her.

"It's horrible."

"It's lovely. It's just too broken – it keeps falling off the tree."

"So bin it," Kurt said.

"No," Elle had said, and she'd placed it carefully back into the box.

Rose had knocked on the door and before Elle yelled, "Come in!" she was sitting on a chair directing Kurt as to where to put the figurine of Joseph Elle always insisted on hanging on the tree. "A bit higher than that – after all, he put up with an awful lot."

Kurt wasn't looking forward to Christmas Day as he was back with Irene and she was determined they spend Christmas with her mother. During crisis talks Kurt had promised to make more time for his girlfriend so he couldn't back out of her mother's invitation to Christmas lunch without being accused of welshing on their agreed terms.

"Just dump her," Rose said, with her usual tact.

"I love her, Gran. I don't want to lose her." Then he added, with an ironic twist of the mouth, "At least, not until I'm over second year."

Jane laughed. "That's your idea of love?"

"You know what I mean," he said, placing a bauble on the tree.

"No," Jane said, "I don't."

"Yeah, well, Mum, when it comes to love you're hardly the greatest example."

"Thank you, son. Happy Christmas."

Elle looked around at her family. Her mother sipping from a mug pretending it was tea. Her sister and her nephew engaging in good-natured sniping. Her little cottage was lit up, full of Christmas cheer, and Elle felt content. When they left she went for a nap and when she closed her eyes she saw her father hanging from the rafters of his home office and, under him, herself sitting on the floor playing with her dolls. She looked up to watch him swing and when he stopped she tipped him so that he'd swing again. She had been seeing this image since Jane had told her about their dad. Every time she was alone, eyes open or closed, she saw the same image. In her head she heard him crying and gasping, struggling, gurgling and dying.

I'm sorry, Dad, I should have known but I know what to do now. You won't be alone any more. I'm so sorry you waited so long. I'll see you soon.

Then she fell asleep.

*

Since they had slept together that one time, Tom and Jane had not defined their relationship and neither of them was in a particular rush to do so. They didn't talk about having sex and were able to put it to the back of their minds so that they could still be friends. They behaved as if that night had never happened. It was Frankie who broached the subject with Tom one day when she met him in the fruit section of the local supermarket they shared.

"It was nice of Jane to come to Breda's funeral," she said.

"She was fond of her," he said.

"She's fonder of you than Breda."

"Oh, Frankie, please don't."

"You like one another," Frankie said, "and that's a good thing."

"And what about Alexandra?"

"Let's get a coffee," she said.

They dropped their baskets and went to the coffee shop next door. When they were sitting with coffees in hand Frankie made the point to her brother-in-law that she had long been dying to make. "You need to move on."

"Easy for you to say."

"It's not easy for any of us to say. We all loved Alexandra but, Tom, it's been a year and a half – you know the statistics, and you know what the liaison officer has said time and time again."

"People are found all the time," he said, but without his old conviction.

"Bullshit. Wake up and get off the sofa. You're wasting your life. Start up your company again or start up another or go to college or travel the world or buy a fish shop or join the monks, but do something, Tom, something other than chasing a ghost." And while she was waiting for his response she bit down on her muffin so hard she caught her tongue. "Ouch! I keep doing that."

"I do like Jane," Tom said, after Frankie had composed herself.

"Good."

"No," he said, "not good."

"Why is it not good?"

"Because I don't know if I could ever love her."

"Well, of course you don't. The first few years Eamonn and I were together I wasn't sure that I even liked him, let alone loved him."

"Finding Alexandra will always be at the back of my mind."

"The back of your mind is better than the front."

"If only I knew what happened," he said.

"We might never know."

"How's Ben?" he asked, changing the subject.

"Good days and bad days," she said. "He's staying with Kate and you should visit."

"I don't want to intrude."

"You're family."

"Not any more," he said, and she didn't argue because since Breda had died it was hard not to feel that Tom's final link with the Walshes had been truly severed.

When he returned home he picked up a message from Jane: "Hi, Tom, Jane here, just wanted to invite you to Christmas dinner. I've got a huge turkey. Rose and Elle will be there but please don't hold that against me. Kurt is now going to Irene's so there will be plenty of food and we'd love to see you."

Tom sat on his sofa and thought about what he was

doing with his life, what he wanted, what he didn't want, where he would go, what he would do, and he didn't have one answer to any of those questions. The only question he didn't have trouble answering was yes to Christmas dinner with the Moores. *Where else would I go?*

Leslie and Jim didn't make it to Florida. Leslie became sick with a very nasty flu that necessitated her staying in bed for the duration of the holiday. Because she woke up with the flu on the morning they were due to fly out she didn't bother to tell anyone she was staying at home. Jim moved in to care for her and she spent most of the first two days asleep. She woke long enough to have some of the Christmas dinner he had made, but she was miserable, shaking and sweating like a pig, so she was put back into bed and was asleep again within half an hour. Jim spent the day with Leslie's cat, eating chocolates, drinking beer and watching classic films. It was his favourite way to spend Christmas anyway.

Elle and Rose were already at the table when Tom arrived. He had brought a few bottles of wine and a large Christmas pudding. He and Jane kissed each other on the cheek at the door and then he followed her into the kitchen.

"Rose," he said, leaned in and kissed her.

"Tom," she said.

"I have something for you," he said, and handed her a very expensive bottle of wine.

She instantly recognized it for its taste and worth. "Tom, you shouldn't have," she said, holding it with a vicelike grip.

"It was the least I could do. Elle, this is for you." He

handed her a book on meditation. "Apparently it's the new cool thing to be doing," he said.

"Thanks," she said.

"Jane, this is for you." He handed her a box with a ribbon.

"But you've already given me wine and a pudding!"

"Open it," he said.

She did so, and it was a round-the-world itinerary. "What's this?"

"I was thinking it was time I saw the world and I was wondering if you'd like to come with me."

Elle and Rose stayed silent while Jane gawped at the itinerary. "I can't," she said. "I'd love to but I can't."

"Why not?" Elle said.

"I have responsibilities," she said.

"I think you should go," Elle said.

Rose stayed quiet.

"It's not today or tomorrow," he said. "I don't even know when I'll go myself but I just want you to know that if I do go I'd really like you to come with me."

Jane smiled and Elle nudged Rose, whose face remained frozen.

"Well, that's a lovely gesture," Jane said, and just as she was kissing his cheek for a second time the doorbell rang.

Jane answered, wondering who was calling to her house during Christmas lunch. It was Dominic. "What do you want?"

"Just to see Kurt," he said.

"Kurt's in Irene's," Jane said, closing the door.

"Janey," he said, holding the door, "please forgive me – it's Christmas Day."

"You are something else!"

"I know," he said. "But I miss you, I miss Kurt, I miss Elle but not sleeping with her, I miss this house, I miss our odd little family – Jesus, I must be losing my mind because I even miss Rose."

"I heard that!" Rose shouted from the kitchen.

"Come in," Jane said.

Dominic followed her into the kitchen and she set a place for him at the table. Tom stood up and shook his hand.

"Nice to see you again, Tom."

"It's nice to see you," Tom said.

"Elle, it's good to see you," Dominic said.

"You too, Dominic."

"Rose," Dominic said.

"Dominic," Rose said. "I'd better be careful what I drink today or you might try to throw the leg over me too."

"Well, you watching what you drink would certainly make a nice change."

Jane served dinner and they all ate happily. Afterwards the men insisted on doing the dishes.

"So," Dominic said, while washing a pot, "you and Jane."

"We're friends."

"Are you gay?"

"You know I'm not."

"Well, then, you're not just friends."

"We're undefined."

Dominic thought about it for a few minutes. "Good for you," he said.

Later, when everyone was in the sitting room battling over a game of Pictionary, Kurt returned from Irene's, complaining that he'd just endured the worst duck dinner ever and that he was starving. "I mean, who does duck at Christmas? And it was dry as an old dear's —"

"Excuse me?" Rose said.

"Sorry, Gran."

"I should bloody think so!" She pointed at Dominic. "Did you hear that? That's you!"

Dominic went into the kitchen with Kurt, plated up some food and heated it in the microwave. Then they sat and ate together, again. Rose and Elle decided it was time to leave, Rose so that she could entertain her bridge friends who were due at nine and Elle because she was tired.

"It was a perfect day," Elle said to Jane, and Jane hugged her. Elle had been so different since their chat that she really felt maybe her mother and the doctor were wrong and Elle was fine after all.

When they'd gone Tom and Jane sat together on the sofa.

"That was a big gesture," she said, referring to the itinerary.

"It feels kind of silly now."

"Don't be like that."

"'Here's a piece of paper with lots of countries written on it,'" he said, and laughed.

"You should do it alone," she said.

"I don't want to."

"You should get away from here and find yourself again."

"I didn't know I was lost," he said.

"Well, you are and I'd love you to find yourself with me but I know it's too soon."

"For you or me?"

"Probably for both of us," she said.

327

He nodded and patted her leg. "I think you're my best friend."

"I'm glad," she said.

Leslie woke up and walked into her sitting room in a drugged haze. Jim was passed out on the sofa with her cat passed out on top of him. She looked at the clock: it was 10:05 p.m. She poured some water into a glass, threw some tablets into her mouth and drank until the glass was empty. As she was passing the counter on her way out of the room she saw the message light blinking. She pressed the button and it was Elle. She sounded sleepy and happy. She sounded at peace. "Hi, Leslie, I know you're in Florida now and I hope you and Jim are having a good time. He's a good one. I had a silk dress delivered to your house on Christmas Eve. I hope Deborah took it in for you – it's beautiful and really feminine so when you wear it I hope you think of me."

Leslie looked at the box covered with bows that Jim had signed for the previous day but that she hadn't had the will or strength to open. She smiled at her friend's kindness.

"I just wanted you to know that I've loved being your friend and joining you on your journey. You inspired me because you grabbed on to life and that was right for you. I hope you don't hate me for letting go because that's what is right for me."

Leslie's smile faded. What was she saying?

"Tell Jane that I love her and I always have, and Kurt too and my mother. Tell them to be happy for me, and please be happy for me too. If I could cut out the part of me that's rotten I would, but I know that I can't now and I can't bear to be here any more. I've left notes for Jane,

328

Mum and Kurt buried in the back garden. Jane will know where. Forgive me."

"Jim!" Leslie screamed.

Jim shot up. "What's going on?" he asked, sitting up straight and rubbing his eyes like a child.

"Get up, get up, get up!"

He jumped up and followed Leslie into the bedroom.

"What's going on?" he said, and grabbed Leslie, who seemed to be running around in circles with her nightdress half off and her trousers half on. He held her in place. "Calm down," he said.

"Elle's killing herself," she said.

"What?"

"Elle left a message on the answering-machine, saying goodbye and forgive me."

Jim ran into the kitchen and checked the time the message was received. "Nine twenty," he said. "What time is it?" He looked at the clock on the wall. It read 10:20 p.m.

Leslie was dressed and running around looking for shoes.

"Leslie, stop. Call Jane." He handed her the phone.

Leslie stopped and looked at the phone. "I don't know her number. It's in my mobile." She ran around looking for her mobile and when she found it in her jacket the battery was dead. "Christ!" she roared. "Fucking hell!" She ran around the apartment looking for the charger and found it in the bedroom. She plugged it in and turned on her phone. "Come on, come on, come on," she said, as the phone was taking its sweet time. Jim stood calmly beside her. The phone came on. She dialled Jane's number. It rang out. "No, no, no!"

She dialled again.

*

"Hi, Leslie, sorry – the phone was in the bottom of my bag," Jane said. "Oh, my God, how is Florida?"

"Go down to the cottage now!"

"Have you been drinking?" Jane asked. Tom had his coat on, ready to leave, and she winked at him.

"Jane, Elle left a message on my machine saying goodbye, she couldn't be here any more. She's left notes for you in the garden. She asked us to forgive her. Go down to the –"

Leslie didn't get to finish her sentence. Jane was off and running from the sitting room to the hall and into the kitchen. Dominic and Kurt were eating chocolates and drinking coffee. Jane raced past them and wrenched the door open. She ran down the steps and across the garden, passing her mother's witch hazels, her roses, the graves of Jimmy, Jessica, Judy and Jeffrey, and reached Elle's cottage door. She practically ran into it. It was locked so she banged on it, screaming, "Elle! Elle! Elle, it's Jane! Elle – Elle, please answer the door!"

She was pulling the latch like a madwoman, slapping the door and kicking at it.

Then Tom, Dominic and Kurt were beside her.

"What's going on?" Dominic asked.

"It's Elle – she's killing herself!"

Tom moved her aside and started to kick at the lock. He kicked once, twice, and on the third kick the lock broke and the door swung open. Jane was first in, followed by Tom, Kurt, then Dominic. She ran into the sitting room and then the bedroom, screaming Elle's name. Elle wasn't in either room. She ran to the bathroom door and it was locked. "Elle, please – please open the door!"

Tom and Dominic both started to kick the door down. Kurt stood with his hands on his head. The door broke open and Elle was lying in the bath, one hand dangling over the rim, her wrist bleeding. She was conscious and crying but clearly drugged. Jane grabbed her other hand and it wasn't cut. The dangling wrist didn't appear to be bleeding enough to kill her but nobody in the room knew how much blood she had lost or which drugs she had taken. Kurt got a clean tea-towel and tied it around her wrist while Tom called an ambulance, Dominic emptied the bath and he and Jane wrapped Elle in towels.

Elle was sobbing. "I was too scared, Janey," she said. "I was so happy to go but then I thought, What if it's worse on the other side?"

"It's okay, I've got you now," Jane said, but she was struggling to keep it together. "What did you take, Elle?"

"Lots of things."

"Make her stand up, walk her around," Kurt said, from the doorway.

"Are you sure?" Jane said. "I don't want to aggravate the wound."

"Listen to him, he's doing medicine," Dominic said.

"Yeah, but to be fair, Dad, I saw it in *Almost Famous*." He shrugged. "Honest to God, though, I think it's the right thing to do."

Jane and Dominic lifted Elle out of the bath and walked her into the sitting room. Tom ran outside to guide the ambulance men in from the front. Elle passed out on her second round of the room.

"Elle! Elle! Oh, please, Elle, wake up!"

Rose slept through it all.

Jane went with Elle in the ambulance and Tom drove Dominic and Kurt to the hospital. Elle was unconscious the whole way.

"She'll be all right," the ambulance man said. "Just a cry for help."

Jane nodded numbly.

Tom, Dominic and Kurt travelled in absolute silence except for when Tom rang Leslie to tell her where to meet them.

In the hospital Elle was taken away and Jane returned to stand with the others. "You should all go home," she said.

"No way, Mum, I'm staying," Kurt said.

"I'm not going anywhere," Dominic said.

"Me neither," said Tom.

"She's going to be fine," Jane said. "Honestly, you should go home."

Leslie appeared through the door, sniffling and coughing, shaking and looking as if she needed a bed herself. Jim was behind her carrying the hot-water bottle he'd made her hold in the car.

"Where is she?" she said.

Jane burst into tears. "If you hadn't been at home!"

"Not worth thinking about," Leslie said, hugging her. "I was – that's all that matters."

They sat waiting for word of Elle's condition. Within forty minutes a doctor came out to tell them that she was bandaged, there was no damage to her artery and her stomach had been pumped. He said he would talk to Jane in the morning about what would happen. She thanked him and Kurt hugged her.

It was after midnight when they all made their way out

of the hospital. Tom insisted on driving Dominic, Jane and Kurt home.

When Dominic got out of the car he leaned in at the window. "If this has anything to do with me, Janey . . ."

"It has nothing to do with you, Dominic."

"Okay, good. I'm glad she's going to be okay," he said, and walked up his driveway.

When Kurt got out of the car, Jane told him she'd follow him in a minute. When they were alone she thanked Tom for everything and kissed him. When she pulled away she smiled at him. "I really do think you should go away," she said. "Have adventures for both of us." She got out and he watched her drag herself up the steps to her house.

He made it home half an hour later. He walked up his stairs and fell asleep as soon as he hit the pillow and didn't wake up until his doorbell rang the next morning. He answered it in his robe. His liaison officer was standing outside, clapping her hands together in an attempt to beat the cold out of them.

"Trish?"

Trish nodded, her face saying it all.

"Where?" he said.

"In the Dublin mountains."

"When?"

"Christmas Eve. A man was walking his dog."

"And you're sure?"

"The dental records match," she said, and she handed Tom the necklace that Alexandra always wore, the one he had given her for their first wedding anniversary. It was engraved, *Alexandra, I love you. Tom.*

"How did she . . .?" He couldn't bring himself to finish the question.

"We won't know for a while yet," she said gently.

"Who could have done that to her?" he asked.

"Tom, I promise we'll do everything to find the person or persons responsible."

"And if you don't?" he said quietly.

"You bury her, you let her go and you move on," she said sadly.

"It's over."

"It's over."

"Oh, God," he cried. "Oh, my God, my poor, poor love!"

Trish knelt in his hall and took his hand. "She's safe now," she said.

Chapter 17

Apes & Angels

The heart runs on hope, my friend,
let hope be your horse,
open the tattered maps once more
and let's set a course,
gonna fight, gonna fight,
gonna fight just to love again.

Jack L, *Broken Songs*

January 2009

When she was stabilized Elle was moved from Accident and Emergency in Vincent's Hospital to St Patrick's Psychiatric Hospital, where she remained as a voluntary patient for three weeks. It was difficult accepting her illness but a diagnosis was also a long time coming. The doctors were kind and reassuring, and for the first time in a long time she felt safe. She would be on medication for the rest of her life and she wasn't sure how she felt about that. In fact, Elle wasn't sure how she felt about anything. The doctor explained that it might take time to get the drug cocktail right but he promised they'd get there in the end.

Elle was scared that she wouldn't be able to paint because she believed absolutely that it was her demons that drove her, inspired her and elevated her to a place far from the humdrum of normality and numbness. She was told that her talent wouldn't be affected, but she seriously doubted that and she knew if it was affected in even the slightest way she would sacrifice her new-found peace. But for now she was okay. She'd talk and she'd listen and she'd take their advice on coping skills, stress management and goal-setting, which she did anyway in the form of writing to the Universe, and she'd swallow what she was given even if it made her feel numb because for now numb was good.

Rose was beside herself when she woke on the morning of St Stephen's Day to find Elle had tried to do what her father had succeeded in doing so many years before. She cried and she shook and instantly aged, and Jane found herself hugging her and calling her "Mum".

"Don't cry, Mum."

"I thought she'd be okay."

"I know. Me too."

"But I should have known better."

"All we can do is our best, Mum."

"But I didn't do my best, Janey," she cried. "I'm so sorry I've made such a mess."

"It's okay."

"It's not okay!" her mother shouted. "I shouldn't have let this go on for years! I shouldn't have made you responsible for her, and I shouldn't have told you not to involve doctors because it didn't focking *work*! She could have died, Janey. My fault – again my fault!" Rose was trembling and beating her chest.

Jane wasn't sure if she was cold, in shock, or suffering from DTs. "Dad wasn't your fault, Mum."

"Of course it was. I left him alone and I knew he was in

despair, I left him alone because he was in despair, and I left him alone because I was focking sick of it!" Rose was rubbing her hands in an attempt to stop the violent shaking.

Jane had no clue what to say or do as she had never witnessed her mother in such distress – neither had she ever thought her capable of it.

"When your father died I was angry and sad and bitter and in such pain, and I left you two girls to fend for yourselves. I know I did and I'm not proud of it but you, Janey, you took over. You took care of me and your sister and you did a good job. You're the strong one, Jane, you've always been the strong one – that's why I pushed you so hard. We need you. We always have."

"I thought you were disappointed in me."

"I'm disappointed in myself – you just remind me of it, that's all," Rose said. "I am sorry, Janey, I am sorry."

She was sniffling and Jane felt such an overwhelming warmth for her mother it was unnerving. "Let's just be kinder to each other," she said, and Rose nodded.

Jane held her mother tightly, and when Rose composed herself Jane took a tissue out of her pocket and dried her mother's eyes.

"I hope you hadn't snotted in that," Rose said, and their tender moment was over.

Elle didn't have any visitors during her first week in St Patrick's but after that Jane and Rose came most days. At visiting time she'd sit in the glass annexe that overlooked a lush garden, and her visitors would join her there. On Rose and Jane's first visit together, Rose was not behaving like herself, much to Elle's confusion.

"This is lovely – isn't it lovely, Jane?" Rose said.

"It's lovely, Rose."

"You look fantastic, really beautiful," Rose said to Elle.

"I look terrible," Elle said, and looked at Jane for a hint as to what was going on in her mother's head.

"No, you're lovely," Rose said. "Isn't she, Jane?"

"No, she's right, she looks terrible," Jane said.

"What's going on?" Elle asked Jane.

"Rose is scared that if we're not nice to you, you'll try to kill yourself again," Jane said, and she wasn't laughing.

Jane was angry, and Elle knew it. Rose blushed the way her elder daughter did on most days but not that day.

"You're angry, Jane. I understand," Elle said.

"You understand?" Jane said, pointing at Elle. "Oh, good, because I understand too! I understand that you were desperate and scared and out of your mind – trust me, after two years' dealing with a colicky baby I do understand – but what I don't understand is you lying to me. I came to you, I asked you if you needed help and told you I'd be there to help you, and you lied and lied and lied. You made me doubt myself and if you'd died you would have made me complicit in it."

"I didn't mean to – I didn't want to – but everything was so muddled and unreal and I wanted to be okay. I wanted to be kooky, arty Elmore, the genius painter. I wanted it to be okay to suffer for your art and then it wasn't okay – then the world tipped sideways and I felt like I was barely clinging on. I got tired and all I could focus on was letting go."

Rose was silent and pale.

Jane shook her head. "If you ever try to kill yourself again I'll follow you into the next world and I'll kill you

338

there too." Jane's tears fell and she allowed Elle to bear witness to her pain and her broken heart.

"I'm so sorry, Janey."

"Don't be sorry. Just don't do it again."

Rose took Elle's hand in hers and for the first time Elle noticed her mother was trembling. "We love you, Miss Elmore, whether you're kooky or crazy or a little bit of both, whether you're an artist or a dinner lady we love you – but Janey's right. If you ever put us through that again, hell will be a holiday."

Elle smiled. "Okay, Mum."

"Right," Rose said. "Now, Jane, let's get out of this focking kip before I see someone else I know."

Kurt and Irene called once a week.

"How's medicine going?" Elle asked one day, while they ate beef sandwiches that Jane had sent in a picnic basket; it also contained three types of salad dressing and four types of salad, a large bag of lettuce and three cupcakes.

"Good," he said. "It's hard, though."

"Too hard," Irene said. "I never see him."

"You're seeing me now," he protested.

"And look where we are! No offence, Elle."

"None taken," Elle said.

"The last time we went out was well before Christmas," Irene complained to Elle. "We're in college, for God's sake, and we went out more when we were in school."

"My exams were after Christmas, I'm just finished them, and I told you we can go anywhere you like tonight," Kurt said, clearly annoyed at having to repeat himself.

"Yeah, well, I'm not in the mood tonight."

Kurt raised his hands to heaven. "You see?" he said to Elle.

"Nobody goes out in January, Kurt," Irene said.

Elle decided to change the subject. "So how's nursing, Irene?"

"Hate it," she said, shaking her head. "I'm thinking about leaving and doing modelling."

Elle looked at Kurt who raised his eyes to heaven. "Modelling?" Elle said.

"Mum has a friend in London. She says I've got great cheekbones and a good attitude."

"Well, then," Elle said.

"Still," Irene said, "I'm not sure I'd like modelling. I might do a beauty course or something. I'm not really sure so for the minute I'll stick with nursing but I swear I'll never make a nurse. People are foul."

Leslie came every day except the day she had an appointment with her consultant. She would arrive bringing books or chocolates or both. "You can never read enough or eat enough," she said.

"You're too good to me," Elle said.

"You're right, I am," Leslie said, "and as soon as you're well enough remind me to give you a kick in the hole."

"That's lovely language."

"Isn't it? I heard it coming out of the mouth of a ten-year-old as I was making my way over here."

"Is it possible to be depressed that you're depressed?" Elle asked.

"I'm sure it is. I know I'd be depressed if I was depressed."

"I just wish I could look into the sky and make sense of it all," Elle said.

"The answer to life's problems isn't in the sky," Leslie said. "It's in Jack Lukeman's songs."

Elle smiled. "Really?"

"Absolutely. In fact 'I've Been Raining' changed my life – well, that, a nosy girl called Deborah, a cat with the shits, a broken lift and a surgeon."

"So, name the song that will change my life."

"Hmmm." Leslie thought about it for a moment or two.

"Time's up."

"No," Leslie said, batting her away. "Give me a second." Then she grinned. "'Universe'."

"'Universe'?" Elle arched an eyebrow.

Leslie cleared her throat.

"Don't tell me you're going to sing it?"

"I'm better than you," Leslie said. She cleared her throat again and began to sing. "'Oh nothing lasts for ever . . .'"

"Dun, dun, dun, dun," Elle sang, imitating the trombone.

Two male patients on their way back from a smoke stopped at the door to enjoy the show.

"'You can cry a million rivers . . .'" Leslie sang, and pointed at Elle, who nodded and got ready to imitate a trombone once more.

"Dun, dun, dun, dun . . ."

> "*You can rage it ain't no sin*
> *but it won't change a thing*
> *'cos nothing lasts for ever . . .*"

Leslie reached out and embraced Elle. "Sing it with me, Elle."

Together they sang:

*"There's a universe inside
where the two of us can hide
and there's nothing to be frightened of,
a flash of light a raging star
don't you know you're not alone,
ah there's nothing to be frightened of."*

A nurse stopped beside the two male patients and looked at the two girls singing, arms wrapped around each other. She smiled before she went about her business. The two men clapped.

"Thank you, thank you, we're here all week!" Leslie said, and Elle laughed. They sat silently for a moment or two, then Leslie looked into Elle's eyes. "Well? Did it work?" she asked.

"You're right – I'm cured," Elle said, and laughed.

"I hate to say I told you so." Leslie smiled at her friend. "It's going to be all right, you know."

The first chance Jane had after Elle was stabilized, she made her way down towards her mother's rose bushes and the graves of the gerbils, Jessica, Jimmy, Judy and Jeffrey. She walked the correct distance between them and started digging. Rose and Kurt appeared from their respective doors and followed her to the spot where Elle had told Leslie she'd left her final goodbyes. Kurt and Rose were silent while Jane dug. When they heard the shovel tapping on the tin Jane turned to face them and Rose nodded for her to continue. She cleared the soil from the top of the tin and picked it up. She opened it, exposing the three notes folded inside. She set it down on the ground and took a lighter out of her pocket. She looked once more to her mother and she nodded again. Jane leaned down and set the paper alight. It went out so she lit it again and when it looked like it was going to go out again Rose reached into her pocket, pulled out a hipflask and sprinkled some booze on it causing it to reignite and burn until there was nothing left.

"Aren't you even curious?" Kurt asked, as they made their way back to the house.

"No," Rose and Jane said in unison.

"I am," he admitted, "a bit."

Rose put her arm around her grandson as they walked. "It wasn't Elle's time to say goodbye, so let's just be grateful for that."

Jane found it hard to get rid of all her anger. The people in St Patrick's Hospital had told her that this was a perfectly natural reaction and they attempted to explain her sister's mental state to her. Jane found it hard to accept that Elle was unwell. She had been so desperate to believe her when she'd explained away her symptoms, and now she felt so selfish and stupid.

It was her son who got through to her. "Mum, you do the best you can but you're not perfect. No one is, except maybe me."

"She could have died," Jane said.

"We all could die any day and not because we want to. Elle is just like the rest of us."

"Oh, yeah, and what's that?"

"Fucked up," Kurt said, and Jane laughed for the first time since Elle had tried to kill herself.

*

Alexandra was buried on a Sunday morning. The church was packed to the rafters. Tom stood at the top of the church with Alexandra's father, her brother, his wife, her sister and her husband. The priest spoke warmly of Alexandra, her mother Breda and the entire Walsh family. He spoke warmly of Tom and his fight to find her. He hoped that he could now find peace as he had no doubt that Alexandra had.

When Leslie told the Jack Lukeman camp that Alexandra had been found, Jack offered to sing at her funeral. The family were blown away by his kind gesture so he sang Breda Walsh's favourite hymns for the girl who had died on the way to pick up tickets for his show. Tom got up and spoke about his wife, how they'd met, how they'd fallen in love, the reasons he'd loved her, the reasons he would always love her. He spoke about their plans and dreams and disappointments. He spoke about her sense of humour and he ended by reading from the last note Alexandra ever wrote to him.

"Alexandra always had the last word in our house so I think it's only right that she gets the last word today. 'Tom, When you are shopping can you pick up the following: bread, milk, water, spaghetti, mince – lean! Make sure it's lean and not the stuff they call lean and charge half price because it's not lean. I want lean cut right in front of you and I don't care how much it costs.'"

The crowd laughed, and Tom read on: "'Tin of tomatoes, basil, garlic, wine, if you don't still have a case or two in the office and make sure it's not Shiraz. I'm really sick of Shiraz. If you want dessert pick something up. I'm meeting Sherri in Dalkey for a quick drink at five. She has the Jack Lukeman tickets so I took money from the kitty to pay for them. I'm taking a ticket for you so if you don't want to go text me. I'll be home around seven thirty. Your aunt called. She's thinking about coming to Dublin next weekend. Try and talk her out of it. I'm exhausted and can't handle running around after her for forty-eight hours straight. Your aunt is on cocaine. I'm not messing. An intervention is needed.'"

Again the crowd laughed a little and smiled at the words from a girl who couldn't be boring even writing a shopping list.

"'Oh, and washing-up liquid. We badly need washing-up liquid, and will you please call someone to get the dishwasher fixed? OK, see you later, love you, Alexandra. PS When somebody close to you dies, move seats. God, I love Jimmy Carr.'"

The crowd clapped, and Tom looked down to where Jane was sitting beside Leslie, and she nodded and smiled because he'd done her old friend proud.

Tom led the mourners to the graveside and Jim held Leslie and Jane held on to Elle, who had been allowed out of hospital to say her own goodbye. Rose stood to the side with Kurt and Irene. Alexandra's family bowed their heads in grief and in gratitude that the worst of their suffering was over. Whatever the police investigation might uncover, Alexandra was safe now. The priest anointed the coffin and said his prayers. Jack sang as they lowered her into the ground. When everyone had gone Tom was left alone, staring at the mound of fresh flowers covering his wife who had been dead for more than a year. Jane let the others go to the car and joined him. She slipped her hand into his and he squeezed it.

"The inquest will take at least a year," he said. "I don't even know if I can bear to hear the details."

"She's at peace now," she said. "That's what matters."

"I hope so," he said. "I'm going to go on that trip."

"Good," she said.

"You're sure you won't come?" he said, turning to look at her.

"This is something you have to do on your own," she said.

"Too soon."

"Too soon."

Together they walked away from Alexandra's grave and to the waiting cars. Tom stopped and turned to look at it one last time. *If somebody close to you dies, move seats, you said. So that's what I'll do. I love you.*

Epilogue

15 March 2009

Dear Tom,

As you know, the post-mortem revealed that Alexandra died of asphyxiation. What it didn't reveal was that she was a fighter, but you already knew that. Our forensics team found skin cells under her nails, and although this DNA is not currently on our database we believe that it is only a matter of time before we find the person responsible for her death and when we do Alexandra will help us put that individual away.

On a personal note I just want to say that I'm so sorry for your loss. I've never said that out loud and I wanted to. Although I didn't ever meet your wife, through you I came to know and care for her. Trust that no matter how long it takes we will keep looking and we will get justice for you, for her and for her family.

Now, remember what I said – live your life, you've lost enough.

Sincerest regards,

Trish Lowe

Patricia Lowe

Family Liaison Officer

Clontarf Garda Station

Subject: You're not going to believe what I'm doing
20 August (3 days ago)

Tom,

It's only been eight months and it feels like a lifetime has passed
since I drove you to the airport. It's been fantastic to keep up with all
your adventures through the blog. Good old Leslie for setting that
up. As you know, she and Jim are engaged but did you know that
she's opting for a breast reconstruction? Probably not. I only heard it
through Elle and she wasn't supposed to say anything. Anyway, I'm
delighted for her. How's India? The last time you blogged you had
the trots. I hope the situation has resolved itself and you are no
longer a slave to your bottom half. I'm writing to tell you that I
applied to study medicine as a mature student and I got in!!!!! I
know it sounds insane but the gallery isn't doing a lot of business at
the moment and, let's face it, the way things are going we'll probably have to shut our doors in a few months. Elle isn't ready to paint
yet and when she does I think it's healthier for her to work with
someone else. I've told her and she agrees. I have money saved and
besides I know I'd love doing medicine. I'm so excited. I'm going to
be starting in the College of Surgeons in October, which I'm very
relieved about because Kurt would have had a fit if I'd joined him in
Trinity.

Elle is well. She's taking some time off and she's reading a lot about
her condition. She's looking at alternative therapies and Christ knows
what else. I swear if she read that painting your arse red and dancing
the conga helped she'd do it, but so far so good. She's working with
her doctors and she seems happy. I don't really know any more. I just

have to trust that she'll be okay. Maybe when I'm a doctor I can find a cure. I'd put in one of those smiley faces that people do to suggest they're joking but I've forgotten how to.

Anyway, I just wanted to tell you my news.

I miss you.

Jane X

To: Janemovingon@gmail.com
From: tomtheroamer@gmail.com
Subject: You're not going to believe what I've just done
21 August (2 days ago)

Jane,

I am so proud of you. I think it's amazing and brave and I know that you can do it because you have proved you are capable of so much. I also know that you will make a fantastic doctor because you're kind and caring and even when those around you are driving you up the wall (How is Rose by the way?) you have the patience of a saint. I wish you all the luck in the world but I know you don't need it.

I left India yesterday. My head and my arse had an argument and my arse won. I wish I could have stayed on but honestly the water was killing me. I'm en route to Kenya and I can't wait. I have an old pal living there. He's actually part of a construction team building houses so I'm thinking about sticking around there for a while and working with him. It will be good to get my hands dirty again. I hear the Niall Mellon Township Trust is looking for volunteers to build homes in South Africa in March so I'm going to head that way and give them a hand, although I think I have to get sponsorship. Tell you what – if you come out I'll sponsor you and you can sponsor me. Think about it, ten days can change not just their lives but yours too.

I really miss you too and I look forward to the day I see you again.

Tom X

From: Leslie.sheehan@yahoo.com
To: Janemovingon@gmail.com
Subject: I don't believe you!
22 August (1 day ago)

Jane,

I just got an email from Tom congratulating me on getting new tits!!!!! I can't believe you told him. Mortified!

Leslie

From: Janemovingon@gmail.com
To: elmore@gmail.com
RE: I don't believe you!
10:20 p.m. (3 hours ago)

See Leslie's mail, I think I just landed you in it!!!! Sorry.

Jane

From: elmore@gmail.com
To: Janemovingon@gmail.com
cc: Leslie.sheehan@yahoo.com
RE: I don't believe you!
1:20 p.m. (1 hour ago)

No problem. These days I blame everything on the medication.

Elle

From: Leslie.sheehan@yahoo.com
To: elmore@gmail.com
RE: I don't believe you!
1:21 p.m.

Elle,

You just cc'd me into that mail so now I know your dirty little tricks!

Leslie

From: elmore@gmail.com
To: Leslie.sheehan@yahoo.com
RE: I don't believe you!
1:22 p.m

L,

You see, I would never have done that if I wasn't on medication!

xE

Acknowledgements

The first time I heard Jack Lukeman sing we were both teenagers. His voice was as big then as it is now and it's something I'll never forget. He was a kid and he could silence a roomful of adults with just one bar of "Summertime". I've witnessed his talent and career unfold over the past twenty years and some of my best times have been hanging out with one or all of the Jack camp. I was there in the beginning, when Jack led the Black Romantics and they played night after night in the Da Club. I took my turn selling the first album *Wax* during the interval. Once or twice I was roped into carrying gear through the streets of Dublin heading for 38 South Circular Road, which was the Jack base camp for all of the nineties. So many demos were recorded there; so many people lived there on and off, Jack in the back flat, David in the front, Martin upstairs, there was always something going on. Football, EU canned meats, comedy gigs, phone calls to and from America in the middle of the night, drums, bass, vocals, drinking, smoking, laughing. When I think about the nineties I think about 38 SCR and it always makes me smile.

The first time I conceived the smallest kernel of the idea for *The One I Love* was while standing on a balcony with Martin, looking down at the crowd at a sell-out show. On stage Jack was singing and doing his thing, but it was the crowd that captured my imagination. They were in awe, transfixed and completely silent. I made a joke to Martin that we should set up a church, the Church of Jack, and make some real money. The image stayed with me and over the years, seeing a lot of the same faces come to show after show, the idea of fans becoming friends wouldn't let go. I spoke to Jack, Martin and David about the idea for this book two years ago, and not only were they really supportive but they gave me *carte blanche* to incorporate all Jack's mat-erial and I'm so grateful to them for trusting me not to f**k up. If you read this book and your interest in Jack Lukeman is piqued, his website is www.jacklukeman.com. I hope you enjoy his music as much as I do.

So to all in the Jack camp, beginning of course with Jack Lukeman, thank you for the songs and the laughter over the past twenty-something years. Martin Clancy, you are and always will be one of my best friends, and I'll be forever grateful for the day you walked into my world. David Constantine, that night in Northumberland Road, me on crutches, the meter out of coins and a lunatic screaming, "I've gone blind" – that was our Vietnam. I love you, man! Myra Clancy, you rock, and Patricia Clancy, I can honestly say there isn't one of us that you haven't mothered at some point: thank you.

I'd also like to thank Ken Browne. When my husband introduced us fifteen years ago, Ken was a guitar player in a rock band. We lost contact and didn't see him for years and when we reconnected we discovered that he had transformed into an incredible artist. He, like me, is inspired by music and uses it in his work. He's energetic with the ability to say more in a minute than some say in a lifetime. He's deeply passionate about his work and when I'm around him he reminds me how lucky we are to be in a position to be creative and to do the things we love doing. (When my pal Enda reads this he will yawn and make an unseemly gesture with his right hand. Apologies, Enda, I'm finished; the luvvie has left the room.) I asked Ken if I could pick his brain for this book and I also asked if I could include him, and he was kind enough not only to grant me my wish but also to act excited about it. So, thanks again for your enthusiasm, exuberance and for the beautiful painting that rests on my sitting-room wall. For anyone who wishes to view the works I mention in the book, his website is www.kenbrowneart.com

OK, luvvie bit over. I'd like to thank all my other pals who I've mentioned in the three other books, my family, and everyone at Penguin, UK and Ireland, especially Patricia Deevy and Michael McLoughlin, Valerie Kerins for being as good a PR agent as she is a friend, and Faith O'Grady my ever-patient agent. I'd like to thank Rowohlt Germany, Pocket Books USA and Poolbeg Ireland for all their support and hard work on my behalf. I'd like to thank my husband for his love, support and kindness, and finally I'd like to thank anyone who has taken the time to read these acknowledgements!

Permissions

Jack Lukeman lyrics are reproduced with the permission of Lukeman, Constantine and Clancy.

Chapter 1: "Universe" (Lukeman, Constantine).

Chapter 2: "Fear Is The Key" (Lukeman, Clancy); "Don't Fall In Love" (Lukeman, Constantine); "Move On" (Lukeman, Constantine); "Bedsprings" (Lukeman, Constantine, Clancy); and "Georgie Boy" (Lukeman, Constantine, Clancy).

Chapter 3: "You Can't Get Bitter" (Lukeman).

Chapter 4: "So Far Gone" (Lukeman, Constantine, Clancy).

Chapter 5: "Authentic Fake" (Lukeman).

Chapter 6: "Little Man" (Lukeman, Constantine) and "Edge Of Town" (Lukeman, Constantine).

Chapter 7: "Chocolate Eyes" (Lukeman).

Chapter 8: "Numero Uno" (Lukeman) and "Metropolis Blue" (Lukeman, Constantine).

Chapter 9: "No Goodbyes" (Lukeman, Constantine).

Chapter 10: "Lost In Limbo" (Lukeman).

Chapter 11: "Simple And True" (Lukeman, Constantine).

Chapter 12: "Open Your Borders" (Lukeman).

Chapter 13: "Everybody's Drunk" (Lukeman, Constantine).

Chapter 14: "I've Been Raining" (Lukeman).

Chapter 15: "Happy Death" (Lukeman, Constantine) and "Rooftop Lullaby" (Lukeman).

Chapter 16: "I Ain't Crazy" (Lukeman, Constantine).

Chapter 17: "Apes & Angels" (Lukeman).

For further information on Jack Lukeman please go to: www.jacklukeman.com and for Martin Clancy please go to: www.martinclancy.eu